# THE RAVEN NAELO SAGA
## BOOK 2

# MORTAL GUARDIAN
## INTO THE INFERNO

### R. A. FISCHER

**HELLBENDER BOOKS**

an imprint of Sunbury Press, Inc.
Mechanicsburg, PA USA

**HELLBENDER BOOKS**

an imprint of Sunbury Press, Inc.
Mechanicsburg, PA USA

FIRST HELLBENDER BOOKS EDITION: July 2025

Set in Adobe Garamond Pro | Interior design by Crystal Devine | Cover design by Sienna Rose | Edited by Sarah Peachey.

Publisher's Cataloging-in-Publication Data
Names: Fischer, R. A. author.
Title: Mortal guardian : into the inferno / R. A. Fischer.
Description: First trade paperback edition. | Mechanicsburg, PA : Hellbender Books, 2025.
Summary: Raven Naelo defies her father, the king, and enters the Abyss Realm with a motley crew to reclaim her sister's stolen corpse. As her dragon magic grows unstable, she must face deadly foes, wavering loyalties, and the haunting echo of her father's warning: Beware the balors.
Identifiers: ISBN 979-8-88819-318-1 (softcover).
Subjects: FICTION / Fantasy / General | FICTION / Fantasy / Epic | FICTION / Fantasy / Action & Adventure.

Designed in the USA
0  1  2  3  5  8  13  21  34  55

*For the Love of Books!*

Ashley

# PROLOGUE

The sky rippled with radiant colors as Draconia, goddess of dragons, the embodiment of ancient majesty and terrifying grace, descended from the heavens. Her form blended humanoid elegance with draconic might: limbs armored in peach-toned and wine-dark scales ending in razor-sharp claws, vast wings veined in crimson, and a crown of twisted horns framing a face that was both regal and fierce. Iridescent scales rimmed her eyes, highlighting the gold-slitted pupils floating in liquid silver pools, gleaming like a dragon's hoard. Her irises burned with the wisdom of centuries and the promise of wrath.

Long silver hair cascaded like smoke over her shoulders, starkly contrasting the glistening teal-blue runes embroidered into her flowing, sorcerous robes. She sat tall on the leather saddle, a figure of grim, sovereign power.

Beneath her soared Krea'tion, the great dragon known as Mother of All Dragons, moving with impossible grace for a creature of her size. Her obsidian scales shimmered with hints of purple, like starlight trapped beneath the night's surface.

*I risked everything to bring Krea'tion into the Mortal Realm*—Draconia's oldest creation, the dragons' lifeblood. And if her plan worked, it would finally be time. *Time for the dragons to return home . . . to the Fey Realm, where they belong.*

Krea'tion touched down lightly despite her massive bulk, and the ground trembled beneath her. Dust swirled in russet-brown plumes, welcoming them to this freshly made land—Draakland, the last sanctuary.

Draconia's lips twitched. Her heart should've swollen with pride. *I molded this realm with my own hands.* But there was no time to weigh the risks. No time to breathe. Just the pounding thought: *Now. It must be now.*

Cadence Dow, a Sylvan Draakgoon, stood at the base of the hill—a moon-elf wizened by centuries. Her green hood was drawn low, shadowing her silver

1

brows, but Draconia recognized the telltale hunch in her shoulders and the gnarled staff she leaned upon. Despite her age, Cadence hobbled toward them with surprising speed.

Krea growled and lowered her massive head, allowing Draconia to dismount easily instead of using the folding ladder.

Cadence didn't blink; she couldn't. Her eyes, wide as twin full moons, tracked the impossible length of Draconia's serpentine neck, the horn-crowned head that turned toward her with an almost curious elegance. The older woman reached up and stroked the dragon's snout as smoke coiled from its nostrils, lazy and ominous, curling around rows of fangs longer than her arm. "She's . . . incredible," Cadence said, running a hand over Krea's scales again. "I've never seen a dragon of such vastness."

Draconia nodded. "I wish this were a ceremonial visit." She quickly caught Cadence's elbow before the elderly moon-elf could kneel. "You've earned the right to stand beside me, but it's time to reunite Krea'tion with her kin."

Without another word, Cadence led the way toward a nearby grove as Draconia followed closely, scanning every corner of the now-empty egg nursery. The rustle of hay and dragonwood trees greeted them like old memories. "I'm afraid the breeding ground has slowed down a bit," Cadence offered, her voice tinged with regret.

Draconia stopped short, her gaze narrowing on the vacant nests. "But where's my hatchling?" she asked, her voice sharp with rising concern.

Cadence turned, puzzled. "Where's who?"

Draconia's stomach knotted. The air suddenly felt heavier. "Krea'tion's offspring. I need to rebirth Krea'tion's spirit into a younger physical body."

Cadence froze. The blood drained from her face, and her expression morphed from confusion to alarm. "I-I'm sorry. No egg arrived."

For a moment, silence stretched between them, thick and unbreathable. Then Draconia stepped forward, her voice low but trembling with anger. "That egg was marked for delivery a month ago. Where is it, Cadence? I entrusted it to my remaining Draakgoons. It was supposed to hatch here. Time flows faster in the Mortal Realm!"

Cadence lowered herself shakily onto a stool. "I've protected this land for over five hundred years. I would know if someone delivered an item of great importance."

Draconia bit her scaled lip with a slow breath that rumbled through her chest. *Fools! I should've delivered it myself.* Without another word, she stormed away while Cadence struggled to follow, then stopped as Draconia mounted

Krea again. "We will return," the goddess snapped. Her voice was a whipcrack of restrained rage. She leaned forward, whispering to the dragon. "Find your offspring."

Krea roared, her voice echoing across the entire world of Pángorbis. Her body gleamed with astral light in a blink and launched into the sky, tearing over the Pangean Ocean.

By the time they reached the western coast of Euphrasia, dread weighed in Draconia's gut like a stone. Krea dove suddenly, wings folding, heading for the Suttiir River.

Before they landed, the stench of rot hit her. Her heart pounded. They touched down in a clearing stained with death. Insects buzzed hungrily over what remained of the egg—a cracked, empty husk oozing with something dark. The black scales were removed, exposing the soft, unnatural skin as if it had never been allowed to harden. Claw marks and bite wounds covered the areas. Small animals fled into the underbrush, stomachs full of what should have been a goddess's heir.

Krea wailed—a haunting, guttural sound. Her pain echoed across the realm, vibrating in Draconia's bones as she slowly approached the shattered egg.

Draconia spotted a hole inside—something had drained the life from it. *Not just killed it. But consumed it.* A tear slid down the goddess's cheek. She hadn't cried since the day Natus, the material god and her father, banished the dragons to the Mortal Realm over a thousand years ago. But this was worse than banishment. *This is a desecration.*

"We were ambushed," a voice rasped as Draconia turned sharply, her hands aglow with magic. Krea snarled beside her. A sapphire scale-armored Hydra Draakgoon—a once-beautiful elf, now reduced to a limping wreck. One of her white, blue-trimmed wings was shredded, and half her face bore burns and bruises. She dropped to her knees, panting. "I'm Draak-kin of Hydro, Devanna."

"What happened, young Draak-kin?" Draconia asked with an icy voice as a hurricane of fury and heartache rumbled inside her.

Devanna coughed. "The wysard school, Waterfront. They attacked. I was the only survivor . . . I fought, and I bled. I starved for a week. I even killed curious bugbears that came sniffing around."

Draconia's voice caught in her throat. "The headmaster broke the accord. I gave him knowledge—for peace." Her claws tensed at her side. *Elora.* The name snapped like a fault line in her mind. *She knew.* Rage simmered, silent and sharp. *Justice could still be served.*

Devanna hesitated. "When I returned . . . a gnome and elf were feeding on the egg." Her words dropped like stones. "Then a balor arrived. Killed the elf."

Draconia's stare pierced like a blade. "And the gnome?"

"Took a portal along with the corpse with the assistance of the Realm Guardian."

"And the transport? A copper dragon, Bakahrrato?"

"He dropped the egg after being severely injured but escaped east. He fell shortly after passing the river. I was with him until he ordered me to assist with the battle, but when I returned, he was gone. Then I protected the egg until—"

"Until you failed me."

Silence.

*Killing her and Elora is still an option. But I already lost so many of my Draak-goons. My Draak-kins.*

Devanna's sky-blue eyes saddened, almost reading Draconia's thoughts. "The balor took the Artifact of Souls off the dead elf."

"Are you certain?"

"I swear on my life."

*The relics! So, the headmaster doesn't have them all yet.* Draconia stepped forward, gently touching Devanna's torn wing. *I could destroy Natus with them.* A golden light pulsed from her hand, and the injury vanished.

"Thank you," Devanna gasped, flexing the new limb. "You are merciful."

"I'm rational," Draconia replied through clenched teeth. "And let's hope you're right. Meanwhile, you'll assist Draak-kin of Sylvan, Cadence Dow, in Draakland. The time for vengeance on the headmaster and Elora will come after I deal with my father."

Devanna bowed. "As you wish."

"Ride with me, young Draak-kin."

The two climbed up the saddle ladder onto Krea's broad back, the dragon mount's glossy black scales rippling like liquid armor beneath them. With barely a beat of her wings, Krea let out a low, resonant growl. The air sparkled, warping like a heat haze, then tore apart in a jagged spiral of light as she lunged into the Astral Realm.

They burst through the veil and landed with a thunderous impact before the gilded front gates of the High Council, their arrival echoing across the courtyard like a war drum.

Draconia unfolded the ladder from the saddle. After she descended, her talons clanked against the white marble. "Return Krea'tion to the sanctuary," she ordered curtly, glancing over her shoulder.

Devanna nodded, swiftly rolling up the ladder and securing it. With a sharp tug on the reins, she and Krea vanished into a swirl of silvery mist, tearing back into the Mortal Realm.

Draconia turned sharply and found Elora Clover already waiting. Six High Council guards flanked her, spears crossed over armored chests with unreadable expressions.

"What's this?" Draconia sneered, sweeping her cloak behind her. "A welcome party?"

"Natus requires your presence," Elora said, her voice level, but her fingers clenched tightly around the hilt of her staff.

Draconia snorted, the sound dry and sharp. "Since when does a god speak through a mortal?"

"Not through me," Elora replied, then she stepped aside. "Through them."

From beyond the gates, more figures emerged. Their robes trailed like smoke. The unmistakable presence of divine power thickened the air. At the center of the procession stood Solas, goddess of energy and Draconia's sister. Her auburn skin glowed faintly as if lit from within.

Draconia's smile thinned. "I suppose you agree with this absurdity—letting mortals sit among gods."

Solas hesitated. A breath caught in her throat. "You disobeyed Father."

"I protected my creations," Draconia snapped. Her voice echoed with barely contained rage. "Felix tricked my dragons into creating the Shadow Realm, and I helped Fharla create the Mortal Realm so she could reunite with her brother. Our father cannot forever cast the dragons aside. They are slowly dying out in the Mortal Realm."

"He can," Solas said softly. "And he will."

A beat of silence passed. Draconia's jaw tightened, the muscles in her cheek flickering. "Fine," she hissed through her fangs. "How do I reach Father? No portal has been open to his chamber for centuries."

Elora met her stare. "Stand in the portal chamber. The great Natus will open it for you."

"The *great* Natus," Draconia mocked, brushing past the elf with a flare of her cloak. "Silence, peon."

Solas stepped forward, her steps soundless on the marble. "I'll escort you."

They walked through the vast, echoing hall of the High Council. The sixteen stained-glass windows depicted scenes of heroic battles and legendary figures from the history of the realms, casting a kaleidoscope of colors onto the marble floor. Torchlight danced along the mirrored walls, and distant hymns hummed through the stone like ancient memories. They bypassed the holding cells to finally reach the portal chamber.

"If I don't return," Draconia muttered, her voice low, "inform Fharla to care for the dragons."

Solas stopped, her breath catching. "Don't say that."

Draconia smirked sideways. "Should I request that new demigod of luck instead?"

Solas gave a faint grin, her voice almost a whisper. "He'll forgive you."

Draconia's gaze turned cold. "Somehow, that doesn't comfort me."

The portal chamber's massive doors groaned open, heavy with age. Beyond them, the chamber stretched vast and silent, lit only by a semi-circle of five pulsing, red portals. Their glow flickered like dying embers, throwing jagged shadows across the obsidian walls. It felt like stepping into the mouth of something ancient and hungry. The sixth gateway opened to her father's chamber.

Solas stepped close, brushing a kiss against Draconia's cheek. "Goodbye," she whispered.

Draconia didn't respond. Her throat was tight. She wanted to say something—anything. *She knows what I'm walking into . . . and she's too afraid to say it out loud.*

Solas turned and fled down the corridor, her footsteps quickly swallowed by the silence.

Draconia stood frozen for a heartbeat, the echo of Solas's farewell lingering. Her sister's eyes had said what her words hadn't: *This might be the last time.* Draconia didn't look back. Pride wouldn't allow it. She stepped forward, the doors sealing behind her with a sound like the closing of a tomb as she stared at the rare sixth portal.

The gateway thrummed with pressure as if it recognized her and had been waiting. Draconia didn't flinch. She stepped through. The heat cracked in the air around her, unnatural and electric. Behind her, the portal hissed shut with a final, whirling snap, severing the world she'd known. *There's no turning back now.* Inside, the air was thick with a chill that slid under her tough skin like frostbite.

Natus sat upon a throne carved from star metal and bone. His gaunt fingers tapped a slow rhythm against the armrest, each strike echoing like the tolling of a funeral bell. He rose—deliberate, ancient, inevitable. His armor groaned with the weight of forgotten wars. A horned helmet veiled his face, but the power radiating from him pressed against Draconia like a storm wind—immense, merciless. The scythe he dragged behind him shrieked against the stone, its edge singing of her death.

Draconia's breath caught in her throat. Her heart thudded against her ribs, loud enough to betray her, telling Natus she feared him. Her immortality suddenly seemed to slip away. Still, she didn't step back. She couldn't. *I will not stand down—for my dragons.*

She swallowed, forcing steadiness into a voice that wanted to tremble. "Father . . . It's been—"

But the blade was already in motion.

No sound. No pain.

Only darkness.

Draconia's spirit circled Cenergy, the light of life, her divine essence never returning to the soul pool. In the physical world, she was gone. The egg lay shattered. The cry of dragons faded into the wind.

But fate is not so easily silenced. A spark lingered in the hush between realms, where starlight clings to torment and time forgets its shape—not in a cradle of scale, but in the quiet heart of a newborn half-elf girl. A nameless soul pulled from the Astral Realm by the ancient song of birth. She would not know if her name was written or if her body was forged in dragonfire when she rose. A soul hurled not into peace but . . . into the inferno.

But the world would remember the Draak-kin of Krea'tion.

# CHAPTER○ONE

# AWAKEN THE DRAAK-KIN
# WITHIN

C urled into herself on the winter-hardened dirt road, Raven fought for breath—with each inhale, a struggle against the winter air clawed at her lungs. Her body rocked slightly, forming a cradle in the mud. Cold seeped into her skin—a stark reminder that her armor was still in her room. *I don't deserve it.* The pulsating brightness above her stabbed at her vision. Still, there was something there—a rhythm, a flicker—like how Carya danced barefoot in the sunlight with shadows rippling around her like wings.

Raven's limbs trembled, her heart fluttering like a trapped bird. *I wish I could have danced with you. Just once.* After pulling her knees to her chest, she embraced them. She hummed soothingly as if blocking a thought, then began singing, "A basket . . . full of carrots . . ." swaying slightly. A song to block out the funeral's thorns.

But the pain of her sister's burial flooded every fiber. The memory's razor scraped every nerve. The thought of Carya's wake hit like a second death. That aching silence, the too-tidy flowers, the way she stood apart from everyone, arms crossed like invisible armor. Wearing the put-off demeanor like a newly equipped shield.

Now, every missed visit, every unsent letter, every cruel word muttered came back swinging. Every regret struck a critical hit. *I was selfish.* The outside world disappeared briefly as Raven raised her bandaged hand and traced Carya's name in the thick grime with her finger. *I'm so sorry.*

A familiar, husky voice drifted in from the shadows as she lay numbly, staring intently at the letters. "Rise."

*Baka?* The name clawed at the edges of her memory, and panic surged up her spine. She lay momentarily as if it were just her imagination playing tricks.

"Rise . . . Draak-kin of Krea'tion." Raven jerked upright, the darkness pressing in, thick and suffocating, like a burial shroud. Dirt clung to her breeches as she pushed herself up, jaw clamped tight, wiping away tears.

With effort, she forced herself to raise her chin to meet the unseen speaker with a glare she didn't feel brave enough to own. "Of all the people or creatures to welcome me to the Astral Realm." She brushed herself off. "I didn't expect the spirit of a copper dragon."

Her hands twitched toward her weapons instinctively—one dagger was missing, the other left behind when she collapsed. The void offered no clues, only the constant throb of light and the taste of stale air and acid on her tongue. Her gut tightened. *Where are the others?* She strained her ears. Nothing. No voices. No footsteps. Just her. Alone.

"Accept . . . the truth . . . Krea."

"Stop calling me that!" she snapped, though her voice trembled. The echo mocked her as the dragon's chuckle stirred the air somewhere in the dark. "And what truth?" she asked, dreading the following realization. "That I'm dead?!"

The laugh came again—Baka's hoot—but it no longer echoed from caves or shadows. It spiraled from the center of the blinding orb. "You're being . . . reborn." *Reborn?* The word thudded in her chest. Her skin prickled. "With the gift . . . of dragon tongue."

"Dragon tongue?" she repeated, voice hoarse. "What does that even mean?" No answer came. But she felt it—deep, ancient, coiling inside her. And then, instead of retreating from the warmth rising in her chest, Raven drew a deep breath and whispered, "Then show me." Her body answered. A wordless instinct trembled behind her teeth. Her lips moved. The words surged through her—not foreign, not forced, but hers. Chosen. "*Zhar ven draak-kin solas.*" The syllables felt heavy with power. She clapped a hand to her mouth. *I understood that.* Her breath steamed again as she stated, "Seek out the living Draak-kin."

The orb's glow no longer pierced her eyes—it pulsed softly in rhythm with her heartbeat. Her skin gleamed, just for a moment, light rippling across it like sunlight on scales. Her veins lit faintly with a bright purplish hue before fading as Baka spoke. "Call . . . for your skin."

"My skin?" Raven shook her head while inspecting her body. She held up her hand. "Why does acid not burn me?"

"You have . . . all the traits . . . But call . . . for your skin."

"All the traits of Krea? But—Oh, you mean my armor? I can't. It's too far away."

Baka's voice rang out clear and stern. "Call . . . for your . . . skin."

Raven sighed, giving in. "Tolth-Armis." Her armor appeared, wrapping her like a blanket, providing warmth like the hug she needed. "But how?"

"The scales . . . of Krea'tion. The armor . . . forged by my father . . . Plathorax." After Baka's final words, the orb vanished. A heartbeat later, the darkness—the gloom womb—lashed toward Raven like a recoiling serpent, too fast, too violent. It struck with a pressure that crushed the air from her lungs. She didn't move as the new reality slammed into her.

Colors smeared. Shapes twisted. And then—bodies. Scattered. Still. Panic clawed up her throat as she staggered forward, the world tilting. Then—movement. Her friends. Alive. Relief slammed into her with enough force to buckle her knees, but it didn't last. The necromancer, Jarz, and her sister were gone.

"Plathorax?" The words trembled out of her, half-breathed, half-spoken. They didn't feel like hers. Nothing did. *How did Gideon receive armor from the Father of the Metallic Dragons?* Her ponytail cracked like a whip in the wind as she jerked around, eyes searching, pulse screaming. Then, she witnessed Gideon descending like a celestial through the heavens. And for a moment, the terror receded. But her body still shook. She rushed to him without thinking, not for safety, but to anchor herself to something real. "I'm so sorry," she breathed, voice thick.

He held her tightly, warmly, and steadily. But even as he reassured her, Raven couldn't shake the feeling of dislocation—that a part of her was still in the darkness, echoing with the names Krea and Plathorax. With her cheeks pressed against Gideon's armor, she glanced down at the letters C-A-R-Y-A, still freshly engraved in the sludge, and she gripped him tighter.

Shorte's voice sliced through the reunion like a blade. "That monster converted Carya's corpse into a lich."

The word lich twisted her stomach, and her gaze snapped to where he pointed—toward the bridge, thick with chaos only moments ago. Her mind tried to catch up, but everything moved too fast as she watched Avalann inspecting the corpses. *Carya. Dead. Turned into—*

"I've never seen anyone in the Mortal Realm capable of such power," Avalann stated, her voice brittle, almost hollow. She knelt beside the crumpled body of a headless undead soldier, fingers brushing the corpse. "But the necro captured Jarz, too, and disappeared through a portal over there."

The words barely settled before Raven felt the change in Gideon beside her—a subtle tension, like a drawn bowstring as he stiffened. "What color was the portal?" he asked.

"Blue," Izarra answered, arriving with swift, almost frantic steps. Tears streaked her face as she handed Raven the dagger she had dropped.

While Raven sheathed her weapon, she studied Izarra's expression with empathy. She knew that look—the desperate need for answers, for something solid to hold onto when everything had been ripped away. *I can't lose another family member.*

"They're still in the Mortal Realm," Gideon replied, placing a hand on Izarra's shoulder.

Raven observed how gently he did it. The tenderness in his eyes, the calm authority in his voice. She admired but resented it. He always seemed to know what and how to say the right things while she struggled.

"What do they want with him?" Izarra's voice cracked, sharp and small at once.

"They want Jarz because he's powerful," Gideon replied, but Raven could tell he didn't know. A rare flicker of uncertainty passed over his face, but she noticed it. And it scared her. Gideon activated the gem in his gauntlet. The red glow triggered the Mortal Guardians' rings, and their stones pulsed in response.

Once the blue portals flickered to life, they stepped through their personal passages to Gideon's camp—Raven last, always watching, constantly checking the angles. The moment her boots hit the snowy ground on the other side, the cold bit her skin, but the silence unnerved her. No wagon. No noise. Just snow. She scanned the area as they waited. And waited. The portal was late. That meant something. *This isn't right.*

A glint of blue sparks ignited hope, then it was gone. Izarra's cry, "Jarz!" jolted Raven's heart as Izarra sprinted toward the collapse of light, desperation trailing behind her like a scream.

Raven lunged after Izarra but stopped. The anguish was raw, and sharp, like looking into a mirror. She didn't scream, but she felt it inside. And for the first time, she couldn't tell whose pain she felt more—Izarra's or her own. The words caught in her throat as she tried to speak. *I should've—*

"Why did you all just stand there?" Izarra screamed, turning on them with tears streaking her cheeks. "Why didn't you try to help him?"

"He's still alive," Gideon said, voice low.

*I want to believe him.*

"Something happened to him!" Izarra shouted again. "Gideon, you have to do something!"

As Gideon tried to reason with her, an ache of helplessness thudded through Raven like a second heartbeat, drowning out explanations of options, logic, and possibilities. And then Shorte snapped. "What a damn coward!"

Gasps. Everyone turned.

Shorte huffed. "Not Gideon, the necro-fairy. Using the dead against us. It's immoral. I'd like him to try to summon with my mace up his arse! You should have finished him while you had the chance—"

12

"All right, Shorte," Gideon interrupted while Raven stepped forward instinctively, her hand on Shorte's arm. A grounding touch meant more to her than to him as Gideon tried to keep things calm. *Shorte has a point. Why didn't Gideon end the necromancer's reign of terror?* But she wasn't listening anymore. Not until Gideon stated: "I'm teleporting you all back to Omlett. I'm going to Fellswar's Claim alone."

Her heart lurched. Before she could second-guess herself, Raven stepped forward. "I'll go with you." She didn't plead—she challenged. Avalann fell into step beside her, silent but solid. A swell of gratitude pressed against the tight knot in her chest.

Gideon's gaze flicked between them. His expression was unreadable, but Raven held his eyes without flinching. The silence stretched, brittle. "No," he said finally, voice flat. "You're returning to Omlett."

Raven's jaw clenched. "You're making a mistake." The words landed harder than she'd intended.

Gideon looked taken aback, but not enough. Not enough to change his mind. He turned away, shutting her out with the same finality as his answer.

Avalann tensed beside her as she let out a soft, scornful sound—half sigh, half snarl—and then pivoted on her heel. Her boots dug into the mud as she stalked off, shoulders rigid beneath her cloak.

Raven didn't need to hear the muttered Elvish to know it was a curse. *I don't blame her. Not this time.* "You'll need someone who's seen what I've seen," she called out. Then, without waiting for permission or a response, she stepped through the portal last. Her fingers brushed the hilt of her dagger. *If he won't let me help him, I'll find another way.*

The gateway opened onto the noiseless crossroads by the Omlett Inn. Raven's boots landed hard on the dirt road. What had once been a center of laughter and commerce felt hollow and gutted. Smoke lingered in the air like a warning.

The others cursed Gideon's name as they limped toward the Inn, but their voices faded. Raven didn't follow. Her tongue still burned with the syllables of the dragon's tongue: "*Sestrix, si tepoha wux di wer thurirl vur wer myvhh.*" *Sister, I love you with my heart and soul.*

*Soul.*

The word slammed into her like a fist, sending a pulse of fear through her—until her hand found the cold weight at her neck. Relief flooded through her that the relic was still there. *The Artifact of Stolen Souls.* She clenched it tight. "Thank Blade," breath catching. "I didn't lose it." Followed by a louder, steadier promise: "Carya, I *will* set you free."

# CHAPTER TWO

# GRIEF, THE SHARPEST BLADE

E ugor and Mara arrived at Suttiir, where the vibrant Elven village now lay in desolation. They brought their horse-drawn carriage to a halt, and Eugor helped his wife down. Together, they approached the stone fountains with measured steps. The once pristine water features that flowed clear and bright now stood dry. Their marble basins were cracked like eggshells. Images of children laughing and darting past the stone arches on festival nights surged through his mind.

Several of Mug's iron golems, massive and imposing, patrolled the area, their metal joints creaking with each step. One golem bore gouges along its side, and its faceplate had been twisted into a semi-permanent sneer. As the metal giants passed, a child hiding behind a collapsed cart peeked out, staring in fear—unblinking.

King Edlin Luhnar and Queen Baela Luhnar of Suttiir stood tall by the dais, flanked by their royal guards. Their spines were unbent beneath the weight of mourning. Though weariness shadowed their eyes and sorrow tightened their mouths, their crowns sat firm, their hands clasped in still resolve—a portrait of sovereign endurance. Time and stress had stolen the golden fire from the king's hair, leaving behind pale threads of silver at his temples, like frost clinging to autumn leaves. Queen Baela clutched her shawl tighter around her shoulders, protecting herself from the cold as they waved the Naelos over.

An elf mage dressed in a blue robe, his eyes weary but vigilant, stepped forward to halt them. Eugor's vision blurred momentarily, and he felt the uncanny tug of a presence watching through the spell. A gust of wind formed and surrounded them, blowing down their hoods and ruffling their hair. The air carried a scent of crushed pine and burned sage. Once the spell ended, the mage nodded, satisfied.

"Are you sure?" King Luhnar asked, his voice tinged with concern as the mage nodded again, his expression one of exhaustion. The king turned back to the couple. "We had to be certain you are . . . well, you." He extended his hand.

Eugor took it. "We understand," he replied sympathetically, noticing dark patches on his friend's skin. "Are you well?"

"Of course," the king responded, though his voice lacked conviction. "If you would follow us to the infirmary."

Along the way, Eugor observed the elves salvaging reusable lumber from the ruined buildings, their movements mechanical and despondent. The scent of burnt wood hung heavily in the air.

Shops and homes that had weathered centuries were now smoldering ruins, a grim testament to the recent devastation. *Thank Blade that Omlett still stands.* He winced. *Coward's gratitude. Their children go hungry, and I give thanks for my unbroken walls.*

They arrived at the makeshift infirmary in the gutted heart of the village. Two of the king's guards flanked the entrance, their faces expressionless beneath soot-streaked helms.

Inside, the air was thick with the mingled scents of blood, sweat, and something sweet—lavender oil. Elves lay sprawled on cots like broken dolls, their skin pale, their breaths shallow. Healers moved among them in silence, their hands swift and strangely detached, as if performing rites rather than treatment.

A low, wavering chant drifted from the far end—thin and cracked, rising like smoke. It was the sound of someone dying, a resonance all too familiar from Eugor's days as an assassin. The rustle of cloth and the breathy moans of the wounded filled the air as if the infirmary had begun to weep.

King Luhnar gestured to a cot where a young elf lay, barely more than a child, her petite body mottled with old soot and dried blood. Her once-yellow tunic was stiff with grime, charred in places. Thick scabs crusted over patches of healing skin, raw and uneven beneath the grime. Dust and ash clung to her lashes like gray frost. She stared at nothing, lips parted and cracked as if she had cried out long ago and never finished the plea. The child's eyes fluttered at their voices but did not blink. Her bandaged arm twitched a sluggish, instinctive movement.

"This is what we've been reduced to," King Luhnar said softly, his voice fraying at the edges. "Our people . . . our city . . ."

Queen Baela placed a comforting hand on her husband's arm. "We will rebuild," she said firmly, though tears dampened her lashes.

Eugor nodded, his heart heavy. "We are here to help in any way we can. Suttiir will certainly rise again."

As they moved toward the next tent, Eugor froze. Two children were rummaging through the blackened timbers of a collapsed home. Recognition hit him like a blow. "Elira," he murmured. *The weaver's daughter.* He had seen her weaving autumn flower garlands outside her family's stall a couple of months ago. Now, she clutched a scorched doll to her chest and held tightly to her younger brother's hand, which trembled with fear.

Mara gasped and rushed toward them, dropping to her knees. She gathered the girl into her arms, speaking gently, while the boy clung to his sister's side, hushed and shaking.

Eugor watched Mara momentarily—how swiftly she moved, how naturally she opened her arms. Even here, amid the wreckage, his wife carried grace like a birthright, creating space without effort. A quiet awe rose in him as if her kindness were the last thing left standing in a world turned to ash—until the guards parted the flaps of the bereavement shelter for the king and queen.

As they cleared past the first set of cots, he spotted them. *No. No. No.* Eugor frantically blasted past the guards. He stepped inside and staggered. The smell hit first—damp earth, bitter incense, and something sour beneath it, like rot sealed too long in silence. The air thickened as the flaps fell shut, pressing in on his lungs. Two bodies, barely recognizable, lay on cots—still, broken. His breath caught. The world narrowed to the shapes he had once called Amil and Adar.

Eugor's knees nearly buckled at the sight. All the mental preparation he had after receiving the news had failed. Their bodies were disfigured and ruined. The necromancer had twisted them, puppeted their corpses into something that mocked the memory of who they'd been. Arrows pierced their skulls. "Self-defense," he muttered, barely hearing his own voice. "There was no choice." But the words did nothing to hold back the wave breaking inside him. He had failed them by not arriving in time.

For a breathless moment, he couldn't move, couldn't think. The world seemed to tilt, narrowing into sharp, unbearable detail. There—his mother's silver comb, still resting on a folded cloth beside her pillow, gleaming faintly in the dim light. And just beyond it, his father's boots, dust-caked and cracked, as if waiting for the man who would never wear them again.

His breath came in short gasps. Eugor's chest ached. Anguish reached up from the floor and slammed into him, dragging his ribs inward. He knelt, touched their hearts, and prayed to Blade. *Son, please guide your grandparents' souls to meet your sister in the Astral Realm. Let them rest together in peace.* He crossed his mother's hands over her chest as tears blurred his vision.

King Luhnar stepped forward, his voice subdued but firm. "My condolences, Eugor. Your parents were the very heart of the elder council. They will be missed."

Eugor's throat tightened. The words, though kind, belonged in someone else's story—one where he hadn't just buried his daughter, one where these deaths weren't stacked upon an already bleeding heart. "I'd like to be alone for a moment," he said, his voice rough as gravel.

Edlin gave a solemn nod and touched Eugor's shoulder reassuringly. His grip was steady, but his eyes mirrored the same exhaustion and sorrow that clung to everyone in Suttiir. "Of course. And remember you are more than welcome to use my hunting cabin if you need privacy."

Queen Baela lingered for a breath longer, her lips parting as if to offer comfort. But the king lifted a hand—gentle, brief, and unmistakable. A silent gesture.

She bowed her head in understanding, her silver circlet catching the lantern light as she turned and slipped quietly from the tent. The flap closed behind them with a muted whisper. And then it was only Eugor and the dead.

Time passed, marked only by the flickering of lantern light and the composed rustle of healers tending to others in the tents. Eugor remained kneeling beside the cots, unmoving, numb. *I don't even know if it's high noon. I don't care.* The tent was a tomb, heavy with silence and memory.

The image of Mara appeared through his blurry vision. She wrapped her arms around him, her embrace warm and grounding. Eugor leaned into it instinctively, like a tree bracing against the wind. The silence between them wasn't empty—it was dense, a heavy shroud of things neither had the strength to say aloud. Their pain settled like dust in the lungs.

"I'm here," she murmured, her voice cracked. "They will reunite with Carya in the Astral Realm."

Eugor didn't respond. His throat was thick, words caught beneath the tide of sorrow.

Mara guided him gently to the floor beside the cots, sitting with him in the dim light of the bereavement shelter. "You shouldn't have to carry this alone," she said, wiping the soot from his cheek with the edge of her sleeve. "Not all of it."

Eugor's lips twitched into something almost like a smile. "I keep thinking I'll run out of tears," he said, voice rough, "but they just keep coming."

"Then let them," Mara whispered, gently brushing a lock of hair from his face. "You don't always have to be the strong one."

He swallowed hard, staring at the ground. "How much more can one heart bear?" His voice cracked. "Is this what I deserve? Retribution for all the lives I took when I was young—an assassin who never wept until now? For every cut I dealt, every silent death I caused . . . is this the price?" He looked up at her, searching for answers. "I've survived wounds, poisons—even decapitation. But this . . . the grief—" He paused, breath catching. "It's the sharpest blade . . . because Mara . . . it hurts."

A hush fell, her head resting gently on his shoulder, their fingers laced together. The torment between them wasn't just for Eugor's parents—it still burned hot and raw from Carya's death.

Mara's breath hitched in her throat, and her body trembled slightly against his. "She should never have gone out to the front line," she said suddenly, her voice tight with pain. "I should have kept her closer."

Eugor closed his eyes, guilt knotting deep in his chest. "She wanted to help. She believed in the mission. In protecting others."

"She was murdered, Eugor. Torn from us like"—her voice cracked—"like she was nothing. To the emotionless creatures that ravished her, she was nothing."

He didn't try to argue. The image of Carya rushing around the tent helping others haunted him, braver than he'd ever been at that age. *But Mara's right. Whether emotionless beings or a simple dagger, they were weapons. My poor daughter was murdered.*

"I still hear her voice sometimes," Mara said softly, tears slipping down her cheeks. "In the hall. In my dreams." The words fell like stones in the quiet as he held her hand tighter. "I'm not ready to let go."

"Neither am I," Eugor murmured. "But she's watching. Somewhere in the Astral Realm, she's waiting. Just like my parents are."

Mara nodded, tears slipping silently down her cheeks. She pulled a soft cloth from her satchel, gently wiped the tears from his cheeks, and brushed the dust from his tunic.

Eugor gave a faint, broken smile. "Sometimes I wonder if the pain is all left to prove they were real. If I stop feeling it . . . does that mean I've let them go?"

Before she could argue, a soft voice called from the tent's entrance. A guard held the flap open as Queen Baela called in. "Mara, dear, please, I require your assistance briefly in the recovery tent."

Eugor kissed Mara gently. "Go, I'll be fine."

"Are you sure?" Mara glanced back, asking permission even though she didn't need it. He gave a slight nod, and her lips pressed thin as she followed the queen with hesitant steps.

Once Mara was gone, Eugor's composure shattered. His hands trembled. A scream built inside his chest, clawing to get out until it broke free like thunder crashing in a cathedral. With a strangled cry, he flipped the nearest empty cot—its metal frame clattered violently against the ground. He grabbed a nearby stool and hurled it across the tent, where it splintered into pieces against a medical desk. Another cot followed, upturned with enough force that its legs twisted. The tent walls trembled with each anguished outburst. Blood welled along his knuckles from where a jagged leg of a cot sliced him. *Proof I'm still alive.*

Eugor's chest heaved, breath ragged. His hands trembled as they curled into fists, knuckles pale beneath the strain. A shudder tore through him, soundless, violent—like something deep inside had cracked wide open. And when nothing was left to break, he dropped to his knees amid the wreckage, shoulders shaking, head bowed. The silence that followed was deafening.

Mara paused at the entrance, silver bracelets chiming softly as she drew back the flap, then returned to his side, scanning the scattered wreckage. "Oh, Eugor," her voice tight with concern. She knelt, resting a hand on his shoulder. "I thought something had happened to you."

He didn't dare to look at her. "I just—I couldn't hold it in anymore."

Mara nodded, giving his shoulder a gentle squeeze. "I know." They sat silently, letting the charged stillness settle between them. She rummaged through the shattered remains of a first-aid kit, found a crumpled bandage, and gently wrapped it around his injured hand. "But it's getting late, dear," she finally said, her voice soft but steady. "The clerics will need to prepare your parents' bodies for the ceremony. Perhaps we should wash up, too."

Eugor gave a faint nod, letting her guide him back toward the castle. He glanced back. His parents still lay there peacefully among the destruction he caused.

The castle's silhouette loomed against the twilight, its towers casting long, mournful shadows over the ruined village, like fingers reaching back through time. Its stone walls gleamed coldly in the moonlight, untouched by the flames that had devoured everything else.

Within the inner courtyard, children gathered in lines, bowls in hand, as clerics offered warm stew and kind words. The scent of herbs and broth drifted through the air, momentarily dulling the sharper odors of smoke and decay.

Eugor paused just beyond the gate, his gaze settling on the line of young faces—hollow-eyed, dirt-streaked, as they clutched their bowls as if hope might be ladled next. His throat tightened. Some of them were the same size as when he used to carry Carya on his shoulders through the castle gardens. *She would've found a way to make us laugh, even now.*

He stepped forward, his boots crunching on grit and scattered leaves. The scent of thyme and root vegetables stirred something warm and shameful. He hadn't eaten all day, but the hunger in his belly felt obscene in a place like this. *What right do I have to feel hungry when these children's entire lives have been burned to the ground?* He clenched his jaw, nodded silently to the clerics, and moved on. There was no comfort here—only reminders of war.

Eugor and Mara found a brief haven in a serene chamber, where shallow basins of warm water steamed in the still air. Mara stood beside him, her hands trembling as she pinned back her tangled hair. Eugor scrubbed at the dried blood on his knuckles with slow, mechanical strokes, watching the water blush pink. They washed in silence. After a day of filth and sorrow, the act felt almost sacred. They changed into fresh royal tunics provided by the castle steward—gold for Mara and crimson for Eugor, echoing the evening sky.

Eugor straightened and quickened his stride, the warmth of the bath and clean tunic lending him a fragile calm. He took Mara's hand, and together, they stepped into the ballroom, which glowed with a hushed radiance. The light from chandeliers pooled softly on the marble floor, its warmth at odds with the misery that hung in the air. They maneuvered among the gathered mourners before crossing the threshold to the open field where the funeral awaited.

The firelight wove restless shadows over the sorrowful crowd, each flickering a whisper of misery. The scent of incense and burning wood created an atmosphere of reverence and sorrow. Mara's grip tightened around Eugor's hand as they watched the silk-wrapped forms of his parents be placed upon one of the dozen pyres.

The high priest stepped forward, arms raised. His voice rang clear as he invoked the sacred elements: "Earth—Bearer of Life and the Cradle of Death, we invoke you. Air—Breath of Life and the Wind of Change, we invoke you. Water—Nourishment of Life and the Cleanser of All, we invoke you. Fire—Warmth of Life and the Flames of Death, we invoke you."

The final words melted into silence. Then the pyres caught, flames blooming upward with a gentle roar, bathing the mourners in golden light.

Eugor leaned in, his voice barely more than a breath. "I love you, Mara."

She turned to him and whispered, trembling, "I love you, too."

Eugor turned slightly, noticing a figure standing at the edge of the tree line, half-shrouded in shadow. *Celeste.* Her presence struck like a heartbeat of memory. Before he could fully process it, a light touch settled on his shoulder.

He turned. A hunched figure stood before him, wrapped in a threadbare traveler's cloak, hood drawn low.

"I'm sorry, my friend," the stranger murmured.

Eugor's breath caught. The voice, weathered and low, tugged at something buried deep.

"Do I . . . know you?" The figure tilted its head. Beneath the oversized cowl, a pair of ice-blue eyes glinted. Recognition surged. Eugor staggered back. "Gideon?"

The disguised guardian grinned, a lopsided and unmistakable expression.

"Are you out of your mind?" Eugor hissed. "The High Council sent word to every kingdom and village searching for you." He let the last sentence ring loud enough for others nearby to catch. Then, lower, under his breath: "Why here? Why now?"

"I couldn't let you and Mara face this alone," Gideon said. "I wasn't there for Carya. I—"

Mara gasped, her hand flying to her chest as the voice hit her like a jolt.

"You look awful," Eugor muttered. "I don't think Raven would approve— but she'd be glad you're here."

Gideon opened his mouth to reply, but Celeste emerged at his side before he could speak. "You're insane," she murmured. "The mages are on high alert. They're scanning for illusions since the attack on the king."

"I came to pay my respects," Gideon protested.

Eugor sighed. "Gideon, maybe—"

"Fine," Gideon said quickly, voice low. "Eugor—I need to talk to you. Something happened at Omlett."

"Is Raven all right?" Mara asked.

Gideon nodded. "She's fine. But—"

Celeste covered Gideon's wrinkled lips as a nearby guard snapped his head toward them, suspicion etched across his face as he started their way.

Eugor's gaze flicked to the incoming authority. *It's a High Council guard. Take control.* He straightened, his voice rising, sharp and theatrical. "How dare you!" he barked at the old beggar, ensuring the High Council guard caught every word. "Barging in like this in search of coins."

Celeste slipped her arm through Gideon's and began guiding him away. "Come on," she said gently, a teasing smile on her lips. "Let's find you something warm to eat."

Eugor scoffed under his breath and wiped his hands nervously on his tunic. "Can you believe the nerve of that sickly beggar?" he muttered loud enough and coughed. "I think he was contagious."

The guard's glare lingered on them for a beat longer, then, apparently satisfied, gave a curt nod and moved on through the crowd.

The funeral fires had burned low, the last prayers uttered into an ash-laced wind. As the mourners drifted off in slow, hushed clusters, Mara stepped beside Eugor and gently wrapped her arms around his waist, resting her head against his back. For a moment, neither of them spoke.

Then, quietly, Mara asked, "Do you think Raven is really safe?" Her voice was soft, but the strain beneath it was unmistakable—worry sharpened by the return of ghosts, by all they'd already lost.

Eugor placed a hand over hers. "If Gideon says she's fine, I believe him. But we'll know more soon." He didn't say what they thought—*safe is a fragile word.*

"Why don't we go to the cabin?" she asked softly, her voice a balm. "You've been through a lot today."

Eugor didn't answer right away. The warmth of his wife's touch grounded him, but his eyes remained distant, locked on the broken skyline of Suttiir. The flames still flickered in his peripheral vision, dancing ghosts of the people he'd lost. "I just need a little time," he murmured at last. "Alone. For a bit."

Mara turned him gently to face her, eyes searching his with so much love. Her fingers brushed a loose strand of hair behind his ear, lingering there longer than necessary.

"All right," the words threaded with ache. "But don't vanish for too long." She kissed him—slow, lingering, as if trying to memorize the shape of his lips and his breath's warmth. Then she rested her forehead against his, the space between them full of everything unspoken. "I'll go seek the queen," she murmured. "She's probably already requesting my presence."

Eugor watched Mara slip into the thinning crowd, her silhouette lit in flickers by the dying embers, the stars keeping a silent vigil overhead. He nearly called her back to feel her hand in his a moment longer. But he didn't. Instead, he turned, pulled a torch from its sconce, and disappeared into the trees, the castle lights fading behind him as he moved toward the village.

# CHAPTER THREE

# UNDEADLY BOUNTY

The Mortal Guardians grumbled as they dispersed, Raven still reeling from Gideon's decision to leave them behind. Shorte ascended the stairs with heavy steps, his hand clenching the Inn's handle. "Why bother training us if we can't do our job?" he muttered, bitterness thick.

Raven's voice cut through the tension. "Guardians," she called, her gaze fixed on the broken city beyond the Inn. "We can't leave them like this." Her tone allowed for no argument, and none was forthcoming. The group halted, drawn to the sight of bodies lining the streets—faces they knew, lives they failed to save.

Avalann stepped beside Raven, placing a hand on her shoulder. "You're right."

"How's your side?" Raven asked, glancing over, her tone softer now.

Avalann looked mildly surprised. "Mending. Your mother's healing is something else."

Raven nodded, but her thoughts stayed on the scene before her. She forced herself forward as they moved in pairs—Izarra and Shorte clearing the stage while Mug Cogwheel tended to what remained of his golems. Raven and Avalann began the slow, dreadful work of aligning the dead along the roadside. She focused on each body, treating each as more than debris. *These were names. Stories. Futures.*

The stables offered a sliver of peace. Ghost greeted her with a subdued nicker, and Krit nudged Avalann's shoulder affectionately.

"At least they're safe," Avalann murmured, brushing Krit's muzzle.

"Thanks to the two strangers," Raven replied, her fingers threading through Ghost's mane. "They saved Thomas, too."

The mention of his name made Grail whine. Both women turned instinctively, their hands moving over the warhorse's trembling body.

"Better?" they asked together, and the smallest smile broke the tension.

"At least we have something in common."

"Maybe," Avalann replied, her voice carrying a flicker of uncertainty.

A distant chant drifted to them. They turned to find High Priest Stone-Prayer at the fire pit, his voice rising in solemn prayer. The Guardians began laying the bodies on the pyres.

Raven scanned the rows, her heart lurching with each familiar face. *How many more will we lose before this ends?*

Two guards approached. "We'll take it from here, princess," said a dwarf, gruff but respectful.

"Where's Captain Plunkett?" Raven asked.

"He was severely injured," the other guard began, but Raven stepped closer, urgency burning in her.

"Is he alive?"

"Yes, milady. The captain will never walk again, but he lives."

Raven released a breath, as if surrendering a weight, she'd carried too long.

Mug arrived just then, an oil-stained rag in hand. "I'll build him a mobile chair."

"That would mean more than you know," Raven replied, her voice steady despite the sting behind her eyes.

Avalann turned to face him. "Does Shorte know?"

"Aye, Mister Stone-Grin left in a hurry to visit his uncle," Mug confirmed. "I'll head to the prison soon to visit him and get measurements for the chair." With a brief squeeze of Raven's hand, he turned and left.

Raven watched the burning pyres as the sun set, painting the sky with vibrant hues of orange and pink. The smell of charred flesh hung heavy in the air, a grim reminder of the day's tragedy. *We survived, but at what cost?*

When Raven and Avalann reached the tavern, Izarra was waiting at the Inn's door. Her face bore a guilty expression with an apologetic glaze.

Raven shook her head. "You have nothing to apologize for. I left my post—I made that choice." She gripped her friend's hands. "And I will find Jarz."

Izarra's eyes filled with gratitude. "Now I know what it feels like . . . to lose someone I care for."

Avalann groaned, her voice breaking the moment. "Oh, come on. Hug already—I'm thirsty." She pushed past them with a smirk. "Too slow, rogue."

Inside, the Inn was eerier than Raven had ever known it. She watched as Avalann approached the bar, laying her bow aside.

"May I?" Avalann asked.

Raven gave a curt nod.

Avalann vaulted the counter smoothly and poured herself a drink. Izarra slid onto a nearby stool, her presence still. The red-haired elf behind the bar, always quick with her hands and quicker with her temper, slid a mug across the surface toward the half-nymph without a word.

Raven turned away, her gaze drifting to the room's far end. There, she spotted Thomas seated at a table with two unfamiliar faces. Their expressions were taut—too still. A chill crept down her spine. The steel dagger she'd given Thomas caught the light like a warning. Its tip was embedded in the wooden table. Dread pooled low in her stomach.

Avalann gulped down the last of her ale. "I'll search the rest of the Inn." She grabbed her bow and strolled toward the sleeping rooms.

Raven glanced back toward Izarra. "Could you please retrieve my staff? It's in my bedroom," she requested politely as Izarra nodded, setting her drink down and heading toward Eugor's work chamber. Raven turned her attention to the new arrivals as she settled at the table across from the passed-out paladin and secured her dagger. "Thank you."

"No problem," the human warrior replied, gently lifting Thomas's head to check his breathing. "He's a fighter."

The rogue nodded in agreement. "I'm Raven Naelo."

"We know, Princess," the tiny elf in brown-furred armor chimed in. "I'm Gooey, from Spires Hand."

The warrior beamed. "But everyone calls her Gobs because her full name is Gooeybeans." The druid elf flushed crimson, burying her face in her hands while the warrior casually lifted a hand. "Ashley Nell."

Her eyes caught Raven's attention—not red from exhaustion, but something more profound. They twinkled, reptilian, slit like a snake's. *Is it an enchantment, bloodline, or something worse?*

Raven hesitated. Waterfront's headmaster warned her that touch spells can linger or bite. But she pushed the voice aside and clasped Ashley's offered hand. Her grip was firm, solid. "Thank you," she said. "For protecting Thomas. And the animals. I owe you both."

"Actually, Princess—" Ashley's voice dropped, her usual confidence softening into something quieter. Her dragon-slit pupils met Raven's eyes. "We're even now."

Raven blinked, confused. "I'm sorry, I don't understand."

Ashley hesitated, then spoke more gently. "Do you remember the old man you saved from the bugbear raid a couple of years ago?"

Raven's brow lifted. "My first mission."

Ashley nodded. "He was my grandfather." Her voice cracked slightly. "Our family owed you a debt ever since."

Raven's breath caught. "How is he?"

Ashley glanced down, her fingers curling slightly on the table. "He passed. A fortnight ago."

The words hit harder than Raven expected. "Oh . . . I'm sorry."

Ashley gave a faint, bittersweet smile. "They said it was natural."

"He died from heart failure," Gobs added with blunt clarity. "I told him to cut back on salt intake, but he didn't listen."

There was an awkward pause, but Raven didn't mind it. Her gaze lingered on Ashley—the grief behind those strange, fiery pupils—and she felt the weight of that old mission settle on her shoulders in a new way.

"Gobs, I thought you nagged him to death." Ashley jokingly nudged Gobs, then winked at Raven. "We were able to spend more time with him before he left for the Astral Realm. For that, we'll always be grateful. He would sit and tell the children in our town about the mighty elf hero and her friends."

"Half-elf," Raven corrected.

"But you look like an elf," Ashley countered.

"No—she resembles a human," Gobs amended, laughing.

The two friends exchanged amused glances and nodded in unison, "Half-elf."

"Anyway, thank you," Ashley replied, returning to Raven.

Raven nodded, the weight of Ashley's words settling into something solid—something proud. "You're welcome," she said, her voice steady. "I'm glad I was there when it counted."

For a moment, the air around the table shifted. Gratitude passed between them in softened looks and expressions. Raven sat a little straighter, not out of pride but purpose. *I made a difference. We saved a life. A life that mattered.* "My friends and I did what we had to do," she stated, her voice steady as she tried to grasp the nature of the two companions before her. "Just like you both did here. Thomas would have died, and so would Ghost, Grail, and Krit."

"Which one is the unicorn?" Gobs's hands tapped on the table with excitement.

"Ghost. She's—"

"Pregnant!" Gobs's sudden interruption caused Raven's jaw to fall open. "Ah, you didn't know," she added sheepishly.

"You must forgive her candor. Gobs is a druid." Ashley tittered, nudging her friend. "Druid senses. She can detect new life in the most unusual ways and sometimes gets overly excited about it."

Raven raised an eyebrow with a crooked smile. "And what about you?"

"I'm not pregnant," Ashley teased. "Oh, you mean . . . I'm a warrior from Penn's Woods. We came here searching for a wizard named Astrick Fake. He has a bounty on his head, and we're here to collect."

"I'm afraid you're too late," Raven explained somberly, watching Thomas for any reaction. "A succubus killed him. We believe he was working with her and a necromancer."

Gobs and Ashley exchanged a concerned glance. "Do you still have the body?" Ashley asked, her voice grave.

"No. Cremated." Raven's voice cracked just slightly.

"A damn shame." Ashley's shoulders slumped slightly. "We really could have used the coin."

"We just lost ten gold pieces," Gobs added, her expression reflecting a mix of disappointment and resignation. "I guess we can return to the east and look for work there?"

Raven nodded sympathetically, understanding their predicament. "I'm sorry we couldn't have met sooner."

"It's not your fault," Ashley replied with a small smile, trying to lighten the mood. "Guess we'll have to find another way to make ends meet."

"What if I hire you?" Raven asked impulsively. "There's—"

"All clear in the north wing," Avalann shouted, returning from searching the Inn's rooms. The archer joined the group at the table with sharp eyes, assessing the newcomers briefly. "Friends or foes?"

"Friends," Raven said simply.

Avalann nodded in understanding, then turned to the newcomers. "Welcome to Omlett Inn," she greeted, her tone respectful yet guarded. "But I'm going to check on the south wing."

"So! What do you need to hire us for?" Gobs asked excitedly.

"I want to place a bounty"—the need for revenge rushed through her—"on the necromancer."

Ashley glanced at Gobs. "That's a dangerous request."

"Name your price," Raven retorted abruptly.

"Four platinum pieces." The warrior wiggled four fingers as the druid looked worried.

"Done." Raven walked to the safe under the bar. *I'm sure my father won't mind.* She retrieved two platinum pieces and tossed one to each of them. "Two PIPs now, the other half when he's brought to me dead or alive."

"Or undead?" Ashley grinned.

"Either way. We think he's in Fellswar's Claim," Raven responded calmly as the two women stood from the table.

Ashley offered one more handshake, and Raven shook it firmly. The warrior smiled, her grip solid yet reassuring. "Deal." Raven couldn't ignore the bloodshot redness in Ashley's cornea. As she let go of her hand, she turned to her friend. "Gobs, we need to contact the *Squid*—have Saven portal us to the Claim."

"But you hate portals," Gobs retorted, frowning.

"I'll do it for the coin." Ashley gave a determined nod, then turned back to Raven. "Did I overhear that the necro abducted someone?"

"Yes, our swordmage, Jarz Fisker."

"We'll make sure to locate him as well." Ashley swiftly downed the remainder of her drink.

Gobs approached Raven with a warm smile as she gently took Raven's other hand. "Make sure you get plenty of rest, stay away from the ale, and drink plenty of water," she instructed earnestly, whistling a tune as she approached the door.

Ashley retrieved her backpack and turned back to Raven. "Nice eyes, by the way. You can tell a lot about someone by their eyes." The warrior caught up to Gobs at the door and paused. "Oh, and I would take Gobs's advice to heart. She's never wrong about these things." Ashley and Gobs exited the Inn with a wink, leaving a sense of bemusement.

Raven sighed, her concern deepening as she moved to sit beside Thomas, gently pushing his untouched mug of ale aside. *Give up ale?* She scoffed at the thought as she ran a hand through his messy hair, her expression a mix of worry and tenderness. "What am I going to do with you?"

"Carya," Thomas moaned again, his voice thick with emotion.

Her heart sank at the name, and tears welled. The weight of loss and uncertainty pressed heavily upon her as she tried to comfort her friend. Raven bowed her head. "I'm still here," she whispered. *For now.* Her thoughts wandered back to Baka and Krea.

The Inn door slammed open. Shorte strolled in, oblivious to the tension he shattered. He grabbed a mug of ale from the bar without hesitation before joining Raven at the table.

"That ale's Izarra's," Raven informed him with a hint of annoyance.

"So, I guess she'll pay," Shorte quipped, taking a sip and settling in. "Where is everyone?" He glanced around the nearly empty Inn.

Before Raven could answer, Avalann entered from the south corridor, bringing a bit of urgency to the atmosphere. "Cyndi's alive and is caring for Brugg," the archer announced, moving swiftly to the bar. "He's laid up with injuries."

"How bad is it?" Raven inquired.

"Some deep scratches across his face, chest, and legs." Avalann poured herself another drink. "They're in his quarters."

Shorte, ever the provocateur, nudged Thomas with his mug. "How's the dragon fodder doing?" he asked in a tone that grated on Raven's nerves. She shot him a look of irritation, but the dwarf just shrugged and took another drink.

Avalann sat beside Shorte, her expression serious as she joined the conversation. "How's Buzz?"

"He's fine." Shorte wiped ale from his chin. "I'm staying with him to help with the new chair. Knowing Mug, there will be some tweaking to do." With that, the cleric returned to the bar for another round of drinks, his manner gruff, but his loyalty to his friends was evident.

Raven glanced around, taking in the familiar faces and the weight of their recent losses and challenges. Gratitude washed over her for the companionship and support of her friends, even amid their rough edges and quirks.

Izarra appeared, cradling the staff and circlet in her arms. "Sorry I took so long," she said, slightly out of breath. "I checked your house—everything looked fine. It feels . . . empty now that your parents are in Suttiir."

"Thank you," Raven said, her voice warm with gratitude as she took the staff and slid the onyx circlet into place.

"But I also found this," Izarra added, holding a smooth, dark bracelet. The onyx band glinted under the light, almost absorbing it. "It was wrapped around your staff. Looks like something's missing—or maybe it fell out."

Raven flipped the bracelet around, inspecting the piece of jewelry with curiosity. *Oh, Mug.* Her fingers delicately retrieved a flat, gray stone from her coin pouch; its surface was smooth and cold. She took a moment, her brow creasing in concentration, and with precision, aligned it with the center of a sleek bracket on the onyx bracelet. The muted gray of the stone contrasted sharply with the dark band, creating an oddly harmonious combination.

"Great, she has a pet rock," Avalann quipped, turning to Shorte as he took a deep swig of ale.

The timing was precise. Raven had barely braced herself when ale erupted from Shorte's mouth and nose in a glorious spray, droplets catching the lantern light like fireflies before splattering across the table—and all over Thomas. Shorte doubled over, coughing and laughing, his beard dancing with ale beads as he wiped his face with a rough, calloused hand.

Thomas sat in stunned disgust, lifting his soaked arms with a grimace that drew another round of laughter from the group.

A smile cracked on Raven's lips. It surprised her how easily it came, how much she needed it. The sound of honest and unguarded laughter filled the space between them like a balm. In the middle of uncertainty and half-buried heartache, it was a moment that reminded her they were still mortal. *Still together.* But she kept eyeing the remaining friends and thought about the ones they'd lost. *We're not done yet.* She gripped her staff and stood. *Not by a long shot.* "Shorte, clean up this mess by the time I return."

# CHAPTER FOUR

# WATERFRONT BOUND

Raven moved noiselessly through the low-lit corridor toward Brugg's quarters, her boots barely whispering against the stone floor. She paused at the familiar door on the left and knocked twice softly, respectfully. Cyndi's voice invited her in, and Raven stepped through, heart already bracing.

Brugg's room was warm despite the winter winds creeping through the two open windows. As always, he insisted they stay open—said the cold reminded him he was alive. The mantel was cluttered with small treasures: a chipped wooden whistle, a child's ribbon, and the green "Welcome" plate Raven's mother had etched carefully. That piece drew her eyes. She hadn't thought of it in years.

The room held pieces of him everywhere, each one tugging at her. Drawings from children—one of her and Carya swinging off his massive arm. A dire-bear pelt sprawled across the floor, the trophy from a hunt he'd once taken with her father. She could still remember the laughter in their shared stories after that hunt.

Brugg lay still in his bed, a battered giant confined to quiet suffering. The bed creaked slightly under his weight—oversized but not quite built for an orc of his stature. His green skin was pale, and his breathing was shallow. Bandages soaked through with dark blood wrapped his legs, and his face was a mess of swollen flesh and jagged claw marks. Cyndi knelt beside him, dabbing at a fresh cut on his cheek.

After setting her staff against the wall, Raven moved closer, her throat tightening. "How is he?" she asked, her voice low.

Cyndi offered a thin, tired smile. "Still with us. Barely." She adjusted his blanket. "He kept me alive."

Their voices stirred the sleeping orc, and Brugg slowly opened his eyes, his gaze shifting between them.

"Hey, you big lug," Raven said in Orcish, forcing a smile.

Brugg's attempt at a grin ended in a wince. His voice rasped out one word: "Family."

It hit harder than she expected. She nodded, but her voice was heavy. "What happened?"

"Just Brugg being Brugg," Cyndi explained with a fond smile, her tone tinged with admiration. "He fought like hell. Broomstick, rake—anything he could find. But then a group of undead orcs arrived. Familiar faces. That's when he stopped fighting."

Raven blinked, not quite believing. "He just stopped fighting?"

"Family," Brugg muttered sadly in Orcish.

Cyndi continued her account, her hands deftly checking the bandages. "Then they overwhelmed him. But luckily, a warrior and a druid stepped in and saved his life."

"They saved Thomas and some of our stable friends," Raven added, her voice tinged with gratitude.

Cyndi nodded, her attention focused on her task. "The druid cast a healing spell and bandaged him up."

"You know you'll end up with an eye patch like Buzz," Raven teased gently in Orcish, trying to lighten the mood.

Brugg coughed in pain, attempting to chuckle. "Me . . . hurt," he managed to say in the common language, his voice strained.

"I know," Raven rubbed his bulky green arm. "Rest."

Brugg grasped her hand, his fingers closing around hers tenderly. His smile widened to reveal a chipped front tooth. "Gideon—naked," he mumbled suddenly, his lips twitching in amusement. "Wait . . . for . . . Raven."

"Gideon naked?" Raven echoed, raising an eyebrow suspiciously as Brugg chuckled again, his laughter interrupted by coughs. Eventually, he grew still and closed his eyes.

Raven exchanged a bemused glance with Cyndi, who shrugged with a smile. "He's been through a lot," Cyndi remarked gently, grabbing his large hand. "He must have taken some serious hits to the head, but I'll take care of him, Princess."

As Raven stood by Brugg's bedside, she couldn't help but feel a mix of emotions—gratitude for his bravery, concern for his injuries, and a touch of amusement at his unexpected comment about Gideon. Her smile softened as she nodded at Cyndi's reassurance. "Thank you. I know he's in good hands."

Raven collected her staff and returned to the common area. As her fingers curled around the smooth wood, a storm of fortitude built inside her. *Enough waiting.* "I've decided," she said flatly as she rejoined the others. "We're not sitting around anymore."

Avalann straightened and muttered, "About time."

"Indeed!" Shorte yelled, slamming his mug on the table.

Raven leaned against the counter, her gaze sweeping over each of them. "We need to find Jarz and deal with this necromancer. I'm not going to wait for bounty hunters. We have skills and resources—we need to use them."

Shorte nodded thoughtfully, scratching his beard. "Aye, we can't sit around on our arses as Guardians of the Realm. I'm with you."

"We need to find a way to Fellswar's Claim," Raven said, her voice low but resolute.

The dwarf let out a dry snort. "Too far to ride on a horse, and then we would need to find a boat."

"No one's ever dared to set up a portal receiver there," Avalann added, arms folded tight across her chest. "Too dangerous. Too wild."

Izarra hiccupped and swung her mug in a lazy arc. "And in case you missed it," she slurred, "our wizards aren't here."

Shorte leaned toward Raven, mouthing, "She only had one drink!"

Raven's staff cracked against the stone floor, silencing them as Izarra jerked upright. "There are portal scrolls to Waterfront," she said sharply. "And Waterfront has wizards. Capable ones." One by one, the others nodded.

"It's worth a shot," Avalann replied, breaking the silence with a determined look. She adjusted the strap of her satchel with precision. "Where can we get Waterfront scrolls?"

"Maggie's," Shorte revealed, his voice a low murmur that carried a hint of reluctance, glancing at Raven briefly before continuing. "You plan to break into Maggie's shop again?"

"Do we have a choice?" Izarra questioned. "Jarz is out there somewhere with that maniac. So I'm in." Avalann and Shorte nodded in agreement.

Raven raised her staff, closed her eyes, and chanted as she summoned her familiar, a raven. The bird came to life and sat on the staff's end as she telepathically gave it a message. "I need to tell my father what happened here at Omlett, and that we're heading to Fellswar's Claim."

"That's just a bit creepy," the cleric muttered as Avalann opened the front door. "Have you named that thing yet?"

"No, but I was thinking about Shorty since she can be a bit stubborn," Raven said teasingly. She opened her eyes and watched the bird fly past the archer and out the front door. The dwarf glared at her murderously.

After surveying the town and assisting citizens along the main road, the Mortal Guardians finally reached the magic shop by sundown. The group dismounted from their animals by the eerily quiet cobblestone building. The surrounding shops had shattered windows, and the wooden doors were splintered, traces of recent turmoil. Maggie's shop, however, stood resolute—an oasis of calm amid chaos. Colorful, rectangular stained-glass windows curved around the door frame, catching the last remaining sunlight in a dazzling display of blues and purples.

"I'll go alone," Raven said.

"By all means," Shorte allowed, stepping aside.

"I'll be back shortly." Raven's voice was barely audible against the hushed night. She cautiously approached the heavy oak door, her footsteps echoing softly on the cobblestones. The ornate bat knocker, wrought from iron, loomed eerily in the moonlight. With a deft hand, Raven retrieved her lock pick from her ponytail and set to work. The tumblers moved quickly, and the lock clicked softly. *Cookies!*

The door creaked open.

As Raven crept around the shop, the air thick with the scent of ancient magic and herbs, she searched through one intriguing object after another. Cabinets of powders and liquids lined the walls, their contents shimmering with latent power. Several magical staffs stood sentinel in the corners, their intricate carvings seeming to pulse faintly with inner light. Displayed prominently were various animal skulls, appendages, and preserved body parts suspended in eerie green liquids inside glass jars. Nearby, bookshelves sagged under the weight of candles, small cauldrons, and weathered spell books.

Raven methodically searched each shelf for the scrolls. At last, she spotted a golden box radiating a faint aura on the top shelf behind the polished counter. She climbed onto the table ledge and stretched toward the container. Yet, as her fingers brushed against the cool metal, a mysterious force yanked it from her grasp, returning it gently to its place.

"What the spell?!" Raven hissed. Undeterred, she tried again, only to encounter the same inexplicable resistance. A soft yet commanding voice echoed behind her as she poised herself for a third attempt.

"Raven?"

Raven froze, caught off guard by Maggie's sudden appearance—and the flicker of blue sparks dancing along her fingertips. The raw energy crackled in the air, a reminder of just how close they'd all come to death not long ago. Maggie's eyes were ringed with fatigue, but her stance was rigid, ready.

"I didn't mean to startle you," Raven said, steadying her breath and nodding toward the scroll. "We need to get to Waterfront."

Maggie's expression flickered—fatigue, something haunted. "Just knock next time," she said, though her voice lacked bite.

Raven hesitated. "How are you holding up?"

Maggie glanced at her for a long moment, then shook her head. "I'll mend. Eventually. Not all wounds bleed." There was a silence neither of them moved to fill. Then Maggie exhaled sharply, gesturing to the scroll. "Take it, Princess Naelo," she said, turning. "Show her out."

A force nudged Raven toward the door, a gentle reminder from Maggie's unseen servant to depart respectfully. She took the hint, realizing she had perhaps overstepped her bounds with the shopkeeper. "I know the way," she muttered softly. *I'll apologize later.*

Once outside, she quickly broke the seal and unfurled the parchment, revealing intricate hieroglyphs glowing with a faint blue hue. Without hesitation, Raven channeled her focus into casting the spell. The air around them shimmered as the magic took hold, forming a swirling vortex of blue light. The portal hummed softly.

"Does anyone know the location of the portal receiver in Waterfront?" Izarra's voice quivered with nervousness.

"That's a damn good question, blondie," Shorte growled, the clang of his mace against his shield ringing like a war drum. He trudged toward Izarra, blue energy throwing harsh light across the lines of his rugged face. "But I don't care 'cause it's one step closer to where we need to be."

# CHAPTER FIVE

# BLOOD BROTHERS

Aushade emerged from the sparkling portal. He squinted, adjusting to the morning light that bathed the muddy road. Ahead, two undead elf minions struggled, dragging a young mage by his arms. They halted abruptly as the portal sealed, dropping the mage unceremoniously onto the damp ground, where he sprawled face-first into the muck. Aushade approached with amusement.

The young mage groaned, his face smeared with mud, and lifted his head from the ground, sneering. "Where's your ride?" he inquired, his voice strained yet surprisingly composed. "I think she needs to be milked." A wry smile twisted his mouth.

Aushade's expression hardened. Without a word, he gestured casually, and one of the lifeless elf minions lumbered forward, its decaying fingers extending toward the prisoner's dirty face.

The mage's bravado faltered as the cold, rotting digits pressed against his lips, forcing their way into his mouth. He gagged and thrashed, desperately dislodging the foul intrusion. With a violent twist of his head, the mage tore the fingers from the minion's grasp. Before he could spit out the putrid remnants, Aushade's hand clamped over his mouth, driving the severed fingers deeper into his throat. Panic seized the wizard's eyes as he clawed at the necromancer's arm, fighting for air amid the suffocating assault.

Aushade's stare remained impassive, watching with detached interest as the struggle intensified. "Two things are going to happen," he instructed calmly, his grip unyielding. "No more insults"—he watched the mage scowl in acknowledgment—"and no incantations." He held the threat there until the mage nodded vigorously in agreement. "If you try," Aushade continued, his voice low and menacing, "I'll have them rip out your tongue." He waited until the mage's expression registered genuine fear before slowly retracting his hand, allowing the dismembered fingers to fall to the ground.

The mage coughed and retched, spitting out the remains of bile and mud. "Understood."

"Want some milk to wash it out?" Aushade quizzed, his tone mocking yet edged with a dangerous undercurrent. Though tempered by the reality of his vulnerability, the wizard's glare burned with defiance. "Remember," he added coolly, meeting the mage's gaze with an intensity that conveyed his authority, "you're alive because I have allowed it."

"Why?" The mage's voice was hoarse as he lay on the ground, still catching his breath.

Aushade regarded him for a moment, then offered his hand. The young man hesitated briefly before reluctantly grasping it. They walked toward the Grey-Holg Inn, the structure sagging like a drunk in the wind. Aushade's bag knocked against his hip, the artifact within emitting a pulse, faint but insistent. It was reacting again, drawn to something. Or someone.

Aushade watched the mage's twitching fingers drift toward the satchel. *He senses it, just as I hoped. Still useful, for now.*

Off to the side of the inn, a shape hunched against the warped fence, draped in death and silence. Aushade stopped cold, breathing shallowly as he noticed the undead female. The air thickened. "Keep moving, mage," he said, voice low but sharp as flint. He gripped the bag tightly. Whatever stirred in the artifact was drawn to *her*, and that was a complication he didn't need.

But the mage stopped. Aushade turned, irritation rising.

The mage's face had gone pale, staring at the corpse like it was more than just another pitiful thing dragged back from the brink. "I know her," he said, voice hollow.

Aushade glanced back, his expression betraying a flicker of interest. The undead minion, clad in a dirty, white burial gown, stood motionless, its expressionless face staring at the village. "My prize." Aushade reached into his bag swiftly. He retrieved a silver box, its surface engraved with intricate symbols. The undead female turned toward them slowly, emitting a mournful moan as the box emitted a haunting wail in a feminine voice.

"That's a lich phylactery," the wizard indicated, his voice tinged with recognition and concern as he examined the silver box.

"So you're familiar with them?" Aushade asked, his tone curious yet guarded, his focus never leaving the undead minion nearby.

The mage continued to inspect the metal box thoughtfully, running his fingers over the engraved runes. "That's a shite substitute for a real one, though." His brow furrowed with disapproval. "It won't contain the soul for long."

"Well, you work with what you got," Aushade stated, his voice betraying a hint of annoyance, grabbing it back. He carefully returned the box to his bag, securing it. "I need you to make a real one in the form of a necklace, and I won't take a—"

"I will," the swordmage interrupted firmly, his tone resolute and unwavering. "If that means Carya keeps her soul and some of her consciousness."

Aushade nodded slightly, acknowledging the mage's pledge. "She must have been important to you," he remarked, pushing open the heavy door of the crumbling Grey-Holg Inn and gesturing for the mage to enter first.

"She's family," the wizard answered tersely, his face mere inches from Aushade's. His eyes briefly flickered at the bandage on the necro's cheek. "Did you get a boo-boo?"

"Sit," Aushade snarled, his voice sharp as he pushed the prisoner into the gloomily lit inn and slammed the heavy door behind them.

The young mage complied, settling onto a rickety wooden stool.

"Drink?" Aushade asked casually, striding toward the dusty bar and setting his worn duffel bag atop it. He picked up a mug in each hand, sniffing them individually. "Not much of a selection. Water, ale . . ." He placed the mugs on the bar, then hesitated at the third. With a sudden jerk of his head, he recoiled. "Or piss."

"Water," the mage replied grimly.

Aushade turned his attention back to the prisoner just in time to see the flicker of blue light pulsing from the mage's ring. A surge of magic sparked to life. A portal flared open before he could react. "Jarz!" a woman's voice cried from the other side.

*I was right.*

The mage lunged for the duffel bag, panic in his movements. Then he spun toward the portal, ready to escape.

"AUSHADE!" the necromancer shouted, straining over the portal's growing hum.

The name struck like a blow. The mage froze mid-step. "How do you know that name?" he demanded, his voice tight with shock and suspicion.

"I know lots of names," Aushade said cryptically. "Stacia. Ausharz. Jarz."

His calm words halted the prisoner's frantic struggle.

Jarz hesitated, then dropped the bag. He reached down, slid the glowing ring from his finger, and set it on the nearest table—just as the portal collapsed.

"Check the phylactery."

Jarz opened the bag and pulled out a small box, placing it beside the ring. "Still functional."

Aushade slung his pack onto the counter and took a thoughtful sip from his mug. "I'll admit, I expected you to portal out. You must be curious."

"I figured you'd have killed me already," the mage replied bluntly, eyeing Aushade warily. "How do you know those names?"

"The wings—" Aushade began, his voice softening with a hint of reminiscence. "I saw your blue water wings on the battlefield."

The mage furrowed his brow, a mix of confusion and guarded interest on his face. "You captured me for my water wings?"

"Those wings aren't just for cosmetics, are they?" Aushade interrogated, his tone probing deeper into the mage's motives.

"I cast them before a battle," Jarz explained, his voice tinged with defensiveness. "Just like how you turn your magical mount into a Nightmare—it's just a spell."

"But why the blue water wings?" Aushade's curiosity drove him onward.

The mage shot back with a flicker of defiance, "Does it matter?"

"It's a simple question," Aushade insisted, his tone firm yet patient.

Jarz hesitated momentarily as he wrestled with memories. "For my brother, Aushade Fisker," he finally admitted, his voice softer now, mingled with sorrow and longing.

Aushade's expression softened, a flicker of understanding crossing his features as he processed the revelation. "I see." He placed his ale on the bar with a deliberate *clunk*, then turned his back on the younger man, his movements intentional and focused. He retrieved a bundle of sticks and a folded blue cloth from his bag, the items that had sparked recognition from the wizard. A sharp gasp escaped Jarz's lips as realization dawned. "I made this for you," he boasted, facing his brother, and he quickly assembled the wing contraption. "I found them, but you were gone, Jarz." *Now I find out if the risk of bringing him here was worth it.*

The wizard stood in awe, fixated on the familiar contraption taking shape in the necromancer's hands. "Aushade?"

With a swift motion, he removed his helmet, revealing a bandaged cheek and a face weathered by battle. "Yes, it's me." His voice conveyed emotion as he finished assembling the wings. "It's been a long time." He extended the contraption toward his younger brother, a silent offering filled with unspoken memories and a promise of reconciliation.

Jarz stood frozen, his eyes wide, as if he had seen a ghost, until his face flushed red. Without a word, he reached out, snatching the branches and blue cloth from Aushade's hands and throwing them violently onto the inn's dusty floor. "You killed all those elves—dwarves—gnomes." His voice trembled with anger and hurt. "You attacked us! You killed your family!"

Aushade staggered backward, his confusion evident as he struggled to comprehend his brother's accusations. "I—" His gaze darted between Jarz and the discarded wing contraption.

Jarz huffed bitterly, pointing outside with a shaky hand. "Carya was our cousin, and you had your horde kill her, too."

The necromancer frowned deeply, his brow furrowing with regret. "I didn't know who Carya was. I didn't know you were alive and on that battlefield. I would have never—"

"Father always told us we had two paths to take, and you chose to become evil by killing those innocents—"

"The orcs are not innocent!" Aushade fumed, his anger palpable as he slammed his ale against the wall. "They took everything from us. We had a peace treaty allowing humans to establish a town in Fellswar in exchange for a place in Western Euphrasia. And they broke it, catching us off guard."

"What then?" Jarz pressed, his voice softer but insistent. "Once you got your revenge on the orcs, what made you decide to attack so many people?"

Aushade hesitated, his expression darkening with inner turmoil. Memories of battles and betrayals flashed through his mind, each decision weighing heavily on his conscience. "They were supposed to pay," he murmured, his voice laden with bitterness. "But it spiraled out of control. Power, revenge—it consumed me."

Jarz regarded his older brother. "Why?"

Before Aushade could answer, a swirling red portal materialized in the inn. Instinctively, he drew his sword, ready to defend against any threat that might emerge. However, to his surprise, only Courtlynn and Floxy, her companion, stepped through the portal's flickering veil.

"Aushade, you had me worried," Courtlynn said with relief and affection, pressing her lips hard against his. Her body leaned close, but he gently pulled back, releasing her embrace.

"I thought you returned to the Abyss?" Confusion stained his concern as he studied her face.

"Not yet." The succubus's gaze momentarily flickered toward his younger brother. "The battle was over, and you were gone. I wanted to make sure you were safe."

"What have you done?" Jarz interjected sharply, his stance defensive as he summoned his sword and shield, eyeing the succubus with suspicion.

Courtlynn tilted her head, curiosity piqued as she looked past Aushade to study his brother. "Who's this?" Amusement laced through her tone.

The young wizard stood defiantly. "Go back to the Abyss, demon!"

Courtlynn giggled softly, a hint of sarcasm in her voice. "Aren't you adorable?"

"Enough!" Aushade scolded firmly, stepping between them to defuse the rising tension.

"When did we start taking prisoners?" the succubus asked casually, staring at the mage with a calculating glint. "He would make a powerful soldier for your army."

"The mage is none of your concern," Aushade responded, his tone cold and dismissive. "I'm questioning him, nothing more. I'll dispose of him when I'm done."

"Very well." Courtlynn shrugged as she opened the front door. Floxy darted outside eagerly. "My master's army is ready. It may be some time until we see each other again, my dark pally. Will you miss me?"

"You know I will." Aushade watched Floxy as the demon fox returned, dragging the undead female minion Jarz had called family. "Where do you think you're taking her?" he demanded, his voice rising angrily.

"My master needs a demon leader. Her power will surely help him win the war," Courtlynn explained rationally.

"You told him about the soul?" The sting of betrayal burned.

Jarz snickered from his place, unable to resist a jab. "You can't trust a demon."

Courtlynn hissed at the mage, her face twisted with malice, then turned to Aushade, her expression softening. "You don't understand, my love. I can't lie to my master. I'm bound to him."

"I didn't capture her for Draklor," Aushade asserted, pushing Courtlynn away from him. "She's to stay here with me."

Her smile faded. "You need to know your place, my love. He will come for her if she doesn't return with me, and I don't want to see you get hurt."

Aushade huffed, his frustration evident. "I can take care of myself."

"Just trust me." Courtlynn batted her lashes to soften him. "I'll watch over her in the Abyss, and once the war is over, I'll return her to you." She gave Aushade a peck on the cheek, her lips lingering momentarily.

"Please don't let this evil demon take her," Jarz pleaded, his voice cracking with desperation.

With a swift motion, Courtlynn opened an orange portal. As the swirling vortex came to life, she cast a final glare and hissed at Jarz. Then, with a graceful sweep, she took the metal box from the table, her attention never leaving

Aushade's. "Until we meet again." The flirtatious succubus kissed Aushade once more before stepping through the portal with Carya and Floxy in tow, disappearing into the Abyss.

"Now I understand," Jarz scoffed bitterly, "that succubus got inside your head and seduced you into killing everyone."

"It's not like that," Aushade retorted sharply, pointing to the sword and shield. "I told you, no incantations."

Jarz dismissed his magical items with a wave of his hand. "That creature will say and do anything to complete its master's bidding. How can you be involved with someone like that?"

"You don't know what I went through, brother." Aushade's temper burned with suppressed rage. "And by the looks of your fancy armor and spells, you were probably raised in the luxury of Waterfront. So don't you dare judge me!"

"I don't have to—*brother*," Jarz sneered back. "All of Western Euphrasia already has."

The necromancer moved closer, his anger flaring. He grabbed Jarz by his armor, effortlessly lifting him off the ground.

Jarz paused, his expression softening. "You're right," he replied as the necromancer released the mage, dropping him unceremoniously onto the floor. "A wizard rescued me."

"Figures," Aushade muttered darkly.

"Do you remember Henry Owens?"

"Barely," Aushade replied, though the name triggered a faint memory.

"Well, he created a portal by the throne room to save as many people as possible. I happened to be wandering around the chaos, calling out your name. Father was defending the portal and grabbed me by the wings," Jarz explained, his voice heavy with the weight of the memory. "He ordered me to go with Owens. But we did wait for you until Father ordered him to go when a group of orcs entered the Royal Hall."

Aushade sighed, the weight of his past heavy on his shoulders. "I was trapped in the training yard by those orcs." He paused momentarily before continuing. "I fought my way back to the house and found Father's body crumpled on the stairs. I rushed to him and tried healing spells, but it was too late. Then I was surrounded by war orcs."

"How did you defend yourself?"

"Not sure. I was fifteen, frightened, and desperate," Aushade responded, recalling the memories of the orcs charging the courtyard. "I tried to copy Father's resurrection spell and somehow animated the corpses on the steps."

Jarz's voice was barely a whisper. "Including our father?"

"Including our father," Aushade repeated, retrieving a leather-bound book from his bag and holding it out for his brother to see. "But the orcs didn't stand a chance."

"Father's spell book," Jarz breathed, reaching for the fragile item with reverence. He hungrily examined the ancient text, peeling each page like a delicate flower. "Where did you find it?"

"I was studying it in the courtyard before the attack," Aushade replied, watching his brother closely. "What is it?"

"It's Father's notes on Uncle Eugor's resurrection," Jarz responded, still absorbed in the journal. "Eating a dragon egg apparently bonded a dragon element to his body."

"Let me see," Aushade demanded, stepping closer behind his brother. "I haven't read those notes in over a decade. Is it permanently infused, or is it temporary?"

Jarz flipped the page, scanning the text. "He kept a record of our cousins. With normal blue eyes, Carya shows minimal signs of dragon traits, blah, blah—here! Raven Naelo was born with purple eyes—question mark."

Aushade glanced over Jarz's shoulder, shaking his head, and read, "Eugor reported that she was immune to acid at age three." He paused, considering. "I think these are traits of a black dragon."

"Seems like Eugor knew all along and was working with our Father."

"Do you think she can spit acid?" Aushade rubbed his bandaged cheek thoughtfully.

"It's possible. Izarra told me about Raven casting darkness during her eighteenth birthday party."

"Who's Izarra?" Aushade asked, intrigued by the new name.

"We have to take this back to Omlett," Jarz suggested, ignoring the question. "We may be able to resurrect Carya."

Aushade sighed deeply. *I know what I must do.* "You can take it back."

"Return with me," Jarz urged. "Turn yourself in and give the Naelos the book as a goodwill gesture."

"Are you insane? They would execute me on the spot. Besides, I'll need to retrieve Carya from the Abyss." The brothers stared at each other, the weight of their decisions hanging heavily between them.

"I guess this is goodbye?" Jarz questioned solemnly.

"For now. I have to make the long journey back to Fellswar's Claim."

His younger brother created two blue portals with a flick of his wrists. "This one will take you there, and I'm returning to Omlett."

Aushade grabbed his bag and helmet, facing the portal. Before he could move, his brother pulled him into a quick hug. For a moment, Aushade stood there, stiff and stunned, the weight of the embrace hitting harder than he expected. It had been years since he'd felt anything like it—solid, familiar, real. Then Jarz stepped back, casting water wings with a flick of his hand before vanishing into the Omlett portal with the book tucked under his arm.

Aushade swallowed hard and turned toward the Claim's portal. The physical embrace of the hug clung to him as he stepped through. Emerging on the other side, he found himself in the familiar landscape dotted with cinder cones, small craters, and volcanic fissures stretching out before him.

Dominating the scene was a massive volcano, its peak rising sharply into the sky, a plume of smoke and ash billowing from its crater. Rivers of lava snaked down the sides, cooling and hardening into solid rock, while older flows formed lava tubes and caves. In some places, the surfaces were black and glassy, with cracks revealing the bright orange and red glow of molten rock beneath.

The ground was rugged and uneven, covered in hardened lava flows that twisted and turned, creating jagged formations. The vegetation was sparse, but hardy plants and pioneer species slowly reclaimed the barren land, adding patches of green to the otherwise dark and rocky terrain. In some areas, steam vents hissed, releasing sulfuric gases.

The necromancer drew in a shaky breath, the acrid stench clawing at his throat. *Home, sweet home.* His chest still ached where Jarz had grabbed him—a sudden, desperate hug he hadn't known he needed until it was gone. *I found my brother all because of his love of wings.* He squeezed his eyes shut briefly, holding onto the feeling, hoping it could fill the hollow yawning wide inside him. *I can rescue Carya. I have to. I have to make it right.* Because if he didn't—if he failed again—there would be nothing left of him worth saving. But he sensed something was wrong. The air felt heavier, laden with an unsettling stillness. Spinning around, he scanned the area and saw his minions lying headless. The once formidable warriors now resembled discarded puppets, their lifeless bodies sprawled haphazardly.

"No!" Aushade mumbled in terror as he dashed up the spiral staircase, his heart pounding like a war drum. Taking two steps at a time, he reached his throne room and pushed open the secret compartment to his bed chamber, breathing a sigh of relief when he saw it undisturbed.

A lone figure, chained to the wall, staggered within the limits of his chains, his ragged breath echoing in the room. Aushade reached out and turned the corpse to look at him. The familiar features, now gaunt and hollow, met his gaze.

"Father . . . Jarz is alive. You and Mother would be very proud of him." He threw down his bag with a heavy thud. "Unlike me, who has only brought agony and death." His voice cracked, laden with remorse and anguish.

Aushade glanced down at his table and studied the battle map he had meticulously drawn. Once symbols of strategy and power, the lines and markers now felt like chains binding him to a fate he no longer desired. He stared momentarily at the spot marked "Omlett," his vision blurring with unshed tears. "I'm done fighting, Father. I want the suffering to go away."

His eyes burned from holding back tears as he placed his hand on his father's forehead. The skin was decaying but unyielding. Whispering, "Morior," he witnessed the final flicker of his father's essence dissipate, and the body fell lifelessly to the floor with a dull thud. "I may join you and Mother in the Astral Realm soon."

Aushade removed his armor, each piece falling away like the burdens he carried—guilt, loss, unfulfilled promises. He searched for a shovel by the equipment shed. The cold metal was a stark contrast to the warmth of his hands. His brow dripped with perspiration as he dug his father's grave, each stroke of the spade biting into the earth, a rhythmic sound—a lullaby to his grief. Memories of his father—teaching him to hold a sword, to stand tall in the face of adversity—flooded his mind, each one a painful reminder of the man he had lost. With each stroke, he welcomed the sweat to camouflage the tears streaming down his face.

He patted the earth one last time, sealing his father's body to become one with the world. The grave was a modest mound, but to Aushade, it was the end of an era. He stood over it, the silence around him deafening. The wind blew through the trees, carrying with it the ghosts of his past.

As he reached for his canteen, the acrid scent of smoke lingering in the air mingled with the damp, earthy aroma of the forest. A flicker of light protruding from the dark wooded area of dead trees caught his attention. *Who would even dare?* Suspicion and curiosity warred within him. Too exhausted to retrieve his armor, he approached the source, armed with only the shovel, its metal edge gleaming faintly in the dull light.

He found an empty camp, a solitary fire casting eerie shadows on the surrounding trees. The odor of burning rotted wood and slightly charred meat assaulted his nostrils, making him grimace. "You're courageous for trespassing here," Aushade yelled, inspecting the fire pit. "I know you're here. There's barely any ash."

Rustling in the fallen leaves made Aushade's grip tighten on the shovel. The forest air was thick with decaying foliage, yet the smell intensified as he fought against the creeping plants, which snared his feet and raced up his body. Struggling to free his legs, he pried the shovel between the roots, leveraging his weight against the relentless force of the vines.

A small humanoid creature in the distance waved, its movements almost teasing. The distraction was brief but enough to draw Aushade's attention. A figure emerged before him, moving with a supernatural grace. A new scent hit him: a blend of leather and something metallic. Before he could raise the shovel, a female voice spoke, her tone laced with mockery and menace. "Oh, there's plenty of ash."

A quick blur flashed before Aushade's eyes as the impact of a heavy, blunt pommel connected with the side of his head in a sickening thud. Pain exploded in his vision, and the pungent smell of iron filled his nostrils as blood trickled from the wound. There was a moment of stunned silence as if the world held its breath. The force of the impact reverberated through his skull, a brutal symphony of bone and metal. He staggered back a half step, balance slipping. A confused flicker of discomfort crossed his face as the woman drew back for another strike before his legs gave way.

He crumpled to the ground, consciousness slipping away like sand through his fingers, the only sound remaining the dull echo of the blow. Darkness swiftly followed. The last thing he heard was a smug woman's voice stating, "Oh, honey, that was way too easy."

# CHAPTER SIX

# A LUCKY SECRET

With each step Eugor took down the old dirt road, memories rose like spirits from the ruins. This had once been Eugor's neighborhood—the corner where he'd raced Gideon, the ivy-covered wall he'd hide behind to give Celeste a scare. Now, it was all blackened stone and twisted timber. The trees he once climbed stood like charred sentinels. Windows that had glowed with candlelight now gaped, shattered.

Eugor was accompanied by the crunch of his boots against the ground and the ache in his chest. He didn't know what he hoped to find among the wreckage. Only that something in him needed to remember.

When Eugor reached the shattered remains of the Naelo cottage, he stopped cold. The roof was no more—*not collapsed, but simply gone*, ripped away as if the sky had swallowed it whole. Charred beams jutted upward like the broken ribs of a beast, pointing to nothing but open air. Only fragments of walls clung to the foundation, scorched and crumbling.

Amid the ruin, the old stone stoop remained—tilted, cracked, but defiant. Eugor stepped forward and sank to his knees, hands shaking as he dropped the torch and brushed aside blackened splinters. Each movement was careful, and reverent, as if he were unearthing bones instead of memories.

The sound of a portal opening behind him broke the silence as a bright light washed over the darkness, lighting up the debris.

"Do you remember this spot, Gideon?" Eugor asked, managing a hollow chuckle, still fixed on the stone.

"I do," came a soft, feminine voice, cracking with emotion as Eugor turned swiftly. Celeste stood holding a light orb, clad in golden armor, her white wings tucked in neatly, her blue eyes dulled by sorrow. "It's where I gave you our son," She released the orb, allowing it to float over the rubble. "And asked you to raise him."

"I wasn't expecting you," Eugor said, his voice faltering.

"Gideon is safe." She moved closer, her expression softening. "I thought you might end up here. I'm so sorry about your parents . . . and Carya."

A lump rose in Eugor's throat, sudden and thick. He swallowed hard, then nodded. "Thank you. It's kind of you to disobey the council to be here."

Celeste gave a faint smile. "It's been how long since we saw each other?" She reached for a stray lock of his white hair as he stepped back. Her hand dropped, and she laughed softly. "Age has been good to you."

Eugor grunted, trying to hold the line against her presence, to keep her charm from slipping past the armor he'd forged from years of silence and woe. But it pierced through anyway, quiet as memory, sharp as regret. The image returned: her back to him, walking away across the hillside, the wind tugging at her robe. In his hands, a fistful of wildflowers and a wishful thought, she would change her mind.

He turned from her now, fixated on the wreckage at their feet. "Are you here to help," he muttered, "or just to torment me?"

Celeste didn't answer. She dismissed her wings and armor with a whisper, stepping over the splintered remains like they were nothing. "So—Gideon and Raven?" she asked, too casually.

Eugor groaned as he heaved aside a scorched beam, splinters biting into his palms. "Will you stop?"

Celeste didn't answer right away. She crouched beside what remained of a hearth, brushing ash from a half-melted pot as if it might still be worth saving. "I thought you'd be happy. Raven's with the next best elf in Euphrasia."

*Happy.* The word stung. Eugor turned away, shoulders stiff, but not before his eyes flicked to her—how her tunic clung to her slender frame, how the years had softened her instead of wearing her down. Time had kissed her gently, while it had carved him hollow.

He grunted, straightening with effort. His joints ached. His back throbbed. He felt like an elf hewn from the ruin he stood in. "How's Tier?" he asked, voice hoarse as he kicked at a pile of crumbled stone.

Celeste's face dimmed. She pushed a broken chair aside with her foot. "Wish I knew."

"Long story?"

"Something like that." She knelt to tug a charred tapestry from beneath a beam. Ash flurried upward like soot-colored snow.

"And my son?"

"Our son is . . . well," she said, hesitating. She stood, brushing her knees. "He's been assigned to the High Council and is busy watching over the Astral Realm."

Eugor blinked. His hand rested on a half-collapsed archway, steadying himself. He hadn't expected pride to sting so much. "Assigned to the High Council . . . that's a big responsibility."

She nodded, then bent to shift a shattered oval mirror. Her reflection cracked and flickered in the broken glass. "It is." Celeste nudged a charred timber with the toe of her boot, frowning at whatever lay beneath. "But Blade's grown into it. Guardian Misty Meliae says he's remarkable. But I think she may have an infatuation with him."

A bittersweet satisfaction swelled in his chest. It comforted—and hurt. "I wish I saw him more."

"I do, too." She didn't look up this time. Her hands were already buried in the rubble again.

They continued working in silence. Residue clung to their fingers, and the smell of burnt wood never quite left the air. Eugor uncovered a half-burned trinket box. Inside were the charred remains of Blade's keepsakes. A cracked mirror. A faded ribbon. A miniature wooden horse. His breath caught. *Blade used to run through these halls, laughing. Clutching that horse. Clinging to my leg when he was afraid of the dark.*

"Is it hard?" Eugor asked quietly, staring into the box. "Seeing him. Not being able to tell him who you are?"

Celeste met his gaze. "He knows . . . in a way."

"What do you mean?"

"I visited him in secret when he was little. I told him I was his guardian protector. I waited until he was asleep . . . I didn't want you to know."

Eugor exhaled slowly. Hurt and understanding battled for space in his chest. "I always thought he meant Gideon."

She glanced away, brushing dirt off her fingers. "I couldn't stay away."

"I waited," he murmured. "For you to return. I thought maybe—one day—you'd change your mind."

She froze. "I know. I thought about it every day. But I knew you'd protect him."

"He missed you. I missed you," he said, voice tightening. "He believed the fairies took you to be their queen."

Celeste gave a small, wistful smile. "That's not far from the truth."

"I never told him. To protect you. To protect him from the council."

She nudged his shoulder lightly. "Are you going to stand there sulking or help?"

A tired laugh escaped him. He turned back to the wreckage, removing shards of pottery—his mother's, once displayed proudly above the hearth. His thumb traced the glaze, now dulled and cracked.

They worked in tandem, clearing the worst of the damage. The house stood like a skeleton—walls charred, beams half-collapsed. Blackened frames where memories once lived.

"Over here was his room," Eugor said, voice catching. He stepped across broken glass and splintered wood.

Celeste bent and picked up a singed piece of parchment. She turned it over—a child's drawing. A fairy on a throne, labeled *Mother*. Above her, a winged figure hovered in silver crayon. A tear slipped down her cheek. She folded the parchment gently, almost reverently, and tucked it inside her armor. Her fingers lingered. "Do you remember the day Gideon and I graduated?"

He scoffed. "The day you assassinated my heart."

She gave a dry chuckle. "Assassinated? That's pretty extreme, even for a rogue."

"Is it, though? Part of me died on that hillside when you left for the Fey Realm." Eugor turned toward the rubble just in time to catch a snowball to the neck. He stiffened. "Celeste," he said, voice flat, brushing the snow from his collar like it could wipe away the sting beneath it.

She was already forming another, her grin careless and cruel in its lightness. "Answer this. Would you rather I'd told you I was leaving or that Gideon would one day court your daughter?"

Eugor didn't flinch, but the question hit harder than the snow itself. "I'm not answering that," he muttered, turning away as another snowball struck his ribs. He whirled on her. "Celeste!" But she wasn't even looking at him as she pointed.

When he turned, Mara stood at the edge of the ruins, snowball in hand. Her face was solemn, but her eyes sparkled with mischief. The cloak she brought for him lay by her fur boots.

"What are you—" he began, but she let it fly. It thudded against his chest. Eugor blinked, stunned by the moment—by her. He crossed the distance slowly, snow clinging to his tunic like ash. He leaned in and kissed her cheek, his hand lingering on her shoulder.

Mara's smile was soft, steady, and bright, like spring daring to return. And in that quiet, impossible warmth, something inside him stirred. Not healed, not whole, but breathing again. Her smile warmed him more than a campfire ever could.

Celeste joined them, her tone shifting. "I'm Celeste Wynndrik," she said, offering her hand.

"Mara," she replied, shaking it firmly.

"I've heard a lot about you—from Gideon," Celeste said as Mara smiled politely. "Is Euwee always this cranky?"

"Well . . . Euwee is . . . we're hurting," Mara said softly.

Celeste's face dropped. "I understand," she said remorsefully.

Mara's gaze steadied on her husband. "But darling, you didn't answer her question."

Eugor exhaled through his nose and turned back to the rubble, unwilling to meet either of their eyes. *Some truths are easier to bury, like the dead.*

"It was a pleasure to meet you," Celeste said, donning her armor again. "And good to see you again, Euwee."

"You're always welcome at the Omlett Inn," Mara offered gently.

Celeste gave a final nod, summoned a red portal, and stepped through.

The silence she left behind felt heavier than all the wreckage they'd sifted through. Eugor stood unmoving, heart thudding in his chest. "Blade's mother," he said, at last, the words barely more than a breath.

Mara inhaled softly. "But she's a Guardian—" There was no accusation in her voice. No pressing, no demand. Just calm eyes, offering space, not judgment.

"That's why I never told anyone. Only three people know. And it has to stay that way."

Mara stepped forward and wrapped her arms around him. "I understand."

Eugor didn't resist. He let her hold him—let the weight of grief, regret, and long-buried love settle into the warmth of her embrace. And for the first time in what felt like ages, he allowed himself to rest—truly rest—in someone else's understanding. They stood together in silence, watching the last glimmer of the light orb fade into oblivion. The past settled around them like snow: soft, cold, and inescapable.

No more words came. None were needed. When the moment passed, Mara gently took his hand. "Come," she said softly. "Let's leave this place."

Eugor nodded, retrieved the dimming torch, and followed the forested trail beyond the village. The trees whispered above them—ancient, indifferent—bearing witness. Near a moss-covered stump, fireflies flickered briefly, their gentle glow seeming to mock the night's heaviness with careless beauty.

The stars were already scattered across the sky, silent witnesses, by the time they reached the hunting cabin—hidden deep in the royal woods, where grief could breathe unheard.

A welcoming fire crackled in the hearth, casting a soft glow across the cabin. A generous cut of meat, heavily seasoned, turned slowly on a spit, the scent filling the room with comfort.

Mara paused in the doorway, taken aback. "You . . . cooked?" Her voice held no suspicion, only surprise—a quiet marvel that pierced the sadness they carried.

Eugor took her hand gently. "I wanted to surprise you with something nice."

She glanced at him, then at the fire, her expression unreadable. "When did you find the time?"

"I asked Miss Cyprus to hunt before returning to duty," he admitted. "She wouldn't take a coin. Said it was the least she could do for us."

Mara exhaled softly, watching the slow-turning spit. "And the castle chef?"

He gave a tired half-smile. "Emptied my pockets without shame. But worth it."

Mara shook her head and smiled. She stepped closer, resting her head briefly against Eugor's shoulder.

He lingered in the moment before stepping away to pull out a weathered wooden chair. Despite its age, the wood gleamed with careful polish. He gestured for her to sit. They settled at the rough-hewn table. Eugor sliced the venison with practiced ease, plating it alongside a chilled melon salad—an unexpected but thoughtful pairing.

Before either reached for their utensils, Mara bowed her head. "For your parents. For Carya." Eugor followed suit, lowering his head beside hers. The silence between them said all the rest—pain, love, memory—spoken without words.

"This is absolutely delicious," Mara complimented him, her voice soft with admiration.

"Of course it is," Eugor replied with a flirtatious smile. "I didn't cook it."

After their meal, Mara gracefully rose to gather the empty plates, carrying them to the worn wooden counter, then paused. Her gaze drifted to the narrow twin bed tucked into the far corner of the cabin. Her fingers lingered on the counter's edge. "Maybe we should have stayed at the castle," she murmured, a blush coloring her cheeks.

Eugor pushed back his chair with purpose. He moved to the stone fireplace and carefully arranged a few candles and a half-filled bottle of wine on the mantel, their flames casting a soft, golden glow across the room. Then, swiftly, he gripped the table's edge and tipped it onto its side. Flower vases clattered to the floor, and the last dinner rolls scattered across the room.

Mara hesitated, then joined in with a humorous laugh as she threw her chair into a corner. "The king will not be pleased," she teased lightly.

"It was an ugly table anyway. I'll have Mug craft him a new one." With determined strides, Eugor swept away the pelts from the bed and spread them in front of the crackling fireplace. They retrieved their drinks and settled down, leaning comfortably against the furs and the bed frame.

Mara rested her head against Eugor's chest. In a soft, almost reverent tone, she whispered, "Living like kings and queens."

"No other way," Eugor murmured, his voice soft with affection. He gently loosened her bun, letting her hair fall around her shoulders, his fingers drifting through the strands where the firelight coaxed out rich shades of red. "Do you ever regret leaving the comfort of Fellswar's castle for a fool with a wild dream of running an inn?"

She smiled. "I only regret not meeting you sooner." He sighed, and she leaned in, tracing the scar along his neck with a teasing finger. "You really should've lost your head sooner."

"We did meet under unusual circumstances."

"Maybe," she whispered. "But I felt like I knew you already. My brother never stopped talking about you."

"I owe Ausharz everything for my second chance."

"But when the orc attack came and I lost my brother and nephews, you were there for—"

"I know," he said gently. "I remember."

"These last few days have been so difficult," her voice barely rising above the fire crackle as Eugor said nothing, his eyes fixed on the flames. "I gained a nephew when I found out Jarz was still alive, but I lost a daughter." The silence lingered between them, broken only by the slow collapse of burning wood, like the sigh of something too tired to keep holding on. "I think we should return tomorrow," she said, her tone edging into a plea. "We need to check on Raven. She keeps blaming herself for what happened . . . and I'm afraid she's slipping." Eugor turned slightly, listening. "Before we left, she spent all her time at the Cache Tavern. She hardly spoke to anyone. And now, with Gideon's cryptic message about Omlett . . ." Mara hesitated, her voice tightening. "I'm scared, Eugor. Something's not right."

"Brugg and the others will watch after her," Eugor said, brushing a lock of her hair away.

"It's unlike her to not check in with us."

"True, I haven't seen that message bird of hers in days."

Mara let out a soft, weary laugh. "I remember when it brought me a message that said 'sugar cookies.' I told her, 'You're in the Fey. Make your own.'"

Her laughter, fragile and warm, broke mid-breath. A sob caught in her throat instead. She covered her mouth as tears slid down her cheek. "I should've said, 'Yes. Come home.'"

"Gideon said she was fine. We can decide about our stay when he returns with a report about Omlett. Suttiir needs help, and I promise we will only stay a couple of days if all is well at home."

The creak of the cabin door suddenly broke the stillness, and Eugor hurried to open it, expecting to find Gideon, but no one was there. Outside, the whisper of wind through the tall pines underscored the eerie silence of the night. A parchment lay on the steps, a finely drawn portrait of the Queen of the Fey gracing its surface. Celeste's eyes in the drawing were just as he remembered them. He folded the parchment with a shaking hand and tucked it into his coat. *Oh, Celeste.*

Before Mara could speak, a raven flew into the room, wings silent as a shadow. It landed on the hearth and delivered its message directly into Eugor's mind: *Father. The necromancer attacked Omlett. He escaped with Jarz. I'm going to Fellswar's Claim.* The room seemed to hold its breath. Then, as suddenly as it came, the bird vanished.

Eugor rose to his feet. "We have to go."

"What was the message?" The words punched the breath from her lungs.

"She's putting herself in grave danger." Eugor grabbed a parchment and quickly scrawled a message for the king. A portal flared open before them as he stepped outside—blue light spilling across the snow.

Gideon stepped through, back in his usual form. His golden armor shimmered under the moonlight, his hair tied back, his expression tense. "Eugor. Omlett—"

"We know," Mara cut in. "Raven sent a message."

"She's safe," Gideon assured.

*Safe. There's that word again.* Eugor growled, "Raven's going to rescue Jarz."

Gideon's brow furrowed. "I ordered the group to stay put." He muttered a curse. "*Shercor.*" Tilting his head, he paused, listening. A breeze stirred, faint and cold, carrying a wind message. "The Guardians used a scroll. They're in Waterfront."

Eugor's grin spread slowly, sharp with knowledge. "Do they know what they've walked into?"

"I doubt it," Gideon said, a smirk tugging at his mouth. "I never told them."

Mara glanced between them. "Told them what?"

Eugor glanced at her. "Where do you think we got the idea of a truth zone for our prison cells?"

Gideon opened a portal with a casual flick, the magic unfurling in a swirl of deep blue light. "They're in one of the realm's most secure—and honest—areas."

Mara exhaled in relief, her breath a soft plume in the cold air as she stepped through, following Gideon.

Eugor's gaze swept the treeline, every shadow a potential threat. *Are we being watched? Is Celeste still stalking about? Did King Luhnar send spies?*

Just as he turned toward the portal, a sound sliced through the stillness. It wasn't a branch or the wind but a faint, clean swoosh of a blade cutting air. He froze. That sound was etched into his bones—the last thing he'd heard before the balor took his head. His stance shifted, alert, hand near his weapons. The last thing he wanted to do was to desert Suttiir in its time of need. But Raven needed him, and he could not fail her. *I'll send Avalann back with supplies.*

But even as he stepped through, the sound lingered—like it was waiting.

# CHAPTER SEVEN

# NOTHING BUT THE TRUTH

The portal to Waterfront flared open, a blue and luminous sight.

Raven gripped her staff tightly, fingers whitening. Her heart was a weight lodged deep in her chest, but she locked her doubts behind a familiar wall. "Let's go," she ordered, her voice steady even as her stomach twisted. *No hesitation. No second-guessing.*

After stepping through the portal, Raven's senses were assaulted by chaos. The air crackled with unfamiliar energy, and the scent of new leather filled her nostrils. Her bare feet met cold, smooth wood. The soft glow from the fireplace flickered uncertainly, casting eerie shadows across the room. *Is this a trap?!*

Shorte, always quick on his feet, shoved the others backward, his urgency evident. Avalann's bare skin brushed against her own, and Raven recoiled, realizing with horror that she was naked. Her weapon was gone. Her hand flew to her throat. Panic rose within her as she instinctively reached for the artifact hanging around her neck, only to find it gone. "What the spell?" Raven shouted, her voice echoing off the chamber walls. *I lost it. Great. The one thing Blade trusted me with.*

The frantic but composed cleric pointed toward the wall. "Look! Robes!" Shorte exclaimed.

They fumbled toward the garments, grateful for any barrier against their vulnerable reality. Raven clutched the rough robe like a shield, and caught the flicker of Avalann's embarrassment, the giggle bubbling from her lips. Part of Raven wanted to snap—to scream that this wasn't funny—but laughter meant they were still alive for now.

Despite the chaos, Shorte covered his eyes with trembling hands. "Well, this is awkward," he grumbled.

"I'm not sure what your problem is with nudity," Izarra remarked casually. "It's the most natural thing in the world."

Their easy banter skimmed over the surface of Raven's unease, but it couldn't banish the coiled tension in her gut. She forced herself to play along, adjusting the robe and masking her fear. "This is *my* bedroom," Raven said, scanning the warped but familiar features.

Izarra's brow furrowed. "Did you cast the right portal?"

"I did," Raven insisted, but the words felt brittle. She crossed the room, scraping fingers at the faux stone of the mantel, willing the secret panel to give. It didn't. *Something is wrong.* "Ogre poop!" she cursed, a rare slip of childish frustration breaking through her practiced calm.

"What's wrong?" Avalann asked, concern pinching her brow.

"The necklace Blade gave me. It's gone," Raven confessed.

Shorte snickered. "If you didn't notice, everything's gone."

Raven fought back the urge to snap at him. She crouched low, inspecting the hidden compartment—nothing. She had hoped, irrationally, that her artifact might have survived, tucked safely away. *Another foolish hope crushed.*

"It's like the magical ebony tree portrait at the Inn," Izarra noted, her voice soft as she glanced at her reflection in the tarnished copper mirror. "We need to find a way out."

"But there aren't any knights in armor chasing us," Shorte pointed out, his frame relaxed as he lounged on the edge of an old, creaky bed. "You sure it was the right scroll?"

Raven huffed in frustration. "Yes, it had the Waterfront seal. Why is everyone questioning me?"

"Reckless," Avalann blurted out, then quickly moved her hand over her mouth.

"Impulsive," Shorte said, then scratched the back of his neck, eyes darting to anything but her. Raven caught the shift—the way he shrank into the pause that followed.

Izarra held her answer but winced suddenly, grabbing her side. "Temerarious," she managed through clenched teeth.

"What in the Abyss does that mean?" the dwarf asked, his brow contracting in confusion.

"They all mean the same thing," Raven replied coldly. *They mean you make mistakes.*

"I'm sorry, Raven," Izarra pleaded softly, reaching out to comfort her friend amid the tension.

"Me too. I didn't mean it harshly," Shorte expressed.

"I'm not sorry," Avalann said firmly, her voice cutting through the tension. "You can be rash sometimes, harming the group someday." Everyone paused, their gazes turning inward as they pondered her words.

"All right, something is going on in this room." Shorte's lips curved with amusement as he broke the heavy silence. "Who's your favorite dwarf?"

"Nice try," Avalann smiled weakly, then suddenly hunched over, clutching her side. "Mister Plunkett," she cried out through gritted teeth.

"Hmm . . . It's not my Uncle Buzz," the dwarf laughed heartily. "Care to try again?"

Avalann shot him a nasty look, still gripped by the discomfort. "You are," she managed to answer with relief.

"I knew it!" Shorte's face gleamed with satisfaction.

Avalann straightened, but her expression clouded. "But I'm not sure after today."

"We must be in a truth zone," Raven surmised, her voice tinged with realization. "We have them in holding cells at the prison in Omlett."

"My turn!" Avalann declared roguishly.

"Oh, no!" Shorte protested, covering his ears with his fingers. "La la la—"

"What is your true passion?" Avalann pressed on with a glint in her eye.

"I can't hear you . . . la la la—" Shorte continued, trying to drown out the question amid the discomfort of the room's effects.

"Wait for it," Avalann mused, tapping her fingers thoughtfully on her arm.

"We should stop and try to figure out how to get out of here," Raven suggested, concerned as Shorte rocked back and forth in discomfort.

"La la . . . cooking!" Shorte suddenly blurted out, his voice filled with both relief and embarrassment. "I love cooking."

Avalann bit her lip to stifle a giggle, exchanging glances with Raven, who amusedly shook her head. "Don't give me that," she teased. "He started it."

"There's nothing wrong with being a chef." Izarra glanced at Shorte.

"There isn't," Avalann agreed, "unless you're a dwarf."

"It's a respected profession among elders," Shorte defended himself, his face reddening. "For dwarves who can't do much else."

"You need to eat. Entire villages need to eat," Izarra countered with a puzzled expression. "I don't see the issue."

Shorte shrugged, his embarrassment evident. "I'm done talking about it."

"I did enjoy the oat cake you made for my birthday," Raven admitted, her tone softening. "Back at camp."

Shorte's stunned expression almost made her laugh. "You remember that?" he asked, displaying a half-grin.

"Yes, and we're in a truth zone, so I'll admit it could have used a bit more seasoning"—the rogue smiled teasingly—"but it meant a lot."

Shorte chuckled. "I didn't have many ingredients to work with."

"Now, let's focus on finding a way out of here," Raven urged, redirecting their attention. They began scouring the room for any clues that might aid their escape. *This version of my room still contains Carya's old bed.* "This is my room, but it's not how I left it this morning."

"How is it different?" Izarra asked.

Raven's mind flashed to Gideon's armor—the gleam of metal that once stood in the corner like a noiseless sentinel. "Gideon's armor was here in the corner."

"Wait," Avalann interrupted, her eyes widening. "How did you get his armor?"

"Blade," Raven answered simply. "He brought it to me."

"You saw Blade?" Avalann asked, surprise evident in her voice. "How was he?"

"Good, I suppose, for a demigod," Raven replied, her tone thoughtful.

"Why the sudden interest in Blade?" Shorte questioned, raising an eyebrow at the archer's revelation.

"As a child, Blade was my instructor at the archery camp before ascending to become a demigod. That's why I'll cherish his bow as long as I draw breath," Avalann answered affectionately. "He was my first infatuation." She blurted out as everyone eyed her. She bit her lip. "We need to find our weapons and get out of here."

As if in response to their conversation, the door blinked out, replaced by a young wizard, an apprentice in robes, with a nervous grip on his wand. His cropped blond hair and stubble beard gave him a slightly disheveled appearance.

"Finally!" Shorte exclaimed, pushing himself up from the bed.

"Stay back!" The mage's gaze flicked from one of them to the next, sweat beading at his temple. His wand quivered. "What is your business here at Waterfront?"

Raven stepped forward, shielding the others as instinct took over. "We need a portal to Fellswar's Claim."

"And you are?" the wizard pressed, his wobbly wand still trained on them.

"I'm Raven Naelo, and this is Shorte Stone-Grin, Avalann Greenorr, and Izarra Lyte."

The man flinched mid-step, shoulders giving a short, jerky twitch. "What business"—he cleared his throat—"do you all have in Fellswar's Claim?"

"We need to dispose of a particular necromancer," Shorte responded firmly.

"A necromancer that resides in Fellswar's Claim," the mage repeated.

"Yes," Avalann confirmed, her gaze steady.

"I'll discuss your request with the headmaster," the mage replied cautiously. "I'm Apprentice Donavan, and I'll oversee your stay here."

Shorte's stomach let out a loud growl at that moment, and his face turned crimson with embarrassment. "Didn't have suppa'," he mumbled sheepishly.

"I'll bring you dinner while you wait," Apprentice Donavan offered before disappearing through the open doorway. The door shimmered back into place behind him with a soft hum.

Avalann stepped forward, her fingers curling tightly around the iron bars. Her voice was low, thoughtful. "Something about this place doesn't feel right."

Raven tilted her head, studying her. "I didn't think you had feelings," she said before she could stop herself. The words were barely out when she threw her hands over her mouth.

Avalann shot her a sharp glare but said nothing, returning to the bars with renewed focus as Raven mouthed, "Sorry."

Moments later, the door creaked open, revealing two witches clad in dark, flowing robes. They carried a steaming cauldron between them, the rich aroma of herbs and spices wafting through the air. After setting it on a side table, they hurriedly exited, their cloaks whispering against the floor. The last witch, a tall figure with silver streaks in her hair, flicked her wand, and four canteens and bowls materialized beside the soup. With a final nod, she vanished, the door magically sealing behind her.

"Complementary soup!" Shorte announced, his eyes twinkling with interest. He dipped a finger into the hot stew and tasted it thoughtfully. "Needs another pinch of salt." The others chuckled, their laughter echoing softly as they each grabbed a bowl, the warmth of the soup a comforting contrast to the cool, dimly lit room.

"There's no silverware," Izarra observed, glancing around the room.

Shorte shrugged and dipped his bowl directly into the cauldron, slurping down the savory broth. "No need."

Raven shrugged at Izarra and followed the dwarf, Avalann close behind. She kept her senses sharp, the comfort of the chamber never quite sinking past the edge of her nerves.

They settled around the table, and as they ate, talk turned to old memories of Gideon's camp—stories. Raven listened, letting the laughter and easy banter wash over her. It was like being wrapped in a blanket she didn't quite trust, but she clung to the moment anyway, grateful for it.

Shorte's booming laughter startled Raven as she masked the flinch by reaching casually for her drink. He was finishing his third bowl like a man possessed, and she watched with awe and concern. Then came the sound—a deep, ominous rumble from his gut that cut through the room like a warning bell. "Where's the privy?" he barked frantically as they scanned the room.

Raven glanced at Avalann, who was already mid-panic.

"Oh no," Avalann breathed, urgency flashing across her face. She sprinted to the door and pounded on it. "Donavan, help! We've got dwarf business!"

Raven's hand drifted toward her hip before she caught herself—*an old habit.* She exhaled through clenched teeth, watching as the door flickered, then vanished, revealing Donavan's confused face on the other side.

Without missing a beat, Avalann pointed straight at Shorte. "He just picked up a side quest—finding the privy."

# CHAPTER EIGHT

# THE HAUNTED HUNTED

Donavan nodded once, sharp and sure, and gestured for Shorte to follow. Without a word, they disappeared, the front door blinking back into existence with a soft, smug click.

Raven's brow furrowed. *I despise locked doors.* She yanked the handle anyway—no give. *Figures.* She reached slowly for her hair tie and patted lightly. The lock picks were gone, too.

"How long does a dwarf business usually last?" Izarra asked, grimacing and clutching her stomach.

Raven noticed how pale she appeared and how she shifted from foot to foot. "You, too?" she asked, her gut doing slow, angry somersaults.

Izarra nodded miserably. "Liquids go right through me."

"That's funny coming from a water nymph." Avalann giggled—too loud, too bright—and then clamped a hand over her mouth. Regret splashed across her face.

Raven wasn't amused. *Something's wrong.* "Maybe we should all go," she suggested, about to knock on the door when it disappeared before her hand could reach it.

"Let's go," Donavan's voice echoed as if he had anticipated their need. The apprentice led them down a flight of stairs just as Shorte emerged from another chamber, adjusting his robe.

"Must be the peppers." The dwarf blushed as he followed Donavan back up the steps.

As the three ladies made their way down the hall, a soft voice spoke. "Raven." The rogue turned but saw no one else. She glanced around briefly, suspicion pricking her senses, before joining Avalann and Izarra at the privy chamber.

Raven crossed her arms inside and murmured, "Ed-Osite." Testing her invisibility spell, she waved at the apprentice and approached a woman dusting books nearby. She gestured with her hands but received no response, confirming that her magic was working.

Raven dashed around the circular chamber, scanning for another door amid the smooth stone walls. Finally, she spotted one that stood out, its surface marred by black silt from what seemed like a past fire. As she approached, a purple tribal heart mark glowed faintly on the door, accompanied by a whispering gust of wind that carried a message she couldn't quite decipher. Amid her search, Raven overheard Donavan's question from outside the privy chamber: "Where's the other one?"

"She's still inside," Izarra replied nervously.

Deciding she should return, Raven whirled around, only to collide with someone. Startled, she saw an older elf with a trimmed gray beard and receding gray hair—*Headmaster Taiker*. She gasped, attempting to sidestep him, but he moved to block her path once more. "Headmaster!" her voice cracked. "You can see me?"

"Of course, child," the elder elf replied calmly, his demeanor kind yet authoritative as Raven instinctively dismissed her invisibility spell.

Donavan skidded around the corner, sputtering apologies. Taiker waved him away like he was nothing but a gnat. "It's fine, Apprentice. Return the other two to their chambers."

"You mean cells?" Raven interjected pointedly, feeling the tension rise.

"Miss Naelo," Headmaster Taiker said, his voice calm but not unkind. "You're not a prisoner."

Raven bristled at the word prisoner, though she didn't show it. Her hands remained at her sides, her fingers relaxed, her mind already mapping the exits. *Then why do the walls feel like they're listening?*

"You teleported to Waterfront of your own free will. But even for a guardian, unrestricted movement here isn't permitted. We deal in dangerous, sensitive things that require . . . discretion." His eyes swept the room, lingering on her companions. "I suspected the arcane assassin might wander my halls—invisible." His gaze paused just over Raven's shoulder. "And I gather the delicate blond is the half-nymph, a warlock bound to water." He nodded slightly toward Izarra. "The red-haired elf, clearly the archer." A glance at Avalann. "And the dwarf, there is no mistaking a cleric's posture." He turned his attention back to Raven. "This isn't a cage, Miss Naelo. But don't mistake vigilance for hostility."

Raven exchanged a glance with Izarra and Avalann, realizing they had been identified based on their abilities and appearances. "Great observation."

"Not really." The headmaster grinned knowingly. "I have Gideon's list of current recruits. We were very proud when the Realm Guardian chose Mister Fisker."

*So he knows about us.* "That's why we're here," Raven stated firmly. "Jarz is being held captive by a necromancer who resides in Fellswar's Claim. We need a portal there."

"I see," the headmaster responded thoughtfully. "We shall create one in the morning."

"Thank you," Raven replied with a nod, her attention drawn back to the purple tribal heart mark on the mysterious door.

"What is it?" Headmaster Taiker inquired.

"This mark." Raven reached out to inspect the door.

"That room has been vacant since the Dragon Wars," Taiker explained as he graciously opened the door.

The moment Raven crossed the threshold, her skin buzzed—like stepping through a spiderweb of static. She paused. The room was wrong. Scorch marks clawed the walls, and ash dusted the edges of a melted chandelier. "I can see why," she muttered. "A fire destroyed this place." She stepped forward lightly, her boots brushing aside a thick carpet of dust and debris. A shattered wardstone pulsed faintly in the corner, like a dying heartbeat slowed by a thousand years. Protective glyphs etched into the walls had faded to scars, their meanings lost. This was no longer a sanctuary of knowledge. It was a graveyard of forgotten power, and something deep beneath the rubble still remembered the fire.

"Miss Naelo," Taiker's voice came behind her, too calm. "We repaired this room centuries ago."

"No, it's—" Then Raven saw her. A woman in the far corner, silhouetted in green firelight. Dark skin. Silver curls. A cloak the color of poison. She cradled a flickering fireball in her hands. Raven's breath snagged in her throat as her hand instinctively reached for her dagger—but touched only empty air. "Who is that?" she asked, pointing.

Taiker blinked. "Who's who?"

The woman was gone.

"I think you need some rest, child," the headmaster suggested kindly, placing his hand reassuringly on Raven's shoulder. "You should return to your room, and we will provide the portal in the morning."

"But Jarz—"

"I know Mister Fisker, and he'll be fine."

Raven turned to leave, and the air snapped. A rush of cold surged up her spine as the woman's face exploded into view, inches from her own. Eyes glowing green. Mouth stretched wide.

"Draakgoons!" she screamed.

Raven recoiled instinctively, a strangled cry tearing from her throat as she stumbled back, arms raised to shield herself. Her knees hit the stone floor with a thud. Then—nothing. The face vanished like smoke in the wind.

The headmaster's cold hand gripped her arm, grounding her. "Miss Naelo?" Taiker's voice had lost its sternness. He knelt beside her, concern lining his face.

Power buzzed through her limbs—too much, too fast. *Magic? Fear? I can't tell.*

"Are you all right?" the headmaster asked again, softer now.

She stared past him, heart hammering. *What the spell was that?*

Raven surveyed the room, but it appeared pristine and undisturbed, devoid of any signs of a fire. "I'm fine," she replied, her voice shaky with confusion. "But I think you're right. I need to lie down."

Supported by the headmaster, Raven entered the chamber. Izarra gently lifted the rogue's chin and inspected her with interest. "You look like you saw a ghost."

Shorte handed her a canteen of water. "You do seem paler than usual."

Raven lay back on the bed, recounting her unsettling experience to them, describing the woman and the strange words she had shouted.

"I always thought you were a bit of a loon," Shorte teased lightly, attempting to lighten the mood.

"Goon," Raven corrected, taking a sip of water. "Not a loon. Draakgoon."

"What's a Draakgoon?" Izarra asked, her brow creasing.

"I've never heard of it," Avalann admitted, her expression thoughtful. "And I've been around a long time."

Shorte scratched his head, deep in thought. "There's the Gooners, the dragon protectors from long ago."

"Remember Cee's theatrical performance of the dragon wars?" Izarra recalled, a hint of amusement in her voice.

"The Dragon Wars were long ago," Shorte explained thoughtfully. "Stories were passed down in my family, but I've never heard of the Draakgoons either."

Despite the lingering tension, Avalann teased, "You probably didn't pay enough attention."

"You better watch—" Shorte began but winced in pain, cutting his retort short. "Fine! You're right. I didn't."

"Maybe they were soldiers during the Dragon Wars," Raven mused aloud, her voice trailing slightly as she stifled a yawn. "Lost wizards, perhaps."

"Many wizards died in that war," Avalann remarked solemnly, her gaze distant as if recalling ancient tales.

"So did many dragons," Izarra added softly, settling beside Raven on the bed. "To the point of extinction."

"I think Taiker is hiding something," Raven stated suddenly, her tone serious.

"Oh no, another Raven conspiracy theory!" Avalann exclaimed with a shake of her head. "This truth room is getting annoying!" She glanced at Shorte, who patted the bed and stretched out, clearly seeking comfort. "I don't think so."

"Oh, come on," Shorte protested good-naturedly, making himself comfortable on the bed. "There's no other place as cozy as this."

"I'd rather sleep in the jaws of a dire-bear," Avalann quipped, finding a spot against the wall.

"Ouch," Shorte chuckled, undeterred by her comment.

"Maybe someone should take the first watch?" Avalann suggested, catching the oversized blanket Shorte reluctantly tossed her way.

Shorte huffed lightly. "Get some rest," he advised, pulling up a smaller throw blanket. "You worry too much." With that, the group settled into their makeshift accommodations, the room gradually growing quieter as fatigue and the day's strange events took their toll.

"Yes, get some rest," Raven agreed softly, exhaustion pressing down on her. "We'll need it."

Sleep took her, but something colder stole her deeper.

A green shimmer broke through the dark. The woman again. Cloak curling like mist, eyes alive with unnatural light. She raised a hand, not in warning, but in invitation.

Raven followed. She didn't remember standing. Her limbs obeyed the pull before her mind could catch up.

The door—the one with the purple heart mark—peeled open as if waiting. The mark melted like wax in a fire. She stepped inside. "Who are you?" Raven's voice barely echoed. The air swallowed it. The word *Draak-kin* swept through the air like a hushed secret.

Scorched walls loomed, blistered with ash. Torn tapestries clung to iron hooks like skin on bone. The scent of old smoke coated her tongue. A blackened podium rose at the center—its surface gleaming with unnatural heat. A book sat there. Leather cover. That same mark burned into its front. Raven's fingers hovered. *Don't touch it.* She felt it anyway.

Raven gently lifted the old book and cautiously opened its fragile pages, revealing an intricate illustration of a black dragon, followed by a red dragon, each page depicting another dragon type. *This is written in Draconic.* She stopped briefly in a chapter explaining the first dragon created, Krea'tion, and her two offspring, Kaleidris, Mother of the Chromatic Dragons, and Plathorax, Father of the Metallic Dragons. Flipping farther, she saw instructions on how to spawn dragon protectors. They forced humans to consume dragon eggs. *My father consumed one.* She turned the page to find out what would happen after they consumed it, but the page was torn out. *Ogre poop.* The map on the other page suddenly burst into flames, causing her to drop the book.

The woman in green appeared before her once more, her fluorescent green eyes capturing Raven's attention as she placed both withered hands on the rogue's shoulders. "Help," she implored softly before a blinding light engulfed Raven's vision.

"Miss Naelo," a stern voice interrupted her reverie, pulling Raven abruptly back to reality. "Miss Naelo." Headmaster Taiker's voice echoed with anger.

Raven stirred groggily, realizing she was no longer in the bedroom; instead, she was back in the Dragon War room. "I don't know—" she murmured, disoriented, trying to gather her thoughts, "how I got here."

"I've tolerated your excursions long enough." Taiker's voice was sharp as he gripped her arm firmly, guiding her back up the steps.

"Ow, let go!" As they ascended to the top of the stairs she pulled away. Apprentice Donavan was lying unconscious before the chamber door.

The headmaster hurried to check the young apprentice's pulse and breathing. "He's alive." He turned his stern gaze back to Raven.

"I didn't," Raven protested weakly, her mind racing with confusion. "I couldn't have."

"Somebody had to," the headmaster said sternly, his grip tightening on Raven's arm as he forcefully ushered her back into the room. As he spoke, the air crackled with magic, sealing the entrance behind them with a wave. "I'm increasing security on this wing. Consider it a cell now, Miss Naelo."

The transition was abrupt. The plush beds vanished, replaced by unwelcoming stone slabs that lined the walls.

Shorte, unperturbed by the transformation, let out an exaggerated huff. "A stone slab the whole time?" He grumbled, rolling over and resuming his snoring as if nothing had changed.

"A slender lady in a green cloak was standing there," Raven shouted, desperation lacing her voice. "It had to be her."

"There's no one with a green cloak roaming this building," the headmaster explained, his voice edged with concern. "I assure you, it was just you and Apprentice Donavan."

"What's going on?" Avalann interjected, her voice groggy as she sat cross-legged on the floor, wrapped in a threadbare blanket.

"I'm in the truth room," Raven blurted out, ignoring her friend's confusion. "She had bright green eyes."

The color drained from the headmaster's face at the description. "Apparently, the young apprentice's losta-lotus soup wasn't potent enough for you elves."

"The losta-lotus?" Avalann muttered, her words slurred as the elderly wizard recited an Elvish incantation, flicked his wand, and then briskly exited the room. "What did you do now?"

"Nothing—" Raven began to protest, her words faltering as she staggered against the doorframe. As Taiker left, sealing them in, Raven slumped against the wall, brain whirring.

Avalann adjusted her blanket, eyelids heavy. "Losta-lotus," she mumbled. "Rare Fey flower . . . weakens Elven resistance. Shouldn't've had that eating contest with Shor—"

"Shorte," Raven corrected, voice thick. She belched and winced. "Ugh. I don't feel—"

"Take your dwarf business—" Avalann began, but her words broke off. "Elsewhere." Her body sagged sideways, collapsing against the hearth like a puppet with its strings cut.

Raven's breath hitched. Her vision blurred at the edges. *The soup.* She tried to stand. Her knees didn't listen. Her arms weighed twice their size. "What . . . what the spell?" The room tilted and a magical slumber began to drag her under.

# CHAPTER NINE

# A GUARDIAN'S BURDEN

Gideon patrolled the road between Suttiir and Omlett as the sun rose. The landscape bore the scars of recent conflict, and as he journeyed south toward the Inn, he noticed the dismantled, rusted-out iron golems strewn along the path.

With vigilance, he knelt beside one of the fallen golems, the shards of rusted metal around its joints a testament to the fierce combat it had endured. His fingers traced the edges of the metal fragments, remnants of a powerful Rust Metal Spell that had rendered these formidable constructs inert.

Standing tall once more, Gideon brushed the residue from his hands, his expression tinged with determination and weariness. The signs of battle were everywhere, patches of dry blood stark against the dirt road, a grim reminder of the violence that had unfolded.

Gideon lowered his head momentarily, a silent acknowledgment of the golems' valiant but futile effort. With a determined huff, he continued his patrol, his resolve unshaken despite their overwhelming odds. The road ahead was long, and his sense of duty was the only thing that kept him moving forward.

He observed Miss Crinkly's shattered bakery shop window a few feet away. As Gideon entered, the early morning light filtered through the broken window, casting fractured patterns on the floor strewn with glass. He carefully navigated the debris, his boots crunching softly with each step. Gideon's gaze swept over the damaged, toppled display stands and the remnants of delicate pastries reduced to scattered, trampled crumbs. The air carried a faint aroma of burnt sugar mingled with the unpleasant scent of decaying flesh.

Miss Crinkly had always been known for her generosity, especially during Dragomas, when she delighted in giving sweets to children. The community and Gideon, who knew her warmth and kindness well, would keenly feel her absence.

Despite the devastation, there was a glimmer of hope: Eugor had mentioned that Miss Crinkly's sister, Brena, from Clear Springs, would take over the bakery. But Gideon didn't care about the shop. *I failed Betty. I failed Omlett.*

The community's resilience was unmistakable—their grit showed in every effort to rebuild, even with the scars of violence still fresh. Gideon wanted to fix everything: the shop, the town, the people shattered by loss. *Did I make a mistake not killing the necromancer when I had the chance?* Finding Jarz was the only path forward, but every lead had gone cold. Even the undead stronghold at Fellswar's Claim gave up nothing, but wiping it out had brought a grim satisfaction. *At least I put a dent in the necromancer's army. Now, helping Eugor comes without the fear of the council's backlash. With the flox and succubus involved, I finally have the justification to act.*

Closing his eyes briefly, Gideon pictured Betty's face, a small kindness lost. He would remember her. Then, like always, he would move on. Because moving on was all he could do.

Gideon stopped by the prison yard and spotted Buzz'diir in his new mobile chair—a rough assembly of gears, leather straps, and stubborn will. The contraption creaked across the stone floor, but the security chief commanded it like a warhorse.

"Mister Anderson! What are you doing? Patrol the riverbank—I don't want another ambush," Buzz'diir barked, his voice cutting through the noise like a whip. His sharp and alert guard didn't hide the weariness etched deep into his weathered face. The recent injuries hadn't dulled his edge; he just added a layer of gravel.

A young guard stumbled past, nearly colliding with Gideon as he hastily dropped a glove. Buzz'diir clicked his tongue. "These damn youngins are still rattled by the attack," he muttered, spinning his bulky chair.

"Shouldn't you be resting, Mister Plunkett?" Gideon asked as he approached the dwarf.

"I'll rest when I'm dead," Buzz barked as he rolled over to pick up the fallen glove. His long beard caught in the spokes of the chair, and he cursed under his breath. "Damn it."

"You need a shave," Gideon teased, trying to lighten the mood in the grim surroundings.

"I need new legs and an eye," the dwarf spat as he untangled his beard from the chair's mechanics. "I guess you wouldn't have a spell for that?"

"I'm sorry, Mister Plunkett, I don't, but I have one to hide the gray from your beard, if that helps."

Buzz'diir grumbled, his brow furrowing as he considered Gideon's offer. "Shouldn't you be out looking for that bastard who raised the dead?"

"I'll continue the search after I retrieve Raven and the others. They teleported to Waterfront."

The dwarf stopped his chair and glanced at Gideon with a mischievous grin, the lines of age and experience etched deeply into his weathered face. "Do they know?"

"I doubt it," the guardian chuckled, but the sound faded quickly. His wry smile straightened into a thin line. "As for the necromancer—" he paused, voice dropping. "I'm not sure where he is."

Buzz huffed impatiently, his bulky form shifting restlessly in the cramped confines of the chair. "And the council?"

"They wouldn't help even if I asked." The guardian glanced out the small window, noticing the morning sun beginning to lighten the sky. "I need to go. Eugor's waiting."

"Tell that elf he needs to visit me," Buzz'diir instructed gruffly, his tone leaving no room for argument. "Tell him, don't make me wheel my arse over there."

"Will do. Let me know if you need anything." With a nod, the guardian made his way out, his heavy boots echoing faintly on the cold stone floor.

"I already told ya, legs and an eye!" the dwarf called, his voice echoing in the corridor.

Walking on the roads of Omlett, Gideon chose to take the route to the Omlett Inn on foot instead of using the convenient portals. It felt strange, almost uncomfortable, but he needed the time to steady his swirling mind.

As he pushed open the Inn's heavy oak door, Eugor was already waiting at the far end of the hall, just finishing the ritual of locking his work chamber door with a deft twist of his fingers.

Gideon started toward his friend when movement at one of the tables caught his eye. A figure was slumped over, arms wrapped protectively around a thick book, breathing softly in slumber.

"Jarz?" Gideon's voice carried surprise and relief as he and Eugor approached.

The young mage stirred, his eyes snapping open with confusion and alertness. "Gideon. Eugor."

"I'm glad to see you're all right." Gideon reassuringly patted the mage's shoulder.

"How long have you been here?" Eugor asked with a smooth, commanding voice that cut through the quiet of the morning. He settled into the empty chair beside the swordmage.

"Since high moon," Jarz replied sheepishly, wiping away a small pool of drool that had collected on the cover of his beloved book. "I searched everywhere for Raven and the others. When I arrived at the Inn, it was already locked up for the night, so I used a portal to wait inside. I figured someone would eventually show up."

"Where did he take you?" Gideon's voice sliced through the tense air.

"Grey-Holg," the swordmage answered, his voice strained. "But it doesn't matter now. I'm sure he left once I . . . escaped."

"I checked there right after annihilating his army at Fellswar's Claim," Gideon confirmed, his brow furrowing.

"Was he there?" Jarz questioned, his knuckles whitening around the edge of the table.

"No," Gideon growled. "The bastard was gone, leaving the unanimated corpses to rot. I should've killed him." He clenched his fists.

"Why?"

"No man should be so disrespectful to the dead."

"He has to be a demon," Eugor asserted with conviction. "No man would show such disdain for the fallen."

"Who is he?" Gideon pressed.

Jarz hesitated, his eyes darting to the worn leather-bound book before he answered. "I'm not sure, sir."

"Well, I'm delighted you've returned safely, son," Eugor said, his tone softening as he rose from the table. "Help yourself to the pantry if you need food or the bar for a drink. Aunt Mara is home. She will tend to your wounds."

"Thank you." Jarz stood, the weight of his recent encounter evident in his weary movements.

"Your uncle and I must retrieve your friends from Waterfront," Gideon informed him, the air around him shimmering as he conjured a portal into existence.

"Wait!" Jarz called out, lifting the weathered book. "I think we can save Carya. This was my father's spell book and journal."

"The same one"—Eugor choked up, his hand instinctively rubbing the scar around his neck—"that saved me?"

"Yes. The necromancer removed it from my childhood home." Jarz showed the weathered spell book to Gideon, whose brow furrowed in curiosity and concern. The tome exuded an ancient aura, its pages crackling with latent power.

Gideon hesitated for a moment. "Eugor, you stay. I'll gather the troops." He watched as Jarz carefully inspected the spell book, running his fingers over the embossed letters that glowed faintly in response to his touch. "Hopefully, this won't take long."

With a resolute step, Gideon approached the shimmering portal that hummed. As he crossed the threshold, the world around him twisted and warped, and with a sudden rush of wind, he found himself standing at the imposing main gate of Waterfront, the institution for mages and mystics.

The dark storm clouds, heavy with rain, rolled ominously in from the Pangean Ocean, casting the last rays of sunlight into a fiery orange glow that danced on the churning waves. The salty tang of seawater mingled with the sharp scent of wet earth as violent gusts of wind whipped through Gideon's wings and tousled his blond hair.

"Halt!" shouted a guard dressed in mage attire from the window of his tower, squinting against the gust and rain. "State your name and business!"

Gideon steadied himself against the battering wind, his voice firm and unwavering. "Gideon Grindal. I'm here to visit the headmaster."

The young guard disappeared momentarily, seeking shelter from the storm within the tower. "One moment," he called back, his voice slightly muffled.

Gideon shook his head as he waited, the corners of his mouth twitching into a faint smile. "Mages these days," he muttered. "Can't even stand a little storm."

Moments later, the large metal gate creaked open against the force of the wind. "My apologies, Guardian," said the young mage, struggling to close the heavy gate behind them. Raindrops splattered against his robes, which bore the emblem of Waterfront Academy.

"No need for apologies," Gideon replied, his voice carrying over the wind. He looked at the young guard with interest. "What's your name?"

"Thees," the guard answered, pushing open the interior door to allow Gideon inside. "Enjoy your stay."

Gideon nodded appreciatively, rainwater trickling down his face. "Hopefully, it won't be too long," he said with a cynical smile, but Thees stood at attention with a serious expression. "Did you graduate yet, Thees?"

"No, sir," Thees replied respectfully. "I'm still a second-year apprentice."

"Word of advice?" Gideon offered, his voice lowering slightly as he leaned closer.

"Yes, sir."

Gideon looked at the young guard with a hint of wisdom in his eyes. "Don't hide in the tower because of inclement weather."

Thees hesitated for a moment. "But we all do, sir."

"I know," Gideon replied with a warm smile, his gaze distant momentarily. "My classmates did, too, but that's why I'm a Realm Guardian, and they're not."

The guard furrowed his brow, clearly puzzled. "Because you stood in the rain?"

Gideon chuckled softly, the sound carrying a mix of amusement and something more profound. "When no one else would. Just let that sink in."

"Yes, sir," Thees responded earnestly, adjusting his cloak hood against the driving rain. With renewed purpose, he pushed open the gate, its metal hinges groaning faintly, and stepped out to resume his patrol along the perimeter of the prestigious Waterfront Academy.

As the storm continued to rage overhead, Gideon watched the young mage go. He knew that within the academy walls, young mages like Thees were learning not just spells and incantations but also the invaluable lessons of courage and duty that would shape their paths in the realms to come.

Gideon shook his wings, dampened by the gentle patter of rain. He entered the courtyard, where raindrops collected on the clear dome overhead. He dismissed his wings as students bustled along the cobble streets, ducking under awnings and hurrying from one building to another. The modest buildings lining the roadside were crafted from local rock, their bright white walls adorned with stunning shades of blue roofing.

Near the bakery, a young girl sat on a weathered bench, engrossed in a spell book balanced on her knee. She absentmindedly nibbled on a freshly baked muffin with one hand, her gaze flicking occasionally to the fountain at the courtyard's center. First-year apprentices took turns practicing spells, their efforts reflected in the changing hues of the water. Nearby, a mischievous young elf flicked his hand, causing his friend's textbook to erupt in flames—a testament to the magical antics that enlivened the academy's atmosphere.

As Gideon approached the main castle, its grandeur was unmistakable. Rising over five hundred feet tall, the castle's walls were adorned with stained-glass windows that shimmered under lightning flashes. Giant marble steps wound their way to the cathedral-like doors, where the headmaster stood waiting, his presence a reassuring beacon amid the magical noise.

"Mister Grindal," the elderly elf beamed, his silver hair catching the light as he stuck out his arm in a gesture of warm welcome, "such a pleasure for the Realm Guardian to visit."

"Headmaster Taiker," Gideon greeted warmly as he clasped the headmaster's forearm in a firm handshake. "How have you been?"

"As well as expected," Taiker replied with a twinkle in his eye, his ageless face crinkling into a smile. "What brings you here today?"

Gideon sighed, a hint of amusement playing on his lips. "We both know why I'm here." He released his grip.

"Ah, yes." Taiker chuckled softly. "My visitors."

"I'm sure you treated them well." Gideon slightly raised his eyebrow.

"Of course, of course." The headmaster gestured for Gideon to follow him deeper into the ancient halls of the academy. They passed through the main entrance, where small study chambers were filled with students. Through one door, a young human wizard conjured four glowing light orbs that hovered above him. An elf in an adjacent room reached outward, and bursts of colored light shot from her hands.

"I see this place hasn't changed much," Gideon observed.

"You know I don't like change," the headmaster responded, his voice tinged with nostalgia. "That's how things get lost."

They entered another building complex that held the visitors' chambers. A female and a male human stood at the entrance, clad in simple robes, and holding staffs.

"Two guards?" Gideon asked, raising an eyebrow. "Isn't it usually just an apprentice who draws the short straw?"

"We did upgrade the security around here." The headmaster's voice echoed softly through the stone chamber. "It's the new standard."

"Thought you didn't like change?" Gideon teased, eyeing the heavy oak door the headmaster had opened with surprising ease.

"It's not that big of a change."

As Gideon stepped into the room, he immediately sought out Raven. She lay pale in the middle of the wood floor, with no blanket to shield her from the cold. Izarra and Shorte were sprawled on separate beds, their forms barely visible under thick covers. Avalann's messy red hair tickled her pointy ears as she slept soundly near the fireplace, a blanket at her feet and her robe pulled tightly around her.

"You could have supplied better sleeping arrangements," Gideon huffed, glancing back at the headmaster.

"We aren't some overnight tavern."

Moving swiftly but gently, Gideon knelt beside Raven and reached out to shake her awake.

Raven squinted, looking disoriented. "Gideon?" Her voice was barely above a whisper.

"There's those purple eyes," Gideon said softly, brushing a lock of hair from her face.

Raven reached out, her fingers trembling slightly as they traced his jawline. "Are you really here?"

"Of course." His heart tightened at the sight of her fragile state. "Let's go home."

"Jarz?" Raven asked, her voice tinged with worry.

"He's safe, back with your father," Gideon whispered, his gaze never leaving hers.

"How?" Raven's voice cracked as she sank gratefully into his embrace.

*Was she drugged?* "Watch her, please," Gideon instructed, his voice urgent as he handed her over to Taiker. She pulled away from the headmaster's grip, her slender frame propping against the wooden wall for support. The glow of the hearth flickered in the chamber, casting long shadows that danced across their weary faces.

Gideon surveyed the room, noting the fatigue etched on each guardian's features. A thick haze hung over them, sapping their strength and clouding their minds. Only a potent drug could render elves vulnerable to the charms of sleep spells—a troubling realization that tightened the knot in Gideon's stomach.

"Niece," he called gently, his voice cutting through the heavy silence like a blade. Avalann glanced up with a struggle, her lids heavy with exhaustion. "Time to rise," Gideon prompted as she stumbled to her feet, swaying like a reed in the wind before bracing herself against the warmth of the crackling fireplace. "Help me with the others," he ordered, moving swiftly to Shorte as Avalann trudged to the half-nymph.

*Perhaps the promise of exertion might snap the dwarf from his unnatural stupor.* "Mister Stone-Grin," Gideon called out firmly to Shorte, who lay sprawled under a tangled mess of blankets, oblivious to the urgency around him. "Wake up, or I'll have you run ten miles more around the lake."

Shorte grunted as he struggled to disentangle himself from the cozy embrace of his bedding. He finally sat up, blinking rapidly to clear the fog from his mind.

Gideon watched with unease as his niece, fear etched deep into her face, cradled the unconscious half-nymph. Avalann gently brushed Izarra's tousled hair away from her serene features—a tender gesture amid the rising tension.

"Jarz, stop! That tickles," Izarra mumbled drowsily, still caught between sleep and waking.

"She'll be fine," Gideon assured himself more than anyone else, though his frustration was intense. "Do I have permission to use a portal to Omlett?"

"Of course," the headmaster responded. "I'll have my handmaidens retrieve their personal items." He gracefully exited the room, leaving a somber atmosphere.

Gideon concentrated, summoning his powers to create a shimmering portal to the Omlett Inn. The gateway hummed softly as it stabilized, revealing the empty Inn filled with the warmth of the flickering hearth.

With a supportive hand, Gideon guided Izarra, Shorte, and Avalann through the portal, their forms blending momentarily with the ethereal energies swirling around them. As they stepped through to the other side, the familiar comfort of Omlett's welcoming embrace enveloped them.

Raven stood firm, her eyes locked with Gideon's. "I can't leave yet," she insisted, her voice tinged with urgency.

"Why?" Gideon's brow crumpled with concern.

"My necklace!" Raven clutched the area where her pendant should have been hanging, her fingers trembling.

He clenched her shaking hands until they stopped. "You have to go. I'll wait for your belongings."

Raven closed the distance between them, her voice barely audible. "And there's something here, calling to me."

Gideon sighed, his gaze searching hers. "There's powerful magic in this place. You're an arcane assassin, not a mage. It might be overwhelming for you."

"It didn't affect the others." Raven gripped his hands. "Gideon, I'm not imagining this. I saw a symbol or mark and a woman wearing a green cloak. She was calling out from a burnt room. You have to trust me."

"I do," Gideon said softly.

"You do?" Raven flinched, her breath puffing out in a sharp gasp.

"We're standing in a truth room," Gideon replied with a slight smile. "But I don't need this room to verify that I'll always trust and love you."

"I love you, too," Raven responded, her voice filled with relief and affection, kissing him tenderly.

Their moment was interrupted by a pointed cough from the headmaster. Four women, the headmaster's attendants, entered the room carrying the guardians' belongings. The woman carrying Raven's gear paused, placing it gently on the bed and handing her Blade's charm. Raven quickly fastened it around her neck, a reassuring weight against her chest.

"Are you sure you want to stay?" Gideon asked as she nodded solemnly, her gaze steady. "Headmaster, we would like permission to stay for a few days. Raven needs access to advanced training spells, and this would be the ideal place for it."

The headmaster bit his lip, contemplating the request. His piercing green eyes flickered between Gideon and Raven. "Of course, Mister Grindal," he finally replied, his tone measured yet accommodating, "anything for one of my greatest students."

"Thank you."

"You may use this chamber." Taiker gestured to where they stood. "We will deactivate the security spells and transfer the other guests in this wing to the west wing. That should give the two of you some privacy."

"Thank you for converting the cold cell back to my bedroom," Raven remarked, her voice laced with a hint of sarcasm. She eyed the guardian standing nearby, who bristled but remained silent under the headmaster's gaze. "I'm sure Gideon wouldn't have appreciated the stone slab beds."

The headmaster grunted. "If you'll excuse me." He adjusted his robe, casting a final stern glance around the room before turning on his heel. The heavy wooden door closed with a decisive thud behind him.

Raven eyed Gideon suspiciously. "That was surprisingly easy."

"A little too easy." He paced the room restlessly, his senses on high alert. "What happened to everyone? You were acting as if you were under a heavy sleep spell."

Raven sighed, brushing a lock of black hair behind her ear. "The headmaster mentioned lotus flowers in our soup earlier. It didn't affect Avalann or me as quickly as the others." A silent understanding flickered in her expression. "I'm guessing it's our elf heritage at play."

"It would seem so." Gideon's attention moved to the unfamiliar tapestries on the wall. "Must have been the losta-lotus variety. But Celeste doesn't allow that flower to be harvested anymore." *At least, I thought she didn't.*

Raven moved closer to him, her expression softening. "Then Taiker cast a sleep spell before he left."

Gideon tensed, his features tightening with concern. "Why would he risk doing that, though?"

"Maybe because we all appeared so dangerous, you know, in our fluffy robes," she teased before kissing his lips tenderly.

He gently placed his forehead against hers, locking gazes with her. "We have to be on guard," he murmured, his voice tinged with unease as Raven nestled against his chest.

Her voice trembled. "I think Taiker is up to something."

Gideon tightened his embrace, a mix of protectiveness and resolve in his tone. "I think you might be right."

# CHAPTER TEN

# BROKEN LEASH

ourtlynn explored the small kitchen, her wings tucked tightly against her back as she navigated the cramped space, irritated by the inconvenient design. *Human habitats were not built with wings in mind.* She noticed an ornate cabinet with its doors ajar and peered inside, the light catching on the shimmering surfaces of ornamental plates and glasses. The scent of polished wood mingled with the faint aroma of spices lingering in the air.

She rolled her eyes at the old wizard's latest string of curses, then found herself drawn to a ruby-encrusted goblet shimmering nearby. She reached out, her long fingernails tracing the intricate gold inlay with a delicate touch. The cool metal made her shudder as she marveled at humans' obsessions with gems. The chalice felt heavy and solid in her hand, a stark contrast to her delicate form.

After reluctantly closing the cabinet doors, she moved to a counter where an antique-looking bowl sat, filled with various fruits. She selected a pear, its smooth skin yielding slightly under her grip. The faint, sweet fragrance promised more than it delivered. The unexpected bitterness made her wince as she bit into the fruit, her sharp teeth cutting effortlessly through the flesh. The tart juice coated her tongue, reminding her of how long it had been since she'd eaten real food.

She chewed slowly. The pear's texture was grainy and unfamiliar, and she swallowed it with difficulty. But each bite was a necessity. Energy was scarce without her usual means of sustenance, the intimate and invigorating act of seducing a man. The mundane act of eating human food left her feeling hollow. No amount of human food or sleep had the same revitalizing effect as the carnal energy she craved. She sighed.

The coughing caught Courtlynn's attention. An older man was seated, stooping over his worktable in the corner. She crossed into his work chamber, and the air filled with the acrid scent of burning incense and the musty odor of ancient tomes. "Is it ready yet?" *Finding a wizard who can craft a phylactery necklace for the right price has taken far too long.* Her master's army had already begun its attack, but he needed this item to control the lich. It wasn't until Courtlynn reached the small village of Sonny-Mikula, in the far east of Euphrasia, that she finally found one.

Silas, the wizard, glanced up with a magnifying glass attached to a leather headband, enlarging his face. "You can't rush these." His hunched figure was silhouetted against the light orb. His gnarled hands moved with surprising dexterity as he twisted thin metal around the empty glass case. The clinking of metal and the occasional muttered incantation filled the otherwise quiet room. "Holding a soul is more delicate than catching fireflies."

While waiting for the necklace, Courtlynn continued moving around the cottage and forced herself to eat more fruit, each bite a struggle against her distaste. The house was filled with curious artifacts and trinkets. Her fingers brushed over a wood carving of a knight in black armor, and she couldn't help but smile. The intricate details captured the knight's stern visage and powerful stance perfectly. The image of Aushade entered her mind, his presence as vivid as the carving before her. *I wonder what he's up to. He's the first mortal I genuinely miss being around.* The image of how he looks at her appeared in her mind, bringing an unsolicited smile.

The taste of the fruit lingered bitterly in her mouth, contrasting the warmth of her memories. Aushade's rugged features and fierce loyalty were etched in her heart, an unexpected but welcome attachment to her otherwise solitary existence. She sighed softly, tracing the carved lines with a wistful finger before returning to the wizard and his painstaking work. The anticipation of completing her mission mingled with the bittersweet thoughts of her past, creating a tumultuous mix of emotions.

The scraping of a chair made Courtlynn turn again to see Silas approaching her. His wrinkled hand shook as he dropped the chain into hers. She held it up to the light, watching as beams reflected through the glass casing. Wrapped around it was decorative metal wiring forming an ebony tree in the center.

With a fluid motion, she pulled a pouch from her belt and dumped the coins onto the table, the metallic clinks echoing in the small room. Silas handed her a piece of parchment. "Here's the incantation for the soul transfer."

"Aren't you cute?" Courtlynn responded, tossing the half-eaten pear at him. "My master has been doing this for a very long time. He doesn't need your incantation."

Silas stretched his arm out more insistently for her to take it. "But her soul—"

"I'd like that figurine as well." She pointed to the toy that reminded her of Aushade.

"But that's not for sale," Silas replied, then paused as she squinted at him with murderous intent. He hurried to the shelf and retrieved it for her.

"Thank you," she said, placing it inside her now-empty coin pouch. "I'm feeling a bit peckish, so be a sweetheart and create a portal for the Third Layer of the Inferno-Plane, please." *Thank you. Please. I'm spending way too much time and energy in the Mortal Realm.* Her irritation simmered beneath her composed exterior.

"But the Realm—"

"Don't worry about the Guardian."

Silas removed a portal scroll from a drawer and hesitated before creating a swirling red portal to the Abyss. "Your master should use that incantation to feed the phylactery," he insisted, holding the parchment again. "Souls could be tangled when fed."

Courtlynn glanced at the portal, its fiery edges casting an eerie glow over the room, and then back at the wizard. She snatched the parchment from his hand, not bothering to hide her impatience. "Fine. Just be glad I'm in a good mood." She kissed Silas's cheek quickly before stepping into the gateway.

As soon as she emerged on the other side, she knew something was wrong. Jagged molten cliffs framed the area, housing honeycomb-shaped tents that were unmistakably not part of the Third Layer. *That senile wizard teleported me to the Second Layer.*

Above her, a squad of humanoid wasp creatures, known as wasptoids, flew in tight formation, their massive wings creating a gust of wind that blasted her red hair out of place. The buzz of their flight was a low, ominous hum that reverberated in her bones. Below them, a regiment of humanoid mantises, called mantoids, marched past her, their moss-green armor glinting dully in the harsh light. Each creature towered over her at nearly ten feet tall, roughly the size of ogres in the Mortal Realm.

*That old fool dropped me behind enemy lines.* It was clear the Third Layer's attack was happening in full force, and she had landed in the wrong place. Courtlynn quickly assessed her surroundings with growing frustration and followed the mantoid squad, hoping they would lead her to a way out. She hadn't gone far when a wasptoid buzzed sharply at her.

"I'm lost," she explained in the common language, hoping they would understand. The bee soldiers buzzed again and waved over one another, creating a knot of anxiety in her stomach.

The two wasptoids conversed in their buzzing language, their mandibles clicking and antennae twitching. One of them removed their helmet, revealing a sharp, insect-like face with multifaceted eyes glinting with curiosity and suspicion. The wasp soldier stared at the succubus intently, his gaze piercing and unyielding.

A twinge of nervousness bit her as she maintained her composure. "I was sent here by mistake," she continued, her voice steady despite the circumstances. "I need to get to the Thir—Seventh Layer."

The wasptoid tilted his head slightly, studying her with deliberate stillness. After a tense moment, he buzzed something to his companion, who nodded and flew off. The remaining wasptoid turned back to her. "Follozze meze," he said in a surprisingly clear and resonant voice, motioning for her to follow.

She fell into step behind him, her senses on high alert. The landscape around her was a chaotic blend of molten rock and jagged cliffs, each step a reminder of the precariousness of her situation. As they moved deeper into the Second Layer, Courtlynn couldn't shake the feeling that she was being led into a trap, but she had little choice.

"Why iz you here?" the smaller wasp asked in the common language, his antennae twitching with curiosity.

"A bad portal." Courtlynn tugged at the strap of her satchel, fingers twitching. "I was trying to get to the Seventh Layer."

"Zeventh Layer," the wasp repeated, his mandibles clicking thoughtfully. "The layer of the zuccubizz and incubiz."

"Exactly." She pointed at herself. "Succubus." Before the wasp could respond, a loud commotion erupted in the distance. Wasptoids flew in wounded soldiers, some missing their wings and stingers, while others were covered in green blood that oozed from deep gashes.

Courtlynn took a sharp breath as she witnessed the chaos. The air was thick with the scent of burnt chitin and the metallic tang of blood. The buzzing of distressed wasps and the groans of the injured created a cacophony that set her nerves on edge.

"We'z at war," the smaller wasptoid stated, his tone grim.

Courtlynn suppressed the urge to roll her eyes. *I know.* Annoyance simmered beneath her calm facade. The wasps buzzed at each other, their wings creating a symphony of uneasy vibrations, before guiding Courtlynn to a tent where an elder insect sat on a rock. The elder's carapace was duller than the others, his corneas clouded with age. The smaller wasp buzzed, explaining her presence and predicament.

The elder nodded slowly and rose, motioning for Courtlynn to follow. They walked through the camp, weaving between injured soldiers and frantic medics.

Finally, they reached the portal system, a series of swirling, glowing exits that shimmered with different hues. "Zeventh Layer," the elder wasp said, pointing to a radiant blue exit.

*I know how it works.* Courtlynn managed a polite nod. "Thank you," she said awkwardly, her voice tinged with reluctance. *I can't believe I'm thanking my master's enemy. I've been around humans far too long.*

The elder didn't respond, as his attention shifted back to the camp. Courtlynn took a deep breath and stepped toward the portal, the blue light enveloping her. As she passed through the cooler air of the Second Layer, the warmth increased until it reached the more familiar environment of the Seventh Layer.

She emerged on the other side, the landscape instantly recognizable. The Seventh Layer was a realm of heat and seduction, the air thick with the scent of exotic flowers and the sound of distant, haunting melodies. The sight was familiar and strange after so many eons. Black obsidian buildings with leather curtains lined the shores of the lava river, Flamma. Brimstone's sulfuric scent invaded the air as the molten river's glow cast eerie shadows on the pathways. Hundreds of naked residents moved about, their presence a reminder of the primal, seductive power that permeated this realm. *It feels like an eternity since I've socialized with my kind*, but she no longer had time to delay. *I'm glad Tessk had the new Cubbis Council pardon me.*

She glanced around, taking in the familiar sights and sounds, before setting off toward her destination. Her master's army would be waiting, and the phylactery necklace she now carried was crucial to their success. Despite the unexpected detour, she had managed to get back on track. As she moved through the Seventh Layer, the image of the elder wasp lingered in her mind. She couldn't shake the feeling that her time in the Mortal Realm had changed her in ways she was only beginning to understand. She sighed and pushed those thoughts aside, focusing on her task. *There will be time for reflection later.*

Courtlynn moved swiftly toward the portal systems and entered the Third Layer portal. Then, she scurried to the war portal to her master's camp and returned to the Second Layer. This time, she emerged on the right side of the battlefield. The scene was chaotic. Wasptoid and mantoid soldiers fell from the fire demon army's deadly blows.

Still, the wasptoids managed to push the invading army back, their resolve apparent despite their losses. The acrid smell of burnt chitin and the screams of the wounded filled the air as it did on the other side of the battlefield.

Draklor, Courtlynn's master, stood at a stone table, his eyes fixed on his beloved battle map. His messenger, Gimp, hovered beside him, arched over in anticipation of relaying a new message. The undead female, with her lifeless eyes, stared out at the carnage, a metal box clasped in her hands, its blue light fading ominously. Courtlynn entered the chamber, holding the necklace aloft with pride.

"It's about time," Draklor snapped, snatching the necklace from her. He studied her briefly, his brow tightening. "You look ill, child."

"I'm fine," Courtlynn responded, her voice steady despite exhaustion.

Draklor's hand cupped her cheek, his touch cold, clinical—like a butcher sizing up a carcass. "You need to recharge. After all this time in the Mortal Realm, I'd expect you to be bouncing off the walls with all the male energy you've soaked up."

"I'm fine," she lied as exhaustion clawed at her bones. The Mortal Realm had drained her slowly, mercilessly, but she refused to let him see it.

"Fine," he echoed, his voice like ice cracking. Then his hand snapped across Courtlynn's face, a backhand that dropped her to her knees. Agony bloomed, sharp and immediate, burning her skin and rattling her teeth. She tasted blood. Still, she refused to cry out. "Wipe that grin off your face," he hissed.

Courtlynn tilted her head, hair veiling part of her face, a flicker of fire curling at the edges of her composure. He might have knocked her down, but he hadn't broken her. The tilt of her chin held defiance, but something quieter lingered beneath—not quite surrender, but not resistance either.

Draklor's eyes narrowed, but he said nothing more about her condition. Instead, he turned his attention to the necklace. He examined the intricate design closely. Satisfied, he handed it to Gimp, who scurried off to prepare the phylactery, placing the necklace around the neck of the mindless, undead creature. The creature stood soundlessly, still clad in an old, white ceremonial gown, its features vacant and lifeless.

"Because you were late, my armies were unorganized," Draklor continued, his voice a low, menacing growl. "They needed a leader out in the field, and if you had taken any longer, I would've had to retreat." He turned toward the battlefield, the carnage and chaos a testament to the critical situation.

Gimp fluttered over and offered his hand to help Courtlynn to her feet. She accepted, rubbing her jaw as pain pulsed through her face. Her cheek throbbed as a knot formed, a physical reminder of her master's wrath, but she forced herself to stand tall, her mind racing with the implications of his words. But she couldn't afford to show weakness. "I apologize, Master," she said, her voice steady. "It won't happen again."

Draklor pressed his hand to the lich's chest, fingers splayed with unnatural precision. Courtlynn felt the shift before she saw it—an oppressive hum in the air, thick with old magic. His voice dropped into an incantation, low and guttural, each word vibrating through the chamber like a curse etched into the world's bones.

Dark energy poured from him, coiling through the room like smoke, seeking something to consume. Courtlynn's stomach turned. She knew that magic. She *hated* that magic. It clung to everything, seeped into the skin, and left things changed.

The lich twitched. A flicker of movement, then another. Color crept slowly into its gray, decayed flesh. Courtlynn's fists clenched at her sides. *That thing isn't alive—it's pretending, wearing the shape of a woman. And Draklor is feeding it.*

Then the necklace lit up. Blue. Cold. The glow settled in Courtlynn's core like a warning bell.

The soul transfer had worked.

"Lady Chaotica," Draklor announced, his voice rich with pride and poison.

Courtlynn's heart thudded—*Lady?* The undead creature, now taller, burning with an unholy light, stood obediently. *That creature is no lady.*

Draklor held out Tessk's old staff, which he had stolen from the Cubbis Council. "You will lead my demon army," he commanded, his attention fixed on the lich like a proud god admiring his monster.

The betrayal hit harder than the slap, but Courtlynn didn't flinch.

The new subordinate studied the war map intensely. The lich held the staff firmly, looking regal in her new position. Courtlynn jerked back when the creature spoke for the first time. "Yes, my master," the lich responded, her voice surprisingly smooth and authoritative.

Draklor moved behind Lady Chaotica, stroking strands of her strawberry-blond hair with a possessive touch. "We shall conquer this layer, and you will be by my side for eternity." His tone dripped with sinister intent.

"Master," Courtlynn pleaded, trying to regain his attention and favor.

"Gimp, get this useless creature out of my sight," Draklor ordered, his gaze never leaving the lich. "Unless she needs another reminder of her incompetence."

Courtlynn's stomach turned as she rushed out of the chamber, the weight of her master's rejection heavy on her shoulders. *After everything I did for that ungrateful bastard.* She clung to the hope of finding solace. *Aushade, he'll understand.*

As the succubus made her way through the camp, the sounds of battle raging outside reminded her of the immediate dangers. But her mind was already turning to thoughts of escape and finding Aushade. *I need a plan, and I need it fast.* Her loyalty to Draklor was fraying, and she had to look out for herself now more than ever. *I know too much, and my master knows it.*

Courtlynn stepped back through the war portal to the Third Layer, her mind racing with a strategy. Hurrying through her master's chamber, she found Floxy fast asleep. The creature's ears twitched as it sensed the succubus approaching. She neared the cage stealthily, her heart heavy with conflicting emotions. After unlocking the cage, she released Floxy, who whimpered softly in recognition.

"I should destroy him with his flox," Courtlynn stated bitterly, eyeing the last tail. Instead, she gestured for Floxy to follow her, and together, they made their way to her chambers. The room had smooth obsidian stone walls that glistened from the candle chandelier, casting reflections that twisted and writhed like the shadows of tormented souls. At the center of the room, a lavish, crimson velvet chaise longue dominated the space. Red silk sheets covered her mattress, and lace curtains surrounded her four-post bed, starkly contrasting the harshness of the rough terrain outside. Floxy settled on the bed, curling up with a contented rumble.

Courtlynn began to meditate, reaching out with her mind for the only person who could help. "Aushade, where are you?" Moments passed, but she couldn't sense any connection. Frustration and worry gnawed at her, but she pushed them aside. After gathering a leather shoulder bag containing her whip and other essentials, she and Floxy returned to her master's chamber, passing the guardian still secured to the wall. Draklor had subjected him to terrible torture; his body roasted up to his chest, with only a few feathers remaining on his wings.

A tear welled in Courtlynn's eye as she approached. "I'm so sorry," she murmured, her voice barely audible. The prisoner's chest moved slowly with labored breaths, and she leaned in closer, listening. Suddenly, Tier screamed in pain, and Courtlynn flinched back in horror. As she regained her composure, the guardian fell limp again. "Forgive me," her voice thick with regret as she gently plucked a feather from his damaged wing. "I will reunite you with your love. I promise."

Courtlynn and Floxy continued their journey to the Second Layer, the roars of triumph echoing from the front lines. She followed the sounds of cheering to find Draklor's demon army celebrating their victory. Her master knelt before a demon lord, being promoted to the rank of general as a wasptoid wearing a gleaming gold helmet lay in the center of a black stone slab.

*He finally got his wish,* Courtlynn noted bitterly, observing the scene with disdain. Lady Chaotica, gripping the staff that marked her newfound authority, stood proudly behind Draklor, radiating ambition and power. As Courtlynn approached, she could feel the jealousy emanating from the undead servant, an unspoken rivalry brewing between them.

The air was thick with the scent of death and victory, the flickering torch-light casting shadows that danced across the faces of the assembled demons. Courtlynn's wings twitched nervously as she prepared for what would come next. *That should have been me.*

Gimp frantically flew over to her. "Courtlynn, it's not wise for you to be here."

"Why?" she asked, staring at her master with hatred.

"Lady Chaotica," Gimp responded nervously, "the lich has great power."

Draklor rose with a predator's grace, each step deliberate, ominous. The air pulsed with menace as he marched forward, the edge of his vorpal sword catching the chamber's light as if it hungered for blood. "I did it," he sneered as he passed, his voice a blade of its own. "No thanks to you."

Courtlynn's breath caught, fury and helplessness tangling like wire in her throat. But she refused to cower. She spun toward him, her voice sharp and defiant. "Then I guess you don't need me anymore."

That stopped him. Draklor turned slowly, eyes burning like twin furnaces beneath his brow. "You're mistaken, my dear," he growled, the term of endear-ment poisoned. "This is just the beginning."

Something inside her cracked. No more dodging. No more hoping for escape through compliance. Courtlynn straightened, though her legs trembled. She drew in a breath that scraped her lungs raw, and summoned every fragment of her unraveling resolve. "I want to be released."

A dangerous silence fell. One that reeked of punishment. Still, Courtlynn held his gaze, her heart hammering. Never again would she play the role he'd forced upon her.

Draklor stormed toward her, raising his hand as Courtlynn flinched and covered her face, but the blow never came. She lowered her hands and saw Lady Chaotica standing between her and their master.

"Very well. You're free." The balor lowered his hand, annoyed. "But you're banished from this layer." He waved at a nearby guard posted by his tent. "Make sure she is gone before I return," he ordered, grabbing the lich's hand. "I have a new companion."

Courtlynn stood there, stunned and betrayed, as Gimp and Floxy departed with the other demons. The weight of Draklor's dismissal settled heavily on her shoulders. She watched without a sound as Lady Chaotica glanced at her with an expression that might have been a pity, though it was hard to discern behind the undead creature's impassive facade.

Draklor, now accompanied by his new protégé, disappeared through the portal, leaving Courtlynn alone with the demon guard.

"You heard the master," the demon guard stated gruffly, stepping forward with his spear gripped firmly in both hands. His stance was clear and menacing, a silent reminder of her newfound vulnerability in Draklor's domain.

Courtlynn swallowed her pride and met the demon guard's gaze, defiant despite the ache tightening in her chest. The bitterness of betrayal burned in her throat, but she forced her expression still. Composed. Controlled.

"I understand," she said evenly, her voice edged with quiet steel. Her eyes swept the camp, every detail etched sharper now, as if she were seeing it for the first time through the cold clarity of her banishment.

The demon guard hesitated, then jerked his spear toward the camp's edge. "You have to go," he grunted, curt and dismissive. "You heard the master."

Her hand slid into her shoulder bag, fingers curling around the familiar grip of her whip. In one smooth motion, she drew it, snapping it to life. Flames ignited along its length with a flick of her wrist. "Draklor is no longer my master." She advanced, flicking her wrist again. The whip cracked through the air, severing his spear cleanly in half. The charred pieces clattered to the ground.

Stunned, the guard stepped back, empty hands trembling. Courtlynn strode past him, her hips swaying with purpose, heels striking the ground like a war drum. "I'm already dead to him."

Behind her, her wings unfurled in full, dark and magnificent. "I can see myself out of this . . . what do humans call it?" She sneered over her shoulder. "*Hell.*"

# CHAPTER ELEVEN

# ARCANE ASSASSIN

S itting in bed, Raven twirled a strand of Gideon's hair as he slept. His chest's peaceful rise and fall brought a soft smile to her lips. Once the first light of day shot through the window, casting a golden glow across the room, she gently extricated herself from the covers. She placed her circlet on her head, savoring the familiar touch of the smooth metal against her skin, then summoned her armor, its protective weight comforting as it settled around her cloth tunic and breeches. *Is today the day I need its protection?* Pausing for a moment, she leaned down and tenderly kissed Gideon, her fingers lingering on his cheek, savoring the warmth of his skin and the quiet moment. *No matter what lies ahead, this will be the memory that stays with me.*

"I don't like it," Gideon muttered, struggling to open his eyes as he gripped a pillow tightly.

Raven styled her hair into a ponytail, using the unique band that held her lockpicks. "I can't pass up the chance to officially earn the title Arcane Assassin."

"Being a Mortal Guardian is a better title," he argued as he sat up in bed. "I don't trust him."

She watched Gideon, bare and unguarded, stretching out the morning stiffness. Her brow creased as she considered his words. Stepping closer, her hands found his waist, and she smiled reassuringly. "Trust me, then. The headmaster is giving me a great opportunity to prove myself."

Gideon huffed, running a hand through his hair. "I know what these trials are like. The combat scale is high. I've seen students hurt and even killed."

Raven yanked on her coin pouch and secured the leather case for her razor wire. "I'm not a student anymore. I had the best instructors: Maggie, my father, and you. Besides, what title did you earn here?"

"War-wizard," he replied, his voice softening.

"A war-wizard," Raven repeated. "And all you bring is peace."

"But if something would—"

"No need for what-ifs. Taiker said it's only a day trial." She patted his bare chest. "I'll return by nightfall." Despite the confidence in her voice, unease coiled in her gut like a tightening rope.

"Just remember, in this trial, anything goes. There are no rules."

"Yes, sir," Raven replied, a teasing lilt in her voice. "And I expect to find you like this when I return." She pulled away with a smile and headed for the door, grabbing her purple cloak from the rack and snapping the clasp together.

He wrapped a sheet around himself, preparing to wish her luck. "May Blade—"

"Not today," Raven interrupted, confidence radiating from her. She reached for her staff, which Gideon handed her with a slight smile. "Luck's for the unprepared."

Apprentice Donavan appeared at the doorway. "Are you ready for your big day?"

"Lead the way," Raven replied, her voice steady. As the apprentice turned to escort her, she glanced back again, meeting Gideon's gaze. He nodded before closing the door.

The walk through the corridors was quiet except for Donavan's footsteps echoing through the empty hall on the way to the headmaster's work chamber. Her escort knocked twice on the solid door.

"Enter," the stern voice called, sending a chill down Raven's spine. Donavan swung open the door. A candlelit chandelier bathed the room in a soft, flickering glow, stretching elongated shadows across the walls. Headmaster Taiker stood behind his desk, his arms outstretched in an unusually welcoming gesture. "Look at you," Taiker said, stepping closer, beaming. "You seem very prepared for this."

"Of course," Raven replied, forcing a smile as her mind raced uncertainly.

"I've admired your armor and staff since the first day you arrived."

"Thank you," Raven replied, trying to dry her sweaty palm on her breeches. "I appreciate this opportunity."

"I would be *lying* if I said this was entirely for you," Taiker responded, "but I'm curious about how well Miss McGee taught you. She *was* one of my top instructors."

"At least you're honest."

"And now you will be tested by the best Arcane Assassin instructor."

"I never thought to ask about applying here."

"We receive hundreds of applications from mages across Pángorbis, most striving to be a war-wizard. That title is rarely given out. As for Arcane Assassins, we don't get many applicants. Those who do attend either drop out or die trying."

Raven remained stoic, not allowing the sudden fear to show through.

"But Miss Naelo, do you have any idea what an Arcane Assassin does? What makes someone survive the training?"

Raven tilted her head and folded her arms, paying full attention.

He smiled without warmth and leaned toward her. "*They kill.*"

Her shoulders dropped as she sighed in disappointment. "You aren't telling me anything I don't already know," Raven replied, though she couldn't hide the edge of agitation in her voice.

The headmaster shuffled over to an ornate cabinet filled with pendants, rings, and other ancient-looking trinkets—each resting on black velvet, gleaming with the weight of forgotten power. His hand drew her to a bronze medallion shaped like a serpent devouring its own tail, pulsing faintly as if it were alive. "It's not just a fancy title to kill evil beings," he said, fingers brushing the glass till he reached a small knob, "but others as well."

"Like?"

He opened the transparent door and removed a thick journal. "Beings who use magic that isn't registered at Waterfront, for example, or people who fail here and continue practicing."

"Like Astrick," Raven mumbled, and then a frantic realization hit her. "Wait, does that mean I would be on that list? What about Izarra?"

He slammed the heavy book onto his desk. Raven flinched at the sharp sound, her pulse ticking like a warning drumbeat.

"No need to worry. Paladin and cleric guilds turn in all the required paperwork. Even Guardian Grindal turns in reports of who is capable of what kind of magic they wield."

The headmaster opened the journal and flipped through the brittle pages. Raven read along, but her mind snagged on that word: *capable. Capable of what?* She folded her arms to keep from rubbing her temples—she hated it when people talked about magic as if it were a disease.

"This institution kept a record of all magi in this book since the year five hundred. Magic can be dangerous in the wrong hands. This institution has a necessary responsibility. A corrupted mage could make your father kill your mother or make you kill someone you love. You could wake up with blood on your hands."

Raven's jaw tightened. She wasn't sure if it was the headmaster's words or how he said *you*—like he saw something in her that even she didn't want to admit. Her fingers twitched at her side, and she curled them into a fist. She shuddered at the thought, her mind racing. "I never thought about it that way."

"Mages disguised as loved ones, or—"

"I get it." Her voice was sharper than intended.

"It doesn't matter anyway." The headmaster slammed the book closed. "Magic is about to be obsolete."

"Why?"

"Dragons are the source of magic in this realm."

"But they're extinct."

"They want us to think that, but they're hiding somewhere."

"I don't know anything about that, but my trial—"

"Oh yes, yes—my apologies. This old fool just rambling on." The headmaster stepped to the side. "Seastral Haven Porta." A blue portal shimmered into existence. "This will take you to Seastral Haven, located on the tropical shore in southeastern Euphrasia."

Raven double-checked her equipment, her nerves prickling. "What's my objective?"

"You will meet my arcane instructor, Alagust Stormryder, there. He will brief you on the quest."

Raven inhaled deeply, trying to steady her racing heart. "Thank you." The headmaster nodded as she stepped through, the blue light of the portal enveloping her. *Shite! He never explained how one survives the trial.*

Raven stepped out to a stunning natural landscape at sunrise, showcasing a series of terraced water-filled pools. The terraces formed by mineral deposits created a layered effect cascading down a gentle slope with palm trees peppered throughout. *I miss my watering hole back home.* The warm hues of the rising sun bathed the scene in a golden glow, highlighting the contours and textures of the natural balconies that overlooked the Pangean Ocean to the south. The morning air was warmer compared to the weather back home. The sky was a gradient of soft oranges, pinks, and blues, reflecting on the calm surface of the pools. To the north, the terrain extended into the distance, with rolling hills and a subtle mist that covered the dense tree line. *This scene is straight from the Fey Realm.*

"You must be Night Breeze," a voice called from the far-left pool, startling her. The mature elf stood nude in the pool, splashing his way over as the portal closed. "Nice armor." He approached with an air of timeless grace, his movements fluid and hypnotic. His short, chestnut hair was wet and tousled, while his piercing green eyes, wise beyond their years, locked onto hers with an intense yet gentle gaze. His pointed ears, adorned with intricate silver earrings, glinted in the soft light. "That's a big staff."

*Likewise,* Raven blushed, her thoughts betraying her. *Damn elves and their casual nudity!* She raised her hand. "I'm Raven Naelo."

"Alagust Stormryder." He stared at her friendly gesture, a faint smile on his lips. "Sorry, I don't—"

"Touch spells," Raven grumbled, still blushing.

"Exactly. But I do apologize. I was expecting another elf with the last name Naelo. I would have worn something more appropriate if I had known Gavan was sending a human."

"I'm a half-elf."

"Ah, that explains your red cheeks. But if you care to join me?"

Raven quickly turned her head. "I had a bath last night." As she spoke, the memory of the warm, candlelit bath she had shared with Gideon sent a pleasant shiver down her. The thought of his touch, the feel of his skin against hers, was enough to make her heart race anew. The scent of lavender still lingered in her mind, mingling with the soft laughter they had exchanged before receiving the news about her trial.

The elf beside her grabbed a towel from a rock, seemingly unaware of her distraction. "Maybe tonight." He wrapped himself and brushed past her. "Follow me." The water beads highlighted the chiseled muscles of his back, which bounced as he strode to the vast, circular tent. "This will be the base of our operation."

A large wooden table dominated the center, covered with a map, scrolls, and various documents. Candles and lanterns were strategically placed to provide ample light, casting a warm, flickering glow.

Raven glanced toward the back. "There's only a double-sized bed?"

"I didn't know you wanted to spend the night, but if you *decided* to, we both know that would suffice."

"I don't—I just—"

"Your mission will be over by sundown, but if you want—"

"Get dressed." Raven turned away from the opening. *Get it together. Stop acting foolish.*

She paced, eyes locked on the tree line. It loomed like a wall of jagged teeth, whispering threats she couldn't quite hear but felt in her bones. The branches didn't sway—they beckoned with crooked fingers curling in mockery, an invitation she wanted to ignore. Shadows shifted between the trunks, stretching and recoiling like something alive. Watching and waiting. *Why do I feel like my mission is in there?* The thought clung to her like a warning—or a dare. After a while, he finally summoned her.

Alagust's armor, a masterpiece of elven craftsmanship, was designed to enhance his agility, stealth, and lethal efficiency. He wore a hooded, dark green and black cloak, perfect for blending into forested shadows. Various pouches for lockpicks and vials for poisons hung from his belt. His form-fitting leather chestplate, reinforced with mithril inlays, provided essential protection without sacrificing mobility. Matching bracers covered his arms from wrist to elbow, while fingerless gloves allowed unmatched dexterity. His tight-fitting leggings, reinforced at the knees and thighs, assured silent, agile movements, and his soft-soled green boots of Elvenkind ensured his steps remained soundless. He glanced at her as she entered. "By midday, our target will be set up to be hunted. Then you have until sundown to find and assassinate our target." Alagust studied the map on the table.

"Who is our target, and why must they be eliminated?"

"We have to wait—" A loud screech cut through the air as something swooped past the tent opening. Alagust dropped to a knee, his hand flashing to the dagger at his belt. A scroll fluttered to the ground. "Interesting," he muttered, unrolling it with caution. Alagust's expression darkened. "I'm not sure you'll like this."

Raven snatched the scroll from his hands, stretched it out, and read aloud. "Target: Prince of Spires Hand. Sixteen-year-old male high-elf. Parents paid for a mage to teach him unauthorized, powerful spells." She dropped the parchment as if it burned her fingers. "I have to take the word of this scroll to assassinate Prince Jerymiah Thorne? This could start a war." *It feels too personal, too wrong.*

"I can create a portal back to Waterfront if you like," Alagust offered, his tone measured but revealing nothing of his thoughts. "I can handle it on my own."

Raven's mind raced. *Is this part of the test?* She squared her shoulders. "What spells did he learn that warrant a death mark?"

"I don't know." Alagust's gaze was fixed on the scroll. "I just received these parchments with my objective."

"You don't question the headmaster?"

"Why would I?" Alagust's voice was firm. "We've kept this realm in check for five decades." He snapped his head straight, staring at the side of the tent.

"What is it?"

"Well, this was unexpected. Our target is here," Alagust said, grabbing the parchment and rolling it up. "He triggered my North Passage alarm." He sighed. "I'm not supposed to tell you this, but I like you."

"Um, thanks?"

"Prince Thorne is trying to be the youngest Arcane Assassin for early admittance to Waterfront." Alagust's voice was tense, scanning the area, avoiding eye contact.

"His target"—her voice dropped to a growl, sharp and unsteady—"is *me*?!"

Alagust pressed his lips together and glanced at her with concern.

Raven's stomach plummeted. Her pulse pounded against her throat like it wanted out. She blinked hard, as if she could shake the words from the air, scrub them of meaning—but they clung, heavy and echoing. *Did the headmaster sign a warrant for my death?*

Her hand shot back to pat the rear pouch—razor wire, still there. Then her fingers gripped her staff, hesitating. *Split it into daggers now, or wait?* She shifted her stance, muscles coiling tight, ready. Her gaze swept the shadows, alert. *Is he already here? Watching? Either way, he's coming.*

"And he's your target," Alagust said, his voice low as the temperature seemed to drop around her. "Head north."

Raven didn't move at first. The words landed, cold and sharp but slow, like blades pushed through the ice. A mission. *Her* mission. *To kill the one sent to kill me.*

She swallowed hard. *A test? A trap? Or some twisted kind of trust?* Her jaw tightened. She didn't know which answer was worse. But her orders were clear, and she would meet him on her terms.

Raven gripped her staff and trekked north along the dirt trail until the edge of the forest line. "ꬿd-Osiṭẹ." She went invisible. The air, thick with humidity, wrapped around her like a warm, damp blanket. The canopy above was a sprawling tapestry of emerald leaves, filtering the sunlight into dappled patterns on the forest floor. Vines twisted and coiled around towering trees, their bark rough beneath a layer of moss. The sound of distant animals and the calls of unseen birds, their songs sharp and melodic, cut through the dense underbrush. A flicker of movement caught her eye—a flash of iridescent blue as a butterfly danced past. The rustle of leaves startled her as some small creatures scurried away into the undergrowth.

The hum of the insects was a constant background chorus that rose and fell like a natural symphony. Branching off to the right, tall coconut trees mingled with bamboo stalks as Raven's steps pressed into the soft, loamy earth, rich with the scent of decaying wood.

She lifted her staff. "Vita Corvus." The bird came to life, shook its feathers, and squawked. *Find Prince Thorne or any sign of someone in the woods.* The raven flapped its wings at her message and shot straight into the air.

Raven glanced up as the midday sun peeked in, searching the sky for her familiar. Shorty was circling an area just northeast of her current location. She moved quickly through the dense foliage, approaching the tree line where it opened to a campsite. A lone figure sat by the fire, seemingly relaxed.

Suddenly, a dart shot from the northwest treeline, striking Shorty in mid-flight. The bird vanished, materializing wooden and lifeless on Raven's staff as she brought it around. "Vita Corvus," she whispered, hoping to revive him, but the bird remained still. *Perhaps I should give him more time.*

"Visus Verum." She activated True Seeing, and the figure by the fire flickered, revealing itself as a glitchy hologram. *I knew it. He's setting a trap.* A flicker of motion drew her to the flat-topped boulder just beyond the clearing, where someone crouched, blowgun poised toward the camp.

Raven moved like a shadow despite the harsh midday sun beating through the dense canopy. The tropical heat was oppressive, but she remained focused, her breath steady and controlled. She slipped between patches of light and shadow, a predator stalking her prey.

The prince lay prone on the boulder, his back to the world, lulled by the warmth of the sun and the false silence of the jungle. His chest rose and fell steadily, his attention fixed on the treeline. He didn't notice the shadow creeping closer.

Raven's gaze locked onto him, cold and calculating. Her hand slipped into her back leather case, finding the familiar coil of razor wire hidden there. The wire was thin, nearly invisible, but its lethal sharpness was unmistakable. She pulled it taut, the metal glinting in the sunlight.

The forest held its breath as she moved in, her body low and fluid. Every rustle of leaves and every distant birdcall was noted and dismissed as she focused entirely on her target. She was close enough now to hear the prince's breathing, close enough to see the faint stubble on his jaw, close enough to spot the nervous twitch of his fingers around the blowgun.

Raven stepped onto a smaller stone and hopped to the top of the boulder to straddle him. She was soundless, but it made him glance back. He shifted his elbows to secure the blowgun again as he overlooked the campsite.

Raven quickly wrapped the razor wire under his chin and yanked as the blowgun fell forward, bouncing off the boulder. She canceled True Seeing as the prince struggled. He split his left palm, trying to pry the wire from his neck. His right index finger slid off his hand as he tried to slip it underneath the coils. The dismembered finger hit a familiar parchment.

*Alagust Stormryder's portrait and name.*

"I'm not his target." Her voice was calm but urgent. Raven released the razor wire, and the prince's hands shot up to his throat, desperately trying to stem the blood loss. Quickly, she shrugged off her cloak and pressed it into his hands. "Here, press this to stop the bleeding."

Alagust emerged from the western treeline, his strides purposeful as he moved past the campfire. Raven jumped down from the boulder, landing lightly. "Please, help him," she urged.

Alagust raised an eyebrow, skepticism etched on his face. "Why? You've already won."

Raven shook her head, her expression serious. "I wasn't his target," she replied, noticing the concern flickering in Alagust's eyes. "You were," she added, then reached for the bloodied parchment beside the prince and handed it to Alagust. "If you save him, we can get answers. Like why the headmaster would betray you."

Alagust's expression hardened as he studied the parchment. After a long pause, he nodded once and dropped it to the ground. "You're right." He pulled a small vial from his pouch and handed it to her. "Let him drink this."

Raven took the container, her hands steady as she tilted it to the prince's lips, helping him swallow the liquid.

"It should stop the bleeding in a moment," Alagust assured her, his tone oddly comforting. He stepped closer, watching Raven keep pressure, her hands trembling slightly. "You need to hydrate before you collapse." He offered her a canteen.

Grateful, Raven took a quick swig. "Thank you," she said, the water cool and refreshing on her parched throat but with a weird aftertaste.

"It was my pleasure," Alagust replied, his voice almost too smooth.

Raven's breath caught in her throat as her eyes locked on the prince. Thin, dark green lines crawled across his pale skin, threading-like veins of rot beneath the surface. From the edges of his jaw, the marks spiraled outward across his cheekbones, splitting like cracks through fine porcelain. His lips paled, tinged with the sickly gray as he gasped his final breaths.

Her stomach twisted. She took a small step back as if distance could shield her from what she was seeing. *No, no, no* . . . Her heart hammered against her ribs, the sound roaring in her ears. "You poisoned him?" she asked, though it barely came out at all. The words scraped her throat like broken glass, rasped on a breath too shallow to carry disbelief. Horror laced her voice, but beneath it, a dangerous current of realization rose.

"I didn't. *You* did," Alagust corrected, his expression unreadable. "But it was either him or me."

Suddenly, Raven's throat swelled, a fiery burn spreading from her mouth to her chest. Panic surged through her as she realized what was happening. "What . . . the . . . spell?" she choked out, her voice stifled.

Alagust watched her with cold detachment, his lips curling into a faint smile. "A simple precaution," he said, stepping back as Raven's vision blurred. "You were both my targets."

Once alive and vibrant, the forest spun as the poison took hold. Raven's knees buckled, and the canteen slipped from her fingers. Alagust caught her as she fell, holding her close as her world narrowed to a painful point of betrayal.

"Such a shame," he murmured, his voice soft and venomous in her ear. "But it is poetic justice if you think about it. Gideon Grindal stole my position as Mortal Realm Guardian, so I stole his love."

Raven's vision blurred into darkness as her body went limp in his arms. Even in the still void, she was aware of a faint buzzing, like the sound of a distant portal. She felt weightless, floating in midair, her mind grasping at the edges of consciousness. *What is happening?*

Suddenly, the comforting solidity of a cot pressed against her back. The faint, almost imperceptible vibrations of a portal opening and closing reached her senses. Slowly, the feeling in her hands returned, her fingers tightening around something familiar—the staff, placed across her in a funeral position.

Raven forced her eyes open. The soft glow from orb lamps and the flickering flames in a barrel cast shadows across the tent's ceiling. Slowly, her mind cleared.

Alagust stood with his back to her, focused on the table where he carefully inspected the razor wire before placing it in a case.

She watched, her breath shallow and hushed, as he tossed more parchment into the barrel, the flames roaring as they devoured the paper.

He kicked the barrel, tipping it over so the burning contents spilled dangerously close to the tent's fabric. Raven squinted as the firelight cast eerie shadows across Alagust's face, revealing his expression of cold finality as he turned toward the portal.

Raven's grip tightened on the staff, her fingers coiling around the worn leather like a serpent preparing to strike. In one fluid motion, she twisted her wrists. A muted click sounded as the staff split down the middle, folding inward with clockwork precision to become twin daggers, their obsidian blades catching the low light like shards of shadow.

Alagust turned his back.

*Fatal mistake.* Raven moved like smoke—silent, fast, impossible to trace. She lunged forward, each step predatory. Her lead dagger speared straight into the center of his back, right between the ribs. The blade sank deep with a wet, muffled crunch.

Alagust stiffened, a gasp choking in his throat. His hands twitched as if trying to reach the wound that he couldn't see, couldn't comprehend.

Raven leaned in close, her lips near his ear. "I guess I'm immune to poison, too," she whispered, voice smooth as ice.

Alagust's body stiffened, his hands twitching at the hilts of the daggers, but before he could react, a second dagger came up under his arm and drove into the soft tissue beneath his collarbone, angled to nick the artery.

She held him there, locked in a grim embrace, until his limbs went slack. Pain and surprise etched into his features as Raven stepped around him. He crumpled like a severed marionette the moment she released him.

Raven stood over Alagust's motionless body, her chest heaving, every muscle trembling with a volatile mixture of adrenaline and wrath. The satisfaction of victory was cold and sharp, but her stomach churned with a nauseous undercurrent, the scent of burning fabric from the tent mingling with the bitter taste in her mouth. She stared at Alagust's still form, her breath ragged, trying to steady herself in the aftermath. *All the traits.* The words felt hollow in her mind, but Baka was right. *The trait of a green dragon.*

She glanced at the portal, energy crackling like a snarl against the roar of the flames. So much undone. So many questions gnawing at her. Triumph thudded in her gut, raw and uncertain—or maybe that was just the poison clawing for a final word.

After securing the razor wire to her belt, she surveyed the destruction around her. *I need to inform King and Queen Thorne about the prince.* Raven grabbed Alagust's dagger and stepped through the portal, the sensation of dislocation momentarily disorienting as the world around her shifted. She emerged into an amber haze of the headmaster's chamber, the air thick with the scent of old parchment and incense.

Raven stepped into the room like a storm breaching its walls, limping, blood still drying under her nails, the poison's metallic sting biting her tongue. Seated behind his desk, Gavan Taiker waited, watching in disbelief. A tremor started in his fingers as he reached instinctively for a quill, then thought better of it. His gaze twitched—not a blink, a flinch. A pulse beat in his temple, rapid and betraying.

The man who once towered over her with quiet certainty now looked like a statue cracked at the base. His throat worked around a breath he didn't take. The unshakable headmaster, the all-knowing, appeared utterly, hopelessly mortal for the first time.

*I dare you to grab my arm again.* Raven didn't smile. Didn't speak. She dropped Alagust's dagger with a sharp clank on the polished desk. Her grip tightened around her staff as she turned. Every step toward the exit dragged the poison deeper into her bones.

She ignored it.

Taiker said nothing. His awe formed into silence. Then, just as she crossed the threshold, he called after her, "Congratulations, Arcane Assassin."

She didn't turn. "*Phuk Parmab,*" Raven cursed in Orcish. *I have work to do. Poison or not, I'm a Mortal Guardian.*

# CHAPTER TWELVE

# IN THE WAKE OF DREAMS

Raven jolted upright, gasping as if a kraken tentacle released her from the depths of the sea. The pillow she'd clung to flew across the room like a discarded shield. Her nightgown clung to her skin, drenched in cold sweat, and her heart pounded—far too fast for someone to be at rest.

She forced herself to take measured, sharp inhales, like she was moments away from letting a dagger fly. "Another nightmare." Slamming the back of her head against the headboard, she winced instantly. Her eyes flicked to Gideon. *Still asleep. Good.* The last thing she needed was a witness.

She reached for the fallen pillow, groaning as her back seized up with a vengeful spasm. "Ogre poop," she hissed, massaging the knot like it had personally betrayed her. *One more ailment for the list.* She collapsed back onto the bed with a sigh that bordered on a growl, staring up at the ceiling as if it might reveal the answers.

The dream replayed in her mind, vivid and taunting. Always the same: sprinting through the endless corridors of Waterfront with the air thick with dread. Behind her was the thunder of something massive that reeked of a dragon, though she never once saw its face. Its roar, deafening, reverberated through every bone in her body. Every door she tried was locked. All except one. *The one marked with that damned symbol.* She always stepped into the dark chamber with hopes, expecting the woman in the green cloak to be there. But every time, there was nothing. Just silence. Just darkness. Just the feeling that she was too late.

Raven yawned and sat up in bed, the soft morning light filtering through the thick curtains. Beside her, Gideon lay sleeping, his long blond hair cascading over the pillow in a golden wave. The familiar heavy woolen covers were draped across his naked body, a comforting yet peculiar reminder of home. *I wonder if he has nightmares.*

She ran her hand across the coarse fabric, feeling the warmth of his skin through the layers. It still baffled her that this room was an exact duplicate of her bedroom at home: the wooden beams, the antique furniture, even the faint smell of lavender. And yet, something about the place made her uncomfortable, an unsettling sensation that gnawed at her insides. *Why would the headmaster do this? Is it an attempt to let my guard down?*

As the moments dragged on, unease coiled tighter in her chest. The walls felt closer now, the silence thick enough to choke on. An uncanny stillness hung as if the room held its breath.

Raven shifted her attention to the window Gideon had conjured to brighten the chamber, half-expecting to find the woman in the green cloak watching from beyond, her presence a silent weight. But there was nothing—only the soft rustle of leaves stirred by the wind.

She sighed and slid out of bed, her bare feet touching the wooden floor. The chill sent a shiver up her spine. *I won't find peace until I find the woman in the green cloak.*

Making her way to the side table, Raven rinsed her mouth with a canteen of water and spat into an empty porcelain bowl. *Yuck!* The acid from her spit training always left a gross aftertaste, lingering like an unwelcome memory.

"I think that was intended for fruit," Gideon mumbled, his voice thick with sleep, his face still partially blocked by the pillow. "You've finished three bowls already."

Raven picked off a mint leaf from the plant and chewed, the fresh flavor battling the sourness in her mouth. "Oh well, we still have another full bowl over there." She stretched her arms, feeling the satisfying pull of her muscles, and rubbed her left shoulder where it felt tight. Slowly, she rolled her neck from side to side, trying to ease the tension that had settled there as she returned to sit at the edge of the bed.

Gideon's hand covered hers, warm and comforting, while his other hand applied gentle pressure between her shoulder blades. His touch was familiar and tender, evoking countless shared moments.

Raven closed her eyes and let his masculine hands work their magic, his fingers finding and kneading the knots with practiced ease. "Good morning," she moaned softly, the words breathy as she surrendered to the sensation of his touch.

"Morning, Miss Arcane Assassin," Gideon murmured, his voice a soothing rumble against her ear. He shifted closer, his chest warm against her back, breath soft on her neck.

A shiver ran down her spine—not from fear, but from the comfort he brought.

"How's that?" he asked.

"Perfect," she sighed, her body melting into his. She tilted her head just enough to catch his gaze, a small smile curling at her lips. "And I like the sound of that."

His lips brushed her shoulder. "Are you going to tell me about the trial?"

She met his eyes for a heartbeat, then pressed a kiss to his forehead. "One day," she said quietly. It was the truth. But not now. She knew Gideon well enough to guess how he'd react—and he wouldn't like what she had to report.

"Maybe you're trying too hard," he murmured, nuzzling her. "This mystery lady . . . maybe she senses your stress."

Raven let out a soft breath, somewhere between a laugh and a sigh. *Maybe he's right.* Maybe her tension was chasing the answers away. Still, she couldn't shake the feeling that time was running out. "Fine. Can we stay in and do this all day?" she asked softly as she traced a finger along his bicep.

Gideon glanced at her with a tender smile. "We could. However, we still have two more traits to test."

"I know, I know. The water and the darkness," Raven said, spitting out the chewed-up mint leaf and grabbing a fresh one. The bitter taste lingered on her tongue, making her scrunch her nose. "I still think the acid is gross."

"It's a great defensive ability," Gideon offered, gently pulling out the leaf and kissing her. The minty taste mingled between them. She smiled against his lips, then stuffed a fresh mint leaf into his mouth.

"You need this, too," she pointed out playfully.

Gideon chuckled, chewing on the leaf. "Let's get washed up and dressed." He removed the herb from his mouth and placed it on the table beside them before extending a hand to her.

Feeling refreshed after a long bath that eased her aching muscles, Raven summoned her armor, the dark plates gleaming faintly in the light. The heat of the tub still lingered in her skin, but the moment the armor settled over her, Raven's thoughts turned cold. She glanced at Gideon. "Who's watching the Mortal Realm?"

Gideon paused, his fingers tracing the intricate runes etched into the hilt of his vorpal sword. "I'm not sure," he admitted reluctantly. "But if I meditate and check, they'll find me."

"Maybe you should just confront them," Raven suggested, her purple boots tapping impatiently against the floor. "You have evidence of demon activity. We don't have to stay. The woman isn't here. Probably just my imagination."

"Patience," Gideon murmured, sheathing the vorpal sword and attaching it securely to his belt. "That room has helped you hone your dragon skills."

Raven scoffed, adjusting her belt with a sharp tug. "Isn't that odd, though? I found the room, and the headmaster was ready to portal me to the Abyss. But he was completely willing to allow us to use it when you showed up." She shook her head. "It doesn't make sense."

Gideon met her gaze, caution mirrored in his expression. "There are deeper currents at play here," he said slowly, his voice low but resolute. "We must tread carefully. The fate of both realms may hinge on what we uncover. And besides, I was his favorite student," Gideon teased as he adjusted his summoned wings.

Raven slapped him playfully on the arm, a fond smile playing on her lips as she watched him finish dressing. Despite their banter, the mention of the harbinger in green lingered in her mind like a stalker. "The woman mentioned Draakgoons," she said, her tone low and cautious.

"Never heard of it," Gideon replied nonchalantly. With a swift gesture, the ornate wooden door in their room shimmered and vanished into thin air. "I've heard of Gooners before, though."

"Shorte mentioned the same." Raven frowned slightly, her brow contracting in thought. The mention of unfamiliar terms in their line of work always made her uneasy, but Gideon's casual demeanor was infectious. She trusted him implicitly, yet the unknown was a persistent worry at the edge of her awareness. She sighed and grabbed two apples from a nearby basket along with her polished ebony staff with the raven atop.

Raven tossed a vibrant red apple to Apprentice Donavan with a gentle smile as she exited. He quickly caught it, a gesture they'd repeated for the past few days. Gideon had insisted on Donavan standing guard outside their quarters, citing routine security measures, though Raven couldn't shake the feeling that there was more to it.

"Ready for some water practice today?" Gideon asked as they walked through the castle courtyard, the cool breeze carrying the scent of blooming jasmine.

Raven nodded eagerly, taking a crisp bite from the apple. "Absolutely. I'm eager to learn."

As they approached the grand front entrance, they passed Master Owens, an elderly wizard known for his wisdom and keen insight. He leaned lightly on his ornate staff, its intricate carvings telling tales of a long past.

"An early start this morning, Master Owens?" Gideon greeted him respectfully.

"Indeed," the old wizard replied, his eyes crinkling at the corners as he smiled warmly. His gaze shifted to Raven, and he paused as if sensing something beyond the obvious. "That's a lovely necklace, my dear," he remarked, his voice low and thoughtful.

Raven instinctively touched the silver pendant shaped like a sword. *Can he perceive its hidden magic?*

"It was a gift from my brother."

Owens raised a bushy eyebrow skeptically. "I don't believe a demigod would give you such a poorly crafted trinket."

Raven quickly glanced at Gideon, who stood nearby with pursed lips.

"Henry," Gideon interjected smoothly, using the wizard's first name. "If you will excuse us, we have a lot of work to do today."

Master Owens nodded sagely, acknowledging the dismissal. With a slight incline of his head, he turned and made his way toward the castle's classrooms, his staff tapping gently against the cobblestones.

Raven huffed, her breath forming a mist in the crisp morning air. "What the spell?" she muttered under her breath, eyeing Master Owens with frustration.

"Henry's old and a bit . . . eccentric," Gideon replied, his voice calm but tinged with a hint of apology. "Please don't pay him any mind. It would be best if you focused on today's lessons. We know you can control your breathing in calm water. But today, we need to push your limits."

Raven glanced back at Henry, who was now muttering to himself and waving his staff exaggeratedly as Gideon pulled her out of the front gate.

The sky was a clear, rich blue, scattered with slow-moving white clouds. Sunlight warmed the beach, glinting off the crystal water. Golden sand carved along the coastline, and seagulls glided overhead, their calls rising and falling with the steady crash of waves.

"It's such a beauteous day to spend on the beach," Raven remarked, her voice carrying a hint of excitement as she gripped Gideon's hand. They descended the weathered stone stairs, and the rhythmic crash of the waves against the ancient rocks grew louder, a constant backdrop to their journey.

Their boots sank comfortably into the soft, warm sand as they reached a secluded alcove. The turquoise waters shimmered invitingly, but Raven felt the weight of them—depthless, heaving, alive. The breeze carried the tang of salt and seaweed, and something colder beneath. She shot a glance at Gideon, catching the flicker of reflected waves in his eyes. Her stomach tightened. "You want to test me in that?"

"Over there," he instructed, pointing to a crystal blue lagoon that shimmered in the sunlight. "Celeste and I swam here often when we were students. But first, I need you to activate your familiar."

Raven gripped her staff, its carved bird staring back with dull black sockets. She focused, channeling her will into the wooden figurine. "Vita Corvus." The blackbird atop the staff shook its feathers and let out a sharp squawk, its pupils briefly glowing purple

"He'll be able to connect me telepathically to you," Gideon explained, his voice low. "This way, if you need help, I will know."

"If you want to know what I'm thinking, just ask," Raven retorted, amusement laced with purpose as she began to unsummon her armor. "Armis—

"Keep it on," Gideon cut in abruptly, scanning the horizon.

"Really?" Raven flashed him a skeptical look. She took a deep breath and slowly waded into the water. "Ah, this is cold."

"Keep going!" Gideon urged, tension tightening his voice. "Remember to breathe."

"Easy for you to say," she muttered under her breath, each step sending ripples through the lagoon. As she moved in deeper, the chill seeped into her bones until, with a mental command—*I'm cold!*—the armor responded. Heat blossomed within, warding off the cold with a comforting warmth. *There we go.*

Raven closed her eyes, heeding Gideon's advice. She inhaled one deep breath and then submerged completely, weightless in the chill embrace of the lagoon. Beneath the surface, the world softened to the gentle rhythm of the waves and the distant cries of seagulls.

Opening her eyes, Raven gazed into the precise, blue depths, where a school of yellow-striped fish darted whimsically among swaying seagrass. Beyond them, vibrant coral reefs burst with life, their colors vivid against the ocean's canvas. Sunlight filtered through the water, casting shimmering rays that danced upon the sandy seabed. Each moment felt like a suspended breath in time, serene and untouched by the world's rush above.

Raven's thoughts drifted to the secret sister spot as she settled onto the ocean floor. It was her haven, a place where solitude wrapped around her like a comforting cloak, shielding her from the chaos of daily life. Here, amid the beauty of the underwater world, she found peace and a connection to something deeper within herself.

Her mind drifted as the muffled sounds of waves churned in her ears. A vision of her mother's face appeared, soft yet distant behind a veil of memory. The blurry image of Mara pulling her out of the water during a swimming lesson at the age of seven flickered into view.

"*You have to kick your legs,*" Mara's voice echoed faintly in her mind.

"*Like how you kick me when I'm trying to sleep. That's why I want my own bed, Mother,*" Carya had retorted, splashing around defiantly.

"*Don't leave me!*"

The images shifted abruptly. Now nine years old, Raven roguishly placed a frog in her sister's washbowl. Carya cried out in disgust, calling out. "*Mother! I want my own room!*"

"*Don't leave me!*"

The scenes continued to whirl. The two sisters, now older, dove into the secret cave to activate the light orb that Gideon had gifted Carya for her eighteenth birthday.

"*I got accepted to be trained by Stone-Prayer. It will be a while until I can swim with you again,*" Carya explained softly.

"*Don't leave me!*"

Each memory bore the weight of unspoken longing and the ache of separation, weaving a tapestry of sorrow. The memories of Carya twisted Raven's heart as she relived the moments. The images didn't quit. The sensation of passing through the portal with Izarra and Shorte to Gideon's camp was vivid—the rush of magic enveloping her, the disorienting swirl of colors as they traversed realms. Amid it all, Carya's voice, "*Don't leave me,*" pierced the chaos, a desperate cry echoing in Raven's mind.

"*Carya!*" Raven gasped, her voice catching. Her sister's face contorted with anguish. Her arm reached out as if to grasp onto something slipping away.

The image shifted abruptly to another memory, stark and bright. It was Omlett's anniversary celebration, the stage illuminated with dazzling lights. Carya stood in a delicate white gown, dancing gracefully with Thomas, her laughter carrying through the air like delicate music. Raven felt a pang of longing and guilt as she watched from the shadows as her sister paused and called out, "*Don't leave me!*"

Suddenly, Raven found herself in a secret cavern, the air thick with moisture and mystery. She struggled to stay afloat in the icy water, her breath coming in ragged gasps. Her mind raced, searching desperately for Carya amid the swirling darkness.

Mentally exhausted, Raven pushed herself to the surface, where Thomas stood bathing in the soft glow of a distant light. She stared at his naked form, the beads of water falling down his chest. A feeling of desire filled her body then quickly changed to shame. *What am I doing?* As she turned, Carya appeared before her, anger flashing in her eyes like lightning in a storm. They argued fiercely, words tumbling like sharp stones, each accusation cutting deeper than the last. Tears stung as she watched her sister run off into the brush, her sobs echoing hauntingly through the air.

"Carya," Raven whispered hoarsely, causing her to swallow some salt water. She could still hear her sister's voice echoing in her head, repeating, "*You left me*," accusing her of abandonment. The weight of guilt pressed on Raven's chest, threatening to drown her in a sea of regret at the bottom of the ocean.

The more she struggled, the faster the sand swallowed her. Raven's frantic kicks only sank her deeper into the suffocating embrace of the soft ground. Panic surged through her veins as cold water filled her throat. Her eyesight flickered between light and darkness.

A frail hand clutched her wrist, offering a lifeline in the gloom. Then, a lady in a flowing green cloak materialized beside her as if conjured by her distress. Her presence was calming yet otherworldly. "*Relax*," she murmured, her voice like a distant siren in a storm. The inexorable pull of the water ceased, though her mouth tasted of salt. "*Breathe*," the lady urged gently.

With trembling hands, Raven focused on expelling the water from her mouth, forcing it through her nose. The salty burn intensified, but she dared not stop. Slowly, she regulated her breath, the sensation of drowning ebbing away. Her vision returned to normal.

Yet a foreign obstruction persisted in her throat, a barrier between life and the watery abyss. *I'm breathing underwater—I'm breathing underwater*, she repeated frantically in her mind, her thoughts racing to Gideon, her only hope. She kicked off the sandy seabed, surrounded by schools of fish darting away as she rose. Her movement became more powerful, pushing against the water's resistance until finally breaking through the surface with a splash. The obstruction in her throat vanished as she gasped for air under the open sky. Soaking wet, she trudged out of the water, full of steam as her armor worked overtime to dry her. Then she collapsed, coughing up seawater.

Gideon rushed to her side, concern etched on his face. "Are you all right?" He knelt beside her.

Raven shivered slightly as the warmth from her armor seeped into her chilled limbs. She glanced at Gideon's campsite, noting the neatly arranged gear and the crackling fire that provided a comforting glow against the gathering darkness.

"How long was I down there for?"

"See for yourself," Gideon replied, glancing up. The sky above them was painted in hues of orange and pink, the last remnants of daylight fading into dusk. "I lost a PIP to your father. I had half a day. He had a full day."

"My father and you bet on this?" Raven asked, incredulous.

Gideon nodded, a cynical smile on his lips as he adjusted the towel around her shoulders. "Oh yes, quite the wager. Even the squad was involved. Jarz had two days, Izarra had three days, but Shorte had you down for two weeks if that makes you feel better."

Raven giggled softly, the adrenaline from her underwater exploration slowly giving way to a sense of amusement. "Like his black dragon story, and let me guess—Avalann gambled I would drown?"

Gideon's expression turned serious for a moment. "Avalann always likes to play the odds. But we all knew better."

Raven grinned, feeling a sense of camaraderie despite the teasing bet. "I guess they underestimated my abilities, because holding a breath and breathing are two different things."

"I agree," Gideon added, his tone softening.

They moved to the fire pit, where a large filet of salmon sizzled and crackled over the flames. Raven's stomach growled loudly, alerting her to how hungry she had become. The rogue swiftly unsummoned her armor, the weight of it freeing her body as she stepped closer to the warmth of the fire.

"The fish should be done." Gideon handed her a warm roll before arranging the perfectly roasted salmon on a plate.

Raven watched his fluid movements as she tore off a piece of the roll, savoring its warmth.

"What happened down there?" Gideon asked, holding out her plate. "You're familiar only said your sister's name and the phrase 'don't leave me.'"

Raven took the meal gratefully, savoring the familiar taste that reminded her of home. She leaned against him as she chewed, comforted by his presence and warmth amid the evening chill.

*My mother would be proud of me for not talking while I chew.* After the last bite, she brushed off her hands and nestled closer. The rhythmic sound of the waves provided a soothing backdrop to their conversation, punctuated by the occasional distant call of seabirds. "I was thinking about Carya. It's like I went into a trance or something down there. Then I realized I was drowning."

Gideon's expression softened, his hand gently stroking her hair. "You scared me."

They sat side by side, watching a large boat glide across the horizon. "Is that a pirate ship?" she asked, her curiosity piqued.

"Possibly." Gideon's arms wrapped around her protectively. "Most ships pass through Mystic Bay to enter the river system."

A sudden burst of red and white fireworks erupted over the water, casting a magical glow over the dark ocean. She turned to him in wonder. "That came from the ship. I hope there's more," Raven said before kissing his hand. Just then, loud explosions echoed from behind them, and they turned to face the mainland, where fireworks lit up the night sky over Waterfront.

"I'm surprised the headmaster would allow that," Gideon remarked, his curiosity piqued. "I wonder who's on that ship?"

"You could fly over and see for yourself," Raven teased, tightening her grip on his arms.

"And leave this?" Gideon countered softly, his gaze lingering on her. "It's not that important."

In the quiet intimacy of the moment, as the distant fireworks painted the sky, Raven whispered, "It's nice to see others enjoying life." She glanced over the shimmering waves, where distant cheers mingled with the surf crash. "I'd like to return to Omlett soon, but first I need to get out of these." Her sandy tunic and training breeches clung uncomfortably to her skin; with a deft motion, she peeled them off and hung them by the fire. The chilly sea breeze prickled her bare skin as she stared up at the now-empty sky, already missing the burst of magic. With a sigh, she turned, only to catch Gideon mid-strip. She stared longer than she probably should have. Her brain shouted *look away*; her eyes didn't listen. "What are you doing?" she asked, trying to sound unimpressed.

He grinned with his breeches down. "What? They got soaked when I was fishing."

"Sure," Raven laughed softly, shaking her head at his innocent excuse.

"I thought we could count the stars." He winked, spreading a blanket. They gazed up at the vast expanse of the night sky as they lay side by side on the soft beach, wrapped in the blanket's warmth. The stars twinkled, casting a serene glow over the tranquil scene. "This wasn't quite what I had in mind," Gideon teased lightly, his voice carrying a hint of amusement.

"This isn't the Fey Realm."

He kissed her, his lips warm against her soft skin. His fingers traced gentle patterns across her back, eliciting a shiver of delight. She cherished these moments of peace with him, the waves' rhythmic sounds, a soothing back-drop to their intimacy. Yet she knew they couldn't linger forever; more training awaited them.

"I understand why wizards are so strict about visitors. To keep the beaches in pristine shape," she said softly, savoring the sensation of his kisses trailing down her neck.

"This place is also dangerous," Gideon said, his voice grave. His breath warmed her ear as he spoke, but there was no playfulness in it—only memory. "These students . . . they're walking storms. One misstep, one surge of emotion, and someone could get hurt."

"Is that why you're training me?" she asked, rolling him beneath her with a smirk. "So I don't accidentally turn someone into an acid puddle?"

He didn't laugh. His hands found her waist, but his thoughts had drifted elsewhere, distant, haunted. "I trained someone once. Years ago. Devanna was gifted. Brilliant. But I pushed too hard, too fast, and she lost control of a fireball." He exhaled, the sound raw, as if he could still feel the heat of the flames. "Three people died before I could react."

Her heartbeat caught as his words sank in. The air between them shifted—no longer charged with teasing tension but with something heavier. She studied his face, tracing the faint shadows beneath his eyes and the tight set of his jaw. This wasn't just caution. It was guilt and grief. She didn't speak. Couldn't. A part of her ached for him—for the pain he still carried, the weight of a mistake that never stopped burning. *After all this time, I'm still learning new things about him.*

"That's why I'm training you," he said, voice steadier now as his eyes found hers again. "Because I won't let that happen again. Not to you. Not to anyone." His hand slipped the tie from her hair. She felt the gentle tug, then the fall of her hair around them like a curtain, softening the world beyond their shared space. "You have more power than you know," he murmured. "But power without control . . . It's not freedom. It's a fuse."

The words settled deep in her chest, humming through her bones. Raven swallowed hard, the truth of it sharp and sobering. For the first time, the idea of her own power didn't excite her—it frightened her. But beneath the fear, there was something else: Resolve.

She studied him, the gravity of his words slicing through the silence between them. "I didn't mean to make light of it," she murmured, sorrow flickering at the edges of her voice.

"I know," he said gently, his hand brushing a lock of hair from her cheek. "But it's important you understand."

A heavy silence settled between them. Then, slowly, almost cautiously, they moved closer, the distance between grief and desire dissolving with every breath. Raven moaned softly as their bodies met, heat sparking at every point of contact. "Am I emotionally compromised now?" Breathless, her fingers drew idle patterns across his chest.

Gideon smiled, a flicker of admiration and want in his eyes. "I think you're the one training me now," he murmured, his voice thick with longing.

He pulled her down into another kiss, and Raven melted into it, the magic in the air crackling around them like it had been waiting for this. For them. The world narrowed to the press of his lips, the heat of his hands, and the pull low in her stomach that left her breathless.

Stars spun lazily overhead, and the sea whispered behind them, but Raven barely registered it. She wasn't thinking about enchantments or danger or training. Just the way his kiss made her feel—steady, wanted, alive.

She kissed him back, slower this time, her fingers curling into his hair as if anchoring herself to him. The scent of sandalwood overrode the salt and sweat that clung to his skin, warm and familiar. She placed her hand over his chest and felt the thrum of his heart beneath her palm as she rested her forehead against his. "I trust you," she whispered, and meant it more deeply than any spell she'd ever cast.

"And I trust you," he replied softly, pulling her closer, their bodies fitting together as if made for each other. Their song rose softly into the night, carried on the wind beneath the moon's tender glow, its soft light settling over them like a blessing. They found solace in each other's embrace, knowing they could face any challenge this magical world could conjure.

# CHAPTER THIRTEEN

# OUT OF SIGHT

At the top of the stone steps, the tower guards were the only people moving about this early. The older guard nudged his partner, and they snickered as they noticed Raven and Gideon approaching.

"Show's over, boys," Gideon boasted, his voice carrying a note of authority.

Raven lowered her head, feeling her cheeks turn red as the guards' amusement rang in her ears. She focused on the ground, the sand crunching softly under her feet.

Gideon placed a reassuring hand on her shoulder, squeezing gently. "Ignore them," his tone gentle but firm. "Let's focus on your training."

She nodded, taking a deep breath to steady herself. As they passed the guards, Raven lifted her chin slightly, refusing to let their teasing get the better of her. "I told you this wasn't the Fey Realm," she muttered as she matched Gideon's stride past the gate.

The couple approached the training area Raven had designated as the Dragon Room. The imposing door stood before them, its surface worn by time. Raven paused, "Visus Verum," activating True Seeing on her circlet. *Maybe the mark has returned this time.* Her eyes glowed faintly as the enchantment took effect, bathing the door in a soft, purple light. She waited—searching for the sparkle of a glyph, a hidden line, anything.

Nothing. Just old wood and silence. She tried again, a bit sharper this time, pushing more focus into the spell. Still nothing. *No sigils. No symbols. No clever traps waiting to be unraveled.*

Her jaw clenched. *This doesn't make sense. There has to be something. Doors like this don't just sit unguarded. Not here.* She narrowed her eyes at the stubborn wood, the magic fizzing out. "I don't understand," she mumbled. "The symbol is gone."

Gideon stepped closer, examining the door. "Are you certain it was this door?"

"Absolutely," Raven insisted, her mind racing. She touched the door's surface, hoping to feel some trace of the mark she remembered. "It was right here, clear as day."

Gideon frowned, considering her words. "It's possible someone erased or concealed it. Or maybe it was an illusion meant to mislead you."

They entered the room, and a surge of energy rushed through her, the same as whenever they came here. The room had an ancient, almost mystical feel, as if it held secrets waiting to be uncovered. They created a training area in the center of the room by moving the desks off to the side, their metal legs scraping against the worn wooden floor. Lining the back wall were empty shelves covered in cobwebs and dust, relics of when this room was bustling with activity. Why had the headmaster blocked this location from being used? *Why can we use it?*

Gideon stood in the middle of the room, his posture relaxed yet alert. "Anything?"

"No," she responded, disappointed, returning to him with a sigh. The room seemed void of the clues they hoped to find, only adding to its enigmatic aura.

He held up his hand and raised a finger as he counted her abilities. "Can spit acid, check. Contaminate water, check. Breathe underwater, check. Immune to acid, check."

*And poison.* Raven groaned. "I'm a monster," The words tasted bitter as they left her lips. Her hands trembled as she folded Gideon's fingers into her own and pressed a kiss to his knuckles—more apology than affection, more desperation than doubt.

Gideon tilted her face up. His touch was steady, a weight that pulled her back from the edge. "Stop."

She blinked at him, not in disbelief but in longing. Her eyes searched his—*is it all right to hope?* She gave the slightest nod.

"The final skill you've shown is the Darkness Spell," he said, voice calm, deliberate.

Her chest rose with a quiet breath. Pride flickered through her like a candle guttering in a storm. "It's . . . hard to control."

He moved behind her. The warmth of his hands on her shoulders bled through the tension. "Close your eyes. Concentrate."

She obeyed, holding her staff tightly as warmth stirred inside her chest. "This room makes it easier to control," she remarked, opening her eyes. Darkness flowed from the rogue, enveloping everything in an impenetrable blackness. Raven activated True Seeing again, allowing her to see clearly in the dark. She observed Gideon moving around, attempting to navigate the obscure surroundings. A purple, heart-shaped mark appeared in a corner.

"Gideon, it's here!" she shouted excitedly, rushing over to the mark. "Do you see the heart?"

"I don't see anything," Gideon replied, his voice strained.

Raven dropped the Darkness spell, and the mark disappeared. "It's gone." She recast the spell with ease, and the heart-shaped mark reappeared. "It's right above the floor." Raven tapped her staff on the spot thoughtfully. "Do you think someone placed something here during the reconstruction?"

"It's a possibility," Gideon replied, inspecting the area with furrowed brows. Waving his hand, he uttered a soft incantation, causing an area of the stone floor to ripple and transform into thick, viscous mud.

Once Raven inserted her staff halfway into the softened floor, she felt it strike something hard, sending a faint vibration up the wooden shaft. "There's something down there."

Gideon approached, examining the mudhole, which churned with unseen currents. He commanded the mud to part with a deft gesture and chanted the spell, revealing a gleaming metal chest. It levitated through the muddy swirls, settling gently onto the floor beside Raven's feet.

Frowning, Gideon muttered a spell, but the chest remained stubbornly sealed. Raven knelt beside it, her cloak stained with mud, and gently wiped the grime away from a small plaque affixed to the lid. Strange runes, ancient and intricate, adorned the label.

"What language is that?" Raven asked.

Gideon's gaze sharpened with recognition. "That appears to be the ancient draconic language," he answered. "I studied it for a semester after learning about the Dragon Wars."

"Can you read it?" Raven inquired, glancing between him and the cryptic inscription.

"No," Gideon admitted. "No mortal can decipher these glyphs unaided."

They exchanged a meaningful glance, their thoughts racing with the implications of what lay before them. "Blade?" Raven murmured. A memory flickered in Raven's mind—a fleeting recollection of bright light and a cryptic phrase spoken by Baka, the ancient guardian who had gifted her. "The gift of the dragon tongue," she muttered aloud, uncertain of its meaning but sensing its relevance to this moment.

Gideon's expression hardened with purpose. "If anyone should intrude, keep them distracted," he spoke urgently, conjuring an unseen servant to assist him. Together, they fetched buckets and began methodically clearing the remaining mud from the hole, driven by curiosity and caution.

"What are you doing?" Raven whispered. "You're making a mess." She watched skeptically as he dumped more mud around the chest. "Fine," Raven sighed as he ignored her. She studied the chest again, the ancient script shimmering and then unexpectedly shifting into words she could understand. "Wait! It says . . . with True Eyes . . . the Nest Lies."

"How could you read it?" Gideon asked as he climbed out of the hole, brushing dust from his hands while the invisible servant kept digging below.

Raven didn't answer right away. Her eyes lingered on the plaque. The fading shimmer of the ancient script still burned into her mind. It had been unreadable—lines and swirls like a language she'd never seen. And then it wasn't. The letters had reshaped themselves, sliding into place as if they'd been waiting for her. "I don't know," she said finally. The words felt thin against the weight of what she'd just seen. "The words just . . . shifted into the common tongue." She glanced at Gideon, unsure whether she wanted him to be impressed or concerned. She wasn't even sure which she was herself.

"I still see dragon gibberish."

Raven crouched beside the chest, its surface oddly warm beneath her fingertips. The keyhole gleamed, small and ornate—harmless enough. She brought it closer, her breath stirring dust from the lid. "It has a keyhole," she murmured, more to herself than Gideon. "I could probably pick—"

A flash. Not just light but *pain*—a needle of brilliance stabbing straight through her eyes. She cried out, the chest slipping from her grasp as she clutched her face, stumbling back.

The world fell into a suffocating blackness as Raven's heartbeat thundered in her ears. She blinked rapidly, but the darkness didn't lift. It clung to her like smoke, thick and unmoving. "Gideon—my eyes," she gasped. "I can't—" Her voice cracked. "Everything's dark."

Hands on her—familiar, careful. His voice tried to be calm, but she heard the tightness beneath it. "Let me look."

Her body tensed as his fingers brushed her temples, steadying her. He was trying not to panic—for her—but she felt it just under his skin.

*The circlet.*

The magic words stumbled off her tongue. "Visus Verum." A plea more than a spell.

Light bloomed again—inside her. Not sight, not yet. A warmth behind her eyelids. She opened them slowly.

Gideon inhaled sharply. "They're glowing . . . fluorescent purple."

She didn't respond right away. Her breath came shallow. *Glowing. That isn't normal.* "Will they stay like this?" The question barely made it out. Not because she lacked the voice, but because she already feared the answer.

"I'm not sure," Gideon admitted. "But we need to leave. Now."

"Wait—what about the chest?" Raven hesitated, torn between curiosity and her worsening condition; her hands returned to cover her eyes.

"There's a parchment inside," Gideon responded urgently, the sound of paper rustling accompanying his voice. "It's blank. I'll try to detect magic writing."

Raven knelt in the dark. Behind her eyes, the world was a muffled void. Her skin felt too tight, her limbs too light, like her body might float away if she didn't ground herself. The faint sound of Gideon's voice reached her—low and urgent. He was chanting now, words shaped by magic and strained breath. An incantation. Then a curse in Elvish—sharp, raw. Another attempt. Nothing.

Behind her closed eyelids, heat bloomed. It wasn't gentle; it clawed its way outward as if something buried deep inside her had been triggered. A flare of panic rose in her chest.

*Is this it? Am I blind now?* She gritted her teeth, trying to keep her breathing steady. Her magic had betrayed her before, but not like this—never like this. Her hands curled in her lap, trembling as her vision remained stubbornly absent.

"Still blank," Gideon muttered, voice edged with helplessness.

The truth of his words stung. Blank. Just another void where her sight once was. Then—like a match lit in a pitch-dark room—an image burst behind her eyes. Not the world around her, but something else, something remembered. A woman. Cloaked in deep green. Eyes that flickered with fluorescent green fire. *True Eyes.*

Raven gasped. The memory struck like a chord in her chest, and with it came understanding—not of the moment but of what came next. "Gideon." Her voice came out clearer than she expected. It didn't shake, even if her hand still did. "Give it to me."

She felt him hesitate for only a moment before parchment pressed against her palm. Warm, as if it had absorbed the heat from her fear. She lifted it slowly, instinctively, until it hovered near her face. A sudden shift. Not vision, not precisely. More like presence—light forming within her, pressing outward. The darkness that cloaked her mind split like silk. A radiant white burst through, blinding in its own right but full of shape, of purpose. On the parchment, lines bled into being—no ink, just light and pressure.

A red outline. Bold and deliberate. *An island.* "I think it's a map," she whispered, though the certainty was already rooted in her. She wasn't just seeing it—she was *knowing* it.

Gideon gasped. "A map of what?"

"Draakland," Raven answered, her voice strained as the throbbing intensified. She barely had a moment to process before the doors burst open with a resounding crash. "Gideon, what's going on?"

"I'll be taking that," the headmaster ordered, his voice smooth yet laced with authority.

"I knew you were up to something," Raven replied through gritted teeth, suppressing a wave of nausea. She felt Gideon move beside her, and then the map was snatched from her grasp. Raven carefully cradled the chest in the crook of her arm, her staff gripped tightly in her free hand.

"That map will help me enslave the dragons and execute their protectors, once and for all," Taiker declared triumphantly, his voice echoing with malice. "Along with this."

Gideon stiffened beside her. "How did you get the artifact?" His voice hit her like a blade gone dull—shaken, cracking at the edges.

Raven's fingers flew to her necklace, grasping the cold metal. *It's here. I feel it. It's real.* "It can't be. I have it right here."

But then Taiker spoke—too close, too smug. "I assure you, Miss Naelo, I have the real one." A strange silence pooled between the voices. Tension, thick and coiled.

"He has it around his neck," Gideon whispered beside her.

She heard it more in the way his breath trembled than in the words themselves. Raven didn't need to see to know he was working fast, slipping thoughts into motion. And then it happened. A ripple through the air—sour and sharp, like a string snapping inside her chest. Raven hardened. The magic didn't vanish—it was *cut*. Unraveled.

It didn't take long for the metal to hit stone. *Clang.* The sound rang too loud in the space. Two buckets, falling with no hands to hold them. Gideon's Unseen Servant was gone.

*Dispelled.* The vacuum it left behind, a hollow pressure in the arcane fabric Raven had grown to know by feel, sent tingles up her arms.

"That's not good," Gideon said under his breath, but Raven didn't need the warning. The spell gathered behind her, his magic trying to twist space. The familiar tug of a portal began to form—then failed, spluttering like a flame in the wind.

*Dead. Just like in the cell.* Raven inhaled slowly through her nose. Her sight was gone, but everything else—the tremors in the floor, the tension in Gideon's voice, the taste of charged magic in the air—was speaking louder than ever. And none of it was saying they were safe.

"Nice try, but I instructed the guards to make this a Dead Magic Zone if you tried anything," Taiker's voice cut through the tension. Footsteps echoed from outside the room—guards, their presence closing in.

"Donavan, step aside," Gideon warned as she felt him draw his vorpal sword.

"Gideon—" Raven whispered, but he left her side. She heard the swift, sharp sounds of bodies hitting the floor. "Gideon!" Her voice rose in panic as footsteps rushed toward her.

"Time to go." Gideon pulled her close to him. "Hold on to everything."

A sudden drop tickled Raven's stomach, the sensation of weightlessness accompanying Gideon's incantation. Moments later, they hit solid ground with a jolt, causing her to stagger.

"Raven," Gideon said urgently, steadying her.

"I'm fine," she responded, clutching the magic chest tightly against her and gripping her staff. She heard the distant roar of a waterfall, the soft chirping of unseen creatures, and the melodious neighs of unicorns. Warm air brushed against her face, carrying the sweet fragrance of exotic flowers. "The Fey Realm?"

"Yes," Gideon confirmed, his voice relieved amid their escaped chaos.

"But how?" Raven asked, her eyesight still shrouded in darkness.

"The mud hole. The DMZ spell was for inside the room. Not underneath it."

"That's why you cleared it out," Raven realized as a smile tugged at her lips.

"Better than the privy," Gideon added wryly.

Raven snickered softly, then focused on the sound of the waterfall nearby. "Our cottage is that way." She felt Gideon's arm supporting her back as his other arm lifted her legs, sweeping her off her feet. "Did I ever tell you—" She paused, pressing her head closer to him. "You smell good, like sandalwood oil."

"You may have. But not on the day I returned after escaping the council," he replied, his voice carrying a mix of amusement and nostalgia. "I believe Thomas told me I smelled like shite."

"My privy elf," Raven laughed softly as he carried her toward their cottage.

Gideon chuckled in response. "Acid breath."

Raven lovingly smacked Gideon with her staff as they entered their cottage's cozy warmth, leaving behind the dangers and intrigues of the mortal world for a peaceful moment of respite. Once he set her down, she reached out, feeling the smooth surface where he placed her hands on the parchment. The map glowed faintly. "It's upside down," she huffed teasingly.

"Sorry," Gideon uttered. "I can't see it."

"Who's the blind one?" she teased back, gently rotating the parchment until north pointed upward. "Draakland," Raven read aloud, her voice tinged with awe and curiosity. "The land of the dragons. It seems to be near a large body of water. The heart symbol I saw at Waterfront is cut in half. I think this is only half of the map."

Suddenly, searing pain surged in her skull, sharp and unbearable. She instinctively covered her face and screamed in agony. Images flashed in her mind—memories of the lady's green eyes from the dragon room and the haunting red eyes of someone familiar, sending shivers down her spine.

"Raven!" Gideon gently moved her hands away. "Let me see."

She frowned, blinking against the persistent purple glow. "Still the same?"

"They're still glowing purple. We need to return to Omlett," he insisted.

"What about the artifact?" Raven pressed, her hand reaching out.

He hugged her tightly, his voice earnest. "I took it from the headmaster."

"May I have it back?" she asked, holding out her hand expectantly.

"I don't think so. It's too dangerous—"

"Blade told me to guard it," she retorted firmly, extending her hand insistently. After a moment's hesitation, the weight of the artifact settled against her chest, its presence both comforting and ominous. "What happened to Donavan and the guards?"

"Unharmed for the most part, but they'll have a headache when they wake up," Gideon said, clearly pleased with himself. "And they'll need to buy a new fighting staff. I cut them all in half."

Raven shook her head slowly, biting back a sigh. *Of course he did.* Typical Gideon—stylish destruction as some kind of art form. As if broken staffs were a mark of progress. She could almost hear the smug curve of his mouth.

"He had a squad of High Council guards portal in," Gideon continued, voice still annoyingly unbothered. "But let's not worry about that. Let's see if your mother can help you. I'll make the—"

Raven didn't even try to hide her exhale this time. "What is it now?" she asked, sharper than she meant, though she didn't regret it.

"Celeste," he responded, like the name alone was a solution. "She's at the front door."

"I saw your portal appear," Celeste's voice explained.

Gideon huffed softly. "At least someone is still working."

"Are you insane? You do know they're still searching for—Raven! Your eyes," Celeste interrupted. "They're glowing!"

"She was injured during training at Waterfront," Gideon explained, "and now the headmaster is working with the High Council."

"Let me see this chest and map," Celeste requested calmly as the parchment slipped from Raven's hands. "And you can read it?"

"Yes," Raven responded wearily. "It's a map of a place called Draakland."

"I've never heard of such a place," the Fey Guardian replied. "Which realm?"

"I'm not sure. I've never seen it in my meditations," Gideon added. "But before we deal with this, I need to get her to Mara to repair her sight."

Celeste huffed softly as hands took Raven's head. "Her mother can't help with this. She needs to stay here. I'll summon our healers and see if the Fey magic can assist."

"Thank you," Raven sighed as the weight of the day's events settled upon her. "I think I need to rest for a bit."

"I'll return with our druids and shamans in the morning," Celeste reassured them as Raven heard the soft click of the front door closing.

"Let's get you to bed," Gideon suggested as he supported her. "We should be safe here for now."

Raven nodded weakly as he lowered her onto the soft bed and gently covered her with a warm blanket. "Stay with me."

"I'll join you in a moment," Gideon promised, smoothing her hair back with a tender touch. "I'm going to Omlett to inform your father of what's happening. Get some sleep. I'll return shortly."

As Raven lay in the darkness of their bedroom, her body exhausted but her mind restless, sleep eluded her. Tossing and turning, she replayed the day's events. Suddenly, two sets of eyes pierced the darkness of her mind—a vivid, fluorescent green and a fierce, fiery red. They burned into her vision with an intensity that jolted her awake.

Heart racing, she sat up in bed, startled and disoriented, as the images slowly faded. A soft and adamant voice whispered in her thoughts. *Find the others.*

The words echoed in her mind, stirring a mix of confusion. *Who are the others? What does that mean?* Raven knew instinctively that the voice carried significance, perhaps a message from the artifact or the mysterious forces now intertwined with her fate.

# CHAPTER FOURTEEN

# THE *SEA SQUID*

Aushade blinked, trying to clear the fog from his mind as he registered the throbbing in his head and his uncomfortable position. His vision wavered, and the coarse texture of the bark grated against his back. *Great. I'm bound to a tree.* He took a deep breath. The salty scent of the ocean filled his lungs, mingling with the earthy aroma of the small forest line. As the beginnings of panic gripped him, he forced himself to stay calm and assess the situation.

The rhythmic crashing of waves against the shore and the distant cries of seabirds told him he was near the coast. The sky turning orange hinted that it was early morning, the first light of dawn casting long shadows across the landscape. "I'm on the island's eastern coast," Aushade murmured, trying to piece together how he ended up in this predicament. Memories were hazy; the last thing he remembered was . . . He failed to recall.

He twisted his wrists, the rough fibers digging into his skin, cutting deeper with every movement. The tree's bark was rough and unforgiving, its hardened grooves biting his back. Aushade's muscles ached from the awkward position, and he could feel the bruises forming beneath his skin. The crisp morning air brushed against his face, contrasting with the warmth of his rising anxiety. He listened intently for any sound that might hint at the presence of his captors or a chance of escape.

His blurry vision, mixed with the bright sunlight, formed the silhouette of a humanoid figure approaching the campfire. The shadow cast fire into the logs, igniting them with a practiced motion. Aushade tried moving, but something scratched his shoulders. He glanced down to see several vine wreaths hanging around his neck, their rough texture adding to his discomfort.

A few feet before him were two hand axes stuck in the sand, their blades gleaming menacingly in the morning light. To the left of him lay his longsword, armor, and a bag of chalices from his castle, their ornate designs partially visible through the opening. His father's crown sat atop the satchel, a stark reminder of his lineage and the honor now being trampled. Anger flowed through him, hot and fierce, as he struggled against his restraints. *I'm going to kill them*, he vowed, his rage renewing his strength.

"She tied those ropes pretty tight," a human female remarked, her voice casual yet tinged with amusement. Clad in leather armor with white fur trim, she approached with a confident stride. Her eyes, sharp and calculating, assessed him as if he were a mere curiosity. The firelight danced across her face, high-lighting her features and the air of authority she carried.

Aushade's gaze locked onto her, a mixture of anger and unshakable grit fueling his defiance. "Who are you?" he demanded, his voice hoarse.

The woman's lips curled in a way that sent a shiver down his spine. "Just someone who found you in the wrong place at the right time," she replied.

"I know where you retrieved the crown from," Aushade stated. "Put it back where it belongs."

"We're not normally grave thieves because it's unlucky to mess with the dead, but we had to make sure you didn't bury the mage," his captor replied, gathering the wreaths near him. Her tone was matter-of-fact, devoid of remorse. "If you had, my client would be very agitated, Mister Necro."

"I set him free," the necromancer said, his focus sharpening as he fixed on the woman. "My name is Aushade."

"That's nice," the woman replied, lowering to one knee before him. She met his scowl with a calm, almost amused expression. "You're blessed that Gobs is a healer."

"Why?" Aushade demanded, his anger simmering beneath the surface.

"I would have let you rot, but she replaced your old bandage with a new one. Which, by the way, smelt like an orc's ass. I'm guessing the wound was infected. You had a fever when we tied you up." She grabbed the wreath from around his head and pushed against the lump on his forehead. He winced, the throbbing intensifying. "It seems I hit ya pretty hard, Mister Aushade." She stood and paced away from him, her movements fluid and confident.

"It's Aushade Fisker," he shouted, his voice tinged with desperation. "Put the crown back, please."

The young woman turned to face him, a glint of amusement in her eyes. "Please? How about that? The necro does have manners." She tossed the wreath toward his head, and he dodged it, feeling the sting of humiliation. "This will be more challenging now that the Daze Spell has worn off." She chuckled, tossing another wreath with a flick of her wrist.

"Will you stop?!" he complained, frustration boiling over as she chuckled.

"No," the stranger replied nonchalantly. "I'm bored."

"Are you a wizard?" he asked, dodging another incoming wreath. "Some type of mage?"

"Why would you think that?" she retorted.

"I just figured it was because you were able to perform the Daze Spell and cast fire on the pit," he stated, narrowly avoiding another wreath. "Your red eyes resemble those of the half-elf with purple eyes."

That got the warrior to drop the rest of the wreaths. She stared at him, her interest visibly sparked. "What do you mean?" she asked, stepping closer, her demeanor shifting from playful to serious.

Aushade seized the moment, hoping to leverage this newfound interest. "The half-elf I encountered before had eyes like yours—striking, unusual, and she had an unusual ability. It's rare to see such a combination of physical skill and magical ability in one person."

The woman stared, scrutinizing him as if trying to discern the truth of his words. "And what do you know about this half-elf?" she inquired, her tone guarded but undeniably intrigued.

"Not much," Aushade replied, sensing a potential opening. "But I've learned to recognize the signs of someone gifted in combat and magic. It's a rare and dangerous combination."

The woman's gaze lingered on him for a moment before the tension in her shoulders eased. "Maybe you're not just a pretty face after all, Aushade Fisker," she said, her lips curling into a thoughtful smile. "But don't think flattery will get you out of those ropes."

"Put the crown back, and I'll tell you more," Aushade demanded, determined and desperate.

She picked up the last wreath, twirling it idly in her fingers. "Not worth the price I'll get for a crown. I have a crew to feed." The woman turned back to the shore and stopped abruptly. "He's here," she mumbled as she looked on the horizon. He turned to where she was gazing. A large ship with two masts sailed toward them. "Gobs! He's here!"

"Who?" Aushade shouted, straining against his bonds to get a better view.

"Our ride," the woman responded, moving closer to the water's edge and waving her arms. "The *Sea Squid*."

He recognized the ship's silhouette. *A brigantine?*

A short elf clad in leather armor with brown fur trim emerged from the tree line, carrying firewood. The stack of sticks hit the beach as the petite elf dropped them and joined the warrior. "Ash! You were supposed to tell me if the spell wore off," she scolded.

"I have it under control," Ash responded, her voice cutting through the tension like a knife. The two women, quickened by urgency, navigated the shifting sands back to Aushade. Ash swiftly looped a lasso of thick vine around his neck, cinching it tight enough to draw a grimace of discomfort. "I wouldn't recommend trying to escape," she spoke through gritted teeth, each word honed like a blade. "This little druid can tighten this so quickly, you'll beg for air." Her fingers deftly worked the vine, tying it securely without cutting off his breath. Finally satisfied, she slashed through the bonds that tethered him to the tree.

Aushade staggered forward, rubbing his neck where the vine had tightened. "Why not daze me again?" he asked, stretching his freed arms to regain some feeling.

"You've been dazed since last night. I'm not sure about the long-term side effects. People tend to pay more for undamaged property," Ash responded, her voice gruff and unemotional.

The druid, a figure cloaked in verdant green and adorned with talismans made from feathers and leaves, gathered their belongings efficiently. "This job was quicker than anticipated," she murmured, her voice melodic.

"We didn't take you for the type to be captured so quickly," Ash added, her tone tinged with amusement. Her eyes, sharp and calculating, scanned their surroundings.

As Ash tugged him forward by the improvised leash that chafed against his neck, Aushade retorted, "I didn't take you as the pirate type."

"I'm not," Ash replied, the hint of a smile playing at the corners of her lips. "We're bounty hunters."

The sound of waves crashing against the shore grew louder as they drew closer to the beach. A rowboat, its wooden frame weathered and sturdy, docked gently on the sand. A lanky male elf with a carefree smile and a spark of mischief about him hopped out of the boat. He wore brown breeches and a white ruffled tunic that fluttered in the breeze. The four rowers, their faces stoic and disciplined, remained in their seats, oars resting across their laps.

The elf warmly embraced both females, exchanging brief words of greeting. He waved his hand with a flourish, and a sparkling portal materialized, its edges crackling with arcane energy.

"Why bring a rowboat if you can use a portal?" Aushade asked snarkily, unable to hide his curiosity.

"Portal sickness," Ash responded, stepping around him. "It's for you." Before Aushade could react, a firm push against his back made him stumble forward, the world around him dissolving into a blur of light and sound as he was thrust through the portal.

After a quick flash, he stood in the middle of a small wooden room. Lanterns hung just outside the iron cell, casting a warm glow illuminating the space. Several holding cells lined the opposite wall, their occupants either asleep or meditating, their faces obscured by shadows.

The room swayed gently, and he felt the floor rocking beneath his feet. His stomach lurched as he realized *I'm on the Sea Squid.* He instinctively reached out, gripping the cold iron bars. "I wish I had memorized that Rust Metal Spell," he muttered. He yanked the vine off his neck, wincing as the rough fibers scraped his skin. He glanced around the dimly lit cell. The awareness of being watched heightened his senses, as a human female approached him. She moved gracefully, her footsteps barely audible against the ship's creaking.

"Welcome aboard the *Sea Squid*," she chirped. "You're in the brig on a brig."

Aushade remained calm as he focused on her appearance. She appeared to be in her mid-twenties, with long chestnut-colored hair cascading down her back from beneath a black leather tricorn atop her head. Her pupils matched the light brown hue of her hair, sparkling with confidence. Her attire spoke of a pirate's life: dark, baggy breeches tucked into knee-high black boots, a red and black-trimmed waistcoat with half-done silver buttons that exposed a ruffled white tunic underneath. A thin rapier hung confidently from her side, reflecting the glint of adventure in her gaze. She was formidable and gorgeous, and commanded attention with her leadership.

He finally spoke. "For not being pirates, you sure have the appearance of one."

"Oh, I am," she bowed with a simper. "I'm Captain Ramzey Porter, and this is my ship and crew."

"But the—"

"We're hired hands for Miss Ashley Nell and Miss Gooeybeans," the captain interrupted smoothly.

"Wait—Gooeybeans?" he repeated, puzzled. "I was captured by a Gooeybeans."

"They're the best bounty hunters in Euphrasia. They bring in the booty for the booty," Ramzey joked lightly, though it didn't amuse him. "If you'll excuse me, I must meet with Miss Nell once she's aboard. We'll be underway after the rowboat is secured." She turned to leave but paused, adding, "We'll supply you three meals daily as long as you cooperate."

"I don't want to walk the plank," Aushade snickered, reclining back on the cot as the captain disappeared up the wooden steps. As the ship swayed gently,

Aushade found it easy to doze off. As he sank into a deep sleep, metal clanking against the iron bars jolted him awake.

"You're not allowed to sleep," Ashley's voice rang out sternly.

"Why?" he asked, turning his back toward her. "Is that a crime?"

The sound of keys jingling broke the silence. "We know you're working with a succubus," the woman stated firmly, her eyes fixed on Aushade as she unlocked the cell door.

"How do you know that?" Aushade retorted, turning to face her.

"I have sources," the warrior replied cryptically, standing tall over the necromancer. She dropped the intricately jeweled crown onto his lap and swiftly exited the cell, locking it behind her. Ashley pulled a sturdy wooden chair over and positioned herself just outside the bars, her gaze unwavering as she observed the necromancer.

He sat up slowly, the weight of the metal familiar but no less unnerving. Awe curled in his chest, but suspicion kept it in check. His fingers hovered for a moment before he lifted the crown, eyes tracking every glint of jewel and engraved line, as if the metal might whisper something he missed the first dozen times. Every gem was intact. That alone told him plenty. A soft sigh escaped him.

He stood, moving deliberately, and placed the crown on the iron hook beside the cot, letting it hang where it could be seen. "Thank you, Miss Nell," he murmured as his fingers traced the smooth edge of the crest.

"It wasn't a fluke." Ashley leaned back in the chair, her tone light but not unarmed. "He does have manners."

He turned to face her again, this time with purpose. "Who sent you?" His voice was quieter now, but it cut deeper. "Suttiir? Omlett?"

Her face shifted—tightened. "Omlett," she bit out, the name landing like a stone between them. That was the one he'd been hoping she wouldn't say.

His jaw flexed as he studied her. *The usual games won't work here. Too sharp, too direct. She's already seen too much.* "How much?" he asked, gaze narrowing. The question sounded like it was about gold, but it wasn't—not entirely. Behind the words, he was measuring: her price, her fear, her loyalty.

"Enough to risk our necks to capture a necromancer in his home territory," the warrior answered wearily, her voice strained as she rubbed her temples. "This whole experience makes me believe in the demigod, Blade."

"Why's that?" Aushade asked as he leaned back on the cot, watching her.

"That was some lucky shite." She grinned wryly, stretching her arms behind her head. "The undead were already headless. I'm assuming you just dug a grave, so you had no armor, you were exhausted, and—" Her expression turned more animated as she sat up straight, her hands mimicking a slow, deliberate walk through the air. "You mosey right into our campsite just as we finished setting up."

The sound of a door creaking open drew his attention back to the stairs. From the upper level descended a short elf with a malicious glint in her eyes. *Gooeybeans.* The name brought a shake of his head, a mix of fondness and annoyance.

"We're on a straight course for Zahgan," the elf reported to Ashley.

"The orc port city?" Aushade asked, his brow furrowing.

"We're docking there to resupply for the long trip back to Omlett," Gobs responded matter-of-factly.

"I thought I—"

"You did," Gobs interrupted sharply. "There aren't many orcs left." The warrior placed her hand gently on the tiny elf's shoulder—a gesture that wavered between comfort and warning as she continued. "It's funny—all the citizens were gone, but the buildings remained intact. It took many years for the survivors to return. They would tell anyone who came to port about the horrors of the Night of the Necromancer."

Aushade's jaw clenched before the words even left him. His throat burned—not from speaking, but from holding too much back for too long. "They're orcs," he growled, the words scraping past his teeth like broken glass. He didn't mean it as a correction. It was a defense. A buried scream. Heat rose in his chest, his fingers curling into fists at his sides. The others spoke of stories—of tales passed through ports and whispered at firelit taverns—but he had seen it. The blood. The silence. The sky darkens in ways that never left you, even years later.

They remembered the aftermath. Aushade remembered the dead faces being resurrected as his own personal army. *They were orcs!* He wanted to shout again. *The monsters that tore my life apart.*

Gobs huffed beside him, bristling. "They were slaughtered—"

"So was my family and my city!" Aushade's fist slammed into the wall with a resounding thud that echoed through the tight quarters. "What the hell is this ship made of?"

"Enchanted red oak wood from the Fey Realm," Ashley responded calmly, her tone softening as she continued. "We didn't know about your family."

Aushade winced, clutching his injured hand while screams and chaos flooded his mind. "We were the first human settlement on the mainland of Fellswar," he explained, his voice quieter now as he paced the floor. "In exchange, the orcs got permission to have a city in Euphrasia. My father insisted we learn to live together. Not all orcs were the monsters people thought they were. He was always trusting." His fingers unconsciously fiddled with the crown dangling from the hook.

Footsteps descended the stairs as Captain Porter entered, carrying a tray of food. She stopped at the landing.

Ashley glanced back at Aushade, her expression softening. "Pull down that peg next to the cot and step to the other side of the cell."

"You don't have to worry about me," he said quietly, unhooking the small wooden peg and stepping back. It revealed a hidden wooden table. "I'm tired of fighting."

The warrior nodded approvingly and unlatched the cell door, gesturing for Captain Porter to enter with the tray.

Ramzey smiled warmly at him. "Enjoy." Aushade hurried to the table and removed the cloth from the tray. The plate overflowed with food; he savagely bit into the chicken breast, savoring the taste of butter and garlic that filled his senses. His thoughts momentarily drifted to Ramzey, admiring how her eyes crinkled when she grinned and how her presence brought a warmth he hadn't felt in a long time. "Hungry?" Captain Porter asked with a dimpled smile.

Aushade's heart skipped a beat, a flicker of nervousness mingling with his gratitude. *It's been a while since anyone but Courtlynn has smiled at me.* A sudden twinge of memory flashed the succubus's face. *No dimples.* Yet, the captain's smile was infectious, and despite himself, his lips curved up instinctively.

"Yes, thank you," Aushade responded gratefully, shoveling the potatoes and carrots into his mouth with gusto. Ramzey placed her tricorn hat next to him, then removed the canteen from over her head and set it on the tray. Aushade reached over and returned her cap with a nod of appreciation. The captain beamed and left, waving her hat at the other two women.

"You should feel privileged," Ashley remarked to the necromancer as she locked the cell door again, her tone teasing. "The captain doesn't personally deliver meals to just anybody."

"Noted," Aushade mumbled with a mouth full of chicken, a faint smile on his lips.

"I don't think she ever did," Gobs added after a thoughtful silence.

"What about the privy?" Aushade asked jokingly, waving the chicken leg in mock inquiry.

Ashley pointed to a small door on the floor. "See that hatch?"

"You're jesting," Aushade responded with a full mouth.

"When you finish your business, just pull the lever next to it. A flap opens to the sea, washing it away. And trust me. You don't want to even think about using it as a means of escape," Ashley warned. "We had one guy stuck in there for days till we reached a port."

Aushade licked the plate clean and slid the tray under the gap of the iron door. Gobs grabbed it and headed upstairs. He approached the hatch and motioned for the warrior to turn around.

"I'll be back," Ashley announced, leaving him to have some privacy.

Aushade held up the hatch, inspecting its size. *She's right. There's no way I can fit in there.* With a determined nod, he pulled the lever, and the hatch flap swung open, dumping the contents into the churning ocean below. The water splashed through forcefully, indicating they were sailing at high speeds.

The bounty hunters returned shortly after. Ashley led the way with Gobs in tow. The warrior pointed at Aushade sternly. "On the cot and face us."

Aushade complied, sitting heavily on the cot and turning to face them as Gobs approached the bars, her voice melodic as she began chanting in Elvish. A strange sensation washed over him. His vision blurred slightly as the magic took effect.

Aushade's sight began to return, blurry as it had been on the beach. An eerie dimness enveloped the room where dark shadows swirled like malevolent spirits around him, unsettling his senses. A faint orb of light hovered over a simple cot, casting a feeble glow that did little to dispel the oppressive atmosphere.

As he slowly sat up, Aushade's gaze fell upon the figure seated on the cot. She remained shrouded in the shadows, her features obscured yet somehow familiar. The low light caught the glint of a silver chain around her neck and the subtle gleam of chalk on her fingers as she delicately sketched. The outline of her form was framed by a distinctive black and red waistcoat and an old-fashioned tricorn hat that hung nearby, evoking a sense of mystery and anachronism.

She glanced up from her sketchbook, revealing eyes that seemed to hold a shared history. In a soft, melodious voice, she murmured an incantation in Elvish, weaving magic into the room. The light orb brightened suddenly, illuminating her features for a fleeting moment before the shadows closed in again, leaving Aushade with more questions than answers.

"You don't look well," Ramzey said, her voice carrying a hint of concern as she gently placed the parchment and charred stick on the chair beside the cot.

He noticed her bare feet and her boots neatly stowed beneath the chair.

"I'm supposed to notify Gobs when the spell wears off," she remarked, her tone matter-of-fact yet tinged with a subtle edge of authority.

"Please don't," Aushade pleaded weakly, his hand gripping his stomach. He reached for the canteen and took a long swallow. The water tasted flat, almost stagnant, but it quenched his thirst and eased his parched throat.

"Still trying to find your sea legs?" She moved closer to where Aushade lay, then gestured sternly toward the hatch, a silent warning not to make a mess on her ship. Aushade nodded faintly, closing his lids against the lingering nausea. The sound of keys jingling snapped them open again. She unlocked the door with a metallic click and extended her hand toward him. "Would you like some fresh air?"

"Sure," he responded with gratitude as Ramzey helped him. "You're brave."

"My crew would kill you in a heartbeat," she replied softly, slipping his arm around her neck and supporting his weight effortlessly despite being smaller than him. "But I also know you wouldn't dare harm another Fellswarian."

"You—"

"You don't remember me, do you?" she teased gently. Aushade shook his head, trying to steady himself on the steps. "It was summer in Fellswar the last time I saw you. I was about eight. My parents visited Zahgan, the orc city, and thought it wasn't safe, so I stayed with my grandfather. He took us fishing. Tell me you don't remember that old, rickety dinghy?"

"Your last name again?" Aushade asked as they reached the second level of the ship. The crew lay sleeping in their cots, and two men stood watch.

"Porter," she whispered warmly, guiding him up another set of steps.

As they ascended to the main deck, the sea air hit his face like a refreshing embrace. Each droplet of the spray sparkled in the moonlight. Countless stars filled the sky, their twinkling reflections dancing on the gentle waves below. A crescent moon hung high, casting a silvery path upon the dark, rolling sea ahead as if guiding their course through the night.

"So, Old Man Porter was your grandfather?" he asked, leaning over the rail.

"Yes," Ramzey replied with a hint of pride, his gaze drifting momentarily to the distant shoreline. "One of Euphrasia's finest shipbuilders."

"The best," Aushade replied warmly, recalling fond memories. "But that dingy scared me."

"The mermaid dinghy," they both blurted out simultaneously, sharing a nostalgic laugh.

"My grandfather used to say mermaids took turns keeping it afloat."

Aushade chuckled as a reminiscent smile played on her lips. "I remember that summer. He took us mermaid spotting—that was you?" Ramzey nodded, a flicker of amusement in her expression. "I visited his shop all the time. He taught me so much about his tools and craftsmanship."

"I know," Ramzey responded softly, her gaze wandering to where the moon cast a shimmering pathway on the sea. "He always wrote back home about how the prince and his younger brother were always at the shop, full of questions. His tools fascinated you, and Prince Jarz loved being on the water."

"Sonny always treated us like family."

"Sounds just like him," she replied warmly, her fingers tracing the weathered grain of the ship's railing, the salty breeze tousling her hair. "When I turned twelve, my parents and I sailed to Fellswar to surprise him. We were planning to stay there permanently, but we arrived on the morning of the massacre. We saw the carnage from the boat, so we sailed to Waterfront." Ramzey's gaze returned to the moonlit sea, where silver waves gently lapped against the hull.

"How did you know it was me who arrived?" he asked curiously.

"Ashley mentioned your name briefly when she returned," Ramzey explained softly. "I couldn't believe it, but I kept it to myself."

He smiled. "Where was your family originally from?"

"Sonny-Mikula village," she answered, smiling warmly at him.

"That's on the east coast of Euphrasia," Aushade noted.

"My great-great-grandfather founded the fishing village along with his wife. They named it after themselves, and my grandfather was named after him."

"I wish—" Aushade began to say, but his stomach chose that moment to growl loudly.

"Stay here. I'll send someone to prepare a dinner plate for you."

"Thank you," he replied with a nod as she strolled toward the helmsman. Aushade closed his eyes, savoring the salty breeze that filled his lungs, the rhythmic sounds of the boat slicing through the waves. Amid the impending danger, an unexpected calm settled over him like a comforting blanket.

A hand suddenly wrapped around his arm, jolting him gently. "Come with me," Ramzey instructed, her voice carrying a hint of excitement. She guided him swiftly across the deck to the ship's starboard side. There, against the backdrop of the darkened mainland, an island loomed, its castle-like structure illuminated by a mesmerizing array of colorful light orbs and torches.

"Is that Waterfront?" Aushade asked in awe.

"Yes," the captain confirmed, reaching into a pocket and producing a small tube with a fuse. With practiced ease, she lit it under a nearby torch. "Watch this."

Aushade's gaze followed the trajectory of the firework as it shot into the sky, exploding in a burst of red and white sparks that danced between the ship and Waterfront.

"Creative," he remarked, his attention drawn back to Ramzey's face, alight with a grin, her dimples deepening.

"Wait for it," she urged, her anticipation infectious as they watched the island expectantly.

Aushade stood transfixed, eyes wide as the sky bloomed in color. Fiery reds bled into molten golds, chased by sapphire streaks and sudden emerald flashes. The bursts unfolded like celestial flowers—flaring, fading, pulsing with a rhythm that felt older than time. By the tenth explosion, he'd lost track entirely, swallowed by the wonder. He'd never seen anything like it.

"You did this for me?" he asked softly, her arm still looped around his.

She scoffed. "Get over yourself. We do this every time we pass Waterfront." Her voice softened. "Maybe next time, you'll get your own private show."

He smiled at that until the thunder of boots on deck broke the moment. The crew poured out onto the railings, cheers ringing across the ship, their faces alight with the glow of another brilliant blast overhead.

Ramzey glanced over at Aushade, who just shrugged, lips quirking. "I don't get it," he muttered, almost to himself. "Why do a few temporary sparks in the sky make people this happy?"

Ramzey didn't miss a beat. "Wow. Putting on the tough-guy act now? A moment ago, you sounded crushed that this wasn't all for you. But hey—if you ever wanna talk, I'm here."

The crew's excitement grew with song and laughter, blending with the crackling fireworks. Each burst was a crackling symphony, illuminating their faces with brief flashes of red, gold, and blue, as the air filled with the scent of powder.

Aushade held Ramzey's gaze as the fireworks painted her face. The light softened her features, but it did nothing to stop the ache in his chest. The moment peeled him open, exposing everything he'd buried—every choice and betrayal. *Does she see it? Do I kiss her? And what about Courtlynn?*

Before he could move—or run—Ashley's voice cut through the night. "What's he doing out of his cell?"

Aushade flinched, guilt giving way to tension as Ashley strode closer, the fireworks illuminating the red in her eyes, making her fury look almost elemental.

"I brought him up," the captain answered, shoving off Aushade's arm with casual dismissal as he stepped between them. "He's been half-dead for days. He needed food. Air."

Ashley's eyes softened, returning to their everyday shade, but her stance held firm, coiled and ready. "If anything happens—"

"I'll take full responsibility." Ramzey's voice was calm yet firm. She accepted a steaming plate from a passing crew member and held it out to Aushade. He hesitated, his stomach twisting from hunger and the weight of everything left unsaid. He accepted it and bit into the shrimp and rice like it might anchor him to the moment.

Ramzey met his gaze again, quieter this time. "Follow me, Aushade."

The necromancer ate more as she led him to the captain's quarters below the helm deck. He hurriedly swallowed the food, his mind racing with questions. "Did you see her eyes?"

Ramzey ignored him, ushering him into the opulent cabin and closing the door behind them. "Welcome to the infamous Captain's Quarters."

Aushade paused to inspect the highly decorated room, setting aside his half-eaten meal. Charcoal drawings adorned the walls, depicting scenes of storms and sea creatures. To the left stood a large bed, its frame intricately carved and draped with silk sheets and oversized pillows. "Why in the Abyss were you sleeping on a cot in the brig?" he asked her.

Ramzey hesitated, caught off guard by his directness. "I had to make sure you were safe."

A massive ebony desk and chair occupied the right side of the room, piled high with navigational charts and letters sealed with wax. In the center, a bronze tub stood, half-filled with gently swaying water, emitting a faint scent of exotic flowers.

"The tub is clean if you want to bathe. I had Saven fill it just this morning."

"Remind me to thank him later." Aushade undressed, pausing with his hands on his breeches.

"I'm not about to leave you alone in my quarters." She toyed as she strolled over and perched herself on the edge of her cluttered desk. "After all, I've been at sea for far too long. Nudity is hardly a novelty around here. No need to be shy."

He stepped into the tub, sighing with relief as the warm water enveloped him. Flickering candlelight danced on the boards, casting gentle shadows. Despite the comforting heat, a chill lingered in the air, causing him to shiver slightly as he hurried through his bath. The scent of coconut from the soap added to the moment's tranquility as she watched. Ever the opportunist, Captain Porter leaped from where she sat after he dunked his head. As he rose, she tossed his discarded clothes through an open porthole. "What in the hell?" he exclaimed, standing up abruptly.

"I'll fetch you a clean set," she promised casually, her lips curling into a flirtatious smile. "Can't have you wandering my ship draped in flowery silk bed sheets, now can we?"

Aushade chuckled as his cheeks warmed. "I thought you said you wouldn't leave me alone in your quarters?"

"The captain's prerogative," she replied, her voice low and teasing. "Besides, a little eagerness won't hurt, will it?"

Ramzey exited as he stepped from the tub onto an exotic rug. He noticed a delicate white robe hanging from the edge of the bed, as if it had been left there intentionally. He strode across the room without hesitation and slipped the robe over his shoulders. Though soft against his damp skin, the fabric barely covered his privates and hugged his chest snugly, the scent of wildflowers wafting from its folds.

Behind the desk, a shelf held bottles secured with leather straps. Aushade reached for one and sniffed cautiously. It carried the pungent scent of a tavern after a brawl or a witch's alchemical experiments with various spirits. He replaced the cork just as the door slammed, startling him. Ramzey's expression darkened into a look that could curdle milk.

"I didn't think you'd mind," Aushade apologized quickly.

Ramzey's anger flickered into a sneer. "That doesn't quite fit," she remarked, tossing him a tunic and breeches. "Try these."

As Aushade changed, Ramzey opened a hidden compartment and retrieved a bottle. She poured a measure of warm liquor into two glasses. Aushade took a sip and, feeling her watching him.

"What was that?" he asked, his voice low.

"Rum," she answered, her tone husky, pouring herself another.

Aushade pointed to another bottle. "And that one?"

"Medicinal alcohol. For disinfecting cuts."

"I'm glad I didn't drink it."

Ramzey giggled. "I'm glad you didn't either. I'd hate to lose my commission for keeping you alive." She approached him, her fingers lingering as she gently removed his bandage. Aushade turned away as she touched the scars, her fingers unexpectedly tender. "They're just scars," she reassured him softly, her breath warm against his neck.

"Why are you being nice to me?" The question slipped out before he could stop it—too raw. He hated how small his voice sounded. "I'm not the boy you remember. I'm a—" The word hovered in his throat, sharp and final, but she said it for him—soft, unflinching.

"Killer. But I witnessed the brutal attack on your home," she said, meeting his eyes with a calm he didn't know how to trust. "I was angry, too, until I found my calling. The water calms me. I changed after meeting Ashley and Gobs. The only time I kill now is to protect myself, my crew and my ship."

He wanted to believe her. He tried to think that peace was something he could still touch. But her words felt far away, like light underwater—visible, but unreachable. *I'm not like you.* He glanced down at his hands. They weren't trembling, but they should have been. They'd done too much. Felt too little. He didn't mean to speak, but the words came anyway. "I got revenge on the orcs . . . but I kept killing." It wasn't a confession. It was a memory, rising like a tide.

Years of silence. Empty nights. Bodies fell and were left behind. Aushade had told himself it was justice—then survival. Then he stopped naming it at all. "I felt numb," he admitted, the truth bitter on his tongue. "Being alone with the dead for so long . . . killing was the only thing that made me feel something." He glanced away, jaw tightening. *They took everything. My family. My home.* And then, slowly, it took him, too. "The orcs stole my humanity."

And the worst part was, he hadn't even noticed it was gone until he tried to remember who he used to be—and couldn't.

"We all have demons. I just don't sleep with mine."

His face scrunched in anger. "Courtlynn is more than just a demon—"

"I'm sorry," she replied gently, opening her wardrobe.

"I think I'm ready to return to my cell."

"A prince shouldn't have to sleep in the brig." Ramzey grabbed a long tunic and sat it on her bed.

"A prince of what? Fellswar's Castle isn't exactly standing anymore."

"Did you build a castle on your isolated island?"

"Yes."

"Then you're right—you're not a prince—you're a *king.*"

Aushade watched Ramzey undress, tracing the lines of her soft, tan skin. She slid into a woven wool tunic with intricate, gold-embroidered sea creatures. The garment fell gracefully to her knees, accentuating her curves far more than the rugged pirate attire. The scent of a rare, spiced incense filled the air, mingling with the salty tang of the ocean breeze that drifted through the cabin's open porthole.

Grabbing the bottle of rum, she poured another glass and downed it in one gulp. Ramzey then retrieved some wrinkled parchments from her desk and handed them over. "The seawater isn't kind to them, but I keep them with me."

Aushade read aloud, "*Dear Rammie,*" glancing up at her.

"My nickname," she replied, fluffing some pillows as she spoke.

"*It's Prince Aushade's fifteenth birthday today; he's becoming such a young man. I'm invited to the castle for the celebration. Can you believe that? This old fool will be mingling with royalty. I wish you were here. You two always got along so well—his eagerness to learn and explore matches yours. I will write to you when I return from the extravaganza. Love you always, Grandpappy."*

Aushade folded the letter carefully, a wistful smile lingering on his lips. The parchment felt fragile in his hands as if it held the last remnants of a lost era. He glanced up to see Ramzey lying in bed, lost in the same memory.

"All the letters are from him." Her voice was barely above a whisper. "But that was his last one."

Aushade placed the parchments gently on the desk, his fingers lingering on the worn edges. "They attacked us at dawn the next day."

"Henry Owens explained how he tried to get Sonny to evacuate, but Grandpappy was stubborn."

Aushade walked to the edge of her bed, his voice carrying a mix of gratitude and sorrow. "Master Owens saved my brother."

Ramzey sat up, surprised. "Prince Jarz is alive?"

"Yes," Aushade confirmed, "and he's in Omlett."

Ramzey's expression shifted from surprise to realization. "That's why you're not trying to escape. We're your ride."

He stood wordlessly, his emotions a tumultuous storm. He hesitated, unsure how to respond, as Ramzey flipped back the covers invitingly.

"Do you finally want to get some real sleep? Or do you want to return to the cot?" she asked, her voice gentle and inviting.

Aushade glanced at the door, then back at Ramzey. The warmth in her eyes and the comfort of her offer were almost too much to resist. Slowly, he moved toward the bed, seeking solace in her presence.

"Courtlynn," he sighed, his voice a soft murmur as he sank onto the edge of the bed, the mattress dipping slightly under his weight. He stared at the floor, his thoughts a turbulent sea.

"Get over yourself," she teased gently, a spirited lilt to her voice as she reached out, her fingers brushing against his arm, sending a delicate shiver. "I'm not competing with your succubus."

"Word does get around." Aushade chuckled softly, the sound rich and warm, as he slipped under the covers. The fabric rustled gently against his skin, a relaxing yet inviting sensation. He kept still, listening to the soft creak of wood and the hush of the sea against the hull. Ramzey's warmth radiated behind him.

Then she giggled catching Aushade off guard—light and sudden, like wind slipping through a cracked window. *Should I ask?* But it was too soft a sound to disturb.

"It's a small ship," she said, voice low, half-laughing, as she shifted just enough for her hip to press back against his, light and deliberate.

The contact startled him more than it should have. A gentle bump, soft as breath, but it echoed through him like a knock on a locked door. Salt hung in the air, clinging to everything—but most of all, to her. He could smell it on her hair, the sun-warmed sea and something sweeter, only hers. He let out a slow exhale, careful not to move. Ramzey was already too close.

"For Grandpappy." Her voice was a gentle caress, the warmth of her presence a comforting balm against the chill of the night.

Aushade sighed exhaustedly, the sound heavy with weariness and resolve. "For Fellswar," he murmured, the name slipping from his lips like a sacred promise, resonating with a deep, shared history.

# CHAPTER FIFTEEN

# IT TAKES A VILLAGE

Eugor shut Raven's bedroom door gently, the soft click echoing faintly in the silent corridor. He sighed and walked down the hall, each step slow and deliberate. The house felt like a hollow shell, its once warm and bustling atmosphere replaced by an eerie stillness. Reaching the landing near Carya's bedroom, he paused, his eyes lingering on the familiar surroundings. The steps to the right beckoned him, promising an easy escape. Instead, he took a deep breath, his chest tightening with dread, and turned.

The door creaked slightly as he pushed it open and entered. The room was precisely as Carya had left it, frozen in time. Books lay scattered across the floor, some still open on her nightstand, their pages yellowed and edges worn. He peered at one, its page displaying a detailed diagram of a poison oak leaf. A note in Carya's neat handwriting was scribbled in the margin: *Do not touch.* A faint smile tugged at his lips.

Her clothes still hung in the wardrobe, a silent testament to her presence. Among them, her wedding gown, a beacon of memories. The white dress, pristine and elegant, contrasted sharply with her practical robes. Eugor stepped closer, his fingers trembling as he touched the sleeve's lace. The delicate fabric felt almost ethereal under his rough fingertips. He closed his eyes.

"Just like Carya," he whispered, his voice breaking. The room, once filled with her laughter and life, was now unbearably empty. The weight of her absence pressed down on him, and for a moment, he could almost hear her voice, see her smile. But as quickly as the memory came, it faded, leaving him standing alone in the silent room, clutching the fragile lace.

Eugor paused when he heard footsteps coming up the stairs. They were too heavy to be Mara's and too light for Brugg's. His heart quickened, anticipation and curiosity mingling as he turned toward the sound. The door opened farther, and a younger elf appeared, clad in green hide armor. His black hair was pulled back, exposing his pointed ears, a stark contrast against his tanned skin.

"Father." The young elf's voice was soft but carried a hint of strength and authority.

Eugor's eyes widened in surprise and joy. "Son!" he exclaimed, rushing over and embracing Blade tightly. The familiarity of his son's presence brought a rush of warmth and comfort.

"I'm sorry I haven't visited you sooner," Blade said, his voice tinged with regret.

"No, no, it's fine." Eugor stepped back to get a better look. "I know it's a busy life, traveling the cosmos. You're here now, and that's all that matters." He scrutinized his son's face, noting the faint lines of weariness and the unmistakable spark of adventure. "You haven't changed much."

Blade glanced down at him with piercing hazel eyes and grinned. "I see age is treating you well."

Eugor sighed, a bittersweet smile playing on his lips. "Everyone keeps telling me that, but having a second chance at life gives you a perspective to enjoy it more."

The demigod's gaze wandered around the room, eventually settling on the white gown hanging in the wardrobe. His eyes softened with understanding. "Carya's room?"

Eugor's throat tightened with emotion. "Yes."

"I'm sorry, Father," Blade apologized, stepping closer and touching his shoulder. "I searched for her spirit in the Astral Realm. When she never arrived, I realized something was wrong."

"There may be a chance to save her," Eugor replied, a glimmer of hope in his voice. "We have Ausharz's spell book, the one with the incantation that resurrected me from death."

"Do you think it will work on her?" Blade asked, his voice tinged with cautious optimism.

"I don't know," Eugor admitted, patting his son's arm. "But since my son is the demigod of luck, maybe we'll get lucky." Blade nodded, a kind smile stretched across his face. "Please stay for a while."

"I should go," Blade replied, indecision creasing his face. "It's been hectic up at the council. The Abyss is at war with itself again. The hunt for Gideon."

"Please. If I could introduce you to Mara, it would mean the world to her."

Blade hesitated, then smiled. "I think I can spare a moment for an introduction."

Eugor led the way down the stairs, his son following closely behind. They went to the kitchen, where Eugor opened a thick oak door, revealing a stony hallway leading to his work chamber at the Inn.

Blade laughed, the sound echoing off the stone walls. "I see you finally built that secret tunnel you always wanted."

"Of course," Eugor replied with a chuckle. "A rogue has to have his secret passage."

Once they reached Eugor's work chamber, his son paused, his eyes drawn to an empty spot on the wall. "My bow—"

"Avalann."

"You finally gave it to her."

"Yes," Eugor replied, standing next to his son. "She earned it."

Blade smiled, a mix of pride and nostalgia in his eyes. "Remind her to keep her elbow up. She always focuses on the target, not the form."

"I will," Eugor promised.

"What did you gift to Raven?"

"My razor wire," he replied, a hint of satisfaction in his voice.

Blade's eyes widened with surprise and amusement. "I bet she was ecstatic."

Eugor chuckled, remembering Raven's reaction. "You have no idea. She's already practicing with it every chance she gets. She's determined to master it."

Blade laughed softly, shaking his head. "That sounds like Raven. She's always had a fierce spirit."

A warm smile spread across Eugor's face. "Yes, she does. Just like you."

They were interrupted as a red portal swirled open, and a guardian stepped through. Her entrance cast an otherworldly glow, momentarily painting the room in crimson hues. She paused, her eyes wide with confusion as she entered the scene.

"Celeste," Blade said, breaking the silence with surprise. "You shouldn't be here. Elora's watching the Mortal Realm until we find Gideon."

"I—I-I know," she stuttered, her voice trembling slightly. "But I just left the High Council, and . . . she's meeting with the other council members."

"She'll be searching for me now," Blade responded, a hint of concern in his voice.

Celeste nodded. "Good. If you can stay here a little longer, Elora will focus on questioning the guardians about your whereabouts. If she goes into her meditation state, she'll see the castoridaens I brought to help Eugor. Just spend some time with your father so they can finish their job."

Eugor's face lit up with a broad smile. "They're here?"

"I created a portal receiver at the construction site," Celeste replied, her demeanor becoming more confident. "They began building and should finish in a few days."

"Thank you," Eugor said gratefully.

"This could cost me my wings," Celeste expressed, her gaze locking onto Blade, "but the children are worth it."

"Children?" Blade asked, puzzled. "Care to fill me in?"

"We're building Starlight Orphanage for the children who lost their parents to the necromancer," the king explained. "They're staying at the barracks for now, but the new building will be north of Mug's golem factory."

Blade's expression softened with understanding. "Well, Elora can keep searching for me a bit longer. I promise to keep her distracted when I return, but I swear she acts like my mother."

An awkward tension settled in the air as Eugor glanced at Celeste, who still appeared nervous. "Blade—"

"Don't," she interrupted as if reading his mind. "Not now."

Blade's head swiveled back and forth between them, confusion evident in his eyes. "What's going on?"

"Celeste . . . is your mother," Eugor blurted out, the words hanging heavily in the air.

"Eugor!" she shouted, her voice a mix of anger and anguish.

He watched as their son stared dumbfounded at him, then over at Celeste, who had a tear running down her cheek. Blade lowered his head, seemingly deep in thought.

"I'm sorry to tell you like this," Eugor continued, his voice filled with regret. "I didn't want the burden anymore. It's the first time all three of us have been together."

"I was carrying you when I went through the guardian ritual," Celeste explained, her voice trembling. "I didn't know what the council would have done if they knew."

"They have one sacred rule," Eugor stated solemnly.

His son finally spoke, his voice barely above a whisper. "You can't produce offspring."

Celeste nodded, her eyes glistening with unshed tears. "I hid my pregnancy, fearing what they might do. When you were born, Eugor took you in and raised you while I committed to the Guardian path. They know it may produce beings with extraordinary gifts."

"*Amil*," Blade said in Elvish, then hugged her tightly.

Eugor watched as his son cried in his mother's arms for the first time. *After all these decades, I can feel the weight of this secret lifted.*

Celeste held their son tighter, her tears mingling with his. "I hope you understand."

"I do," Blade responded, patting her head gently. "I can keep it a secret from the council."

"Elora knows," Eugor blurted out. Both Celeste and Blade turned to him, their expressions demanding more information. "Gideon keeps me informed about everything."

"Elora must have told him when they held him captive," Celeste replied, her voice tinged with worry.

Blade sighed, the realization sinking in. "I never knew."

Celeste grabbed her son's hand, squeezing it reassuringly. "We have plenty of time to catch up on everything."

"Unfortunately, I don't," Eugor replied with a sad half-grin.

"That's your fault," she tittered, trying to lighten the mood. "Who fights a balor by themselves?"

Eugor shrugged, a playful glint in his eye. "I guess I could have found an easier way to retire." He shook his head, the humor fading. "I ensured that Carya and Raven know that fire demons see invisibility. Speaking of demons, any information about the Abyss or Tier?"

Celeste's smile faded, replaced by a look of concern. "He's a prisoner in that forsaken realm. I can feel it."

"The council has spoken with him," Blade stated.

"Tessk has spoken with him. No one else," Celeste corrected, her tone firm.

Blade nodded. "I'll raise the subject again with Elora."

Eugor watched the two of them. *I wish I could have done this when Blade was a child.* Suddenly, a thought jolted him. *The children!* "I have to get to the bar area. It's storytime."

"Storytime?" Celeste teased, her eyes sparkling with amusement.

"Well, we can't miss that," his son responded with a grin. "Is it the retirement story?"

"Of course," Eugor answered as he opened his chamber door, gesturing for them to pass. "It has to be passed down to the next generation."

As they walked through the corridor, laughter and chatter grew louder. The bar area bustled with activity. Children of various ages and races gathered around a cozy fireplace, their faces lit with eager anticipation.

As the three spotted where the children were already seated in a semicircle, their eyes fixed on the crackling fireplace. Mara's voice rang out as she narrated, "Mug and King Naelo approached the big bugbear cave." The children erupted in laughter as the gnome deftly maneuvered a small brown puppet adorned with goggles, representing Mug, while Cyndi animated a white doll with black bristles for hair.

"Puppets?" Blade whispered, a hint of amusement in his voice.

Eugor smirked. "I've never seen storytime with puppets before."

Mara glanced briefly at them before continuing the tale, "The bugbear chief had a magical item around his neck." With a flourish, Cyndi introduced another puppet adorned with a stone necklace and feathers on its head. The children giggled in delight. "The mighty elf defeated the chief and took the artifact."

"I helped," Mug grumbled good-naturedly, bouncing his puppet and eliciting more laughter from the children.

Eugor's gaze shifted toward the bar where Rusty, the owner of Cache Tavern, appeared somewhat sour as he poured drinks. Clearly, Cyndi had recruited him to help with the show, ensuring that the bar's operations continued smoothly while she entertained the children.

Blade chuckled softly, captivated by the lively scene unfolding before them. "They seem to be enjoying themselves."

"They took the magical item and ran into a dragon egg," Mara declared, her voice carrying excitement as she saw the awe in the children's eyes at the mention of a dragon. Mug placed a chicken egg between the puppets with a mischievous grin.

"I'm hungry," Cyndi's bard puppet declared, mimicking Eugor. With a swift motion, she grabbed her puppet and smashed the egg. Laughter erupted among the children as the two puppets comically pretended to devour the contents.

"They need to take this show on the road," Celeste mused. "They've captured your essence, Euwee." She nudged Eugor with her elbow affectionately.

"If I recall, Mug was the hungry one," Eugor responded, feeling a slight flush.

"A big fire demon appeared," Mara continued enthusiastically, drawing Eugor's attention to Cyndi signaling Rusty. Hesitantly, Rusty slumped over to them and stood awkwardly between the puppets.

"Do the roar," Cyndi whispered eagerly.

Rusty rolled his eyes good-naturedly but complied, snapping his hands and curling his fingers into claw-like shapes. "ROOOOOAAAAARRRRR!" he bellowed, causing some of the children in the front row to jump in surprise.

"The fire demon hurt the mighty King Naelo," Mara narrated dramatically as Rusty took the white puppet and theatrically strangled it, then flopped it onto the table. Playfully booing at Rusty's antics, the children eagerly awaited Mara's next move. "But Gideon, the Realm Guardian, flew in, scaring away the demon." Cyndi maneuvered a puppet with wings, chasing the pretend demon back toward the bar. "He then rescued Eugor and Mug, taking them to see his friend. There, he met a lovely young woman." The bard introduced a puppet with yellow and red bristles.

Eugor thought he noticed Celeste making a face earlier, but now she watched the show with her arms crossed over her chest.

"Let's build the Omlett Inn," Cyndi said, imitating Eugor again.

Mug tugged on his puppet, declaring, "I will build a factory."

"Oh, I love you, Eugor," Cyndi's bard puppet purred, mocking Mara. Switching voices to mimic Eugor, she continued, "Oh, I love you, too." With a mischievous grin, Cyndi made the puppets kiss, prompting a chorus of disgusted sounds from the children.

"And they lived happily ever after," Mara finished, prompting the children to applaud.

Eugor glanced at Celeste's bracer and noticed a red gem glowing. Blade observed it, too. The Fey Guardian leaned in and whispered, "I know. I borrowed the idea from Gideon."

Cyndi dropped the puppets and instructed the children to line up. "Mug has gifts for everyone!" Excitedly, the children stood and formed a line. Mara approached Eugor, smiling warmly. His wife paused and kissed him passionately, surprising Eugor. When they parted, Celeste gave her son a peck on the cheek and whispered, "I love you."

"Hello, Celeste," Mara greeted as the Fey Guardian brushed past her. "What's wrong with her?" Mara innocently inquired.

"There's an intruder in the Fey Realm," Blade explained before Eugor could respond.

Mara studied Blade intently. "You look very familiar."

"Mara, this is my son, Blade," Eugor announced proudly as Blade took Mara's hand and kissed it gallantly.

"Charming, just like your father," Mara complimented with a warm smile. "It's nice to finally meet you."

"My father deserves happiness. I know you provide that for him," Blade replied.

"How long are you staying?" Mara asked.

"I should return to the High Council to distract Elora from meditating."

"That would help," Eugor replied, a hint of concern in his voice.

His son kissed Mara's hand again. "Give my best to Raven."

"I will," she replied warmly.

The king embraced his son tightly and whispered, "Be careful up there."

"Always," Blade assured him. "Please tell Avalann I miss her and think of her often."

Eugor watched with pride and worry as his son exited through the front door. He turned to Mara and pulled her into a comforting hug. "That was a great show."

"You enjoyed it?" Mara giggled softly. "The puppets were all Cyndi's idea."

"Her impressions were spot on," he chuckled, his heart lighter despite the impending worry. Together, they finished cleaning the tables and bar area. With the final wipe-down complete, they shared a brief, satisfied smile. It was a routine they had perfected over countless evenings, yet tonight felt different. As they surveyed their handiwork, a sense of camaraderie and quiet accomplishment filled the air as a sudden red portal shimmered into existence.

Gideon stepped through, his expression grave. "It's Raven."

# CHAPTER SIXTEEN

# THE JOY OF FHARUX

Celeste opened the portal just outside Gideon's cottage in the Fey Realm, and the wild wind slammed into her like an old adversary. It whipped her blond hair into her eyes, stinging her cheeks, and bit her exposed skin. This part of the realm had always been volatile—restless like it remembered a storm from long ago and couldn't let it go.

She glanced up. Clouds churned above her, thick and heavy, like a bruise spreading across the sky. The shadows raced ahead of her footsteps as she hurried toward the cottage. It wasn't just bad weather. The realm was warning her—of imbalance, of something shifting.

The door resisted her touch as she yanked it open, the wind clawing at her wings like it wanted her to stay outside. She braced her weight against it, dismissed her wings, and slipped in.

"Gideon?" Raven's voice called—fragile, raw.

Celeste paused at the threshold, catching her breath. "No, it's just me," she replied, scanning the dim interior as she moved swiftly toward the bed chamber.

Raven was curled on the bed, gripping a bracelet like it was the last piece of solid ground she could find. Panic flickered on her face.

Celeste had seen that expression before—on orphans in the wake of wars, on herself in a mirror once, long ago. "We don't have much time," she said, already moving. She didn't give Raven a chance to resist. "I'm taking you to the Fey capital."

She opened the chest beside the bed, her fingers moving instinctively. *Where would Gideon have put her weapons?* The cool weight of the daggers was familiar in her hand. Eugor had let her wield his when they were younger, and for a moment, she was back in her own early days—tight situations, fast exits. She slipped on the boots and tightened the purple cloak around Raven's shoulders.

There wasn't time for softness, not yet. The resemblance of Eugor struck her for a moment.

"What?" Raven asked. "I can feel you staring at me."

"I'm sorry," Celeste responded, "but we need to go."

"But I can't—" Raven's voice cracked.

"I will be your eyes," Celeste said gently, drawing in a breath she hoped sounded steadier than she felt. "Trust me." She wanted to say, *I won't let you fall,* but words like that were dangerous. Promises in the Fey Realm always came with a cost.

They stood at the door again, the wind shrieking like something alive. Celeste raised her hand. The old words slipped from her tongue. "Fharlix Porta." The portal flickered into existence like a blade through the storm.

As they stepped through, Celeste felt the magic pull at her bones—Fharlix didn't just open. It welcomed her. The forest greeted them with silence and scent. That first breath—sweet honeydew and moss—unwound a knot in Celeste's chest.

Emerging into a glimmering clearing, they were surrounded by towering ancient trees adorned with bioluminescent moss. Each gentle breeze brought forth the delicate perfume of the fruits, blending with the earthy scent of the crisp morning dew.

"Do you smell that? These fruits are sustenance for the Fey," Celeste explained, her voice reverent as she admired the beauty around them. "They're imbued with magical properties, offering rejuvenation and clarity to those who eat them." She marveled at their smooth surfaces, reflecting the soft glow of sunlight filtering through the canopy above. "I wish you could see this."

"Me too," Raven said with a heavy sigh, her hand tightening around Celeste's. "Maybe I should have a buffet to see if any would return my eyesight."

The Realm Guardian led Raven along the enchanting forest path, past murmuring streams and delicate fairy rings, each step bringing them closer to the heart of the realm.

"Why didn't we portal into the city?" Raven asked.

"Unlike the Mortal Realm, we do not let people portal into our cities. It's to protect the magic."

"What's it like?" Raven pressed.

Celeste pondered for a moment, recalling the first time she had seen Fharlix. "The city was woven from nature's fabric. Buildings formed of intertwined branches and leaves, their roofs alive with fluttering butterflies and fireflies that create a soft, mesmerizing glow. Each structure is uniquely shaped, blending seamlessly with the natural contours of the forest as if the city grew organically from the earth itself."

"That sounds magical."

"It is. But we need to hurry. Just hold onto me. The trees will become denser." After a serene journey through the woods, they approached the outskirts of Fharlix.

"Do you hear that?" Raven asked in wonder.

"Anyone connected to the Fey can, although I'm surprised you can hear them. It's the voices of the ancient ones," Celeste replied, quickening her pace as they passed the speaking trees. Shimmering vines and glowing blossoms adorned the trunks, illuminating the pathway. The clearing finally opened before them, and even Celeste—so used to its splendor—felt that familiar tightening in her chest as she gazed upon the archway to Fharlix. A masterpiece of nature and magic intertwined. Buildings of living wood and crystal-clear waterscapes greeted them, reflecting the twinkling lights of countless fireflies that danced in the air.

As they entered the city, Raven commented, "I can feel the pulsing energy of the Fey all around me." The laughter of impish sprites, the melodious hum of enchanted instruments, and the rustling of leaves from ancient trees seemed to envelop them.

Celeste guided Raven through winding pathways lined with blooming vines and quaint shops selling trinkets crafted from petals and gemstones. They passed bustling market squares where vendors offered fruits that glowed softly and potions that shimmered with iridescent hues.

Eventually, they arrived at the heart of Fharlix, where the Court of Seasons stood majestic and radiant. Its architecture was a testament to the Fey's connection with nature, adorned with living vines that changed color with the passing of the breeze and delicate carvings depicting tales of ancient magic. *It's where Blade was born.*

In the courtyard, Fey nobles in attire woven from leaves and flowers conversed animatedly, their laughter blending with the soft melodies played by unseen musicians. Celeste led Raven through the bustling court, where she glimpsed sprites weaving intricate patterns of light and nymphs tending to vibrant gardens that seemed to bloom endlessly.

The buildings still breathed with a rhythm older than speech. Their walls formed of living bark and flowering branches that pulsed with quiet, natural magic. Light spilled between the leaves like honey poured too slowly, catching on the curve of vines, the shimmer of winged sprites darting through the air. *It was beauteous. But it was also fragile.*

This was what she had fought to preserve. Not just the city, but the feeling it offered—an ancient, sacred stillness, the kind that reminded you who you were before the world demanded something from you. And yet, each time she returned, Celeste could feel more of it slipping. The songs didn't ring quite as clear. The trees took longer to bloom.

Still, being here settled something inside her. She didn't have to pretend in Fharlix. Not the way she did in the Mortal Realm or even with the High Court. Here, she could let herself breathe, just for a moment.

And now Raven—unsteady but significant—was walking beside her. The girl didn't even know what she was yet, but already, the realm was responding to her like she belonged. *Thread to a pattern, one stitch closer to whatever's coming.*

"Welcome to Fharlix," she whispered, and this time, the words felt heavier. Realer. She hadn't said them with feeling in years. She turned to Raven, who gripped her arm with quiet desperation. "You're in Fharlix," she repeated, voice hushed, reverent. And this time, the words weren't for Raven. They were for herself. "The Fey weave dreams into reality, and every moment celebrates nature's wonders."

Narrow, winding streets led to bustling marketplaces where Fey creatures of all shapes and sizes traded in mundane and magical goods; jewel-like fruits that sparkle with inner light or potions brewed from rare herbs that promise to unlock hidden abilities. The sweet scent of wildflowers and the sound of laughter filled the air as sprites and nymphs darted among the crowds.

"Beyond the city limits, the forest stretches endlessly," Celeste explained. "Ancient standing stones rise from the earth like sentinels, their surfaces etched with runes that glow in the twilight. Towering trees with gnarled branches form a natural cathedral, their canopies guarding secrets of the ages. The magic of nature is intense, weaving its way through every aspect of life. Here, time seems to dance to the rhythm of the seasons, each moment a harmony of light and shadow, and dreams take on a life of their own, blossoming like the enchanted flowers that line our path."

"I wish I could see it," Raven said, gripping Celeste's arm tightly as the sounds and scents of the bustling city filled the air.

"I'm hoping my friend can help you."

"Does your friend know magic?"

Celeste pulled the door open, and metal chimes tinkled. "You could say they do."

A figure clad in a white robe sat near a cauldron as they approached the counter. The shop hadn't changed in years. Crystal prisms refracted the light from the windows, the colors bouncing off the walls. Wind chimes and dream catchers hung from the ceiling beams. A tiny sprite napped inside one of the rainbow-colored glass bowls on the shelf. The young face looked up and smiled. "Celeste, my dear, it's been a while since you stopped by."

"It has been some time, my friend," Celeste replied warmly as wind chimes sang softly and the scent of herbs and potions hung in the air.

"I can't make out the voice," Raven whispered. "Is your friend male or female?"

"They are neither," Celeste answered gently.

"I'm confused," Raven confessed in a lower tone.

"Many are, my dear," the caretaker replied with a kind smile. Their eyes twinkled with a mysterious light. "You can refer to me as an *Elarin*, Elvish for—"

"They," Raven interjected.

"Yes, they," the caretaker affirmed, their smile widening. "The politest thing to do is refrain from using ma'am or sir. Those terms mean nothing to me." Their gaze softened as they continued, "I can identify as anything I wish."

Celeste stepped forward, placing a comforting hand on Raven's shoulder. "Joy'uss, this is Raven Naelo from Omlett."

"A visitor from another realm?" the fluid voice responded with interest as they studied Raven. As they moved closer, their robes shimmered and shifted with each movement.

Raven extended her hand. "Nice to meet you."

Joy'uss took Raven's hand in both of theirs. "Look at those eyes," they said, peering closely. "I haven't seen a pair like that since the Realm Wars."

"Realm Wars?" Raven asked. "That took place right before the creation of the High Council."

Joy'uss patted the rogue's hand, their touch reassuring. "You know your history well."

"Well, Gideon Grindal is a history enthusiast."

Joy'uss's eyes sparkled with amusement. "Ah, Gideon. Still the same, I see," they mused. "You've found yourself among interesting company, Princess Naelo."

Raven asked, "What does that mean?"

"Nothing, dear. Let's figure out who and what you are," Joy'uss said, guiding the rogue to a wooden stool.

"Who am I? What am I?" Raven asked, her voice tinged with anxiety.

"How old are you?" the shapeshifter asked, sitting on the pebbled floor, their flowy orange skirt falling like petals on a flower.

"Twenty-one."

"I see," Joy'uss responded. "Have you experienced anything unusual growing up?"

"Yes, and I believe my brother classified them as traits of a black dragon." Raven adjusted the cuff of her tunic, her fingers trembling.

Joy'uss sighed, a heavy sound filled with unspoken understanding. "I see."

"Will you stop saying that? Cause right now, I can't," she snapped.

Celeste quickly grabbed Raven's shoulder, her grip firm yet gentle. "Calm down."

Raven placed her head in her hand, her shoulders slumping as if the world's weight rested on them. "I'm sorry, it's just annoying me right now," she murmured.

Joy'uss's gaze softened as they observed Raven's distress. "When did your eyes become like this?"

Before Raven could answer, Celeste stepped forward, producing a worn piece of parchment from her satchel and handing it over. "When she read this," she explained. Awe flickered across Joy'uss's face as they accepted the parchment, fingertips gliding over the delicate curves of the Draconic script.

Raven's voice broke through, sharp with disbelief. "Celeste, did you just hand over—"

Celeste didn't flinch, but her breath hitched. *Not now, Raven.* She didn't look at her—couldn't. Her eyes were on Joy'uss, watching their reaction like it might detonate.

"*Minn langniðiar,*" Joy'uss murmured, the words sliding out like a lullaby born before time. The sound settled into the air, too old and sacred to echo.

Celeste felt a prickle crawl up the back of her neck. The room had changed. Subtly, yes—but meaningfully. As if the magic embedded in the map had recognized its maker.

"You can read it?" Raven asked as Celeste held her breath.

"Of course, I can," Joy'uss said, their gaze scanning the parchment with the careful reverence of someone touching a grave marker. "I wrote it. The question is, how are you able to read it? Who gifted you with dragon's tongue?"

Raven answered, "An ancient copper dragon named Bakahrrato."

Joy'uss's hands shook. The parchment nearly slipped.

"Bakahrrato. Is he still alive?" they asked.

"I'm afraid not," Raven said, her voice dipping low. "His soul lingers in a cave through the use of a phylactery."

Joy'uss's expression shifted, softening with something like reverence. "You must be special if you received that kind of gift." They turned and returned the parchment to Celeste.

Celeste's fingers closed around it carefully. The parchment felt warmer now.

Then Raven spoke again. "He called me Krea."

Celeste stiffened. She hadn't expected Raven to say that. Let alone say it aloud. *Don't say that name so lightly.* She watched Joy'uss instead, whose eyes now burned with something far more ancient than curiosity.

"We all exist because of the realms and building blocks of Krea'tion," Joy'uss replied. "This explains what you are, but who—that is a mystery."

Celeste stepped in before the silence could thicken further. Her voice was calm. Measured. But underneath it, something cracked. "She's Eugor Naelo's daughter." Saying it aloud felt heavier than she expected.

It was a truth she had known, accepted, and pushed aside—but here, in the presence of old magic and older eyes, it no longer felt abstract. Raven wasn't just a woman she had sworn to protect but a key someone had long buried—and the lock was beginning to turn.

"A protector, Draak-kin of Hydra, reported the situation to me. He, the elf, who consumed the egg?" Joy'uss yelled. The edge in their voice was sudden, uncharacteristically sharp. Celeste blinked.

Their tone—usually fluid and serene, a melody unto itself—had gone brittle, almost scolding. A strange heat laced their words, and something in their posture changed: too rigid, too still. Their hands, which had moved with the grace of flowing water moments ago, now gripped the edge of the counter, their knuckles pale beneath the shifting fabric.

That wasn't just a surprise. That was personal.

"I don't think my father revered the severity of the situation," Raven replied, her voice impressively steady.

"No, he did not," Joy'uss said, their voice low now but no calmer. "But it might have saved his life if he had drawn air after a very gruesome attack."

Celeste stepped closer. She felt the tension ripple through the room like a pressure drop before a storm. The air had gone too quiet. Even the wind chimes overhead had stilled.

She placed a hand on Raven's shoulder, grounding them both, and spoke carefully—eyes locked on Joy'uss.

"What are you not telling us?" Celeste asked. She knew what fear disguised as knowledge looked like—especially when someone as old as Joy'uss wore it like a new skin.

Joy'uss took a deep breath, their normally serene expression clouded with worry. "Guardian Wynndrick, please wait outside. I'll explain everything to young Raven, but this is not something I can share with you."

Raven flailed for Celeste's hand, finally grasping it after several misses. "Don't leave me—"

"You'll be fine." Celeste gently removed Raven's trembling hand and placed it on her lap. "Some Fey secrets are on a need-to-know basis, even from their guardian." She gave Raven a reassuring hug before turning to leave. As she opened the door, the tinkling of bells vibrated through the shop, the sound both soothing and melancholic. The last words she heard as she stepped outside were Joy'uss's voice, filled with a strange mix of gloom and hope, saying, "Welcome home, Draak-kin."

Celeste's breath caught. She glanced at Raven—this innocent half-elf, a daughter she wished she had, with too many pieces still missing—and she wanted to grab her, shield her, hide her.

But there was no hiding from what that name meant.

# CHAPTER SEVENTEEN

# THE FIVE FORBIDDEN ARTIFACTS

The elderly figure sat poised behind his grand, carved-ebony desk, his posture as rigid as the dark wood itself. His long, bony fingers traced the intricate dragon emblem of onyx, feeling the smooth surface beneath his touch. "Clover Subitis Porta," Headmaster Taiker intoned, his voice a low rumble that vibrated through the air. Red sparks crackled and danced in response, swirling into a shimmering portal.

Through the rippling veil, Elora Clover appeared, sitting with composed grace in her chamber at the High Council. "We need to talk," she said calmly, rising from her seat and unfurling a parchment with a sharp flick of her wrist. "I just received a troubling report about your confrontation with one of my guardians."

Gavan's jaw tightened. "You must be referring to Gideon Grindal. My favorite pupil stole something from me, but his skills were awe-inspiring."

"My guard's report indicates you initiated the attack on him and Miss Naelo."

"I—"

"Gavan, I warned you it was a mistake allowing them to study at Waterfront," Elora interjected, stepping through the shimmering portal into his chamber. It fizzled shut behind her with a soft hiss. "And now they suspect you had something to do with those attacks." She tossed the parchment onto his desk. "You're lucky they sent this to me and not Blade."

"Gideon does this by the book. Which indicates he must contact you," Taiker explained, gesturing toward a chair. "I was not about to pass up the opportunity to watch a Gooner be trained. Young Raven is the most fascinating subject I've studied. She claimed to have seen *our* nemesis, Cadence."

Elora froze. "That's impossible—"

"Indeed."

Her voice trembled slightly. "What did Guardian Grindal take from you?"

"He stole the Artifact of Souls from me."

Elora's brow crumpled. "How did you acquire that? Tessk ensured it was secure with a balor in the Inferno-Plane of the Abyss."

Taiker leaned back, a faint smile playing on his lips. "Well, it ended up in this realm again, causing trouble."

She shook her head. "I still don't understand."

Taiker waved his hand dismissively. "It is not your place to understand. I told you, this plan demands many pawns. The disgraced thespian I hired, a dejected wizard, reported that a succubus and necromancer had the artifact. But we have a more immediate concern." With a forceful gesture, he slammed a thick stack of parchments onto his desk.

Elora jumped slightly. "What are those?"

"The script for the Omlett Inn's upcoming performance."

Her brow furrowed in confusion. "You take issue with a bard's silly play?"

"This is no ordinary story. The performance references the Dragon Wars and the 'Ainu Nehtar' chant to activate the Cenergy Blade! How did they gain such knowledge and access to confidential material from my archives?"

Elora stiffened. "I assure you, it wasn't me."

"I know. You do not come across in a good light in this version. I was thinking of someone a bit more . . . godly."

"Blade," Elora hissed through clenched teeth. They stared at each other, disbelief thick between them. The heavy silence was shattered by the creak of Taiker's chamber door opening and closing.

An elderly man shuffled in, leaning on a walking cane for support. "I hope I'm not interrupting," Henry announced, his voice weathered but firm.

"Not at all, Master Owens." Taiker motioned for Henry to join them. "I need your assistance."

Henry settled beside Elora, his movements slow but deliberate. "How can I help?"

"The Mortal Realm Guardian has absconded with the Artifact of Souls," Taiker said urgently. "They may soon question my motives regarding it and the other forbidden relics."

Elora gasped. "Gavan!"

The headmaster ignored her outburst. "Can you help me?"

Henry's gaze was steady, unwavering. "But why me?"

Taiker walked around his desk and touched Henry's shoulder reassuringly. "I trust you, Henry. You've been by my side since the orc attack on Fellswar."

Elora's mouth gaped. "That was you?"

Taiker's expression remained calm. "Of course. Ausharz Fisker was in my way and had to be dealt with. The orcs required minimal prodding to declare war, but I needed the Book of Wysards. Cleric Fisker denied my request for it several times."

Henry stood from his chair and moved toward a glowing cabinet. "But we never found it."

"Until now. The young swordmage has acquired it. And Owens, since you were close to the boy—"

"Jarz Fisker," Henry interjected, peering up from the display.

"Question him about the artifact's whereabouts and flush out any potential hiding places," Taiker instructed, then paused. "Or keep him from ever using it again."

Henry grunted as his attention shifted to an item in the cabinet. "The Fey Chalice of Natus—how did you come by this?"

Taiker crossed the room, beaming as he admired his prized possession. "I paid a hefty price for that bowl from a contact in the Stone-Grin clan."

Henry's head snapped up, shock evident on his face, and his gaze hardened. "Is it filled with—"

"The Water of Life," Taiker finished, his tone triumphant. "Thanks to Miss Clover."

"Only because you warned King Naelo of the impending threat to Omlett," Elora added, her voice softening slightly.

Henry's eyes bore into Taiker. "Do you have them all?"

"No—but we know where all but one is," Taiker said, moving back to the front of his desk. "I have the basin and water, young Mister Fisker has the Books of Wysards, and Gideon, the Artifact of Stolen Souls. The imbecile Astrick found the Dagger of Chaos among all that pandemonium in the dwarven mines, then lost it in Omlett, but my spies have not located it yet."

Henry shifted uncomfortably. "I may choose to sit this out."

"Nonsense!" Taiker slammed his fist down, the sound echoing through the room. He grabbed a parchment, eyes blazing. "Cessis Nar." His red hands ignited the script's first page into a flame. "Dragons provide us the power to create the material from energy, and we have the energy to destroy it."

Henry appeared uneasy. "The three of us, against all of Pángorbis. I don't like those odds."

The headmaster's smile twisted into something maniacal. "What's the status of Tessk?" he asked, his tone shifting as Elora gestured toward Henry, who remained motionless. Taiker placed a reassuring arm around the elderly man. "It's fine. Master Owens has his share of dirt and blood on his hands."

Elora sighed, her shoulders sagging slightly. "Tessk still has the Abyss Guardian Plumm captive, but I cannot confirm Tier's condition."

"As soon as the balor finishes with the demon army, I'll need them prepared when I gather all five relics," Taiker said, his voice brimming with purpose.

Elora's expression darkened. "You don't know if the Cenergy Blade will function against Natus—"

"That's a risk we must take."

Elora took a deep breath, her shoulders tense. "I understand the plan," she said, her voice steady but strained. "But in my three centuries as a guardian, mortal realm representative, and leader of the High Council, I've seen the portal to Natus open only once—for Draconia, the dragon goddess, who never returned to the council."

Taiker chuckled darkly, the sound low and menacing. "Even gods and goddesses must fall." A cruel smile formed on his lips.

"That's when Krea'tion, the mother of dragons, went into hiding," Elora stated, her voice heavy with the weight of history.

"A rumor said Krea left an egg for Draconia to reincarnate," Henry added, returning to the stool. "Gods' and demigods' souls do not return to the source but flail alone in the void."

"Now you're talking gibberish, my old friend," Taiker replied, his tone dismissive.

Henry leaned forward, his eyes sharp. "I have conversations with the demigod of luck, Blade Naelo, who oversees the Astral Realm. He would know."

"Doesn't matter. That egg was destroyed," Elora said with disappointment.

Taiker's expression darkened. "My wizards were supposed to secure it and bring it to Waterfront," he responded. "I can't help that they arrived too late to find it stripped of its outer shell and eaten." He strolled to another cabinet where five black plates shimmered purple under the light orb. "We did verify it was the egg of Krea'tion."

"I'm glad we don't have to worry about Draconia finding her way back to—"

"Not true," Henry interjected, his tone serious. "There are other means."

"Phylacteries," Taiker grumbled to himself. "But to summon a god or demigod soul from the void would take—"

"Luck?" Henry replied, a hint of a smile on his lips. "High Councilwoman, allow me to talk to Blade Naelo."

Elora nodded, her expression resolute. "Report to me as soon as you know more."

A red portal opened as Henry walked through, and Elora followed, glancing back at the headmaster before entering. "We need to end this soon."

"And we will," the headmaster replied, his voice steady. "All the pieces are coming together."

# CHAPTER EIGHTEEN

# BAKA'S REVEAL

The familiar water ripples against the shore were a nostalgic symphony to Raven's ears. *Gideon's camp*. She inhaled deeply, savoring the bite of the crisp winter air. Shivering, she pulled her cloak tighter, her teeth chattering as the cold seeped through her thin clothes.

"One moment," Celeste stated, her voice gentle and reassuring among the metal clattering. "This will keep you cozy. It's a ring of warmth."

Raven felt her friend's calm fingers take her right hand, and then the smooth ring band slipped onto her finger. A comforting heat suddenly enveloped her, spreading through her fingers and arm. "Thank you," she responded. "What else do you have in there?"

"Rings, lots of rings," Celeste replied with a smile Raven could hear in her voice. "I used to create them while attending Waterfront. Kind of a hobby of mine. I have water-walking, water-breathing—"

Joy'uss tapped their foot impatiently, the rhythmic sound echoing in the quiet. "Let's hurry."

Raven focused on the sounds around her—the rush of the waterfall, the distant calls of forest creatures, and the steady breathing of her companions. "Move me closer to the lake." The group moved swiftly toward the waterfall. Her feet slipped on slick stones as she steadied herself, relying on the familiar sounds and feel of the ground beneath her feet. The rushing water reverberated loudly. She paused momentarily, letting the resonance wash over her. "This camp is so magical. I miss it."

Celeste's voice softened. "I do as well. We had such wonderful times here."

"We?" Raven turned in Celeste's direction. Her smile faltered, just for a breath, before settling back into place. "Do you visit Gideon often?"

"On occasion, for council matters, but I'm talking about when we were younger. Your father, Gideon, and I would come here to *skelma-lut*," the guardian explained.

"That's Elvish, right?" Raven asked, bemused. "But I never heard that before."

Joy'uss burst out laughing, the sound bright and infectious. "It's an Elvish term for swimming without clothes."

"You mean flesh-dip?" Raven asked, mortified, feeling her cheeks flush hotly.

Celeste snickered. "Every summer before Gideon and I went to study at Waterfront."

The thought of her dignified father being so frivolous contrasted sharply with her image of him. An unwanted mental picture of the three friends nude flashed in her mind. Raven shook her head, trying to dispel it. "I—I didn't think I could feel any more ill."

Celeste's laughter rang out, graceful and melodious, like the rippling of a clear stream over smooth stones. Raven couldn't help but smile despite her embarrassment. The ring's warmth on her finger spread to her heart, softening her discomfort.

"Your father was young once, too," Celeste said softly. Raven heard the tenderness in her voice, a wistful tone that hinted at cherished memories. "He and Gideon shared a bond that transcended mere convention. They were brothers-in-arms, in their own way."

A knot of emotions formed in Raven's head, which she couldn't entirely untangle—curiosity, confusion, and jealousy. "But—"

"Enough with the trivial matter. Let's continue before—" Joy'uss's voice was cut off abruptly by a sudden, sharp, crackling sound. "Gideon finds us," they finished with a disappointed tone as the air around them shifted, carrying a faint, familiar energy.

The familiar presence of Gideon, with his unique, authoritative aura, filled the space around her. "Celeste, what are you doing here?!" Gideon asked, his voice sharp.

Celeste's grip on Raven's arm tightened briefly before she let go. "We have urgent matters to discuss, Gideon."

"How did you find us?" Raven asked as she turned toward his voice. Before fully registering his presence, Gideon's strong arm wrapped around her, pulling her close to his armored chest. The familiar scent of sandalwood surrounded her, calming yet disconcerting.

"The gauntlet goes off when creatures from other realms portal in," Gideon explained, a reassuring rumble.

"Thanks," Joy'uss muttered begrudgingly.

Celeste began, "We need Raven to speak with Bakahrrato."

"How will a deceased ancient copper dragon return her eyesight?" Gideon asked harshly.

"He gifted her with the dragon tongue ability," Joy'uss pointed out.

Gideon began, "But—"

"That's enough," Raven cracked, anger flaring. "I don't need your permission or your constant protection. I'm a Mortal Guardian now. I can handle myself."

"In your condition—"

"Celeste and Joy'uss are here. I'm fine," Raven groaned.

"May I remind everyone that the headmaster sent scouts out searching for you and Raven. I suggest we move quickly and return you both to the Fey," Celeste scolded, her tone sharp.

Gideon squeezed Raven's hand in assurance. "Fine."

"Great! Let's go find the big guy!" Joy'uss said happily, clapping their hands. The sound echoed like a thunderclap in Raven's ears, making her flinch slightly.

"One moment," Raven said, turning toward Gideon, taking his hands, and feeling the roughness of his palms against hers. "I want you and Celeste to wait here."

"What?" Their voices were a mix of surprise and protest.

"Joy'uss believes this is something for *Elarin* and me to discuss with him," Raven explained. Besides the distant roar of the fall, the only sound was her racing heart pounding in her ears. *This is a quest I have to undertake alone.*

"Very well," Gideon conceded, then chanted something quickly. The ground beneath her vibrated, trees cracked, and the earth shifted. "This bridge will take you to his entrance. If you are not out by sunset—" He kissed her forehead gently and then pulled away, the warmth of his presence lingering for a moment.

"May Blade watch over you," Celeste whispered.

Raven listened to her retreating footsteps, each one drawing a little more comfort out of the room like breath from lungs.

"Let's hurry," Joy'uss said, gently taking her hand and placing it on the bridge's railing. "I'm right behind you."

The railing was rough beneath her fingers—fibrous and damp, with the faint texture of knotted vines. Raven swallowed. Her other senses were working overtime, trying to anchor her where her eyes could not. She focused on the low hum of the ground beneath her feet, the faint click of Joy'uss's soft-soled shoes behind her, the scent of moss.

She inhaled, slow and deliberate. *You're all right. Just move.*

Still, the void before her was vast. Her foot hovered for a moment before she stepped forward. The cold vines bit into her palm as she guided herself across. They were slick and living, almost like they breathed faintly under her touch. Every step was a test—of trust, of balance, of how far she was willing to go without knowing where she'd land.

*What if I slip? What if Joy'uss isn't right behind me? What if they change their mind?* But doubt wouldn't help her now. Neither would fear. So she continued, blind and unsure, but moving forward nonetheless. Because whatever waited on the other side—answers, identity, something more—was hers to meet.

Her boots remained silent, each step crunching something—*plants?*—under her feet. Once past the bridge, the familiar scent of damp earth and lichen filled the air. *Just like old times.*

"We're here," Joy'uss rejoiced. "I can feel his presence. But there is no entrance, just a rocky cliffside."

Raven raised her hands. "Please guide me to the wall." Soft, silky hands took her shoulder and moved her in place. As she reached out, her attendant gasped, confirming that the illusion wall had disappeared.

The air around her shifted. A familiar coolness and dampness overwhelmed her, bringing flashbacks of Gideon's trial. Shorte held onto one of Avalann's thorns, trying not to sink into the mud. Izarra's water baby fighting the giant skeleton dragon. Jarz's ice shards raining down.

"Raven!" Joy'uss snapped.

"I'm sorry?"

"I asked," her companion said rudely, "can you feel his presence?"

*Was it a mistake to come alone with them?* Raven focused, allowing her other senses to take over. A faint whisper of a voice grew in her mind. *Krea.* Raven staggered to her left, following the voice that called her. The same soft hand on her back guided her. "There should be three stone tombs over here somewhere."

Joy'uss released her hand as Raven carefully tried to navigate over to the area.

"Oh, Bakahrrato, how I have missed you," Joy'uss spoke not in Common, Elf, or Fey but in Draconic.

Raven's instincts were on full alert now. *This was a mistake.* "Joy'uss, what's going on? How can you speak Draconic? Did Baka give you—"

"Always say the full name of a dragon out of respect," Joy'uss interjected firmly.

"You didn't correct me at the shop," Raven snapped back.

The guest's voice softened. "Honestly, I thought Celeste had given you too much fairy dust."

Suddenly, a loud, familiar bellow reverberated through the cavern, echoing off the stone walls and filling the space with its commanding presence.

"Krea . . . may call me . . . Baka."

The sounds sent shivers down Raven's spine, a reminder of the formidable beings inhabiting this magical lair. As the echoes of the roar subsided, Raven stood in the middle of the cavern, surrounded by the mysteries of the stone tombs and the lingering aura of dragons. A mixture of trepidation and awe, uncertain of what lay ahead but steadfast in knowing he held the answers to so many questions. "What am I?" Raven called out. "Why do you call me Krea?"

"Krea'tion," Joy'uss quickly corrected.

"But he calls me *Krea*," Raven retorted, annoyed.

The copper dragon's voice thundered through the cave. "Because you . . . carry her essence . . . young one."

"I don't understand," Raven cried out in frustration.

Baka's course voice echoed, "Your physical . . . body . . . is infused with—"

"Dragon traits. I know. Because my father ate a dragon egg."

"Not just any egg," Joy'uss explained, their voice reverent. "It was the last egg known to be birthed by Krea'tion, which makes it very powerful."

Raven sighed, running a hand through her tangled hair. "Which makes me a Gooner?"

"Don't say that word!" *Elarin* snapped, their voice sharp as a blade. "The wysards used it to demean our protectors, to strip them of their honor and reduce them to mere pawns."

Raven moved backward slowly, her boots scraping against the cold, uneven ground. She could not see the anger on her companion's face, but its force hit her like an anvil, setting off an unmistakable wave of emotion that made her heart race. Instinctively, she slid her hand along her staff, feeling the comforting weight of the ancient wood beneath her fingers. The staff hummed with a faint, familiar energy that steadied her nerves. She took a deep breath, trying to calm the storm of thoughts swirling in her mind. "I didn't mean to offend. I just don't understand what this means for me. For us."

"Peace . . . young one," Baka replied. "We will . . . not harm you."

A hand touched Raven, and she jumped. Joy'uss guided the blind rogue to a ledge to sit. "We created protectors of the dragons. Each family was hand-picked by the goddess of dragons, Draconia, and me. Krea'tion's life force faded once the goddess left the physical realm. So, with the help of Kaleidris's and Plathorax's—her offspring's—magic, she formed a final egg to reincarnate with."

"My father *ate* the egg from the mother of all dragons?" A queasy feeling rushed to Raven's stomach.

"We were never sure . . . since your father . . . never showed . . . any powers," Baka's voice echoed. "However . . . once you . . . your sister . . . were born . . . You were surveyed . . . to see if these powers . . . would develop."

"And have they?" Raven demanded. "Cause I feel like they have."

"It was believed . . . you showed traits . . . a black dragon . . . until you . . . entered my lair. I sensed . . . Krea'tion's essence . . . however faint."

Raven sighed, tilting her head slightly as if listening to the echoes around her. "Is this like a prophecy, or am I the *chosen* one?" A roar of laughter erupted, vibrating through the cave walls. Joy'uss's giggles resonated in the damp air, creating a sonata of mirth. Raven reached out in embarrassment, fingers tracing the rough texture of the cave wall beside her. "A no would have been sufficient," she muttered.

"Your father . . . stumbled upon the egg . . . as Waterfront . . . did everything . . . in its power . . . to down me . . . as I tried . . . to make . . . the delivery."

Raven gasped. "*You?!*"

Joy'uss sighed. "We lost a lot of protectors that day."

"Too injured to help . . . I crawled to a cave . . . assisted by . . . Realm Guardian," Baka said, his voice thick with sorrow. "My son died . . . trying to find . . . a way to keep me . . . alive. Too young . . . perished to the . . . phylactery ritual. My mate . . . Ma'Gamira still alive."

Raven's sightless eyes narrowed slightly. "Where is she?" Her voice trembled. "What *is* she?"

"An ancient red dragon that still roams the Mortal Realm," Joy'uss replied, their tone shifting—calmer, but weighty. "I only informed you because you are now one of us. And we live and die by the dragon code."

Raven stiffened. *Now one of us.* The words clung to her like a mantle she hadn't agreed to wear. A code. Rules. Loyalty. All of it was thrown at her like a language she was expected to speak, as if she'd grown up with dragon blood in her mouth instead of dirt and defiance.

"I don't know this code," Raven said slowly, her voice low and tight. She wanted to shout it, but even that felt useless. How could she follow something she couldn't see? Couldn't touch? No one had prepared her for this—not Gideon, not Celeste. And now Joy'uss was handing her an inheritance she hadn't asked for and a burden she couldn't define.

Inside, frustration twisted in her chest like a tether pulled too tight. Not just at them—but at herself. For not knowing. For needing to.

The ground near the tombs trembled. A deafening crack, like the sky itself shattering, filled the cavern. Dust swirled in the air, stinging Raven's lungs and causing her to cough violently.

"My friend, what are you doing?" Joy'uss cried out.

Baka said, "Krea'tion calls to me . . . through this . . . young one. She will need . . . help . . . protect the others."

The floor stopped shaking, and silence filled the cave once more. Small stones fell from above, splashing into the pool of water. Raven coughed. "Joy'uss, are you all right?" A moment later, an object was pressed against her. She reached up and touched what felt like a vial of something pressing on her chest. "What—"

"It's Bakahrrato's essence," Joy'uss replied. "Watch over it, and when the time comes, Krea'tion will guide you on how to use it to protect the others."

"Where are the others?" Raven asked, but the voice had vanished. Her pupils burned suddenly, and a pain in her head pulsed, making her nauseous. "I just want my eyesight back," she begged. "Please."

Joy'uss whimpered. "I'm sorry—this isn't a dragon trait. Some other source is causing this."

Frustrated, Raven stood and chanted "Vita Corvus," using the raven from her staff to lead her out of the cavern as Joy'uss called out to her to wait. "This was all for naught."

"Raven, do you understand the significance of this?" Joy'uss asked as the rogue pressed forward. "It means you will have more than just black dragon traits." Raven slowed, hesitating as Joy'uss came up beside her. "It means you will have them *all*."

Raven's mind rushed to the memory of the darkness bubble as she lay in the middle of the road. *Baka told me. All the traits. I thought he meant I only had Krea's—but all dragon traits!* The thought echoed in her mind, cosmic and impossible.

"You are part dragon, my dear," Joy'uss continued gently, "and you carry the essence of Plathorax's mother . . . *my* mother."

The word *mother*, spoken with reverence, settled over Raven like a warm blanket in winter. There was something in the way Joy'uss said it—full of memory, of tenderness, of something lost and never forgotten—that loosened a knot deep in her stomach.

The wind stirred around her, not harsh this time but soft, almost guiding. Her skin prickled, not from fear but recognition. The world sharpened—shadows pulled back, and the blurred horizon clicked into focus. "Joy'uss," she breathed, wonder creeping into her voice, "I can see—"

Joy'uss's skin rippled and shifted, taking on a sheen as scales emerged, covering their entire body in a dazzling array of colors that shimmered in the light. The transformation was awe-inspiring and terrifying as Joy'uss's form expanded and grew, muscles bulging and bones lengthening. Their arms elongated and broadened, fingers fusing and extending into formidable, claw-tipped appendages. The sound of bones cracking and reshaping filled the air as their legs morphed into powerful, muscular limbs capable of supporting the immense weight of their new form. A long, sinuous tail sprouted from their spine, lashing and curling with newfound strength and agility.

Their face underwent a dramatic change. The jaw elongated and widened, teeth sharpened into fearsome fangs. Nostrils flared and expanded, and eyes, now slit pupils and glowing with an inner fire, gleamed with predatory intensity. Horns pushed through the skin on their forehead, curving majestically upward, adding to their formidable visage.

With a final, blinding surge of transformation energy, wings unfurled— massive, radiant things that spanned the sky, shimmering like stained glass come to life, each motion rewriting the colors of the air itself.

Raven stood frozen, her breath caught in her throat. The image of the old book stood before her. *No . . . it can't be.* "Kaleidris?"

The dragon—majestic, reborn—answered not with words but with a thunderous roar that shook the cavern. It wasn't just sound; it was a declaration, defiance and memory made muscle and flame.

Behind her, the world shifted again. The ground seemed to tilt, and Raven swayed as darkness crept in at the edges of her sight. The wind whipped through her hair, carrying the electric tang of magic. A blue portal tore open in the air, its core pulsing with violet waves that bled into her vision, then swallowed it.

Darkness again.

"Time's up," Gideon called from beyond the glowing threshold. "Let's get you to the Omlett Inn."

Raven blinked into the black, trying to hold on to the image of Kaleidris— the brilliance of the wings—but it was already slipping. A hand pressed gently to her back. Joy'uss, now in her Elven form, offered a steadying presence.

"Let's go, Draak-kin Raven Naelo," she proclaimed.

Raven took a breath. She couldn't see the path, but for the first time, she didn't feel lost. And for a moment, before stepping into the portal, she allowed herself to believe—not in what she had been, but in what she was becoming.

# CHAPTER NINETEEN

## HOME AGAIN

Avalann stood amid the dappled shadows of the forest, the faint scent of pine mingling with the earthy aroma of freshly cut branches. With practiced hands, she secured two bundles of sturdy branches to the back of Krit, her loyal black horse.

The stoic, strong steed seemed to understand the gravity of their mission. Krit stood patiently, his dark coat gleaming in the soft sunset as streaks of molten gold and fiery orange intertwined with shades of deep crimson and soft pink. The clouds, tinged with purple and lavender, floated like ethereal brush strokes against the vibrant backdrop.

In the clearing, Oslo, her sleek gray wolf companion, bounced after a stick Avalann tossed. His playful yips echoed through the tranquil woods, a brief respite from the heaviness of recent loss.

Surveying the scene before her, Avalann's heart swelled with gratitude and purpose. Hundreds of elves from Spires Hand and humans from Koport and Brindell united in resolution and answered the call to rebuild Suttiir. It had been a fortnight since the cowardly sneak attack had shattered their lives, claiming the lives of many dear friends and family.

Avalann's parents had been spared. They were visiting relatives in the distant high-elf city of Spires Hand. Their imminent return with much-needed supplies offered hope amid the devastation. As gracious as King Naelo was, the supplies he sent wouldn't last long.

Avalann carefully unloaded the branch bundles, placing them among the growing piles near the trunk of a towering elm tree. Volunteers, driven by shared sorrow and resolve, worked tirelessly. They first repaired the shattered ground-level buildings and structures, restoring order and hope to their ravaged city.

As the twilight deepened, Avalann stood momentarily, her gaze sweeping over the flickering lanterns and resolved faces of those who had come to rebuild. She found solace and strength in their collective effort, knowing that together, they would rise from the ashes of tragedy, forging a new future for Suttiir. Builders, suspended by sturdy ropes anchored high in the trees, meticulously laid the foundations for new homes amid the treetops. Each structure was interconnected by a network of bridges, weaving a web of resilience above the scarred forest floor.

Down below, where the city's merchants and prominent elf families once thrived, devastation lingered. The immediate blast had taken its toll, leaving charred fragments and twisted wreckage. The baker's sign, once a welcoming beacon adorned with flourishes of artistry, now hung grimy and obscured by black silt. Piles of rubble marked where the blacksmith's forges had stood, their once-mighty structures reduced to heaps of stone and twisted metal. Melted iron tools jutted awkwardly from the debris, still bearing witness to the violent upheaval that had shattered their world.

Despite the desolation, Avalann's spirit remained unbroken. With each new foundation laid in the treetops and each piece of rubble cleared from the forest floor, the people of Suttiir were rebuilding homes and weaving together the threads of hope and spirit that would once again bind their community.

Avalann stood amid the remains of her village. The butcher's new shop stood as a testament to resilience, its freshly hewn timbers stark against the backdrop of scorched earth and shattered homes. The heart of the village, once pulsing with life, now lay in ruins—mere piles of rubble and splintered wood marked where families had once gathered and children had played.

Approaching one of the crumbled buildings, Avalann recognized it as the former home of Raven's grandparents, the Naelos. *Poor Raven.* Memories of laughter and warmth flooded her mind, contrasting with the cold reality of destruction wrought by the invaders. As the sky went dark, torches and the soft, ethereal glow of wizards' light orbs began to illuminate the village.

"Avalann!" a voice called, pulling her from her reverie.

"Yes, Bailey?" she replied wearily.

"It's Balin," the young male elf corrected gently.

She blushed, embarrassed. "Sorry, Balin."

"It's all right," he reassured her. "The king requests your presence."

Avalann sighed, knowing she couldn't delay. "Fine, I'm going." She sipped from her canteen before whistling for Oslo. The wolf leaped from the butcher's stand, almost excitedly knocking her over. She steadied herself, patting Oslo's fur affectionately. "Ready for a run?"

With Oslo at her side and Krit beneath her, Avalann led the charge through the town toward the castle. The moonlight bathed the castle courtyard in an eerie glow, contrasting sharply with the pristine condition of the court and the king's residence. The sight fueled her anger.

"The necro's plan to destroy innocent civilians," she muttered to Krit, "it's almost like an orc war tactic."

Approaching the drawbridge, a voice called from the eastern guard tower. "Halt! What is your business here?"

Irritation lingered. "King Luhnar has summoned me," she stated firmly as weariness settled in her limbs.

From the opposite direction, a voice called from the western tower, cutting through the fading light of the setting sun. "Avalann? Avalann Greenorr?" The voice was familiar, tinged with both surprise and a hint of relief.

"Yes," Avalann replied, squinting against the horizon's glare, casting a shadow over the moat, making it difficult to see who had called out.

The guard tower doors swung open, and a figure stepped closer, torch-light flickering to reveal Miley, her former companion. "How have you been?" Miley's voice held a mix of nostalgia and concern as Oslo rushed toward her, showering her with enthusiastic licks. "He's gotten so big."

Avalann couldn't help but smile at Oslo's excitement and Miley's familiar presence. "He is—and I'm fine, considering everything that's been going on." Her gaze briefly lingered on Miley's face, still as captivating as ever.

The male guard, Evan, observed the exchange with curiosity. "I take it you know her?"

Miley smiled warmly. "We courted until she decided to leave for Gideon's camp," she answered with her hand resting affectionately on Oslo's head.

"Our separation was mutual," Avalann interjected firmly. "You said you wouldn't wait."

Miley nodded. "I know, and you said I shouldn't." Her expression softened as she added, "But it's nice seeing you again."

"Thank you," Avalann responded sincerely, though mindful of the urgency of her summons. "As much as I would love to catch up, I shouldn't keep the king waiting."

Understanding flickered in Miley's eyes, and she gestured to Evan. "Let her pass."

"Just stand between the two staffs," Evan instructed.

Avalann nodded, snapping the reins to urge Krit forward. The horse trotted steadily between the staffs held by the guards, and she made her way toward the waiting castle, leaving behind the warm glow of torchlight and the bittersweet memories.

Her arrival at the castle courtyard was different than during her previous visits. King Luhnar's generosity in opening the castle to homeless and orphaned survivors was evident, yet the scene was marred by the sight of filthy, malnourished children scattered about. The initial care they received after the war seemed to have waned, leaving many in desperate conditions.

Disheartened but determined, Avalann dismounted Krit and tethered him securely to a nearby post. Oslo, ever loyal and gentle, attracted some of the younger refugees who timidly approached to pet the wolf. Avalann reached into a pouch on her saddle, withdrawing hard peppermint candy sent by Izarra from Omlett. She distributed the treats to the children, offering a small gesture of comfort amid their hardship.

Meanwhile, bards seated on the castle steps strummed soft melodies on handmade instruments, their music echoing through the courtyard. Despite their efforts to uplift spirits, the atmosphere remained somber, weighed down by the suffering around them.

In the distance, Avalann noticed elderly elves laboring to fill a sewer ditch with dirt, which seemed incongruous with the dignity they deserved. The stench of trash and waste hung heavy in the air, adding to the oppressive mood.

Queen Baela, adorned in a regal gold cloak, approached Avalann with measured steps, her chin high but her hands clasped tightly in front of her. "Welcome back."

"What happened here?" Avalann challenged. "Why are these children not being fed? Where's the king?"

Baela's gaze drifted past Avalann, settling on the hungry crowd beyond. "Ever since the incident at Omlett," she said, voice low, "he has become sheltered. Never leaving the castle, refusing to see his advisors, hoarding all the supplies in case of an attack."

Avalann's jaw tightened. She took a slow breath, eyes fixed on the queen. "Where," she said, each word deliberate, "is the king?"

The queen turned her head away. Her fingers tightened slightly on the folds of her gown. "Follow me."

Avalann followed Queen Baela toward the throne room, her boots echoing on polished marble so clean it reflected the chandeliers above. As she stopped at the entrance, the scent of spiced meats and sugared fruit hit her like a wall, so strong it almost masked the rot she'd passed in the trenches outside. Velvet drapes pooled on the floor like blood, and gold-trimmed columns soared above their heads, indifferent to the world beyond the castle walls.

As Baela gestured for her to enter the room, the rings on her fingers flashed—emerald, ruby, diamond—each stone large enough to feed a family for weeks. Avalann's gaze lingered on them a moment too long. Then she saw him.

King Luhnar lounged at the head of an ornate banquet table, his plate piled high with roasted pheasant and boar, spiced figs, and wheels of soft cheese.

He wasn't eating, not yet. He toyed with a silver dagger, slowly peeling the skin from a glossy red apple, the curl dropping to the plate like a discarded ribbon. Avalann's stomach tightened. The clink of silverware had never sounded so violent.

"Come forth, my dear, and sit," King Luhnar beckoned, commanding authority as he inspected the fruit and casually discarded it to the floor. He skewered a piece of meat with the dagger, then bit into it. His eyes, sunken and shadowed, lingered on the dagger he held up for her to see. The blade bore inscriptions in a language that sent chills down Avalann's spine. It was written in the Old Sylvan language, which had died out eons ago. *This shouldn't be in this realm.* "Impressive, isn't it? The spoils of war—taken from the scourge that tried to kill me. This dagger reminds me daily that I can't trust anyone," he remarked.

Avalann approached reluctantly, sitting beside him and feeling the weight of his unsettling gaze. "It looks . . . demonic," she cautioned, uneasy about the implications of such a weapon in the king's possession. Items with Old Sylvan writing were typically kept at the High Council or at Waterfront. *I need to inform Gideon.*

Ignoring her unease, King Luhnar continued, "Your work here over the fortnight hasn't gone unnoticed." He stabbed the meat again, devouring it with a voracious appetite.

"What do you mean, sir?" Avalann pressed to grasp the king's intentions amid his cryptic statements.

"I hired some beggars to survey your actions and report to me this past week."

"You were spying on me?" Avalann's voice cracked with disbelief and frustration, her sense of betrayal growing profound. She had always been someone the king would come to for council. Even at her young age, he trusted and believed in her judgment.

"Your leadership is top-notch according to their reports," King Luhnar continued, brushing off her indignation as he delved deeper into his meal, leaving Avalann to grapple with the implications of his words in the shadow of his authority.

"Thank you," Avalann responded, her stomach coiling. "I think." She could feel the tension in her jaw, the way her lips pressed together as if holding something in—disbelief, maybe, or fury. He was watching. Judging. Measuring her like one of his prisoners.

King Luhnar continued, "General Joro was executed in the attack, and our army was depleted." His attention flickered toward Avalann with a mix of scrutiny and expectation. "Even though I have concerns about Gideon's pupils being in charge of anything, I want to appoint you as the new general to help rebuild Suttiir's army."

Avalann gasped in disbelief. "I would be honored, Your Majesty, but—"

"Very well, it's settled." The king returned his attention to his meal.

Avalann persisted, her resolve firm despite the king's insistence. "But I must decline," she asserted firmly, causing him to choke in surprise. "I'm a protector of this realm, and I must focus on that." She noticed dark, spidery veins across his hand and wrist.

The king wiped his mouth and dagger with a cloth, muttering. Then, with a sudden outburst, he slammed his fist on the table, causing silverware and plates to clatter. "Gideon abandoned us and was nowhere to be found. And you and his other chosen children didn't stop this massacre," he accused, his voice rising as Avalann stood in stunned silence. "Your king has expressed his wishes, and you deny him. Some would call it"—his gaze pierced her—"treason."

"Treason?" Avalann repeated incredulously. "How dare you?"

"To defy a king's order . . . makes you a traitor." King Luhnar's voice trailed off, leaving the threat unspoken but heavy in the air.

Avalann barely heard the final word leave the king's lips. *Traitor.* It rang in her ears like a blow. Her hands remained still at her sides, but every muscle inside her coiled, ready to snap.

*He's not himself. That's not the king I swore to protect.*

The order still echoed: leave Gideons Guild, take control of the army, obey—or be branded treasonous. *Head of the military? Why now? Why me?*

She couldn't leave her friends. *Friends.* Something she thought she would never truly have. *But to disobey . . . it's treason.*

Her pulse quickened. The king didn't see clearly—this wasn't a strategy. This was fear. A kind she hadn't seen in him before, not like this.

"I cannot . . . no. I will not abandon my guild." *Let him call it treason.* She would not be complicit in whatever madness this was becoming.

As King Luhnar continued his dinner in the vast, echoing room, he didn't speak. He simply ate, each bite measured, each chew slow, as if the silence itself were part of his control.

*Something is wrong. Deeply wrong.* Avalann's instincts screamed to move, to go, to escape this room and the man who ruled it. But before she could turn, the heavy doors creaked open.

Two guards entered, flanking an older man whose expression was unreadable. His steps were hesitant, but not fearful—almost as if he already knew what was about to happen.

Avalann stiffened.

"Master Henry Owens!" the king introduced, his voice cutting through the uneasy silence between them. "A master magician from Waterfront."

The aged wizard, clad in a worn brown robe, mumbled about his travels and approached the banquet table slowly and deliberately. His movements were precise, his demeanor calculating, as he selected grapes and other delicacies from the spread before him.

The tension in the room was amplified by the new arrival. "I hired him to protect us against any imposters that may try to take my life," King Luhnar explained casually, though a current of paranoia edged his voice. He glanced at Avalann now and then, as if measuring her reaction to each word.

"Your Majesty, you can't keep living like this," Avalann pleaded.

Luhnar's response was dismissive yet pointed. "As you see, I'm eating plenty to stay healthy and strong."

The difference between his indulgence and the plight of the children outside gnawed at Avalann's conscience. Her focus drifted to Master Owens, hoping for support or reason, but the wizard seemed more interested in his meal than the moral dilemma unfolding before him. His indifference stung, a reminder of the isolation and mistrust that plagued the kingdom. Avalann turned toward the wizard. "Master Owens, you have to know this is wrong."

"I get compensated to dispel illusions," Master Owens replied calmly, his voice unwavering as he selected food with deliberate movements, "not to offer advice on how to run a kingdom."

Avalann felt trapped, torn between her duty to the guardians and her conscience, her loyalty to the guardians and her sense of justice for the suffering people of Suttiir.

"Sir, may I interrogate her in a truth zone after eating?" Henry's request was almost casual. Avalann's breath caught in her throat, the implications of such interrogation echoing through her mind.

"You may," King Luhnar said, tone calm and unwavering, his attention locked on Avalann. "In payment for the two staff out front."

Avalann's heart sank. The king's decision was a betrayal, validating her worst fears and suspicions. She stood, her resolve firm despite the uncertainty pressing down upon her. "Your Majesty," she pleaded once more.

Queen Baela's words echoed in Avalann's mind. *He is not himself.* She had known the king before his descent into paranoia and cruelty, a leader once respected and beloved by his people. She spun in defiance and exited the banquet hall.

As Avalann descended the castle steps, the evening air grew more relaxed, carrying with it the faint scent of smoke from distant hearths and the murmur of worried voices from the encampment below. Lanterns flickered along the paths, casting shifting shadows that danced over the faces of children and adults alike, their expressions reflecting a mix of weariness and hope.

"Children, gather! Grab every type of container or basket you can find," Avalann called out, her voice carrying over the scattered tents and makeshift shelters. The urgency in her tone galvanized the children into action, their footsteps quickening as they hurried to obey.

Krit, her faithful black horse, stood patiently beside the covered wagon, his presence a comforting anchor amid the turmoil. Avalann moved swiftly, securing the wagon and checking their gathered supplies. Her mind raced with logistics—how to evacuate the survivors safely and quickly and ensure they had enough provisions for the journey ahead.

An elder approached her, his weathered face etched with concern. "What can we do?" his voice steady.

"Lower the drawbridge and occupy the guards," Avalann instructed firmly, her gaze scanning the surroundings for any sign of potential obstacles. "Gather everyone, then whistle when they're safely inside the carriage."

"We should be fine. There aren't that many guards left," another adult reassured her, stepping forward to assist. "But we'll get everyone safely on the transport."

The urgency of their mission weighed heavily on Avalann, each heartbeat a reminder that time was running out. She couldn't afford hesitation—not with her kin hurt, neglected, unsure of whom to trust. Her mind was already drawing maps in silence, counting heads and weighing risks. *What would happen to those who would not come? Would the king punish them for not stopping me?* She clenched her jaw. This wasn't just survival. It was strategy. It was stewardship.

Her people were looking to her now—not just as a bow, but as a shield. As something more substantial than fear.

As the children gathered around Avalann, their expressions a mix of apprehension and purpose, she led them toward the throne room. Drawing her bow quickly, she swiftly incapacitated the two guards with precise shots to their shoulders. The guards cried out in pain, their grip on their swords loosening as they slumped against the walls, unable to retaliate.

In the sudden chaos, King Luhnar and Master Owens dropped their food in shock, their faces registering a mixture of surprise and fear as Avalann leveled her bow at the wizard. Oslo snarled menacingly. "Don't even think about it," Avalann sneered, her voice cutting through the air like a whip. "I suggest you don't even breathe."

"Nice bow, Avalann," Master Owens remarked condescendingly, his tone laced with arrogance. "You may want to raise your elbow a bit higher." He subtly moved as if to offer her advice as Avalann tilted her head at the untimely bow lesson.

"What are you doing?" King Luhnar protested, his voice strained with anger and confusion.

"Children," Avalann commanded coolly, raising her elbow slightly, never taking her eyes off the wizard, "load up the food, then return to the courtyard." Without hesitation, the children rushed to the banquet table, hastily gathering all the available food and stuffing it into their containers.

"Avalann, stop this!" The king's command echoed through the room, but she remained resolute, her focus unwavering as she kept her bow trained on Master Owens.

Once the table was stripped bare and the children had darted back to the wagon with their precious cargo, Avalann still held her bow steady. King Luhnar, his patience worn thin, stood and drew his dagger. She swiftly aimed at him, Oslo growling low at the sudden threat.

Owens, seizing the moment, conjured a blue portal and vanished before Avalann could react. The king's dagger clattered against the table as he stared at the archer in disbelief.

"What have you done?" King Luhnar's voice shook with rage and fear, his authority crumbling in the face of Avalann's bold defiance.

Avalann kept the king at bay with her gaze. "Who are you?"

"I AM YOUR KING!" Luhnar spat defiantly, driving his dagger into the table with a resounding thud.

Avalann, her resolve unwavering yet sorrowful regarding their fractured kingdom, slowly returned the arrow to her quiver. "I'm sorry, Your Majesty," she uttered softly. Without another word, she ran from the throne room, her thoughts racing as she hurried to join the survivors gathered in the wagon.

As she guided the wagon toward the drawbridge, she scanned the courtyard for Queen Baela, but she was nowhere to be found. Instead, the guards halted their progress, casting uncertain glances at each other as they faced the determined ranger and the wagon filled with those who had chosen freedom over fear.

"What's going on?" Miley questioned, blocking their path.

"Move aside, please," Avalann pleaded. "The king is mad. I'm taking these survivors somewhere safe, per order of the queen."

"Let me assist you. I want to help," Miley insisted.

"As do I," Evan said, surprising her. "Madness has set over him, and I can't stand by anymore and watch."

"Help me protect the wagon," Avalann requested. "I'm taking them to Omlett."

As Evan whistled for their horses, Miley replied, "Of course. Anything for you."

Avalann pulled on the reins. The wagon rumbled across the bridge just as she heard the king yelling across the courtyard. Oslo ran alongside Krit, with others protecting the rear. *Your reign of terror ends tonight, King Thorya. Thorya*—Elvish for *tyrant*—wasn't his birth name, but it had become the only one worth using.

As they reached the heart of Suttiir, the only light was from their torches and orbs. Most of the volunteers had retired for the night. It was quiet, aside from the children fighting in the cart about personal space and the stewards trying to calm them down. Avalann drew her bow as the sound of another wagon approached them.

"*Amil! Adar!*" she shouted as they approached closer, loosening the tension of her bow.

"*Meleth*, what do you think you're doing?" her mother, Arlene, asked.

"We can't stay," Avalann responded. "It's not safe."

"What did you do now?" her father, Aemon, asked, annoyed.

"We're going to Omlett," Avalann's voice cut through the murmurs like a blade, steady and sure. But inside, she felt the pressure building, pressing against her ribs with every breath. These children were looking to her as if she already had the answers—as if resolve alone could carry them to safety.

She caught sight of Aemon lifting crates without being asked, his quiet presence grounding her more than she wanted to admit. When had her father last followed her lead without question? The thought struck hard, but there was no time to linger on it.

Miley moved beside her, hands swift, shoulders tense. Avalann glanced at her once—really looked—and saw the grief there, carefully masked by motion. She wanted to say something, to reach across the weight between them, but duty held her tongue.

*Later,* she told herself. *If there is a later.*

She refocused on the wagons, checking straps, counting flasks, and scanning for gaps in their plan. The mission demanded everything. There was no room for softness now—not even for family.

"Let's hurry," Avalann urged, her mind racing to move quickly before any pursuit could catch up with them. Given the circumstances, she counted the passengers in her wagon, ensuring everyone was accounted for and settled as comfortably as possible.

"We need one more steward for the other wagon," Avalann noted, focusing on a figure huddled in the corner, hood drawn low. Unlike the others wrapped in ragged blankets, this person stood out with their elaborate cloak. Avalann cautiously addressed the hooded figure directly. "Would you like to join the other wagon?" The figure hesitated before slowly lowering the hood. Avalann gasped. "Queen Baela?!" she exclaimed softly, her voice filled with awe and concern. Her respect for the queen deepened.

The queen nodded, her expression weary yet determined. "I must escape with you. Please, protect me."

"I will," Avalann assured her.

As the wagons began to move, rolling away from the gates of Suttiir under the cloak of night, Avalann felt a surge of responsibility weighing heavily upon her shoulders. Their destination—Omlett—loomed ahead, a place of refuge and perhaps a chance to regroup and plan their next move in the face of the uncertain future that lay before them.

# CHAPTER TWENTY

# A SHORTE VISIT

S horte adjusted his shield and mace as he stood solemnly before a large plaque branded with hundreds of names. The dwarven council had displayed the memorial on the mountainside near the entrance to Iron Cliff. Its polished stone surface gleamed in the morning light, the names etched with meticulous care, each a reminder of the fallen.

He fixated on two names: Molten and Bamrick Stone-Grin. Shorte traced his brother's name with a calloused finger, remembering their hearty laughter and how their eyes sparkled with mischief. Their bodies, like those of many others who had died, were never found. The initial blast of the demon's foxtail had incinerated most dwarves, leaving little more than ashes scattered across the wind.

Flowers and trinkets, amassed at the base of the plaque on top of a memorial, served as tokens of love and memories. Shorte glanced at a small iron figurine of a dwarf warrior, its tiny axe held high in defiance. It reminded him of his brothers' courage in their final moments. "The world will be empty without you, my brothers."

"Pining for the dead will not bring them back, my son," a deep male voice said from behind. Shorte turned to see his father, Barashork, with a bandage still wrapped around his head. He had been injured while leading the elders safely through the hidden mountain tunnels.

*Thank Blade, he's still alive. He always boasted he had a hard noggin.* "I'm not pining," Shorte grumbled, adjusting his weapons belt. "I'm fantasizing about how I will strangle that monster with that demon fox's last tail. It's not the same without Molten and Bamrick by my side. They were always the first to charge, the last to retreat."

Barashork's voice softened, and he placed a heavy hand on Shorte's shoulder. "I know, lad. We all mourned that day. But your brothers' spirits live on in you, in the fight you carry on their behalf. Remember that." His calloused finger pointed to Shorte's weapons. "The mace and shield of Iron Cliff. I hope they've served you well."

Shorte's grip tightened on the handle of his mace. "Yes, Father. They've seen me through the battles since I graduated from Gideon's camp. Thank you for allowing Gideon to obtain the sacred weapons and pass them down to me."

"Whatcha talking about?" his father responded, raising an eyebrow.

"He didn't just portal here and take them," Shorte snorted. "You're the elder in charge."

Barashork chuckled, a deep, rumbling sound. "Your mother insisted," he said, patting Shorte on the back. "Speaking of which, I thought you were assisting her? She planned to visit the infirmary to ensure everyone was healing properly."

A stitch of guilt wound its way through Shorte's gut. "I was, but I wanted to come here first. Pay my respects."

"Well, you've done that," Barashork said gently. "Now, go to your mother. She'll need your strength and support as much as you need hers."

Their mother was the dwarves' best cleric. His time with her as a child, tending to the sick, influenced him to become a cleric. *Carya and I had that in common.* While his father doted on his seven older brothers during their combat training, Shorte gravitated to his mother, wanting to help heal people.

"I'm sure Erack would like the company, too," his father said, interrupting his thoughts.

"I'll meet up with them," Shorte replied. "Any word from Draxxus and Kargos since they left Sand Castle?"

"Your mother received a message this morning. They've been part of the search party seeking survivors in Iron Vale. They will be arriving this evening. Graak was with them, then left for Waterfront a few days ago. I hope he returns this evening. The headmaster graciously offered him training to perform more powerful protection spells, even though Iron Cliff sustained the least casualties since it was the last city along the warpath."

"It'll be nice to see my brothers again," Shorte said, glancing up across the mountain at the sun. "I should go." He turned to head down the path.

"I'm proud of you," his father shouted as he rounded the corner.

Shorte smiled. *That's all I wanted to hear.* He quickened his pace, the path winding down through the bustling camp.

Shorte's miniature horse, Stubby, was tied to a post outside the tent, a reminder of more peaceful times. "You're gaining weight," the cleric said, rubbing the horse's belly. "Have the little ones been overfeeding you with sugar again?" The tiny horse neighed and shook his mane, his eyes bright with affection. "We'll go for a ride tonight and let you stretch your legs."

Nearby, a goat was strung up on a spit over an open fire. The rich aroma of roasting meat filled the air, mingling with the earthy scent of the caves. Shorte walked past, his stomach growling in anticipation. He pushed open the tent flap and entered, the warmth inside starkly contrasting with the cool evening air.

Erack, his brother, lay on a cot with his bandaged leg elevated. His short black hair was unkempt, and his face bore the weary lines of suffering and recovery. Yet even through the fatigue, a spark of mischief lingered in his expression. Erack wiped away the ale that dripped down his triple-braided beard. "Look, my nursemaid has arrived."

"I'm surprised the elf impersonator has jokes," Shorte retorted, laying down his mace and shield. He picked up his brother's bow and examined it with a critical eye. "If you were half as good with this thing as you are with your sarcasm, maybe you would have killed one of those undead bastards."

"Think you're all tough now since you're one of Gideon's chosen," Erack snorted, rolling his eyes. "How many have you killed?"

"Enough," Shorte replied, a hint of steel in his voice. "I know an elf who can teach you how to use this properly."

"Just put it down before you mess up the drawstring. I don't need help from your elf wench."

"She's not a wench," Shorte muttered, feeling a flush rise to his cheeks. "Where's Ma?"

"At the forges to check on the blacksmith, Bovor. The wound on his leg was oozing a smelly, clear liquid."

"That's gross," Shorte said, wrinkling his nose.

"I thought you were a cleric?"

"I am." Shorte smirked, leaning in closer. "I was referring to your face."

Erack grabbed a pillow from under his leg and whipped it at him. Shorte dropped his brother's bow and dashed out, laughing as the projectile narrowly missed him.

With the city of Stone Forge still decommissioned, Iron Cliff was the last city with weapons forges still active in Western Euphrasia. The dwarven council had determined that their top priority was to provide weapons to their allied towns. The sound of hammers striking metal was a constant backdrop, a testament to their grit to arm their people and allies against the undead threat.

Thanks to his father's strategic planning over the decades, he saved hundreds of children by sheltering them in his bunkers.

Shorte found his mother kneeling beside an older dwarf with gray hair who wore leather and an apron. His goggles were perched over his receding hairline, marking him as a seasoned blacksmith.

"I've told you before, drinking more ale won't cure this," Shorte's mother scolded, her tone both firm and caring. "You have to use the ointment I made."

"Vordessa, it smells like petunias. I hate flowers," Bovor grumbled, his face distorted. "They make me sneeze."

"Then next time, I'll create one that smells like horse dung," she replied, banging the container before him. "Use the ointment or lose the leg."

The old dwarf glanced at her nervously, grabbed the canister, and reluctantly rubbed the cream on his leg. The pungent smell of the medicinal salve filled the air, mingling with the scent of hot metal and burning coal.

"Bullying the elders, I see," Shorte teased, smiling. Seeing her made him happy, a comforting constant in his life, no matter the circumstances.

"Just instilling my sense of wisdom," she replied, packing her kit with practiced efficiency. "I'd hoped you would do my rounds with me today. Where did you go?"

Shorte hesitated, thinking about his morning visit to the memorial. He didn't respond, and his mother's gaze softened with understanding.

"My heart aches for your brothers as well, but we must stay strong and help those still here," she said gently. She smiled, a reassuring gesture that never failed to lift his spirits. "Have you seen your father?"

"Yes. Father was at the mountainside memorial. I think he was about to check on the construction. Where is Ahkane? I thought he was in charge of removing the rubble in the mines."

"Your brother was moved to assist with digging out the sewer system—not a word." Shorte bit back a retort. "Draxxus, Kargos and Graak should be here by nightfall," Vordessa informed him as they exited the tunnel, the evening air cool and crisp. "It will be nice to have everyone home again."

*Not everyone.* The thought stung, a sharp reminder of the Stone-Grins' losses.

His mother continued, "Eugor sent a message that your Uncle Buzz is on the mend. He even sent a portal scroll to Omlett for me to visit."

"Glad to hear it," he replied, trying to muster enthusiasm.

"Have you heard from your friends?" his mother asked as they made their way down the path, her tone curious yet gentle.

"It's been a while. Raven's at Waterfront with Gideon. Izarra's been helping with the survivors and children in Omlett while Jarz studies his father's spell book."

"Have you heard from Avalann?" his mother asked, a hint of knowing in her voice. "You've spoken fondly of her."

"She's a tough one, that elf. You should've seen her take down a pack of kobolds. Even when Raven turned her into a misty cloud. That's one elf I would bet on against anybody, even a dwarf. But she's still in Suttiir."

"You ever try courting her?" Vordessa studied her son with a knowing gaze. "I like her."

"Mother, she's a friend."

"Like Carya? You were devastated when she decided to get married," his mother pointed out gently. "You have to open up to people you care about."

"Carya was like a sister to me. I just disapproved of the dragon fodder she ended up with." When his mother shot him a knowing look, he chuckled softly. "Don't give me that. It's not jealousy."

"I'm just saying, if you have feelings for the elf, let her know."

"Avalann has a female paramour—well, *had*—before camp. I'm not sure what's going on right now."

"So she doesn't bond with males?" Vordessa asked, raising an eyebrow.

"She's an elf. They bond with everyone." Shorte shrugged, his expression thoughtful. "Well, you never know."

The path ahead was uncertain, but Shorte knew one thing for sure: with his family's support, he would face whatever challenges came his way. Perhaps, in the process, he would find the courage to explore his feelings and take a chance on something more with Avalann—if fate allowed.

As they entered the family tent, laughter and jovial banter filled the air. A loud, clunking sound followed, drawing Shorte's attention immediately. His older brothers, Draxxus and Kargos, were messing around with his belongings.

"Oye! Arse! That's mine." Shorte stomped toward Kargos and snatched his shield back.

"Come on, baby brother! This stuff is way too advanced for a cleric to wield," Draxxus taunted, waving the mace before him.

"And dangerous," Kargos chimed in, eyeing the mace warily.

"Give it back, and I'll show you how dangerous I am," Shorte responded calmly, holding out his hand expectantly.

"Does the cleric want to duel?" Draxxus teased, tossing the mace toward Shorte. "Here you go, do your worst."

"Just because you're the eldest doesn't mean I won't knock you on your arse," Shorte threatened.

"Don't get blood in the tent," Vordessa warned as she left, carrying a plate of cheese and bread. "I won't have time to clean it up before suppa."

Shorte accepted the challenge, pounding the mace and shield together. He focused his concentration, invoking his dwarven heritage to infuse his skin with the strength of iron. Standing ready, he awaited Draxxus's move. His brother raised the weapon and lunged forward, the mace swinging toward Shorte's head. In a swift move, Shorte deflected the blow with his shield, the clang of metal reverberating in the tent.

Seeing an opening as Draxxus stumbled slightly off-balance, Shorte seized the opportunity. With a quick sweep of his leg, he knocked Draxxus's feet out from under him, sending him to the ground with a thud. "Not bad for a cleric, right?" Shorte quipped, pressing the mace lightly against Draxxus's throat in mock victory.

Draxxus pushed the mace away with a chuckle, his face breaking into a sneer. "Let me retrieve the Diamond Sword and Shield of the Vale, and we'll see who wins. Iron or diamonds."

"That's enough," a rough voice called from the tent opening. Shorte's father and brother walked inside, signaling that supper was ready. Ahkane moved to help Erack from the cot where he had watched the mock duel.

Shorte banged the mace and shield together, returning his skin to normal as his other brothers exited the tent. Stepping outside, he spotted Graak sitting by the fire, conversing with his mother.

"Oye, little brother, I heard your friends Gideon and Raven got themselves in trouble with the headmaster at Waterfront," Graak informed him.

"What happened?" Shorte asked anxiously. "Are they all right?"

"Don't know yet. When I left, the headmaster sent scouts and guards out to search for them."

"I should go," Shorte began, his concern mounting. "Gideon and Raven, they might—"

"Need your help?" Barashork interjected, his tone firm. "Gideon is the guardian of the realm. He can take care of himself." Shorte's brothers snickered at his concern as their father told Vordessa, "Mama, you may serve the meal now."

The seven gathered around the fire, sharing a meal and recounting stories from the recent events. Despite the camaraderie and warmth of the fire, Shorte's thoughts kept drifting back to his friends, torn between duty and family. *I should be with them, not here being treated like a child.*

"Shorte!"

He looked up just as a roll hit him in the face and his brothers roared with laughter.

"I asked you a question, son." Barashork took another piece of meat from the carcass on the spit.

"Sorry, I—"

"Has the guardian updated you on the devastation elsewhere?"

"Suttiir had massive casualties and sustained most of the damage to the town center," Shorte explained. "Thanks to King Naelo and the elf army, they were able to save the castle and the outlying buildings. The gnome and orc villages were not as lucky. All of their coastal and western villages were destroyed. The few gnome survivors hid and retreated to other cities east of the mountains while the orc sailed for Fellswar. King Naelo opened Omlett as a refugee city for those who could not journey."

"Good thing father was prepared," Kargos bragged. "Years of being laughed at for paranoia, no one is laughing now!" The others cheered, raising their ale. Then, a spark of fire and a curse made everyone look to the tent entrance, where Graak's sleeve was on fire.

Then, a thought occurred. "Graak, I want to know how you could afford private lessons with the headmaster of Waterfront," Shorte said, bemused. "Jarz says the headmaster doesn't work with anyone unless it benefits him."

Graak's face dropped with an awkward demeanor. "Despite the rumors, the headmaster is genuinely concerned about our plight."

Their father snorted. "Ha! That elf only cares about one thing. DRAGON MAGIC."

In the distance, Shorte noticed a falcon circling above the head of an elderly dwarf, its flight graceful against the darkened sky. He remembered Carya scattering breadcrumbs in the church garden, feeding the birds in the winter. The thought of her gone tore at his heart. He watched the bird more closely, until he heard his name. He turned to see Draxxus downing his fifth ale.

"I'm just saying," Kragos slurred, "a real dwarf could take out that necromancer with a single swing of his axe." His brother demonstrated, flailing his weapon around wildly.

"Shorte's a softy, mixing potions and frolicking around with elves. He's not a real warrior," Draxxus interjected, as ale dripped from his chin. "Probably hid behind the elf, wetting himself."

"Seriously, if we were in the battle, your friend Caya would be alive," Kragos boasted, staggering to retrieve more ale.

Draxxus snorted. "Yeah. It would've been over in a day if we were there. No fancy spells, no drama. Just blood and bone."

Kragos grinned, leaning heavily on the table. "Instead, they send the tea-brewer and his elf patrol."

Shorte's anger boiled over as he smashed his plate into the fire, sending sparks flying. Everyone's eyes turned toward him in hushed anticipation. His voice cut through the night air, filled with fury. "This comes from the only two among us who haven't seen what that necromancer is capable of. You can't get near him. His undead soldiers multiply with every fallen friend he twists against us. Wave after wave, relentless. You don't know what it's like to watch someone you love die, only to see them rise again and charge at you, their mind gone, flesh-hungry." He held back tears, his mind vividly replaying the nightmare he'd witnessed. How he saw Carya standing beside that monstrous commander, waiting to annihilate everyone she once held dear.

"And where were you, Draxxus? When Ahkane was attacked in Iron Vale and fought his way out to deliver a warning to our father?" Shorte's voice cracked with accusation, each word searing with betrayal. "Or you, Kargos, when Molten and Bamrick stood here fighting to the death to protect our kin!" Neither brother answered. "I'll tell you where. Hiding in Sand Castle, drowning your troubles in drink and women, while the rest of us fought an evil you will never understand!"

"Excuse me for barging in," an elderly dwarf interrupted, his weathered face lined with interest as he approached the group. The falcon perched on his outstretched arm, its keen eyes darting between the faces around the fire. "This falcon has been nagging me until I realized it had a message tied to it. It's addressed to Mister Stone-Grin."

Shorte's father reached out to take the scroll, his brow furrowed with curiosity, but the elderly dwarf hesitated and pulled it back. "Sorry, I meant Mister Shorte Stone-Grin," he corrected himself, offering the tied scroll to Shorte with a respectful nod.

Shorte took the scroll cautiously, his earlier intensity set aside as he carefully broke the seal and unfurled the parchment, scanning each word with relief and concern.

RAVEN IS RETURNING. OPERATION RESURRECTION. PLEASE MEET US AT THE OMLETT INN BY THE FULL MOON. SAFE TRAVELS. —AVALANN.

Folding the parchment carefully, he glanced at the assembled group, his gaze hardening. Shorte swiftly rose from his spot by the fire, his movements purposeful as he gathered his weapons from the nearby tent.

"What did the message say?" Kargos inquired as he watched his brother prepare.

"Sorry, brother, guardian business," Shorte replied with a hint of secrecy, securing his gear onto Stubby. "Graak, how about a portal?"

Graak choked on his ale, struggling to stifle a laugh. "Portals are for lazy elves and humans," he retorted, amusement tugging at his grin. The other brothers joined in, their laughter echoing softly in the night.

Erack joined in teasingly. "Why not ask him for a set of Fey wings? You could fly there."

"Never mind!" Shorte huffed good-naturedly, a faint smile touching his lips. He swung himself into the saddle, his resolve clear in every line of his posture. "You can keep offering your backside to the headmaster for new spells."

The other brothers turned to Graak and pointed, laughing.

"Wait! Is that a new robe?" Draxxus asked, feeling the material.

Graak shoved his brother away, "Shut it!" The other brothers began to bicker, taunting the dwarf wizard.

"Enough!" Vordessa rose from where she sat by the fire, her movements purposeful as she addressed Shorte and his brothers. "It's a long four-day journey. Wait here for a moment." With that, she disappeared into the tent, emerging moments later. "Here, use the Omlett portal scroll," she offered, extending it to Shorte. "Just let your Uncle Buzz know we'll be there soon."

"I will." Shorte dismounted from Stubby and stepped forward to take the scroll. "Thank you," he said gratefully, pulling his mother in for a hug.

He unrolled the portal scroll and concentrated, channeling the magic embedded within. With a shimmering light, a rift opened before him, revealing a glimpse of Blade's church on the other side. Gripping Stubby's reins firmly, Shorte prepared to step through.

But before he did, he turned back to his brothers, a defiant glint in his eye. "Oh, by the way, brothers, you can stay here and pretend to be heroes"—he made a fist and gestured with his thumb toward himself—"but this dwarf is going to the Abyss."

# CHAPTER TWENTY-ONE

# HIGH AMBITIONS

Jarz sat huddled in his thick wool blanket, the coarse fabric shielding him from the biting cold that seeped through the winter air. His father's ancient, weathered spell book lay open in his lap, its pages filled with cryptic runes and diagrams that pulsed faintly with residual magic. Beside him, a disarrayed pile of textbooks sprawled across the frost-kissed ground, their pages fluttering occasionally in the light breeze that rustled the willow's branches.

Above, the sun hung low in the sky, its golden rays casting long shadows over the frozen landscape of Omlett. Chunks of ice drifted lazily downstream along the banks of the Suttiir River. Izarra stood at Raven's water spot, wielding her trident with grace, as Jarz watched her intently. With a flick of her wrist, she channeled magic through the trident, dispersing the lingering mud and decay that Raven's dragon magic-induced swamp had left behind. Though still barren and lifeless, the plants surrounding the water's edge stirred slightly as Izarra's cleansing spell took effect.

Jarz returned to his work, his brow wrinkled in concentration as he compared passages from his father's spell book to the Waterfront books scattered at his feet.

Izarra huffed. "Maybe we can hire Gobs to help revive the vegetation this spring."

Jarz glanced up briefly from the spell book. "Sure, sounds great, dear," he replied absentmindedly.

"Are you even listening?"

"Yes," Jarz answered, finally glancing up. "Roasted vegetables for lunch, sounds delicious." His attempt at humor earned him a sly eye roll from Izarra, who returned to her task of cleansing the water with renewed focus.

"I think Raven will be surprised to see how clear it is," Izarra remarked. "I still don't understand—"

"I think we can do this," Jarz interrupted thoughtfully, tapping a particular page in the spell book, "if any of the traits that saved Eugor passed on to Carya. But according to my father's notes, Raven showed most of the traits."

"I'm sure something passed down," Izarra responded, though Jarz remained skeptical. "Raven told me Carya could hold her breath for a long time underwater. Dragons love treasure, and Carya had a huge jewelry box filled with gold pieces."

Jarz didn't turn the page. His finger froze mid-scroll, and his eyes lifted, narrowing with interest. The journal sagged slightly in his hands. "How do you know all this?"

"The night of Raven's eighteenth birthday party," Izarra answered. "Carya was trying to impress Thomas. She asked me which jewelry matched her dress."

"Huh," Jarz said automatically, then paused. "Did she have any diamonds?" he asked, suddenly thoughtful, considering what they'd need for the ritual.

"I don't remember, but I have one in my necklace back home."

"Not big enough," Jarz responded with frustration. "I'm talking about one the size of an apple."

Izarra paced, deep in thought. "We could travel to Iron Vale. The dwarves mine for precious minerals in the Ril Zorn Mountain Range."

"That will cost a fortune," Jarz lamented, slamming the spell book shut.

Izarra dropped her trident on the ground and moved closer to him. She gently removed the spell book from his lap and climbed under the blanket, sitting between his legs and resting her head against his chest. "I think Eugor would pay anything to have Carya back. Just like I would have given up everything to get you back."

Jarz kissed Izarra gently on the top of her head, savoring her hair's sweet, fruity scent that reminded him of water lotus flowers.

"Maybe Shorte can get one for us?" she suggested. "He's at Iron Cliff now with his family."

"I guess it wouldn't hurt to ask," Jarz replied.

"You could create a portal and visit him. The poor dwarf sounded miserable in his last message."

"I can do it tomorrow once your mother settles in. I need to talk to him anyway."

"About what?" Izarra adjusted the blanket around them.

"We need a cleric for the spell. I'm hoping he can do it," Jarz explained, hesitating.

"He would do anything to get his friend back. *And* to get his hands on that evil necro."

Jarz paused for a moment, conflicted. *Do I tell her?* He gently brushed a strand of hair from her ear and whispered, "He's my brother."

"That's sweet," Izarra replied warmly, her hand rubbing his leg affectionately. "I'm sure Shorte feels the same way about you."

"No, Iz . . . The necromancer. His name is Aushade Fisker."

Izarra stood, her sudden movement whipping the blanket off them both. "What?!"

"I—"

"You waited this long to tell me?"

"I didn't know how everyone would react." Jarz stood and reached out to hold her hands. "He's the one who gave me the spell book."

Izarra bit her lip, clearly struggling to process this revelation.

"Promise me you won't tell anyone . . . not yet," he pleaded.

"I can't promise," Izarra replied, pulling her hands away. "He killed Carya and so many others."

"I know." Jarz sighed heavily. "I don't think even resurrecting her will be enough for everyone's forgiveness."

"No, it won't!" Izarra snapped. "Go to the barracks and ask the children who lost their parents for forgiveness. Of all people, you should know what it's like losing family, too."

Her words struck a chord, and he frowned, knowing the pain of loss all too well. "I lost my brother once and don't intend to lose him again." He searched her expression, hoping she could see the turmoil within him. "Please, Iz."

Izarra closed her eyes and took a deep breath as the heaviness of the situation hung between them like a cloud. "Fine. I promise not to say anything."

Jarz held her close, her head nestled in the crook of his neck. "I love you, Iz."

A sudden cough broke the peaceful silence, causing them to turn. Standing before them was an older gentleman in a wizard's robe, hunched over and leaning on his staff for support. "Master Owens!" Jarz exclaimed with surprise, instantly recognizing the venerable figure.

Henry straightened slowly, his weathered face breaking into a gentle smile. "Jarz, that walk was longer than I expected."

Jarz conjured a sturdy wooden chair with intricate carvings that reflected his mentor's esteemed status.

Though visibly weary, Henry Owens settled into the chair with relief, his worn robes draping around him like a mantle of wisdom gained through years of experience. "Thank you, my son. Just wanted some exercise." Owens chuckled lightly. "I stopped at the Inn, and the lovely bar maiden—Miss Sharp, I believe—said I could find you here. I would've been here sooner, but she asked if I could entertain the little ones with some magic."

A smile played at the corners of Jarz's lips. "She always has a knack for involving everyone in her whimsical ideas. Why are you here, Master Owens?"

"Curiosity," Henry replied with a twinkle in his eye, his gaze shifting to Izarra. "And who's this beauty?"

"Henry Owens, this is Izarra Lyte."

"Star Light," Henry translated with a smile, warmth softening his features. "What a lovely name."

"Thank you," Izarra replied graciously, shaking the old man's hand.

"You have the natural beauty of a nymph. Sylvan nymph?" Owens inquired.

"Water, actually, and only a half-nymph," Izarra clarified gently.

"Ah, fascinating," Owens mused thoughtfully. "Did you know that nymphs are derived from Fey-elves and fairies?"

"My mother has told me the stories of our origin and everything about how Rull Thistle escaped the Fey Realm to create Thistlebane, a sanctuary for all the nymphs stuck here after the Realm Wars."

"You are correct, my dear," Henry said warmly, then turned his gaze back to Jarz with a more serious tone. "Mister Fisker, you haven't returned to Waterfront to visit me in a very long time."

Jarz felt a pang of guilt. "I'm sorry. I've been preoccupied with—" He hesitated, unsure how much to reveal.

"Can't blame you for being distracted," Henry replied gently. "There was a rumor that Gideon's Guardians were in Waterfront, so I went to see for myself. I was disappointed you weren't there."

"Gideon came to the rescue," Izarra interjected diplomatically, sensing the tension in the air.

"You still haven't told me why you're here," Jarz persisted, sensing his mentor might be deflecting.

"Do I need a reason?" Henry countered, a mischievous glint in his eye.

Jarz stood firm, his arms folded across his chest, his expression serious as he confronted his former mentor. "Well, Eugor just chased Waterfront guards out of town. They were hunting his daughter. Now you're here, so . . ." Jarz waited for Master Owens to respond.

"Have you seen the rogue?" Henry asked, his tone shifting to one of focused inquiry.

"No," Jarz replied firmly.

"The guardian?"

"No."

"That's all I needed to ask." Henry nodded thoughtfully. "The headmaster will question me in a truth zone."

Jarz froze, sensing there was more to Owens's visit than he was letting on. "You didn't walk all this way to ask me about Gideon and Raven."

Henry glanced briefly at Izarra, who gracefully excused herself. "I'll get those vegetables for lunch," she said with a smile, kissing him goodbye.

Once Izarra had cleared the area, Jarz turned back, his demeanor expectant and ready for answers. "Spill it, Henry."

Owens began sincerely, "I'm happy for you. She seems like—"

"Henry!"

"All right." Owens sighed heavily, sinking back into the wooden chair. "Elora wants a new guardian for the Mortal Realm."

"Gideon is the Mortal Realm Guardian."

Owens nodded in acknowledgment, his expression grave. "Yes, but circumstances are changing. Elora believes the time has come for a successor."

Jarz's brow furrowed in concern. "Why now? Gideon has been the guardian for centuries."

"He's a fugitive," Owens scoffed dismissively, his tone tinged with impatience.

"And?" Jarz snapped back. The conversation had taken an unexpected turn, veering into ambition, loyalty, and personal convictions.

"This is your opportunity to fulfill your dream of becoming a guardian," Owens continued, his gaze steady. "You'll be the first human to do so."

"What's in it for you?" Jarz asked skeptically. There had to be more to his proposition.

"In return for saving your life, I hope you would vote to replace Elora as the Mortal Realm Representative," Owens stated bluntly, laying bare his ambitions.

Jarz shook his head in disbelief at the audacity of Owens's request. "So you can control the High Council."

"Think about it, my son," Owens urged. "Elora has headed the Mortal Realm for centuries. We could be the first to make a change. We deserve a chance."

Jarz glanced at his mentor, conflicted. "And we've been at peace for centuries," he countered. "None of the other realms have tried to conquer one another."

"We could reshape history," Owens pressed, his voice eager. "Imagine what we could achieve together."

Jarz knelt to be eye-level with the older man, his expression earnest yet resolute. He owed Henry Owens his life, but he couldn't betray his principles, not now. "I've wanted this since I was a boy, but my answer is no under these circumstances. I won't betray Gideon."

"It's because . . . of her," Owens ventured cautiously.

"Leave Izarra out of this," Jarz barked, his protective instincts flaring. "It has nothing to do with her." He stood abruptly and moved toward the willow tree to gather his belongings.

"Do you plan to have children?"

Owens's unexpected question stopped Jarz in his tracks. He turned slowly to face the old wizard. "I don't know, maybe one day," he replied cautiously, grappling with conflicting sentiments and the unwelcome scrutiny of his choices.

"You can still court her, have a family," Owens offered earnestly. "We can change the rules about guardians having children."

"The council created that rule for a reason," Jarz replied firmly, his tone brokering no argument. "Plus, it would be difficult to fulfill my duty of constantly watching over the realm. Not an ideal life for a parent."

"You're sure she's worth giving up your dream?" Owens pressed, his gaze searching Jarz's face as if for any sign of wavering.

Jarz clenched his teeth, frustration bubbling beneath the surface. He hated discussing his emotions, especially with someone who had once been a mentor but now seemed to be pushing him toward a path he wasn't sure he wanted to take. Bending over, he gathered his belongings—textbooks, a blanket, and his father's precious spell book—into his bag.

Before he could finish, Owens's hand gripped his shoulder, turning him around forcefully. "You could be immortal," Owens insisted, his voice almost intensely manic. "Create your legacy."

"We can't control fate, Henry," Jarz replied tersely, pulling away from the older man's grasp.

Owens drew a deep breath. "I know that book," he said as he reached out to touch it. "It changed the fate of the King of Omlett."

Jarz pulled the spell book away protectively, his expression guarded. "It did."

"And I know that the wizards searched all of Fellswar for it," Owens continued in his tone, now probing more. "So, tell me—where did you find it?"

Jarz met Owens with a cold stare, refusing to divulge more than necessary.

"That book is *very* powerful."

"I know. And it will assist me in resurrecting Carya," Jarz stated firmly, waving the spell book for emphasis.

"What happened to your lecture about controlling fate?" Owens challenged.

"This is different," Jarz replied evenly. "I need to fix this, and then I'll burn it."

"You can't destroy it," Owens said firmly.

"Watch me."

Owens's face went sour. "So there's no way of persuading you?"

Jarz shook his head.

"I guess I need to find an alternative plan then." His mentor stepped back and cast a blue portal. "Pray to—"

"Blade?" Jarz finished.

Henry flashed a wrinkled smile. "I wish you all the luck in saving Carya. You're a good man, Jarz Fisker." Then he vanished.

Jarz stared out at the river. *Am I ready for a family?* Clutching his father's book under his arm, he cast a blue portal. He exited the gateway and entered his cottage by Fischer's Docks. Eugor had arranged for them to remain there until the orphanage was completed, and then they could move in with Izarra's mother to care for the children.

He noticed the emptiness. *I guess Iz is purchasing a lot of vegetables.* Jarz walked toward the fireplace and opened a wooden chest where Izarra stored the throw blankets, placing the book under all the covers. He pulled out a clean throw blanket and went upstairs to the guest bedroom to ensure it was ready for her mother. The mahogany-trimmed blue walls were decorated with paintings of oceans and waterfalls. In the middle of the room sat a small decorative bed with white pillows and fabric. Izarra had decorated this space better than their own. He preferred the blue to the bright pink and white of their room.

Izarra's father's medal, a platinum star attached to a red and gold ribbon, hung from a hook above the headboard. *She must be trying hard to impress her mother.* He placed the blanket on the rocking chair before returning downstairs. As he emptied his bag, metal clanked against the stone outside.

Moments later, Izarra burst through the front door, her windswept hair suggesting her busy day. She dropped a basket of food onto the side table, wearing the biggest grin that made Jarz smile back. She threw her arms around his neck, hugging him tightly.

"The castoridaens are almost done!" she exclaimed.

"Great," Jarz replied, returning her embrace. "I take it you walked by the construction site for the hundredth time."

"I was going to Gary's vegetable greenhouse to see what I could salvage. His daughter has enlisted some older children to help her with the farm since her father's gone." The mention of Gary's fate lingered in the air. Jarz nodded understandingly. "I ran into Buzz there. He was testing his new chariot."

"A chariot?" Jarz chuckled, attempting to lighten the mood.

"Mug built it for him," Izarra explained. "That gnome is so creative. It's pulled by a horse and allows someone to stand in the rear. He offered me a ride and escorted me around town. We had to stop at Mug's factory, so I figured I would check the construction progress."

"Sounds like fun."

"He has diamonds," Izarra added with excitement.

"Buzz?"

"No, Mug. You said you needed a large diamond. He has twenty-five of them."

"How do you know that?"

"I counted them. Mug is using them for a secret project."

Jarz leaned in, his lips brushing tenderly against hers, a silent promise of his unwavering support. "Perfect. So, about the castoridaens—"

"They're finishing the roof as we speak. We should be able to move the furniture tomorrow. Mug salvaged shelves, beds, and wardrobes from the homes destroyed in the last storm. His knack for turning ruins into treasures is truly remarkable. Volunteers have built the rest. I hope we have enough to move the children over in a few days."

"You've done an amazing job coordinating all of this." Jarz gave her a quick hug. Moving over to the table, he inhaled the earthy scent of the fresh vegetables. "Should I go get your mother?"

"Yes, please. I'll stay and prepare lunch for the three of us," Izarra said.

"Any word from Raven?" Jarz lightly drummed his fingers on the table's edge, a habit he had when thinking deeply.

Izarra's knife moved rhythmically through the carrots, creating even slices. "No, I haven't seen Shorty lately."

Jarz chuckled. "You mean Shorte?"

"No," she giggled softly, "her familiar."

"That's going to be confusing."

The crisp snap of the knife against the carrots mingled with the aroma of freshly cut produce. "Shorty's last message was about those colorful fireworks at Waterfront."

"Fireworks—at Waterfront. Now that's something you don't see every day," he remarked, a wry smile tugging at his lips. "This is truly the end of days."

"How long does it take Shorty to travel from there?" Izarra asked, focusing on her task.

"Wait, Shorte or the bird?"

"Her raven!" Izarra exclaimed, lightly slapping his arm. "Why don't you have a familiar? I thought all wizards had one."

"There are different types of magic users," Jarz explained, handing her more carrots. "Some create portals, some cast powerful spells, and some, like me, specialize in ancient runes. Familiars are a choice, not a necessity."

"If you had one, what would it be?"

He paused thoughtfully. "Maybe an Arctic husky if I had to choose one."

"Aw, maybe one day."

"I wouldn't take one out of its natural habitat for a pet."

"What if it bonded with you?" she asked, gesturing her knife at him.

"I don't plan on visiting the Arctic anytime soon to find out." He dodged the knife to kiss her. "I'll be back soon with your mother. I hope she packs light."

Stepping onto the deck, Jarz created a blue portal for Thistlebane, Izarra following close behind. "Remember not to stare at the water nymphs," she warned.

"I don't need to, dear, not when I have you."

"Oh, it's not jealousy—they might blind you."

"Right, you mentioned that when we visited after graduation," Jarz recalled, a hint of nostalgia in his voice. "I'll be back short . . . lee."

Izarra shook her head, a playful scowl forming on her lips. "It's Shorty, and you're not funny. But maybe she *should* change the bird's name."

# CHAPTER TWENTY-TWO

# UNWELCOME MAGIC

Izarra deftly finished chopping the last of the vegetables. The sharp scent of onions and the earthy aroma of carrots filled the cozy kitchen. She carefully tossed the colorful assortment into a large cauldron suspended over the crackling fireplace, the simmering broth rich with flavors. Her fingers brushed against the smooth leaves of fresh thyme plucked from a small herb pot perched on the sunlit window ledge, its fragrance releasing a hint of mint as she added it to the bubbling stew. *I hope my mother isn't giving Jarz a rough time.*

A sudden knock startled her. She glanced at the fire and threw a log onto the flames, ensuring they burned and danced warmly. Crossing the kitchen, she opened the sturdy front door to reveal Master Owens leaning lightly on his gnarled staff.

The old wizard lowered the hood of his cloak, revealing a face weathered by years of arcane study, breaking into a warm smile. "My apologies for disturbing you, but Miss Sharp gave me directions to your home."

"It's quite all right," Izarra replied warmly, holding the door open. "Please come in."

"Sorry for the intrusion, but is Mister Fisker home?" Owens asked, quickly taking in the layout of the large, open room.

"No, he left to retrieve my mother," Izarra explained, closing the door gently behind him. "But he'll return soon." She paused, a smile tugging at her lips. "Is there something I can help you with, Master Owens?"

"Please, it's Henry," the old man insisted. "Those are lovely rugs."

"My mother hand-spun them for us as a gift."

Henry reached into the folds of his cloak and withdrew a tied scroll, handing it to her. "This needs to be with his father's spell book."

"All right, Henry," Izarra said as she accepted the scroll and placed it carefully on the sturdy wooden table. "I'll make sure he knows. Would you like a cup of rosemary tea?"

"I can't stay," Henry replied, his gaze drifting toward the closed chest. "But would you put an old man's mind at ease and place that with the book now?"

"Of course," Izarra responded, picking up the scroll and walking to the large trunk. She knew the intricate lock well and opened it, placing the scroll inside. As she turned around, she was startled to find Henry Owens standing uncomfortably close, peering over her shoulder. A shiver ran down her spine. "I'll tell him about the parchment when he returns," she said cautiously.

"Thank you." Henry adjusted his staff with a slight tremor in his hand.

"Are you sure you can't stay for lunch?" Izarra asked, trying to break the tension in the air as the wizard moved away from her, making a small gesture with his hands. *Is he casting a spell?*

"I can't," he answered nervously, fidgeting with his staff.

"Would you like to take a walk on the grounds?" Izarra suggested, hoping to distract him. "Our yard overlooks Fischer's Docks. There's a beautiful view of the ships sailing in and out."

"He always did love the water . . ."

"So do I," she replied with a soft smile. "I guess we have that in common."

"Jarz is a smart wizard," Henry muttered.

"Yes, he is," Izarra agreed, attempting to lighten the mood. "I suppose that's another thing we have in common—except for being a wizard." Henry managed a half-hearted grin in response. She watched him closely, noticing his hands moving again as if preparing to cast another spell. *Jarz, where are you?*

"He has the home secured from portals," Henry observed.

"Yes," Izarra replied, her hand unconsciously gripping her trident. "It keeps anyone from entering or exiting without permission. Or from using magic against us."

"Smart." He stood in the middle of the room as if deep in contemplation.

Izarra's pulse quickened as her senses tingled. "Are you all right, Henry?"

Owens cringed. "I'm sorry, my dear. I must—" Without finishing, he dashed out the front door, leaving it wide open.

*What was that about?* She closed the door swiftly, preparing to set her trident down, as the front door flew open again. She spun and pointed her weapon with practiced instinct at the two figures standing in the doorway.

"Is that any way to greet your mother?" Dawn's voice rang out, breaking the tension as she entered the room. Jarz followed closely behind, carrying a large blue travel bag.

"Mother!" Izarra exclaimed joyously, setting her trident against the wall and rushing to hug Dawn.

"Hello, kiddo," Dawn replied warmly, stroking her daughter's hair. "It's been so long since I've seen you."

"Let me show you to your room so you can unpack," Izarra suggested, pulling from the embrace.

"I didn't bring much," her mother responded with a smile, following Izarra up the steps.

A large wardrobe stood in the corner of the room with its doors open. Jarz placed the bag inside, carefully arranging its contents. Izarra noticed he had laid out the blue blanket as she had asked, but her father's medal caught her eye the most, gleaming amid the familiar belongings.

"Oh my!" her mother exclaimed as she looked around the room. "I might not want to go back."

"Well, you can't return to Thistlebane. You have an orphanage to manage," Izarra said softly, watching her mother approach the bed and gently touch her father's medal.

"Why did you grab your weapon?" Jarz whispered into Izarra's ear.

She bit her lip, considering her response, then mouthed, "Later."

Her mother explored the room, her fingers brushing over dusty books and worn furniture.

"Maybe we can visit Father's grave—if you'd like."

Dawn turned, wiping a tear from her eye. "I'd like that."

"Iz, you should warn her," Jarz breathed into her ear.

She shot him a look that could melt steel. *We need to work on your timing.*

"Warn me about what?" Dawn asked, turning back to them.

Izarra took a deep breath, choosing her words carefully. "We had to rebury him, so the grave is fresh."

"Rebury?" Dawn's confusion was evident, her brow furrowing.

"Mother, a necromancer raised the dead from the Omlett cemetery and used them as an army to attack us." Izarra's voice was steady but laced with sorrow. "I found Father's body before—"

"Did you have to destroy him?" Dawn interrupted, her voice tinged with concern.

"No," Jarz interjected quickly, stepping closer. "When the necromancer departed, his army collapsed."

Izarra continued softly, "I found Father by the river before the security squad arrived."

"They burned most of the corpses to ensure Aushade couldn't use them against us again," Jarz added solemnly, his voice thick with emotion as he mentioned his brother's name.

"That's horrible." Dawn reached out to touch Izarra's arm, her grip trembling.

"I'll let you unpack," Izarra said softly, trying to lighten the heavy mood. "Lunch will be ready soon."

As her mother's attention turned to the wardrobe, Izarra seized Jarz's hand and gently pulled him out of the room. They descended the stairs together, Izarra's mind still preoccupied with Henry Owens's strange visit.

"Master Owens stopped by," she explained as they reached the lower level.

"What did he want?" Jarz asked, his brow furrowing with concern as Izarra opened the chest and retrieved the tied scroll, handing it to him. He untied the string and carefully examined it.

"It's blank," Jarz observed after trying a detection spell for magic writing.

"He insisted I place it with the spell book."

Jarz waved his hand again, attempting another spell, but the scroll remained inert. "I'm not sure what it's supposed to be for. He didn't say anything else?"

"No," Izarra replied. "But he was acting odd. He seemed annoyed by your protections on the cabin. And I'm positive I saw him trying to cast something. It mimicked the same movement you do for portals."

Jarz frowned thoughtfully as he inspected the scroll, then decisively tossed it into the fire. "I should tell you about the conversation Henry and I had. He—" Before Jarz could finish, an urgent knock echoed through the cabin. Together, arm in arm, they answered the front door.

Cyndi stood before them, her expression tense with worry. "Raven's home," she announced urgently, her voice raspy with concern.

As the tension in the cabin mounted, Izarra glanced at her mother, who had emerged from the bedroom, concern etched on her face. "Stay here," Izarra stated softly, reassuringly touching her mother's arm. "We'll return, but make yourself at home in the meantime."

# CHAPTER TWENTY-THREE

# OPERATION
# RESURRECTION

aven clutched Gideon's hand as he guided her to a table near the fireplace at the Omlett Inn. She followed him while he moved, her steps tentative and uncertain. Each time he paused, she stumbled into him, her grip tightening momentarily as if fearing he might disappear.

Her three-day stay in the Fey Realm, where they delved into every form of magic, had not returned her vision, even with the visit to Fharlix. Instead, she had ghostly, wavy purple images that flickered when things moved. *At least I can see that much,* she consoled herself, though the thought offered little comfort. *But how did Kaleidris give me sight?*

Tables and chairs posed an ever-present obstacle, forcing her to navigate with one arm extended. A chair scraped across the floor, and a sudden, jarring noise made her flinch. Gideon's touch on her arm was firm yet gentle as he guided her into a seat.

As she settled, the warmth of the fire brushed against her face, a small solace in the darkness. But her heart raced with a mixture of anxiety and anticipation. Every sound felt magnified, laden with potential threat. Something was brewing in the air, an unspoken tension that quickened her pulse.

"I'll fetch you a drink," Gideon told her.

"No ale," Raven replied, her voice firm despite the lingering uncertainty. A flicker of doubt crossed her mind. *Why am I still following the advice of a druid I don't know?* The Inn smelled like alcohol mixed with burning timber, the scent wrapping around her like a thick, oppressive fog.

"Here you go," Gideon said as a gentle thud came from the table. "I'll inform your father that we're here."

Raven listened as his footsteps faded down the hall, leaving her in an eerie stillness. She glided her hands around the table, feeling for the mug. Her fingers finally wrapped around it, bringing it to her lips. The strong scent of berries filled her nose, a sweet contrast to the Inn's smoky aroma. She took a cautious sip, savoring the flavor.

She closed her eyes and drew in a slow, steadying breath. When she opened them again, a blur of shapes and shadows refused to take form. Her fingers moved across the table's surface, tracing the rough grooves and worn edges she could not see. She only caught glimpses of the flicker of shifting purple waves as the candle flame danced. Motion somehow brought the room to life. The fire's wavering light sketched the outline of a chipped cup, the curve of a forgotten spoon. She leaned in closer, waiting for the next flash and breath of movement to show her the world she couldn't see unless it stirred.

She recalled Joy'uss's voice from Baka's cave. *You'll display* all *the dragon traits.* The urge to test her hand over the candle to see if it would burn was enticing. As she inched her hand forward, she quickly yanked it back when footsteps echoed through the bar area, slow and deliberate. A familiar scent of old leather and a hint of pipe smoke. She turned toward the sound, her heart quickening as her eyesight vanished again. "Father."

"I'm here, Nightbird," Eugor replied, his voice a soothing balm. He moved swiftly to her side, enveloping her in a warm, protective embrace. "Are you all right?"

She sank into his arms, drawing comfort from his familiar presence. "I'm fine." The embrace lingered, filled with unspoken worries and reassurances.

"And your eyes?" he asked gently, pulling back.

"They're the same," she responded. "Celeste tried everything."

"Your mother is still furious you didn't return home. She wanted to help you," her father informed her, his tone soft but firm. "She's out gathering supplies now and gave me strict orders to send you home after this meeting."

"Celeste thought the Fey magic would be more powerful than Mother's clerical skills."

Eugor's voice crackled, "Please don't repeat that to your mother."

Raven eagerly shifted the conversation. "Is everyone on their way?"

"Yes, I asked Cyndi to retrieve Jarz and Izarra. Shorte arrived late last night. Avalann and her parents arrived a couple—"

"Arlene is here?" Gideon's voice was sharp with interest.

"Yes, she and Aemon helped bring the displaced survivors here. Queen Baela arrived with them. She said her husband has been acting mad since the attack on his life. When I was in Suttiir, I thought he looked ill but dismissed it as exhaustion from the war recovery."

"Should I pay him a visit?" Gideon asked with concern.

"No—I'll go after we rescue Carya."

"Another reason to begin this quest," Raven interjected, her tone sharp with intent. She turned her head slightly, scanning the room with sightless eyes, as if willing the world to return to her. Shadows and shapes still evaded her, but she didn't flinch.

*How long should I wait? For someone else to decide I'm ready?* She wasn't used to helplessness. And she *hated* how close it had crept lately—like a second skin she couldn't shake.

Eugor's voice came gently. "Are you sure you're up to this?"

A familiar flicker of doubt surfaced—but she crushed it. "My eyes have delayed this long enough," she said firmly. Her fingers flexed at her sides, the weight of the daggers still familiar, still hers. Sight or no sight, she could still fight. Still move. Still choose. She might be walking sightless, but she wasn't walking backward.

"Ascending into the Abyss with your sight is one thing, but this seems overly reckless," her father pleaded, his voice tinged with desperation.

"Like trying to sneak up on a balor while invisible?" she retorted sarcastically, a dry smile tugging at the corner of her mouth.

"I'll never hear the end of that," her father replied with annoyance.

Gideon grumbled, "I've tried to talk her out of it. She won't listen."

"I'm not sure where she gets this stubbornness from," her father responded roguishly.

"You!" Raven and Gideon responded together, then laughed, the tension momentarily lifting from the room.

"But I have faith in the group that they'll vote on not allowing her to participate," Gideon boasted.

She huffed in frustration. "They don't have a say either."

"Raven, dear, my heart can't take losing another daughter," Eugor said sadly, placing his hand on hers, his touch warm and comforting.

The sound of the front door opening made her head snap in that direction. A set of wavy figures strode in; the footsteps were quick and purposeful, and the air shifted slightly as the newcomers approached the table. A pair of soft arms wrapped around her, and she inhaled the fruity scent of the hair brushing against her cheek.

"I'm so glad you've returned home," Izarra said sweetly, her voice filled with relief.

"Thank you," Raven replied as her friend pulled away.

"Your eyes," Izarra said softly, leaning closer, "they're glowing."

Raven tried to smile. "So I've been told."

"How are you?" Jarz asked, concern evident in his voice.

"Fatigued and nauseous." Raven sighed, running a hand through her hair. "It's probably from this form of sight." Chairs scraped against the wooden floor as the figures around her took their seats.

"So you can see *some* things?" Izarra asked, curiosity lacing her tone.

"Only when things are in motion," the rogue answered, her sightless eyes fixed straight ahead. "It's like a purple blur of movement in a sea of darkness."

"Like a bat," Izarra chuckled, trying to lighten the mood.

"Not exactly," Raven replied, a faint smile on her lips. "Jarz, have you found anything?"

"I studied my father's spell book," Jarz replied, frustrated. "There's nothing about your condition." A sudden ruckus erupted at the front of the Inn, drawing every head toward the commotion.

"Raven's eyes," Avalann murmured to the figure beside her.

"I can hear you," the rogue replied dryly, her voice calm but precise.

"How's that possible?" Avalann asked, louder this time, genuinely bewildered.

Raven shrugged. "Ever since I lost my vision, the rest of my senses kicked into overdrive. Hearing, smell—it's all sharper now."

"I apologize for any bodily function you may have heard or smelled," Shorte said with a snicker. A brief pause. Silence. He huffed. "I guess that excludes the sense of humor."

Raven, unfazed, asked, "Are we all here?"

"Yes," Gideon replied.

"The gang is finally back together!" Shorte exclaimed, his voice ringing with relief and anticipation. "And we're ready for Operation Resurrection."

A low, resonant hum filled the air, accompanied by swirling oval-shaped waves that pulsed from the void. The familiar, sweet scent of wild Fey flowers drifted in as a figure materialized out of nowhere. *I never realized portals made that distinct humming sound.*

"Did I miss anything?" the Fey Guardian asked, her presence commanding attention despite the casual question.

"Celeste, you can't partake in this," Gideon ordered firmly, his tone leaving no room for argument. "You have two marks, and I'm about to leave for the High Council. You should accompany me."

"I'm here to assist," Celeste said, her voice crisp with control. Beneath it, Raven caught a thread of disdain—subtle but unmistakable. "They'll need a Realm Guardian, and it should be you."

"You know I can't," Gideon snapped. The tension twisted tighter, like a wire pulling hard between them.

Raven stepped forward, her voice soft but steady. "It's all right," she said, trying to cut the fuse before it hit the powder. "We understand." Except she didn't. Not really. She couldn't see the expressions being exchanged but *felt* them like heat waves off a forge.

Celeste's calm was applied, like a layer of ice. "But the Abyss is a vast, complex, and dangerous domain," she went on, too composed. "We've been there before, searching for Tier. I'm qualified to guide them."

Gideon's anger was sharp and brittle, coming from somewhere deeper than the moment. "This isn't up for debate," he shot back, iron-hard.

"Am I the only one that disagrees?" Shorte asked, bold and unbothered. "She has the experience. We could use a powerful tour guide."

Then Gideon's voice cracked—not loud, but enough. Raven heard it in the pause before he spoke again.

"She doesn't care about Carya," he said, the bitterness giving way to something raw. "She wants to search for Tier." The room went quiet.

Raven's stomach clenched as she heard the guilt under Gideon's words, the way his breath caught after. Not just anger—fear. The kind you didn't say out loud. The type that haunted you when someone you cared about had already slipped through your fingers once. *Has he given up on his friend?*

A sudden burst of purple waves exploded in Raven's sight, followed by a loud smack that echoed through the room. Gasps filled the air, followed by an uneasy silence. A chill as darkness seemed to envelop her vision, and then tiny wisps of curvy lines, like the breath of unseen entities, broke the eerie stillness of the void.

"If you weren't immortal, I would strike you down where you stand," Celeste threatened, her voice cold and sharp.

An outline of someone dashed toward the front door. "Gideon!" Raven called out instinctively, her heart racing with concern.

"I'll go speak to him," Eugor stated calmly, his reassuring presence a grounding point amid the tense atmosphere. "You'll be all right?"

The rogue nodded, though her worry lingered. "Yes." Eugor gently kissed her forehead before he left, his footsteps fading.

"I'm glad you couldn't see that," Celeste murmured, her tone softening. "But what he said was uncalled for. I may have failed with Tier, but I won't leave that awful place until we rescue Carya."

"I think Gideon's frustrated because he can't help with the mission or my vision," Raven admitted.

"We're in this together," Avalann stated firmly. "But I agree with Shorte. We need Celeste."

"That makes us five strong," Jarz added thoughtfully, resonating. "That may not be enough."

"That's six, Mister I-Graduated-Top-Of-My-Class-At-Waterfront," the dwarf huffed mockingly.

"Raven is in no condition to go," Jarz said gravely. A heavy silence fell over the group.

Raven's jaw tightened. She hated being spoken about like she wasn't there—worse, she hated that Jarz was right. The thought of not helping to search for Carya gnawed at her and lit a fire in her chest that she couldn't act on. Still, she forced a shrug. "Jarz is right," she said, voice light but flat. "I'll just be a burden. Maybe I'll start knitting so you can have new mittens when you return from hell." Sarcasm was easier than saying what she felt—that being left behind made her feel useless, cracked, and painfully irrelevant.

No one laughed, but Shorte snorted. "Don't worry, it's a tough crowd."

Celeste's voice expressed a serious tone. "We're talking about the Abyss. It's not about jumping into the Inferno-Plane. There are too many places to search with just the five of us. The Abyss has several elemental planes, each with multiple layers. Carya could be anywhere."

"We could start in the Ninth Layer of the Inferno-Plane. Home to the flox," Jarz pointed out, his voice laden with the weight of their past encounters. "We saw one during the attack in Omlett, and I saw a succubus, which resides in the Seventh Layer."

"Into the inferno we go," Shorte mumbled. "How did you meet a succubus?" he asked, curiosity tinged with disbelief.

"She was working with . . . the necromancer," Jarz answered.

"You should start there," Raven suggested, her voice steady despite the turmoil in the room.

"But it's still a large task with all the demons, and the High Council watching," Celeste retorted.

"We need more—" Avalann was cut off abruptly by the thunderous thump of the front door swinging open.

Raven's attention snapped to the entrance. "Gideon?" she shouted, but her instincts were off, and she noticed four distinct wavy forms of different heights approaching.

"Hello, brother," a male voice declared with a touch of familiarity.

*Brother?*

The word curled around her like a snake. Raven went still. Her other senses sharpened, reaching for something the darkness no longer gave her. *The voice*—it was smooth, unhurried, almost warm. But beneath it, something cold slithered just out of reach. She couldn't see his face, but the shape of the silence that followed felt too knowing.

A shift in the air—sounds of the battle field, the faint tang of melted metal from her acidic attack. Then memory surged. The necromancer's grip, fingers clamped like shackles around her throat as her feet dangled. The press of his breath, dry and close. The echo of his voice—alien and intimate all at once. *What are you?*

"Princess, I present to you your bounty," a familiar feminine voice said, chilling Raven's spine.

Raven's thoughts raced as recognition dawned. *Ashley?*

"Why you—" Shorte's voice boomed as the waves indicated he stormed toward the prisoner as Raven stood, trying to focus through the chaos of pulsing, twisting lines, making her nauseous once again.

"Jarz, release me," Shorte demanded firmly, his tone brokering no argument. "And tell that pirate to get out of my way."

*Pirate? What the spell is going on?* Raven struggled to make sense of the situation, overwhelmed by the escalating commotion. "STOP!" she screamed, her voice cutting through the noise like a blade. "Leave the necromancer be for now. Jarz, release Shorte."

"Is this a bad time?" Ashley asked, her voice soaked in mock innocence. "Maybe we should come back tomorrow for the reward?"

"Get this dragon fodder out of my sight," Shorte barked, his tone sharp with authority. "Take him to the prison."

"Fine," Raven said, tension tightening every word. "Take him to Buzz."

"Wait! Listen, everyone!" Izarra's voice rose suddenly, sharp with urgency. "Jarz—"

Raven heard the soft exhale from her cousin before he spoke. She knew that sigh.

"His name is Aushade Fisker," Jarz said quietly. "He's my brother."

Silence. Then, a low, steady ringing built in Raven's ears as if her body were rejecting the words before her mind caught up. *Brother. I'm related to that monster?*

The air around her felt different now—thicker, colder. Every shuffle, every breath, every heartbeat in the room sharpened in her awareness. Her fingers curled slightly, flexing as if she needed to hold on to something solid.

And then—Aushade's voice. Calm. Amused. "By the sounds of it, you haven't told them yet," he said smoothly. A beat later, he leaned toward someone nearby and added in a mock tone, "This is awkward."

"You shut your mouth," Shorte declared sharply. "I don't care who you're related to."

"Everyone, stop!" Raven demanded. "Avalann, take Shorte to the bar and pour him a drink. Ashley, take the prisoner over to the corner table. Make sure he stays guarded."

"I'll sit with my brother, too," Jarz added firmly.

"I'll stand watch, too," an unfamiliar female voice said calmly.

Raven began to ask, "Who—"

"She's with us," Gobs clarified.

Raven sank back in her chair, rubbing her temples as the voices in the room softened to a murmur. *My head feels like it's going to explode.*

"Oh, honey," Ashley said sympathetically, approaching Raven and gently tilting her head back. "I see you've discovered True Eyes."

"You know about this?" Celeste asked sharply.

"I sure do," Ashley replied calmly, her voice contrasting with their escalating tension. "It's like the rest of her other trait abilities. Raven, all you have to do is switch it off."

"I've tried everything," Raven mumbled in frustration as the gang quarreled.

"Gobs, get over here," Ashley called suddenly, her tone urgent. An outline of a more diminutive form walked over and stood nearby, chanting something in Elvish.

"Oh dear," Gobs moaned softly, her distress catching everyone's attention.

"What is it?" Raven asked nervously, her heart pounding. Gobs remained silent, adding to the suspense hanging in the air.

"What is it?!" Shorte's voice demanded, the tension thickening as footsteps approached from the bar.

"Maybe we should discuss this in private," Gobs murmured, her voice barely audible over the rising clamor.

"This is my family," Raven stated firmly, her voice cutting through the uncertainty. "They can hear it, too."

"Are you sure?" Gobs asked cautiously.

"Is it?" Ashley's voice sounded shocked. "Oh, honey!"

"What is it?" Raven pleaded, her patience wearing thin.

"Your eyes," Gobs began hesitantly, her voice filled with concern, "they're not something you can just switch off."

"Am I under a spell?" Raven asked urgently, her mind racing back to past encounters. "I was at Waterfront—"

"Not exactly," Ashley replied mysteriously.

Shorte hissed impatiently, "Just spit it out."

"She's with child," Gobs snapped abruptly, her words cutting through the tension like a knife. The room immediately fell silent.

Raven didn't need to see to feel every eye-locking onto her. *I'm . . . I'm . . .*

"Congratulations, cousin," Aushade called.

"You! Shut it!" Shorte shot back sharply.

Izarra enveloped Raven in a tight hug, her voice filled with joy. "Oh, Raven! That's wonderful."

A whirlwind of emotions erupted inside her—joy, fear, and uncertainty—mixing into a turbulent storm. *Gideon's child. Our child.* The thought both warmed and chilled her heart. *How can I protect a child in this dangerous world?*

"Gideon, that old dog," Shorte teased, attempting to lighten the mood with a jest that fell flat.

"Well, she definitely can't go now," Avalann whispered with concern.

"I can still hear you," Raven blurted out, her voice shaky as she tried to hold back the tears that threatened to spill over.

"How far along is she?" Celeste asked, her usually stern voice softened by empathy.

A hand pressed against Raven's stomach. "About thirteen weeks," Gobs said.

Raven's hand instinctively moved to her belly, a mixture of protectiveness and vulnerability washing over her. *Thirteen weeks. Still so early, yet so real.*

Izarra clapped and asked excitedly, "Boy or girl?"

"No, I don't want to know," Raven pleaded as the weight of the responsibility settled heavily on her shoulders.

"The child is stressed and is using your vision as a defense mechanism," Gobs explained, her tone reassuring. "It's like how a bat uses echolocation."

Izarra snickered. "That's what I said."

Someone rubbed Raven's shoulders gently. "Once calm and relaxed," Ashley said, "your eyesight will return to normal."

Raven nodded, grateful for Ashley's comfort but overwhelmed by everything swirling around her. *How can I protect my child when I can't control my abilities?*

"I know what'll help," Gobs said thoughtfully, reaching into her pouch. "Is there hot water?"

"Give me a mug of water," Raven suggested, her voice steadier as Gobs slid a cup into her hands. Raven wrapped both hands around it, focusing her thoughts. "Cessis Nar." Her hands warmed instantly, and the water began to boil gently, a small comfort in uncertainty.

"Impressive," Ashley responded with a hint of admiration. "It's not how I would have done it."

"Ignore her," Gobs interjected, her voice soothing. "I mixed in some peppermint to help you relax."

Raven blew across the rim before taking a sip. The soothing warmth spread through her body, reminiscent of her mother's mint tea, which had always been comforting during childhood illnesses.

"How long will it take for her sight to come back?" Izarra asked anxiously.

"It depends on how stubborn the baby is," Gobs replied.

Shorte snorted. "Well, since it's Raven's . . . it'll be a while."

The room filled with a few chuckles, but Raven only half-heard them. Her hand instinctively moved to her abdomen, resting there gently. *Three months.*

It hit her like a cold wind. Too long. Too quiet. She had imagined so many times what it would be like—being cared for, maybe even fussed over—by someone who *chose* to love her. The kind of care that didn't come with pity or duty. Just presence. Carya would have known what to say. Would have made tea, sat at the edge of the bed, and reminded her she was still herself—even in the dark. *But she's not here.* And Raven couldn't afford to wait for comfort.

"Maybe we should postpone the rescue?" Jarz offered.

"No," Raven said, her voice sharper now. She straightened her shoulders, lifting her chin. "I won't wait any longer." She didn't need sight to move forward. She just needed purpose.

"We can't invade the Abyss Realm with just the five of us," Avalann reasoned. "Even with the Fey Guardian. It's impossible."

"I'll help," Aushade declared defiantly.

"You open that hole of yours again," Shorte warned sharply, "and I'll permanently shut it."

"Carya should still have her soul with her," Aushade continued, dismissing Shorte's threat. "As long as they transferred it to a more permanent phylactery."

"Who's *they?*" Jarz asked.

"Courtlynn and her master, Draklor," Aushade replied calmly.

"So the succubus has a name," Shorte muttered gruffly. "And who's Draklor?"

"A balor—a fire demon," Aushade answered coolly. "The one I helped build a demon army for."

Shorte, his voice brimming with skepticism, began, "If you think we'll trust a—"

"Hey! Fighting isn't helping the situation," Izarra interjected, her voice rising above the noise. "We don't want to put any more stress on Raven."

"It should be her decision," Celeste pointed out. "It's her sister."

Raven's breath came slow and even, but her thoughts churned like a storm tide.

*How can I trust him? Aushade's words are too calm. Too easy. Like he has nothing to lose—or everything to gain.* She shifted in her seat. The edges of her vision, usually dark and formless, sparked faintly. Light and movement. Blurs, like shadows shifting behind a curtain. Her heart fluttered—not just at the sight but at the meaning. *Is this a sign? Is it luck?*

*No. Luck is for the unprepared.* Raven couldn't afford to rely on fate. Not now. She leaned into her training instead—her role as a Mortal Guardian. Breathe. Analyze. Assess risk. *Aushade is dangerous, yes. But so is inaction. So is pride.*

She weighed his threat against what he offered: a way into the Abyss. Names. Knowledge. Maybe even a route to her sister. But trusting him could fracture the group. Already, the tension was pulling them apart at the seams. Shorte wouldn't tolerate it. Gideon might try to rein him in, but not without backlash. *And if he betrays us?* A thought came swiftly, cold and clean. *Then I kill him.* But what scared her more was the doubt lingering underneath it: *What if I hesitate? What if I can't because he's blood?* She hated that the question existed. Hated that no one else could make this call but her.

Raven sat still, feeling the weight of every expectation in the room press against her skin. *I'm a Mortal Guardian. And if I've learned anything, it's that trusting the wrong person can break a world.* She breathed in through her nose, slow and deep, and finally said, voice flat but resolute: "We use him. But if he so much as breathes wrong, I'll end him myself."

"If Aushade helps, I'll help," the unfamiliar feminine voice chimed in from near the prisoner, her tone resolute.

"And you are who, *matey*?" Shorte asked with a hint of sarcasm.

"See what I have to put up with?" the female stranger replied. "More pirate jokes."

"You chose that life," Aushade snickered, amusement coloring his voice. "The donkey and the pirate."

"Well, we know who the ass is," Shorte retorted with a snort. "Now we want to know who the pirate is."

From the corner of Raven's eye, a wavy blur came from the guests' room hallway as the stranger introduced herself. "Captain Ramzey Porter."

"What's the payout?" Ashley asked pragmatically. "The Abyss is no small task."

Raven returned her attention to the group with resolve. "The target is priceless."

"Oh, honey! I'm in," Ashley declared enthusiastically.

"Count me in," Gobs answered firmly.

Raven finished her drink, and a serene stillness settled over her, leaving a lingering sense of peace and contentment.

Avalann began counting on her fingers. "That's nine for Operation Resurrection."

*Wait, her fingers!* Raven could see Avalann's fingers. Relief flooded her as she was about to announce the news, but a voice interrupted her.

"Make it ten," Thomas announced confidently, entering the bar and holding what appeared to be a feather.

"Is that"—Celeste stepped closer to the paladin, fixated on the feather— "from a Realm Guardian?"

"Yes," Thomas confirmed. "From the Abyss, and you won't believe who gave it to me."

"I think I know." Aushade snickered darkly, a hint of defiance in his voice. The paladin noticed the necromancer shackled in the corner and rushed over, landing a punch as chaos erupted again. Shorte joined Thomas, delivering a swift blow to Aushade's stomach. Ramzey and Jarz hurried to intervene, attempting to separate the three combatants before the situation escalated further.

Raven reacted swiftly, grabbing her jeweled dagger and hurling it past the assailants' heads. It lodged into the back wall with a solid thunk. "We need to put aside our differences until we rescue Carya," she declared firmly, her voice cutting through the tumultuous atmosphere.

Izarra's smile was radiant. "You can see again."

The fighting ceased abruptly as the others murmured, retreating to their respective spots in the room.

Shorte's grumble broke the silence. "It's his fault we're in this mess," he muttered, casting a wary eye at Aushade.

Ramzey wiped a trickle of blood from Aushade's face as she helped him stand. Aushade gasped, trying to catch his breath after the barrage of punches.

"I'm going, too," Raven stated firmly, meeting the piercing gazes of everyone in the room.

"Are you sure?" Gobs asked softly.

"I'm going!" Raven repeated, her voice tinged with nervous resolve.

"Oh no, you're not," Avalann replied firmly, crossing her arms. "Elf traditions don't allow expecting mothers to do anything but be pampered by the family."

Izarra frowned deeply. "And I don't think Carya would want you to take that risk."

Shorte snorted dismissively. "I don't know why you two are making such a big fuss. My G-ma went hunting up to the day she had my Ma. Dropped her while gutting a large boar. She still has the tusk mounted on the wall."

"This is different! She's still half-elf," Avalann argued passionately. "And we're talking about entering the Inferno-Plane here."

Raven raised her hand, signaling for silence. "Enough! This is my decision." The group stared at her nervously, awaiting her following words. She took a deep breath, steadying herself. "No one, and I mean *no one*, tells Gideon about my condition." Everyone nodded in solemn agreement except for Thomas, who was nose-deep in another mug, downing more ale.

Gobs stepped forward, her expression resolute. "I'll stay by your side and protect you," she offered quietly but firmly.

Raven scanned the room, expecting further objections, but the silence held. "Good, now we can continue." She motioned for everyone to pull chairs around the table, preparing to discuss their plan. Ashley escorted Aushade and positioned herself near him, casting a watchful eye. Ramzey stood nearby, ready to intervene if needed.

"Where did Celeste go?" Jarz asked, scanning the room.

"And where's the feather?" Thomas chimed in after a belch, his brows furrowed in confusion. "I must have dropped it."

"I bet Celeste took it," Izarra suggested.

"If it's from Tier," Raven said gravely. "I'm afraid she may annihilate the entire Abyss before we arrive."

"We can't worry about her right now," Avalann stated. "We need an alternative plan."

Shorte huffed in agreement. "Gideon was right. Celeste would abandon everyone to free Tier."

"We need to find another way into the Abyss," Jarz suggested, his voice calm but urgent.

The familiar butterflies fluttered in Raven's stomach, a sensation that always preceded their quests. But this time, the stress of losing Celeste and their crucial route into the Abyss turned those butterflies into tight knots. Suddenly, her vision blurred, colors swirling into purple shadows. She sat down abruptly, closed her eyes, and gently rubbed her stomach, trying to calm herself. "It's going to be all right," she whispered, taking several deep breaths to steady her nerves. When she opened them again, relief washed over her as her vision cleared. She could see her friends staring back at her worriedly.

Aushade, standing nearby and still holding a rag from the earlier scuffle under his nose, cleared his throat, drawing everyone's attention. "I can get you into the Abyss."

# CHAPTER TWENTY-FOUR

## REDEMPTION

Gideon paced on the dirt road in front of the Omlett Inn, back and forth, his boots scuffing the ground with each agitated step. He took deep, deliberate breaths to control his temper, but his cheek still tingled from the sharp impact of Celeste's hand. He rubbed it distractedly, the sting a bitter reminder he was still vulnerable. *I can't believe she did that in front of everyone.* The fact of it being a display of public humiliation burned hotter than the slap itself.

As he turned abruptly, his shoulder collided with an elf carrying two woven rice baskets, nearly toppling one. "I'm sorry," Gideon apologized quickly, stepping back. The elf, a slender figure with chestnut hair cascading over his shoulders, merely nodded and continued on his way south, his steps graceful and unhurried despite the near collision.

Gideon glanced around, noticing the townsfolk bustling about, their faces pinched with anxiety. The aftermath of recent events was evident; many residents moved with a sense of urgency, their focus shifting as if anticipating another attack.

The wooden door of the Inn creaked open behind him, then closed with a soft thud. Gideon turned to see his friend approaching with a look of concern on his face.

"You all right?" Eugor asked.

"I'm fine," Gideon replied, though his voice lacked conviction.

As they spoke, a female dwarf and her young son walked by, leading a sturdy mule laden with supplies. The dwarf woman, with braided auburn hair and a warm smile, greeted them cheerfully. "G'day, King Naelo," she said, dipping her head respectfully.

"Good day, Dranna," King Naelo replied, returning her smile. "How's your husband?"

"Dovil is healing from the attack," Dranna answered, her expression shifting to one of concern. "Thank Blade, the fight didn't last long. Damli and I have handled his chores while he's on the mend."

"That's a good lad," Eugor said, ruffling the boy's hair. The child beamed up at him, pride evident in his eyes, before they continued on their way.

Gideon sank onto the Inn's wooden steps, lowering his head into his hands as his thoughts swirled. The sting on his cheek had dulled, but the emotional grief lingered, gnawing at his insides.

"You do realize you aren't the first to feel that hand," Eugor sighed. "If you recall, I said some things before Celeste left me for the guardian position. I still regret it."

"I just spoke the truth," Gideon replied defensively as he looked away, a muscle twitching in his jaw.

"You accused her of not caring about anyone but herself," Eugor responded gently but firmly, leaning against a wooden cart.

"It's exactly what you said that day, now that I think about it," Gideon recalled as he glanced at his friend.

"At the time, I thought she *did* care only about herself." Eugor sat on the steps beside his friend and gave his shoulder a reassuring pat. "But people change. Give her a chance."

"She gave up Blade, thinking only about herself," Gideon argued, frustrated.

"Like you mentioned, it was long ago, and I've moved on. Celeste allows you to have company in the Fey Realm."

"Only because I helped her search for Tier in the Abyss Realm." Gideon's eyes narrowed slightly as he remembered the harrowing journey.

"What's the harm of her looking for him while helping search for Carya?" Eugor asked.

"How can we trust that she won't abandon the others?" Gideon's voice rose with exasperation.

"The same way I trust you. We're family," Eugor said softly, his gaze steady and unwavering.

"It's been so long since you, Celeste, and I were the Inseparable Trio."

Eugor stepped closer, placing a hand on Gideon's shoulder—not to comfort, but to anchor him. "What's really bothering you?"

The guardian huffed, rubbing his temples. "I can't keep hiding from Elora. I need to resolve this. Celeste and I have two marks against us. The High Council will probably oust us."

"I'm sure Brugg could use an assistant." Eugor nudged him playfully, a grin spreading across his face. "You'll need a fallback career after she's through with you."

Gideon chuckled as some of the tension eased from his shoulders. He stood and, with a swift motion, cast a flickering red portal to the High Council. The air around them crackled with energy as the portal stabilized. "Let me deal with this, and when I return, just have that broom ready."

"Deal," Eugor agreed, shaking Gideon's hand firmly. "I need to go check on Mug. He's been busy at his factory on some secret project. I'm beginning to miss that gnome."

"I'm sure he's distraught about that necromancer using the Rust Metal Spell on his golems. He's probably working night and day to ensure that doesn't happen again."

"I guess." Eugor shrugged, a thoughtful look crossing his face. "Maybe I'll take him to get something to eat. He could use a break."

"That's a good idea. Mug always works better with a full stomach. Make sure you visit Captain Plunkett, too."

"I will, and I'll inform Raven that you have returned to the High Council," Eugor said before stepping away from the portal.

Gideon nodded and watched his friend head to the stables as a young woman, who appeared crying, approached the king. With a final glance, he realized it was Lilly Spriglockett. As Eugor hugged her, Gideon thought, *He's a great king.*

Taking a deep breath, he stepped through the portal, feeling the familiar magic rush envelop him. He emerged onto the polished marble floor of the Great Hall, the air filled with the scent of incense. The two guards at the ornate golden doors immediately straightened and escorted him into the main chamber.

The room's grandeur was imposing, with high ceilings adorned with intricate frescoes and towering pillars that seemed to touch the sky. At the head of the room, Tessk, dressed in a flowing red robe, lounged in Elora's chair, his presence both commanding and unsettling.

"I wasn't informed you were in charge now," Gideon sneered, each step deliberate as he closed the distance.

A cold, dismissive voice echoed in his mind—*for now.*

"Get out of my head," Gideon snapped, clenching his fists.

"If you insist, Guardian," the Abyss representative responded, his gravelly voice dripping with condescension.

"Where's Elora?"

The corner of Tessk's mouth twisted among his flanges. "Doing your job."

"I want to see her," Gideon insisted, his voice firm.

Tessk rose, his movements fluid and alien, tentacles flailing disconcertingly. "Follow me." He descended from the High Council bench with an almost serpentine grace, moving through the rear doors with an air of authority.

Gideon followed, the two guards tailing close behind.

The ceredella knocked before opening a side door in the hall into a bright chamber. A mahogany desk trimmed with gold sat in the center, catching the light from Cenergy that shimmered through the window. The chamber walls were adorned with intricate drawings of Elora's former home, Spires Hand, the first Elven city of Euphrasia. The artwork was detailed and vibrant, capturing the splendor of the ancient city. In the corner, on a plush cushion, Elora knelt, her posture serene and meditative.

"Gideon Grindal," Elora stated without opening her eyes, her voice calm and composed.

"Elora Clover," Gideon said, the name catching slightly in his throat as he stepped forward. His fingers flexed at his sides, restless, barely resisting the urge to pace. The formal words came out clipped, tight, as if he were holding back everything he needed to say until the moment allowed it.

"I saw your portal appear in Omlett." She struggled slightly as she stood. Her movements were graceful yet tinged with fatigue. "Leave us," she commanded, shaking her hand and waving the ceredella and the council guards away. Gideon couldn't help but wonder what telepathic message Tessk must have sent her. The trio exited, closing the door behind them.

"Sit." She gestured to the wooden chair before her desk. Gideon complied, settling into the seat as Elora walked to a side table and poured two drinks. The room was filled with the rich scent of mulberry wine as she handed him a golden goblet. "Are you here to return the Artifact of Souls?"

"No, I want to know my status with the High Council."

"Technically, you didn't break any rules," Elora answered, her expression neutral as she sat across from him. She sipped her wine, the goblet looking delicate in her slender fingers. "I held you here as a personal decision. I didn't want you to interfere in the war. But we need the artifact to remain here."

"I don't have it." Gideon eyed the drink warily, deciding against consuming anything until he knew more about his fate. "However, I did get visual proof that the Abyss was involved."

"Is that so?" Elora murmured, a hint of tension tightening her expression.

"A flox and a succubus."

"That's a serious accusation," the high-elf responded coolly, sipping her wine deliberately. Her attention never wavered from Gideon.

"Elora, they used the beast's tails to destroy entire cities, including Suttiir." Gideon's voice trembled with urgency. "The succubus has hidden her aura using an anti-scry spell. I think they've imprisoned Tier."

"That's a grave and dangerous claim," Elora replied.

"I beg you to open an investigation," Gideon pleaded.

"I—" Her words were cut off as the door burst open.

Celeste, wrestling with two guards, stormed into the room, waving a large feather. "Gideon! It's Tier's!"

Tessk quickly approached her, seizing the feather with his tentacles.

"Release her," Elora ordered, standing beside Gideon. Celeste yanked the feather from Tessk's grip and shoved him aside, handing the feather to Elora with shaking hands.

"Where did you get this?" Elora turned the feather over in her hands and examined it closely.

"It was delivered to a human male," Celeste said, her voice tinged with something hollow.

"The succubus," Gideon murmured, piecing it together. "But why would she?"

"Change of heart?" Celeste offered, weariness etched into every word. "It happens to the worst of us."

"Tessk, what do you know of this?" Gideon snapped, turning a fierce glare on the ceredella.

"Nothing, I assure you," Tessk responded defensively, his tentacles twitching.

Gideon charged at him, but Elora swiftly stepped between them, holding up a hand to prevent the conflict from escalating.

"I'm ordering an investigation of the Abyss Realm," Elora declared, authoritative and unyielding. Tessk nodded calmly, though his eyes flickered with something unspoken before he left the room.

"What happens next?" Celeste implored, her voice barely a whisper.

"I'll notify Blade, Ellie, and Ozul to organize the case," Elora answered decisively. "Gideon, you must return to work so I can lead the investigation. You're officially reinstated as the Mortal Realm Guardian. Keep me informed if the succubus or flox return."

"Thank you, I will." Gideon bowed deeply as Elora walked to the door.

The High Council leader turned back, a small, genuine smile softening her stern features. "Glad to have you back, Mister Grindal. We'll keep you informed about Tier. But for now, both of you, get back to work." The guardians nodded as she exited, leaving an air of fierce focus in the room.

Gideon turned to Celeste and took her hand in his. "I'm sorry."

"Me too," Celeste responded, gently caressing the cheek she had slapped earlier. "This is no time for us to drift apart." She removed her hand and gazed out the window, her expression wistful. "It hurts that everyone thinks I only care about myself."

"I know that's not true," Gideon sighed. "You helped me get through my training at Waterfront."

Celeste turned back to face him, wiping away a tear. "And you introduced me to Euwee," she responded, her voice cracking slightly, but she smiled. "I'm aware I hurt him and want to atone for it. That's why I'll do everything possible to return Carya to him."

"I should report you for going, but I won't." Gideon hugged his friend tightly, whispering, "I won't stop you or them, but please watch over Raven for me."

"You should help, Gideon. The Abyss is involved. You have every right," Celeste pleaded.

"I can fight them if they are physically in the Mortal Realm, but I can't invade another realm. I just got my honor back," Gideon responded.

"And you dared to call me selfish. Raven's carrying—" Celeste faltered.

"Carrying what?"

Celeste paused briefly. "A heavy burden. Eugor could lose more than just Carya." She turned away and headed through the circular chamber and down past the holding cells.

Gideon followed her to the Room of Portals, a hexagon-shaped chamber that housed portals to all the realms. The air sparkled with residual magic, and the faint hum of energy filled the space. A cylindrical diamond chandelier hung at the center of the room, casting prismatic reflections across the polished marble floor. A narrow red carpet ran from the entrance to the chandelier, with five additional runners branching off to each archway. Above each arch, the symbols for the portal spells to each realm were intricately carved.

"Maybe I can talk Elora into getting the Abyss to hand over Carya," Celeste mused aloud.

Gideon smirked. "I'll send Blade your way because you'll need all the luck for that."

"If you'll excuse me, I need to return to the Fey to gather a few things," Celeste commented, heading toward the Fey portal. "I had your wagon returned to your camp."

"Thank you," Gideon replied, grateful for the gesture.

Then she turned to him, her expression pained. "How long have I been saying we need to find Tier? Everyone ignored me, accusing me of just being a paranoid lover."

"I went in with you," Gideon countered, his voice edged with frustration.

"That's what I'm trying to explain," Celeste argued, her tone pleading. "It's always just us." She moved closer, taking Gideon's hands in hers. "Raven needs you. Her *family* needs you."

Gideon struggled to hold back his emotions, his heart heavy with conflicting responsibilities. "My family," he murmured. "I can't." He gently released Celeste's hands and turned away, exiting the room with a determined stride. He tried to appear confident, to hide the hurt that gnawed at him.

Returning to the Great Hall, Gideon summoned his resolve, casting a portal that shimmered into existence. Stepping through, he found himself back at his camp. Though he had only been away briefly in the High Council, an entire day had passed in the Mortal Realm. Dark, wintry clouds hung low over the horizon, casting a somber light over the landscape.

His red gypsy-style wagon stood across from the roaring waterfall, a solitary beacon amid the solitude. Once bustling with activity, the camp felt empty and desolate, amplifying the loneliness that weighed on Gideon's heart.

Inside the wagon, the interior was disheveled and cluttered. Crumpled white bed sheets lay in a ball on the bed, papers and spell books scattered across the floor, *just like how my life feels right now.*

Clearing a spot on the bed, Gideon sat heavily on the edge. Memories flooded his thoughts—of Raven, their moments together, and the scroll she had given him that proclaimed her love. The scroll still hung next to the window, pinned by a boot knife. He reached for it, tracing the words softly with his fingertips. "I love you," the words echoed in the confines of the wagon.

Gideon closed his eyes and focused on his duties as guardian to distract himself from the whirlwind of emotions and thoughts about Raven's risky plan. A crimson spark lit his mind, signaling a presence near his wagon. Opening his eyes, he saw Celeste standing at the door, her expression serious and controlled.

"What—"

"There's something you need to know about Raven."

## CHAPTER TWENTY-FIVE

# THE ENEMY OF
# MY ENEMY

"Rise and shine," a melodic female voice echoed through the room, causing Raven to squint against the morning sun. She quickly turned from the sun and curled into a fetal position, clutching a pillow tightly.

"Carya?" Raven whispered, her voice thick with sleep.

"Sorry to disappoint you," the voice responded sadly. "I had your room prepared for you, but it seemed untouched, so I thought I might find you here. I have fresh water for the washbowl and some breakfast."

"Cee?" Raven rolled onto her back, shielding her eyes from the sunlight that streamed through the window.

"The one *and* only—" the bard sang in perfect pitch as she poured water into the washbasin.

"You seem chipper this morning," Raven mumbled as the bard whistled a tune while setting a tray on the desk. "What are you doing?"

"I'm filling in for Brugg while he recovers," Cyndi replied, poking at the logs in the fireplace. "I'm also teaching him how to sing."

Raven giggled softly. "Good luck with that."

Cyndi's eyes twinkled. "Oh, I've already got him croaking out a decent ballad."

"I can't wait for that concert." Raven rolled to her side and pulled a pillow over her eyes. "Now I understand why Carya was always up so early. The sun's so bright."

The mattress dipped slightly, indicating Cyndi sat on the edge of the bed. Raven sensed the bard looking at her through the pillow and lowered it to find the woman grinning.

"You know?" Raven asked, half-amused and half-exhausted.

"If you ever need a nursemaid," Cyndi squeaked excitedly.

"How?"

"I was retrieving food from the pantry for Brugg and myself when the little elf announced it to the Inn," Cyndi explained with a chuckle.

"Great," Raven groaned. "Everyone knows but my parents and Gideon."

"I won't say a word," Cyndi promised earnestly. "But if you need anything, just ask."

"I will," Raven replied with a half-grin.

"There's some sliced fruit for you and a mug of freshly squeezed juice on the side table," Cyndi informed her, standing up. "It's the same plate your sister used to prepare breakfast for Brugg and me every morning."

"Carya?" Raven repeated, surprised, as she sat up in bed. "My sister, Carya?"

"Yes," Cyndi confirmed, her smile warm. "Every morning before she left for the church."

"And here I thought she left early to bootlick the high priest," Raven remarked with a mixture of fondness and teasing.

"She was late quite often. And speaking of late, I need to get downstairs."

"I never knew that about her," Raven responded softly. "I always thought she was perfect."

Cyndi smiled warmly, stopping at the door. "She was close." The soft click punctuated her exit from the room.

The rogue stirred and stretched lazily, blinking against the morning sunlight filtering through the window. Outside, the winter day stretched crisp and bright; the river below flowed serenely under the cold, blue sky. *Such a beautiful view, although I can't wait for spring.*

Raven splashed warm water on her face, awakening her senses as she refreshed herself. Her fingers absentmindedly picked at the fresh berries as her thoughts returned to the previous day's events. The quest had been arduous, revelations unfolding like delicate petals. The necromancer—her own cousin—and the discovery of a child—*my child.*

After finishing the last of the juice, Raven moved to dress for the day, the faint clink of coins in her pouch a reassuring weight against her side. She counted each coin carefully, ensuring enough to settle with the bounty hunters. A sudden draft fluttered the curtains, sending a chill through the room and prompting Raven to reach for her long, weathered winter coat hanging by the door. She slipped it on.

She pulled open the front door, its hinges creaking softly in protest. Outside, the early morning light cast a serene glow over the fresh, snow-covered landscape. Raven buttoned her coat against the crisp air, the faint aroma of pine and wood smoke drifting on the breeze.

The cold wind picked up, swirling around Raven and tugging at her ponytail as she made her way toward Suttiir Bridge, past the somber rows of family burial plots. She paused briefly at Carya's grave, where fresh soil covered the once-open earth, her sister's headstone standing solemnly in place. A shiver ran down Raven's arms, goosebumps rising on her skin as she stood, silently acknowledging that her sister was no longer there.

With a deep breath, Raven crossed the road and veered onto the familiar dirt path that wound alongside the tranquil river. The sound of water gently lapping against the banks soothed her nerves, the rhythmic flow contrasting the turbulent emotions churning within her. The path stretched ahead, lined with frost-kissed grass and scattered leaves.

Farther down, at Fischer's Docks, Raven noticed a tall ship moored, an ornate squid intricately carved onto its bow. Its presence drew her gaze, the craftsmanship of the carving catching the morning light as she continued along the bank.

Memories of the previous night flooded back. Izarra had insisted that she meet her mother, their conversation revolving around Thistlebane and the new orphanage for children left parentless by recent tragedies. *Am I doing the right thing?* Her hand instinctively rested on her stomach, a gentle whisper escaping her lips, "I want you to meet your Aunt Carya. The group will protect us."

Approaching the pier where a ship docked, Raven found herself before two male human guards stationed there. "Is this the *Sea Squid*?"

"Sure is," the taller guard said.

Raven moved to step between them, intent on continuing her path, but the guards swiftly blocked her route.

"Halt," the taller guard interjected firmly, raising a hand to signal her to stop. "You don't have—"

"Permission granted," a gruff voice echoed across the deck, carrying over the gentle lapping of the currents.

Raven glanced up from the dock, squinting against the morning sun. Wrapped in a weather-beaten fur robe, Ashley stood at the ship's railing. In one hand, the warrior held a steaming mug. With the other, she beckoned the rogue to come aboard. Raven nodded to the two guards, who parted to allow her passage onto the small platform that led up to the ship, their eyes watchful.

"Welcome aboard, Princess," Ashley greeted warmly, blowing gently on her drink. Her brown hair was tied in a practical bun, strands escaping to frame her weathered face. "Care for some hot cocoa?"

"No, thank you," Raven replied, her gaze sweeping across the ship's deck.

"Most of the crew are still belowdecks catching some much-needed shut-eye." Ashley gestured toward the stern with a tilt of her mug. "Gobs and I tend to keep watch up here."

As they moved along the deck, Ashley pointed out various features of the ship. "The captain's quarters are below the helm deck," she mentioned, indicating the stern. "But our cabins are forward, under the forecastle."

Entering a narrow passageway, Ashley pushed open a sturdy wooden door, revealing a compact chamber. The space was practical, dominated by a single wooden bed bolted securely to the wall. A small desk provided the only semblance of personal space, creating a narrow aisle between the two fixtures.

"Hold this," Ashley instructed casually, passing her mug of cocoa to Raven. She lifted the bed and secured it efficiently, creating more room in the cramped quarters. Unchaining two stools from the wall, she slid one over to Raven. "It's not a throne, but it'll do. Make yourself comfortable."

"Thank you," Raven replied softly, returning the drink to Ashley and settling onto the stool.

"So what brings you here this early? Thought Gobs and I were scheduled to receive our reward later today."

"I just needed fresh air," Raven admitted quietly.

"And to learn more about True Eyes, didn't you?"

"How did you find out?"

The warrior took a slow, thoughtful sip of her cocoa, her gaze fixed on Raven as if weighing each word carefully. "The legends have been passed down through my village for generations."

"What legends?" Raven leaned forward with interest.

Ashley set her drink on the desk beside her and reached into a drawer, pulling out a small, weathered box. Opening it carefully, she revealed two blank parchments inside. She handed them to Raven, who took them cautiously.

"These are part of the lore of Draakland," Ashley explained, her eyes seeming to glow with intensity as she spoke. "And here are the surnames of known Gooners—or Draakgoons, as you called them. My Great Aunt Mary entrusted these to me."

Raven studied the parchments, her brow furrowing in concentration. "So I'm not the only one."

Ashley smiled reassuringly. "No, you're not alone." She held up one of the parchments, showing Raven a section that displayed a map of Draakland, its contours marked in faded ink. The other parchment listed names—surnames that hinted at a lineage tied to the legendary Gooners.

"And by the way, I didn't come up with the term Draakgoons," Raven admitted. "It's what the lady in the green cloak called them when she spoke to me."

Ashley's expression turned thoughtful. "You met Cadence Albury?"

"I'm not familiar with that name."

"She's a figure of great renown," Ashley explained with a hint of reverence. "According to our family lore, Cadence Albury was the sorceress who saved the dragons from extinction during the Dragon Wars. Legend has it she single-handedly burned down the war chamber at Waterfront, securing dragonkind's survival."

Raven listened intently, her mind racing with the weight of ancient tales and newfound connections. "Besides your eyes, do you have other traits?" Raven asked, her voice tinged with curiosity.

"Not many," Ashley replied, handing the parchments over.

Raven focused, her concentration definite as she willed her vision to glow with a deep purple hue. "I can see it," she murmured, her gaze fixed on the parchments in her hands. "These are similar to the one I found at Waterfront." She examined the map on the parchment. Suddenly, her eyes widened, and her pulse quickened as she pointed to a tribal mark etched on the map. "My map has the other half of this heart."

Ashley leaned in, studying the edges of the parchment. "Look here," she pointed, tracing faint markings near the margins. "Do you see these? They seem to be the top and bottom pieces of different hearts."

"I noticed those marks, but I didn't understand their significance," Raven admitted, flipping to the other parchment and scanning the list of names. "Albury, Mack, Everston, Jules, Nell, Preston. But no Naelo."

"These names have been echoed through centuries," Ashley remarked, her eyes returning to their typical hue.

"I think Cadence is trying to reach out to us," Raven said earnestly, the purple glow fading as she spoke.

"We'd have to sail to Draakland," Ashley responded thoughtfully, placing the parchments back in the drawer.

Raven stood abruptly, her movements purposeful as she opened her coin pouch and emptied its contents onto the desk with a resolute clatter. "This is payment for the bounty, for your help in the Abyss, and to fund our voyage to Draakland."

The coins gleamed in the faint light of the cabin, a tangible testament to Raven's determination and the gravity of their shared quest.

"That's a lot of coins," Ashley remarked, her brow creasing slightly as she counted the PIPs on top of the stack. "Seven, I noticed."

"Is that a yes?"

"I'll need to confirm with Captain Porter." Ashley tapped her fingers on the desk. "But I think we can make it happen. Though Draakland might not even exist anymore."

"I'm willing to take that chance. We'll set sail after we rescue Carya."

Ashley nodded in agreement, her expression thoughtful. "It could take months to reach Draakland by ship. And the baby?"

Raven's enthusiasm waned as she sighed deeply, her shoulders slumping. "Oh."

A soft knock interrupted their conversation. Ashley looked up and called, "Enter."

Gobs poked her head inside, her expression curious. "I'm heading to breakfast. Anything you two want?"

"I'm good," Ashley replied, raising her mug of cocoa. "This is my fifth cup already."

Gobs shook her head incredulously. Her gaze shifted to Raven. "Princess?"

"No, thank you."

"You're eating for two, you know," Gobs pointed out gently.

"I already ate," Raven snapped back.

The druid pursed her lips, casting a disapproving glance at them both before abruptly closing the door behind her with a thud.

"She's just concerned for your well-being," Ashley remarked calmly as Raven huffed in annoyance. "Are you all right?"

Raven nodded briskly. "I'm fine. I must return home and figure out how to tell my parents about all this."

"I'll escort you off the ship."

The air outside was crisp, carrying the scent of salt and adventure as they stepped onto the deck. The morning sun painted the horizon in hues of gold and pink, casting a warm glow over the ship.

Raven walked alongside Ashley, making her way to the port side toward the boat ramp. As they passed the captain's quarters, Raven froze when she spotted Aushade leaning casually against the ship's railing, wrapped snugly in bedding.

"What the spell?" Raven exclaimed. "You're supposed to be in a prison cell."

Aushade turned to face her, his expression nonchalant. "Not now, cousin," he replied coolly, his gaze fixed on the distant shoreline.

"Don't call me that," Raven snapped. "We may share blood, but that's all."

Aushade shrugged indifferently as Raven's frustration mounted visibly.

"And what's with the silk sheets?" she demanded, pointing accusingly.

"They're surprisingly warm in the cold and cool in the warmth. Almost magical." Aushade smirked, his voice dripping with sarcasm.

Raven's temper flared. Without hesitation, she seized a push broom leaning against the ship's mast and snapped it in half over her knee with a sharp crack.

"Enough, cousin," Aushade sneered dismissively, waving her off as he continued to scan the dock.

"I told you not to call me that," Raven growled, thrusting the broken broom handle toward him. Aushade caught it effortlessly between his hands, causing his blanket to slip and fall to the deck.

"Are you really in any condition to be doing this?" Aushade taunted.

Raven's grin was sharp and determined. "Nissrę Nar," she uttered softly. Electricity crackled from her fingertips down the length of the broom handle, coursing through Aushade and bringing him to his knees with a cry of pain. Releasing the handle, Raven stood over him, breathing heavily but satisfied.

Despite the pain etched on his face, Aushade glanced at her with surprise and admiration. "I'm grateful wood isn't the best conductor," he quipped weakly, his leer tinged with respect. "But it still hurts."

"I'm not trying to kill you—yet," Raven retorted with barely restrained annoyance.

Aushade winced slightly as he pushed himself upright, brushing off his robe. "Just don't use that acid spit. I'm still healing from the last one."

"I saw you casting something. What are you up to?" Raven demanded, eyeing him suspiciously.

"Nothing—I swear," Aushade replied, raising his hands defensively.

"Do you want me to scar the other cheek?" Raven threatened, her tone low and dangerous.

"Just wait a moment—they're almost here." Aushade pointed toward the docks.

"Who?" Raven asked. She turned to follow his gaze just as a mangled squirrel appeared, scrambling up the ship's rail and dropping a wildflower at her feet. With a shudder of revulsion, the undead critter scurried off the boat and splashed into the water.

"What the—"

The door of the captain's quarters swung open, and Captain Ramzey Porter emerged, dressed in a crisp white robe. "What's going on out here?" she asked, her brow furrowed in confusion.

Two decayed mice suddenly appeared, dropping a wildflower beside Raven before meeting the same fate in the water as the squirrel. Several more undead critters followed suit, delivering their floral offerings before disappearing into the depths.

"See, no harm done," Aushade mocked, wrapping himself tighter in the blanket. "They're already dead."

"You sent dead rodents to collect wild snow flowers?" Raven exclaimed, a mixture of horror and repulsion crossing her face.

"I have to," Aushade explained defensively. "I'm not allowed off the ship."

Raven huffed in exasperation. "You won't win me over with a bunch of flowers." She brushed the wilted blooms aside with the tip of her boot.

"They aren't for you—they're for her." Aushade chuckled, nodding toward Captain Porter. "To show my appreciation for the hospitality. There wasn't much of a selection."

Ramzey picked up the blue and purple flowers and a few white winter roses. "Thank you." She inhaled the delicate fragrance of the flowers before looking up. "Why don't you put down the broomstick, and we can all talk in my quarters."

"No!" Ashley exclaimed dramatically, her disappointment evident as she and Gobs sat perched on barrels nearby, nibbling on food from a plate and watching the unfolding scene with amused interest. Ashley took another sip of her cocoa, clearly entertained by the unexpected drama.

"Fine," Raven sighed, dropping the broken broomstick and following Ramzey and Aushade. "Nice quarters," she remarked dryly upon entering.

"Thank you," Ramzey responded, placing the flowers gently on her desk. She retrieved an empty rum bottle, rinsed it, and filled it with fresh water from her canteen before arranging the flowers.

"Cute," Raven remarked sarcastically. She began to inspect the room, noting its functional yet comfortable layout, while Aushade settled himself on the edge of the bed, watching her curiously.

Raven glanced from Aushade to Ramzey and back again. "We're just friends," Ramzey blurted out suddenly, breaking the silence.

"That's none of my business," Raven replied evenly, her gaze flickering toward Aushade. "It's just that monsters usually sleep *under* the bed."

Aushade chuckled lightly. "You're funny, cousin. I can see why Jarz is fond of you."

"Call me cousin again," Raven warned, her voice low and dangerous, "and I'll break that bottle so I can cut your tongue into a thousand pieces and use your mouth as a planter."

Aushade's expression turned serious. "One day, I'll be privileged to call you family again."

"Doubtful," Raven spat back.

"Would you like a drink?" Ramzey intervened, trying to defuse the tension. Raven shot her a pointed look.

"Oh, right," Ramzey corrected quickly. "How about some tea?"

"I would like *him* in a cell at the Omlett Prison," Raven stated firmly, glaring at Aushade.

"I'm not going anywhere. I'm done fighting," Aushade retorted defiantly. "I promised you I'd help get the group into the Abyss."

"You may think the war is over, but many people would beg to differ. They would love to get their hands on you," Raven retorted sharply.

"Maybe it's a good thing I'm not allowed off this ship," Aushade replied. "I'm a changed man."

"As opposed to what?" Raven challenged. "A man who mutilated a demon fox to wreak havoc on defenseless families?"

"I didn't realize the extent of the destruction it would cause," Aushade admitted, his voice heavy with regret.

"When did you?" Raven pressed on, her voice cutting through the room like a blade. "After the first city? The second? The third?"

Aushade hesitated, visibly struggling to find words under Raven's relentless scrutiny. "I—"

"Or maybe it hit you after Suttiir?" Raven's voice rose with accusation. "Or when you sent it charging into the heart of Omlett, where your own family lived!"

"I think he understands," Ramzey interjected calmly, sensing the intensity of Raven's anger.

"Does he? What if Jarz hadn't been there? We'd be having a different discussion right now, or one of us would be dead," Raven continued.

Aushade sat in silence, his expression somber.

"You want to be part of this family?" Raven asked, her tone sharp, her attention locked on Aushade. "On second thought, I can't even fathom that— not after what you did to Carya and the others."

"We can save her," Aushade's voice cracked slightly, pleading. "Jarz and I—"

"I'm aware of the plan. But you put Carya in this situation. And what about all the other innocent victims who can't be returned?" Raven shot him a challenging look. "I should make you walk the plank and feed you to the dire-sharks."

Ramzey muttered quietly, "More pirate jokes."

"I want to fix what I can," Aushade declared, standing with his arms crossed. "And if that means I earn your trust by sitting in Omlett's prison cell in a Truth Zone, so be it. But you'll find my answers will remain the same."

Raven paused, considering his words carefully. "I trust Jarz, and if he says we need you, then we need you. But for your own sake, don't leave this ship." Aushade nodded in acknowledgment.

"I won't let him," Ramzey affirmed, her voice steady and reassuring.

"I'll keep you informed when we're ready for the trip," Raven added, softening her tone despite her lingering distrust.

"For what it's worth," Aushade frowned deeply, genuine regret evident in his eyes, "I'm truly sorry."

"We'll see," Raven replied coolly, her expression unreadable, as a sudden commotion erupted outside the captain's quarters.

Raven and Ramzey hurried to the door and stepped out onto the deck. They found Ashley and Gobs standing portside and the crew, armed and looking tense.

"What in the Abyss is going on?" Ramzey demanded, her voice commanding attention as she scanned the scene before her.

"He's insisting on boarding the ship," Ashley growled, her grip tightening on her axes as she stared out toward the docks.

"Who?" Raven asked urgently, rushing to join Ashley at the ship's side. Her heart sank as she saw Gideon approaching, his white wings flexing and his vorpal sword gleaming in the sunlight. Two guards stationed on the docks flew off their feet into the water below. The first guard surfaced quickly, gasping for air and struggling against the cold current, while his heavier companion thrashed about, trying desperately to stay afloat.

"Him," Ashley confirmed grimly.

Raven groaned inwardly. "If you want your ship to remain intact, Captain, I recommend that your men stand down," she advised, her voice tense.

Ramzey hesitated. After a brief moment, she signaled her men to disperse and return to their duties. Meanwhile, Raven hurried down the gangplank to meet Gideon on the dock, her heart racing. She threw her arms around him in a quick embrace, but he gently pushed her away, still holding his weapon at the ready.

"Your eyes?" Gideon asked, his voice relieved as he scanned her face.

"I'm fine," Raven reassured him quickly. "Gobs helped with some herbal drink."

Gideon glanced at Gobs, who waved at him from the ship with a sheepish grin. His expression darkened with anger. "You thought you could keep this a secret?" he demanded through gritted teeth.

Raven's heart slammed against her ribs. *Oh no . . . he knows.* "What?" She was bewildered by his sudden hostility, but she was already bracing herself for whatever came next.

"Celeste informed me," Gideon continued, his tone sharp with disappointment.

Raven's blood turned to ice. *She promised she wouldn't.*

"She did?" Her voice cracked, the edges fraying with panic. She took a shaky breath, trying to hold herself together. "I was going to tell you . . ." Her chest tightened, her pulse racing. She searched his face for answers, but all she found was rage. Her hands instinctively settled over her stomach, the gesture almost protective. "I thought you would be excited," she said, her voice trembling with hurt. Her world felt like it was bending; this was supposed to be a turning point, a moment of joy. But instead, it was unraveling.

"Excited?" Gideon repeated, his voice sharp with disbelief. "Why would I be excited?"

Raven's heart stopped. *I would rather be pelted by a thousand magic missiles than hear him say that.*

He continued, "Why would I be excited that you're working *with* the necromancer who caused nothing but heartache and destruction in my realm?"

"Oh," she replied softly, but it wasn't gentle understanding. It was brittle. Cracking. Shattering. "Oh." Her gaze dropped. She couldn't bear to look at him now. Not with that wide-eyed bewilderment, not when she'd misread everything so thoroughly.

The tension in his posture eased slightly, replaced by genuine confusion. "Wait—what did you think I meant?"

*Don't say it. Don't make this worse. Don't give him something else to be disappointed in.* Raven bit her lip hard, trying to push the storm back inside where it wouldn't show. But her voice came out anyway, low and tight: "Nothing." *But it isn't nothing. It's everything.* She turned away before he could see the emotions battling inside. Her arms wrapped around her midsection—part reflex, part defense.

"He's why I was locked in a High Council cell. The man taunted me, and I'm here for justice," Gideon explained bitterly. His sudden, intense glare at the platform caused Raven to turn back. Aushade, now clad in armor, approached them with his hands held out, as if awaiting capture, as Captain Ramzey and Ashley watched from the ship.

"Take me to Omlett Prison," Aushade stated calmly, his voice resigned. "If it's for the best."

Gideon sheathed his sword and conjured Magic Cuffs, binding Aushade's hands securely. "You're going to the High Council," he declared firmly, his tone brokering no argument.

"No," Raven pleaded urgently, stepping forward. "We need him."

"Maybe it's best to forget about the Abyss," Gideon replied tersely as he created a swirling red portal leading to the High Council.

"But Carya," Raven protested before they could step through the portal.

Gideon paused, his expression conflicted, and then he lowered his head and leaned in to kiss Raven gently. "I'm sorry, dear," he murmured.

"I've promised Raven my help," Aushade interjected firmly as Gideon prepared to escort him through the portal. "I can bring Carya back. Trust me."

"You've caused enough torment," Gideon's voice boomed, filled with righteous fury as he forcibly thrust the necromancer through the pulsating portal. Aushade staggered into the swirling vortex, and with a resolute step, Gideon followed, disappearing into its depths.

Ramzey and Ashley dashed down the narrow steps that led to the dock below. The wind howled around them, carrying the lingering stench of magic from the portal's energy.

"I'm not giving up on my sister!" Raven's voice rang out, defiant as she stood in the swirling haze left behind by Gideon's departure. One hand moved instinctively to her stomach. *Your Aunt Carya.*

Beside her, Ashley tightened her grip—steady, reassuring. "We'll find another way to the Abyss . . . again."

As Raven surveyed the chaotic scene, doubt gnawed at her. *I should have told Gideon the truth, or is it too late?* Her silence felt heavier than ever, knowing the consequences of secrets kept in such a perilous time.

# CHAPTER TWENTY-SIX

# GEARED FOR HOPE

Eugor, wearing his Drizzward cloak laced with crystallized vines that channeled water away, stepped down from the carriage's box. He glanced back as rain poured in sheets, washing the grime from the girl and the machine she called Sengol. *I wish she had accepted my cloak.*

Lilly was soaked to the bone, as if the storm were trying to clean the sorrow out of her skin. Her hair clung to her face like threads, plastered to her cheeks as she wrestled the broken sentinel golem from the cart. She slammed her fist against its side. The metal released a weary creak, more complaint than resistance.

Eugor's frown deepened, tension grinding along his jaw like stone. *Sengol shielded her during the undead assault on Omlett—the same attack that claimed her father.* He exhaled slowly, fogging the cold air. *I might've told her to scrap the thing if not for that.*

Sengol's organic eye snapped toward him, glowing faintly under the rain cascade, as if it had heard him. As if it knew.

The golem wasn't made for tenderness. It had been forged for war—part sentry, part siege engine. Its head was fused to the top of the torso, a single burning eye in the center like a cursed jewel. A jagged metal crown curled above it, sharp and ruinous. There was something obscene about it, this monstrous parody of regality.

A circular orange core pulsed in its chest like a furnace, trying not to burst. *A heart, but one meant for destruction.* Its limbs were broadly segmented, the gear-like joints clanking with each shift. Spikes jutted like broken promises from its shoulders, and the claws were not meant for mercy. It looked like it belonged on a battlefield, not in the rain, not standing vigil over a grieving girl.

*I'd offer her a place with us, but would I do it for the right reasons?* That doubt had festered like a splinter under his ribs since they left for Mug's. Helping Lilly felt right, but so did protecting his daughters. *And now? Carya is gone. Raven is blind but still insists on going to the Abyss with the others. It would be madness to allow her to go.*

As they neared Mug's dwelling—half house, half mechanical jungle—Eugor's boot brushed against a tripwire. A bell chimed with a smug, slight clang.

Mug opened the door, beaming like a gnome who *enjoyed* catching friends off guard. "For a rogue, you missed my trap."

Eugor tried to muster a smile, but it came out lopsided and worn. "It's easy when your mind's distracted." He paused, then, with a sigh, laid the words out bare. "I know this is a lot to ask. And I know you're inexperienced with children, but Lilly wants to stay with you. She trusts you."

Mug appeared baffled. "Children? Isn't she, like, nineteen?"

"Exactly." Eugor gave him a measured look. "She just needs a roof and a bed. Her mother gave her life at Suttiir. Her father defended Omlett. She's got nowhere else." He observed Mug's face, noting the flicker of uncertainty that crossed it. *You built Iron Titans from scratch, but a teenage girl makes your hands shake.*

"I have a lot of projects," Mug replied.

But Eugor saw through that—what he meant was, *I'm scared.* "I get it," he said gently. "But you've always been steady. Reliable. She needs that. Not perfection."

Then Lilly stepped forward, rain sliding off her shoulders. Her voice was soft, fragile. "I want to stay here. With you." Her plea cracked something in Mug.

Eugor could see it. *Push him.* He gestured toward Sengol. "The golem's part of the package."

Mug blinked. "Sengol." He said the name with admiration. Then, almost whispering: "What if I mess it up, Night Breeze?"

Eugor stepped closer. He rarely let emotion show, but it curled around his throat like smoke. "Her parents are gone. She needs *someone.* Someone to say yes."

Mug stalled again, grasping for excuses. "What about Maggie McGee? She always finds a reason to drop in."

Eugor's patience thinned, but he didn't let it break. *You're afraid. So was I.*

Then Lilly stepped under the porch, her lashes soaked with tears. "Please, Mug. Not just for myself, but Sengol." A connection point. *Hope.* "We can work on him together." She ran back into the storm to retrieve a book from a compartment at the back of the construct. "My father infused my grandfather's soul with the machinery." She waved the book as Eugor waited, tension coiled under his ribs as Mug's eyes lit up. "It was my grandfather's dying wish for the last stage of Sengol to be operational."

Eugor didn't speak at first. The rain hissed around them like a warning, but his gaze stayed fixed on the book in Lilly's hands. *Soul-mechanics. It isn't just a theory.* His knuckles whitened against the wooden beam of the porch. "So it's true," he murmured. Not to her. Not to Mug. To the ghost of a fear he hadn't yet named. "You really can bind the dead to metal." He glanced at Mug, half-expecting refusal.

Instead, the gnome was already nodding. Mug's attention darted between the book and Lilly's storm-wet face. "Infused?" he repeated like the word might burn his tongue. But he didn't step back. Didn't argue. Something about Lilly— how she trembled and stood firm all at once—made him believe. Mug rubbed his palms on his apron, his voice quiet. "Your grandfather must've been a brilliant fool." And then softer: "I'd like to meet him. Through Sengol. Now stow the book safely before the rain washes away the ink." Mug exhaled, shoulders slumping like a gnome surrendering to something better than his fear. "I could use a hand around the shop. Plus . . . I can help repair Sengol."

The hug was sudden, messy, and real as Eugor watched and something twisted within him. *This is what hope looks like.*

As the two retreated into the factory, Eugor lingered. Rain slicked down his face, mingling with tears he would not wipe away.

Mug wrestled with the stubborn lock to his workroom, the rusty mechanism finally yielding to his persistence. "Where's Raven when you need her?" he mumbled as the loud bay door rumbled open.

*Even without her eyesight, she would have that open in a heartbeat.* The heavy metal door slid up with a groan, admitting Sengol, the towering golem, into the orb-lit workshop. *Trust Mug to trap light orbs in custom-made sconces that never burn out.*

With her usual effervescent energy, Lilly guided the massive construct to a cleared corner by the sturdy workbench. She grabbed a towel and dried off.

"You can have that space," Mug declared. Lilly's eyes sparkled, sizing Sengol's frame against the available workspace.

Eugor stood against a cluttered workbench strewn with tools and diamond dust, fondly observing the scene. "I think you'll be all right," he reassured Mug, his gaze drifting momentarily to the faded blueprints adorning the walls. "You always watched Carya and Raven for Mara and me when we needed you."

Grizzled and stoic, Mug ambled over to a section of the workshop where large sheets hung from hooks, partially concealing what lay beneath. "Only for an afternoon or evening," he grumbled softly, his rough hands pulling back the cloth to reveal a partially constructed metal talon. "But I owe it to her father. He was a good friend and a faithful employee."

"I'm sure it will only be for a short time." Eugor's attention was drawn back to Mug's work. "Is it ready?" He peered at the intricate framework of gears and hieroglyphs with keen interest.

"Not quite yet," Mug replied with a hint of frustration. "The attacks on the dwarven cities delayed my order of diamonds. Also, I'm changing the material after that necro-nut found a way to decommission my iron golems."

A sudden gasp cut through the workshop's ambient hum. Lilly dashed across the cluttered floor, clutching a large parchment covered in meticulous blueprints. "Is this a—"

"Yip," Mug confirmed proudly, his weathered face splitting into a wide grin, eyes twinkling. With surprising care, he reached into a dented brass case beside the workbench and lifted a pair of worn, soot-stained safety goggles.

Lilly's breath caught as he held them out to her. They were unmistakable. The thick leather strap, the tiny gear fastener her father had added himself, meant to adjust for pressure shifts when steam surged. Her father's touch was still all over them. Lilly's arms trembled as she reached out, fingers hovering over the lenses like they might dissolve if she dared to hold them. "These were his . . ." she whispered, her voice fraying at the edges. "He used to let me wear them when I was little. Said I looked like a 'proper engineer,' even though they swallowed my whole face." She laughed once—a slight, fragile sound that quickly became silent.

"He'd want you to have them," Mug murmured, his voice gruff but kind. "He never stopped talkin' about you."

Lilly nodded wordlessly. And when she slipped them over her head, something shifted. Her breath shuddered out.

Eugor couldn't explain it, not really. Just a subtle change in the air around her. She looked smaller and stronger all at once—like someone who'd been given both a wound and the tool to mend it. He had seen that expression before—on soldiers returning to razed homes, on friends handed a locket or letter left behind by someone who never made it back. That look of sudden weight, of being tethered to someone who should still be here.

Eugor remembered Mivaro. The man who'd patch a cracked boiler with one hand and wipe grease from Lilly's nose with the other. The one who'd laugh in the face of deadlines but never miss a birthday. And now his daughter was wearing those same goggles like armor over anguish.

The thrum of gears behind Eugor seemed to awaken something inside. The ache was sitting uninvited in his chest. They didn't have time for sentiment, not with what was coming. But even so, he let the silence stretch just a moment longer. *Let her have this. Let her become who she needs to be.*

The workshop buzzed with renewed energy. The air was heavy with the scent of oil, metal shavings, and the faint tang of magic lingering from the enchanted blueprints scattered across the workbenches. Each corner of the room told a tale of craftsmanship and innovation, where metal and magic intertwined in a dance as old as the realms.

As Lilly and Mug spread the blueprint, discussing design intricacies and potential improvements, Eugor stepped back. A sense of nostalgia washed over him. In this workshop, the second building built after the Inn, tools, apparatus, and the legacy of Mug's dedication to his craft were now entrusted to a new generation, embodied in the enthusiastic young apprentice who had discovered something astonishing.

However, despite the challenges ahead, Lilly and Mug would face them together, forging a new family united by love and the shared commitment to creating a home. *I hope Lilly can find solace and hope once more.*

# CHAPTER TWENTY-SEVEN

# I DON'T BELONG

Courtlynn, her eyes closed in resignation, dangled upside down from a sturdy black iron perch. The preferred "rest" method for the succubi and incubi never suited her taste. Spoiled by the comfort of Draklor's lavish accommodations and the occasional respite provided by Aushade during her stays in the Mortal Realm, Courtlynn couldn't help but long for the simple luxury of a proper bed.

After parting ways with her master, she found refuge with her friend Vanessa in the tumultuous Seventh Layer of the Inferno-Plane. Remaining in the Abyss posed its risks, the constant danger lurking in its dark corners a reminder of her precarious situation. Yet, with nowhere else to turn, Courtlynn resigned herself to this uncertain existence, hoping against hope for a semblance of stability amid the chaos.

"She appears depleted," a feminine voice spoke, concerned. Courtlynn, feigning meditation, strained to listen without betraying her awareness.

"Can't she find a meat sack?" the voice continued, its curiosity tinged with mild disdain.

"She's chosen to be a solitarian," Vanessa replied softly, her voice betraying a protective edge.

The stranger gasped audibly, then resumed in a whisper, "I'll never understand how some of us fall for these mortal men. Rumor has it she got thrown out of the Third Layer by her master. Is that why?"

"I don't know," Vanessa murmured, her words barely audible over the faint rustle of fabric. "Let's discuss this outside."

As the front door closed, the stranger's voice floated back with disbelief. "How does one throw away the honor of being a balor's companion for a mortal man?"

Last night, like countless nights before, Courtlynn failed to make contact with Aushade. *Did he block me again?* She sighed as doubt crept in. *Maybe the others were right. Perhaps I should give up being a solitarian.*

Courtlynn flipped down from her precarious resting place and stumbled upon landing. Dizziness enveloped her briefly, blurring her vision before fading away. She sat on a cold, uneven stone slab, feeling unusually weak. *I can't protect myself if I lose my strength.*

After a few deep breaths to steady herself, Courtlynn moved to the window. Vanessa's home was nestled by the town square at the heart of their community. It was Courtlynn's favorite spot on their layer. In the center of the village stood a colossal obsidian statue depicting a succubus and incubus entwined, surrounded by vibrant flower beds of blazing stars, sedum, and delosperma. These fiery blossoms were meticulously cultivated to thrive in the relentless heat of the Inferno-Plane.

Courtlynn scanned the square to see if Vanessa was nearby, only to notice a skinny gray imp clad in torn brown breeches wandering aimlessly through the town. Passersby snickered at the creature's plight. *It's unusual for an imp to be grounded instead of soaring through the air.*

As he limped closer to the edge of the square, something about him snagged at her memory—the shape of his ears, the slight hitch in his step.

"Gimp?" she called.

The imp stopped. Slowly, he turned toward the sound of her voice. Recognition bloomed on his face, fragile and bright.

She stepped away from the window, heart thudding as he approached. They met at the threshold of Vanessa's home.

Courtlynn dropped to one knee and opened her arms as Gimp collapsed into her, trembling. "I've got you," she murmured, drawing him in. "You're safe now." He whimpered in pain at her touch. "Your wings?"

"Master burned them," the imp cried, his voice filled with anguish.

"Why?" Courtlynn examined the scars on Gimp's body from Draklor's whip.

"He ordered me to bring you back," Gimp explained bitterly, "to hang you next to the guardian . . . I refused. So he replaced me with a new messenger." His gaze conveyed a mix of fear and relief as Courtlynn took in the extent of his injuries. "He burned my wings, locked me in Floxy's cage, and then abandoned me."

Courtlynn gritted her teeth. "I'm going to rip—"

"Don't," Gimp interrupted, his voice pleading, "I found you."

"I'll ask Vanessa if you can stay, too," Courtlynn offered warmly, patting Gimp's head. "I'm still searching for a dwelling of my own." His face brightened into a grateful smile, revealing his short, pointed fangs as they entered Vanessa's home.

Inside, Gimp's expression turned sour, and his stomach emitted a strange noise. "What's wrong?" Courtlynn asked, concerned.

"I'm hungry," the imp replied, his voice tinged with desperation. "Master didn't feed me."

Courtlynn gently took his little gray hand. "Let's go to the Ninth Layer and find a nice dire-rodent or dire-bat for you." They walked to the edge of the village, where the portals to the other layers awaited. Stepping through, they emerged into a wooden structure on the Ninth Layer.

Courtlynn opened the shack door, which served as a barrier against rodents trying to enter. The layer was dimly lit; intermittent red glows pulsed from the lava streams peeking out underground. "Help yourself," she stated as Gimp dashed off, clumsily pursuing anything small and four-legged. She watched as he struggled, unaccustomed to hunting without his wings. Moving closer to a cliffside, Courtlynn scanned for a suitable nest. "Over here, Gimp."

The injured imp shuffled over, a wide grin stretching across his face, revealing his small, sharp teeth. In the nest nestled against the rocky edge, Courtlynn spotted five baby dire-rats. Gimp wasted no time; he seized one by the tail and greedily stuffed it into his mouth, then grabbed a second, munching away slowly. The remaining babies chattered loudly in fear.

"Just take the nest," Courtlynn instructed calmly, "before their mother returns."

Gimp hastily gathered the nest, struggling to keep the squirming offspring contained, and followed Courtlynn back through the portal.

"Better?" Courtlynn inquired once they returned home.

"Happy," Gimp replied, his voice muffled as he tried to manage the nest and its occupants. The two entered Vanessa's home, where she was repairing a whip.

"What is that?" Vanessa asked, pausing in her work, eyeing the squirming nest curiously.

"This is my friend, Gimp," Courtlynn responded casually, gesturing toward the imp as he finished devouring another rat.

"An imp?" Vanessa asked with disdain, her expression twisting in distaste as Gimp chewed on the rat's tail dangling from his mouth.

"Yes," Courtlynn affirmed calmly.

"What's he doing in this layer?" Vanessa inquired, her tone sharp with suspicion.

"He's been discarded from the Third Layer," Courtlynn explained, her voice softening with sympathy.

Vanessa sneered, her gaze flickering over Gimp's wounded form. "I guess you two have something in common."

"Nessy, let him stay just for a while. He's just a youngling. He'll die if left alone."

Her friend hesitated, staring at the imp for a moment longer before shaking her head firmly. "I'm sorry, but he can't stay. I don't want to be involved when his master comes searching for him."

"Fine," Courtlynn replied tersely, gathering her belongings. As she turned away, her vision blurred unexpectedly, and she staggered, losing her balance as darkness enveloped her.

Courtlynn awoke upside down, disoriented. *How did I get up here?* She observed Gimp and Vanessa engaged in a game of Ignis Alea, a succubi dice game.

"Why the change of heart?" Courtlynn asked Vanessa, still puzzled.

"You should have seen this little guy rush to you when you collapsed," Vanessa replied softly, a hint of warmth in her voice. "He cares for you."

Courtlynn smiled, her heart touched by Gimp's unexpected loyalty, as the imp eagerly rolled the dice, his face lit with excitement.

The game was relatively simple yet engaging. Two players, Gimp and Vanessa, each started with nine six-sided dice. The faces of the dice featured various symbols: two sides displayed a circle, one side an X, and the remaining three sides flames.

As they played, whenever a player rolled a fire symbol, they set it aside and rolled the remaining dice again. However, if an opponent rolled a circle symbol, they could use it to flip one of the fire symbols to an X. Once players ran out of dice displaying fire symbols, they were required to re-roll any X symbols. The objective was clear: a player needed all nine dice showing the fire symbol to win.

Gimp made a pouty lip when Vanessa instructed him to re-roll his dice, a gesture that reminded Courtlynn of her own childhood, where she would pout whenever things didn't go her way.

Dismounting gracefully, Courtlynn approached the table where Gimp and Vanessa were deeply engrossed. She leaned in, watching their competitive spirits and taking pleasure in the simple camaraderie.

"Court, you need to feed," Vanessa said with concern, gathering her dice.

"Re-roll," Gimp interjected eagerly, focused on the game.

Courtlynn nodded, acknowledging Vanessa's unease. "Will you watch over him?"

"Sure," Vanessa replied, setting her dice on the table.

Courtlynn gracefully returned to her perch, preparing to enter the dream world to replenish her energy. *I'm so sorry, Aushade.* Taking a deep breath, she closed her eyes and entered a state of meditation, seeking out dreams to sustain herself. She passed through various dreams, finding reasons not to draw energy from their owners, until she stumbled upon an intriguing scene—a snowy field where two figures battled fiercely.

"Aushade?" Courtlynn observed as one of the figures fell, pierced through the chest by a sword. The victor, wearing a contemptuous smile, caught her attention.

"Who are you?" the surviving man demanded as the snowy landscape transformed into a bustling tavern. A strawberry-blond woman in a white wedding dress appeared beside him, her presence familiar yet unsettling.

Focusing on the woman's face, Courtlynn suddenly recognized her—*Lady Chaotica, Draklor's lich.* "This is your dream," she murmured, her voice low but confident.

"Thomas, who is she?" Lady Chaotica inquired, her gaze flickering with curiosity and suspicion.

"I was just about to find out, Carya," Thomas approached the demon, his sword pointed firmly at Courtlynn. "I'll ask you again, who are you?"

"I can help return your bride. You need only tell me where you are," the succubus replied smoothly, her voice enticing.

"My bride is right here," Thomas responded defiantly, taking hold of Carya's hand.

"You're dreaming, Thomas," Courtlynn interjected softly, her voice a gentle reminder. "It's not real."

"It feels real," Thomas insisted, then turned to kiss Carya passionately.

Courtlynn focused intently, drawing energy from Thomas's intense emotions. She reached into his memories, finding a dark and recent one—a tented infirmary where Carya's lifeless body lay upon a cold stone slab.

"No!" Thomas cried out in anguish. "No, no, bring her back!"

"I can help you," the succubus pleaded urgently, her voice tinged with desperation. "But time is short. Where are you? Tell me, and I can bring her back." Thomas hesitated, his trust strained. "I also have proof that the Abyss Guardian is in trouble."

"I'm at the Omlett Inn, Room Three," Thomas finally admitted, defeat evident in his voice.

"Think about the layout of the Inn," Courtlynn instructed swiftly. "Where is Room Three?" The paladin envisioned a corridor leading from the bar to a door with a distinct number three engraved upon it. "That's it. Now turn around." As he turned, Courtlynn altered her appearance to match Carya's description. She placed a comforting hand on his shoulder and gently guided him to face her.

"Carya?" Thomas whimpered, his eyes filled with tears.

Courtlynn silenced him with a finger to his lips and leaned in to kiss him softly. "I'm here."

As Thomas kissed her vehemently, Courtlynn's body tingled, a blend of excitement and trepidation coursing through her. He gently removed her white dress, the fabric whispering against her skin, and laid her across the bed. Thomas undressed quickly, his urgency evident in every hurried movement, then joined her, continuing their fervent kisses. Courtlynn closed her eyes, letting herself be consumed by the intimate energy he offered, her mind a whirl of desire.

"Carya," Thomas moaned breathlessly, his voice filled with longing. "I missed you."

Though conflicted, Courtlynn couldn't deny the hunger that drove her. She fed on his desire, each touch and peck fueling her with newfound energy. Memories of past hesitations flickered through her mind but were quickly overwhelmed by the intensity of the present. Their bodies moved in perfect harmony, the room filled with the sounds of their shared passion. The intensity grew, a crescendo of emotions and sensations, until they both reached climax, collapsing together in a breathless embrace. For a moment, they lay there, the unspoken connection between them more robust than ever. As Courtlynn slipped back into the white dress, she retrieved a feather and presented it to Thomas. "I need you to take this to Purple Eyes."

"You mean your sister," Thomas responded, recognizing the significance. "Raven."

"Sure," Courtlynn agreed, placing the feather carefully on the nightstand. "Have her take it to Gideon."

"Will I see you again?" Thomas asked, his voice filled with uncertainty.

"If you do as I ask, you may have a chance to see your bride again," Courtlynn assured him as she faded from his dream.

Courtlynn glanced at Thomas, still asleep in his bed, his chest rising and falling with each breath. A sudden commotion erupted outside his room, shouting and hurried footsteps drawing her attention. She knew it was unwise to linger in the Mortal Realm any longer, but curiosity gripped her. Quietly, she opened the door and cautiously peeked down the hall. The noise emanated from the bar area, where voices were arguing. As she started to close the door, a familiar voice cut through the clamor, mentioning her name and then Aushade. Her heart raced with a mix of fear and intrigue. *Aushade's here!* Keeping the door slightly ajar, she strained to eavesdrop on the conversation, desperate to hear more of what her necromancer had to say.

A male voice, vaguely familiar, spoke in an urgent tone. "We need another way into the Abyss."

*They're planning a rescue. Should I?* Courtlynn steadied her nerves, retrieving the feather and tucking her wings in to appear less threatening. With everyone's backs turned, she cautiously stepped forward, straining to hear more. She caught Aushade's voice, mentioning "donkey and the pirate," followed by laughter from a female voice she didn't recognize.

*Who is she?* Moments later, a rough voice responded, "We know who the ass is," prompting a slight smile from Courtlynn. She quickly withdrew into the shadows of the hallway before anyone could spot her.

*Stick to the original plan.* Courtlynn returned the feather to the nightstand in Thomas's room and swiftly cast a portal with her new energy to make her escape. Once back in the Seventh Layer, she made her way to check on Gimp, but what she witnessed made her pause in surprise. Vanessa had the imp engaged in an exercise routine.

"What's going on?" Courtlynn asked, intrigued. Vanessa glanced over with a smile as he squatted, straining under the weight of a large stone.

"I'm building leg muscles," Gimp muttered, every strained breath a testament to his will.

"I see that," Courtlynn replied, impressed. "That rock looks heavy."

"I'm strong," Gimp asserted, completing another squat with effort.

"Look at you, all gleaming," Vanessa teased, causing Courtlynn to blush. "Did you find him?"

Courtlynn shook her head, her expression serious. Vanessa sensed her friend's discomfort and changed the subject. "You lost your solitarian status?" she inquired cautiously, knowing it was a sensitive topic. Courtlynn's glare spoke volumes, prompting Vanessa to backtrack. "I won't ask anymore."

Courtlynn had difficulty sleeping, restless in the tranquil Seventh Layer. She dismounted from her stand, unfolding and stretching her wings. Hanging from the perch had become a comforting ritual, allowing her to gather her thoughts, consumed by jealousy after hearing Aushade's laughter with another woman. Her heart weighed heavily with the realization that he had never shared such moments of joy with her. A strange sense of guilt gnawed at her, compounded by the fact that she had recently drawn energy from another man who seemed to be an adversary. Despite her outward assurances to her friends, she couldn't deny the deep ache of missing Aushade terribly.

She watched the stone dial in the center of the room shift, indicating the passage of time as the Mortal Realm transitioned into night once more. The moon symbol gleamed softly in the darkened space, casting a tranquil glow across the chamber. Courtlynn took a deep breath, letting the serene ambiance of rest time wash over her. She found peace despite the lingering concerns from her recent activities in the Mortal Realm. Glancing around the chamber, her eyes fell upon a smaller perch Vanessa had installed for Gimp in the corner. Like Courtlynn, he rested upside down, a position difficult for his impish species. She recalled waking to the sound of thumps in the past—Gimp falling from his stand in his sleep.

*I think I'll try to search for Aushade.* As she settled back onto her perch, she closed her eyes and entered deep meditation, focusing her energy on sorting through the dreams that floated through the realms of consciousness.

One dream revealed an older man embracing an older woman in a wedding gown, surrounded by an aura of sorrow and recent loss. Courtlynn sensed the heaviness of grief, the sorrow of a recent passing weighing heavily on his heart.

In another dream, a skinny man seduced a young, beautiful wood nymph, their passion intertwined with the natural beauty of their surroundings.

A third vision emerged, depicting a middle-aged, dark-skinned man rallying his squad of paladins, their faces resolute with determination as they prepared to charge into battle.

Courtlynn focused intensely, searching for Aushade among the dreams, but he remained elusive. Her senses strained to pinpoint his presence, wondering where he could be amid the vast tapestry of dreams. Her heart raced with relief and longing as she finally found Aushade's familiar face in one of her scanned dreams. Without hesitation, she appeared before him correctly, disregarding any need for disguise. She knocked the flowers from his hand and kissed him deeply, her emotions pouring into the embrace.

"I've been searching for you. I thought you blocked me again," Courtlynn admitted softly as they parted.

"Never," Aushade firmly responded, pulling her close. "I missed you. I've waited for you every night in my dreams. They may have cast a spell to keep you from finding me."

"Where are you now?" Courtlynn asked urgently, concern coloring her voice.

Aushade sighed heavily, his expression grim. "In a prison cell at the High Council."

Courtlynn's mind raced with thoughts of rescue and escape, her strength of mind solidifying. "I'll find a way to get you out. At least they didn't kill you."

"Yet." Aushade grimaced, weariness etched deep into his voice. "So much has happened, I don't even know where to begin." He gently ran his fingers through Courtlynn's hair, a gesture of unspoken relief.

She yearned to be with him, to feel his presence close. "I'm on my own," Courtlynn whimpered softly.

"What?"

"I have no master. I've been residing in my home layer."

"I'm sorry I wasn't there for you. But I swear I waited for you every night, even took naps during the day."

"We're together now," Courtlynn said lovingly, "but how did you end up at the High Council?"

"Long story short: a pissed-off guardian."

"And the girl with purple eyes?"

"My cousin."

"And the mage you held captive?"

"Brother," Aushade answered, his tone heavy. There was an awkward silence. "Small world, huh?" Courtlynn sensed his hesitation, uncertain if he should divulge more.

"Aren't you going to ask me?" she commented.

Aushade's expression turned bewildered, then softened as he knelt before her in a traditional human way of proposing.

"No, silly!" she exclaimed, pulling him back up with gentle insistence. "You need a portal to the Abyss. Aren't you going to ask me to help?"

"How did you—"

"Small world, huh?"

Aushade smiled warmly. "I knew you gave Thomas the feather."

She nodded as a smile tugged at her lips. "I only found Thomas while searching for you."

Aushade chuckled. "He was probably plotting my demise in his sleep."

"Indeed," she giggled lightly.

"You look amazing." Aushade's touch was gentle as he caressed her face. *Should I tell him about what happened with Thomas?*

"It's all right if you had to recover," he continued, sensing her hesitation. She sighed with relief.

"As long as it wasn't with that ass," he added calmingly.

Her heart raced, and she pulled back slightly, not wanting to spoil the moment, changing the subject. "I want to be with you but can't portal into the High Council."

Aushade frowned and returned to his throne. "I know, it's a DMZ. I doubt the High Council will allow Abyss visitors into the Mortal Realm anytime soon."

She settled onto his lap, eyes glistening with unshed tears. "There has to be a way for us to be together."

He wrapped his arms around her, his voice determined. "We'll figure it out somehow. Will you visit me tomorrow night?"

But before she could answer, Aushade vanished. *Something must have awakened him.* "I'll see you tomorrow night," she whispered as she opened her eyes.

Gimp was there, gently dabbing a tear from her cheek, despair etched into his stare. "Why are you sad?"

Courtlynn hesitated, her voice barely above a breath. "Because I don't belong . . . anywhere."

# CHAPTER TWENTY-EIGHT

## THE PLAN IS AFOOT

R aven stood just outside of the gates to Jarz and Izarra's cottage, pacing. Her blood was still boiling from her encounter with Gideon. *I can't believe Celeste betrayed us.* She heard a giggle and turned to see her friends, arm in arm, strolling past the dock.

"It's about time," Raven snapped. The words left her lips sharper than she intended. She winced, eyes dropping to the ground. "I'm sorry . . . it's just been a bad morning." She smoothed a hand over her arm as if trying to brush the tension away.

"What happened?" Izarra asked.

"Celeste informed Gideon," Raven responded, gripping her arm tighter, "And then he whisked Aushade to the prison at the High Council."

Jarz began, "Why would she—"

"It doesn't matter. We're still going to the Abyss to save Carya. Even if I go alone." Her friends glanced at her with concern. "Jarz, what are we missing for the ritual?"

"Umm . . . just a significantly large diamond." He shrugged apologetically.

"Where the spell are we getting one of those?"

"Mug," Izarra noted casually.

"Mug?" Raven repeated. "He has diamonds?"

"Iz saw them when she was on errands and spoke with Mug."

"Jarz, can you portal us there?" Raven asked, urgency tightening her throat. Her pulse pounded in her ears—too loud, too fast. She couldn't afford to wait.

"It's against Waterfront protocol," Jarz replied, "and I'm not familiar with his factory. I could disintegrate poor Mug."

Raven's mouth tightened into a thin line. "Put us somewhere nearby. I'll break in."

Izarra stared. "What's with the breaking in? First Maggie's and now—"

"To feel like I'm useful," Raven snapped before she could stop herself. The words rang out, too revealing. Heat bloomed across her face. She looked away, pretending to study the ground, her fists curling tight. "I just . . . I need to do something."

Jarz waved his hand, and the air sparked; a blue portal appeared, allowing the three to step just outside Mug's factory.

"Should we knock?" Izarra asked.

"No need," Raven said, eyeing the mechanism. "We just went through this."

Jarz threw up his hands, eyes gleaming with a manic fascination. "Brilliant! We're breaking into one of the most catastrophically dangerous places in Omlett. Golems stomping about, flame-spewing contraptions, and Blade-knows-what abominations powered by *dozens* of diamonds!"

Raven remained unfazed until he mentioned the diamonds. Her eyes flicked toward him, sharp with sudden interest. "Dozens?"

"Yes, he said it was for a top-secret project," Izarra explained. "We don't have to steal—you know he would give you one if it meant saving Carya."

Raven ignored her and crouched in front of the lock. "Just keep an eye out." From the simple black band, she slid out a thin, hidden pick—one of her little tricks. "He tends to have traps." She inserted the pick into the lock, her movements precise and practiced. The metal felt cold, unwelcoming. She coaxed the pins with careful pressure, each faint *click* a tiny victory. Her breath hitched as the last one gave way. "Cookies," she muttered with a tight grin, easing the door open. "Follow me."

The giant stone and wood building was dark and deserted. Piles of debris littered the back corner. A faint, lingering scent of molten metal and earthy magic hung in the air, a reminder of the factory's recent activity.

Inside the golem factory, the air hummed with a symphony of mechanical clanks and hisses. Rows of towering furnaces belched sparks into the dimly lit chamber, casting flickering shadows on massive anvils and assembly lines. Above, makeshift cranes swung heavy loads of enchanted stones, their arcane energies pulsating faintly as they integrated into the golems' cores. Glistening with molten metal, intricate runes glowed faintly on the unfinished golems' bodies, etched by skilled craftsmen who toiled under the watchful gaze of Maggie McGee.

The scent of smelted ore mingled with alchemical solutions, permeating the air with a metallic tang that spoke of ceaseless industry. Amid the organized chaos, the empty seats were for the engineers who meticulously calibrated the mechanisms, ensuring each golem emerged with flawless precision, ready to serve as stalwart guardians or tireless laborers in the city's defense or construction efforts.

"Stay alert," Raven whispered, her voice barely audible over the distant echoes of machinery. She scanned the dark, cavernous space, her eyesight adjusting to the light filtering through the narrow windows above. Shadows danced along the walls, playing tricks in the corners where the debris of bygone creations and forgotten remnants lingered.

Izarra tightened her grip on her trident, the runes etched into its length glowing softly in response to her apprehension. "It feels . . . abandoned," she murmured, her gaze flickering nervously between the looming metal monsters.

"That Rust Metal Spell destroyed a lot of golems." Jarz's voice echoed faintly off the stone walls as he glanced around the factory. "The only intact ones are still patrolling Suttiir."

"Poor Mug," Izarra replied softly, noticing a broken golem that lay dormant near a pile of discarded tools. "All his hard work gone."

The trio continued their cautious exploration, their footsteps disturbing the heavy silence. The ringing of the midday church bell echoed through the expansive building.

Raven's thoughts remained fixed on the vision she had witnessed aboard the ship when Gideon escorted Aushade through the portal to the High Council— a pivotal moment in their quest to reach Carya.

"Are you all right?" Jarz placed his hand on her back.

Raven nodded absently, then moved away, forging ahead of her companions. The usual symphony of Mug's bustling activity—the rhythmic clang of hammers, the occasional burst of Gnomish expletives—was conspicuously absent.

"Gideon will change his mind," Izarra babbled, breaking the heavy silence.

"Aushade's gone, Gideon won't help, Celeste can't be trusted. We're on our own." Raven's voice cut tersely through the factory's sounds. "It's time to move on."

"You should have told Gideon," Izarra blurted out, her frustration evident.

"Well, it wasn't exactly the ideal moment. Gideon was about to sink a ship," Raven replied sharply.

"But—"

"The diamonds!" Raven snapped, her patience wearing thin as they approached the faintly glowing doorway ahead.

"Over here." Izarra led Raven and Jarz through the labyrinthine passages of the factory until they reached a locked door. "Buzz and I were in here speaking to Mug." Raven pulled a lockpick from her ponytail holder as Izarra continued. "He had a cart filled with diamonds. I counted them while Mug helped Buzz add some padding to his—"

"Cookies!" Raven announced after swiftly picking up the lock. It swung inward with a soft creak, revealing an orb-lit room with shelves stacked with dusty books and arcane artifacts. The faint glow of the crystals illuminated the space as a strung-up golem's large eye followed the trio.

"That's disturbing," Izarra blurted as the eye locked onto her as she spoke.

Jarz tilted his head, eyes narrowing as he stepped closer to the figure. His gaze swept over its strange angles, fingers twitching slightly at his side. "I've never seen anything like it," he murmured, as if trying to unravel its secrets just by looking.

They walked farther into the room and discovered something gigantic covered in sheets. It towered from floor to ceiling, its shape imposing and mysterious. Nearby, two large objects were suspended from the ceiling and shrouded from view.

"What the spell is he working on?" Raven eyed the massive, covered object with curiosity.

"Here's the cart," Jarz called over, drawing their attention to a nearby table where several diamonds were laid out, each cut into the shape of talons. "Let's take one that hasn't been modified yet."

"Maybe we should just ask," Izarra's gaze shifted toward the doorway. "I don't want him upset like Maggie."

"He won't mind," Raven responded confidently, moving toward the cart and taking out a diamond.

"Yes, he would," a voice suddenly came from the doorway.

Raven froze, almost dropping the diamond in surprise. Slowly turning around, Mug stood there, holding a sandwich, glaring at them. His small stature seemed nearly comical against the backdrop of the enormous, covered contraption.

"Mug." Raven placed the diamond back on the cart. "We were going to leave you a message."

Mug chewed thoughtfully on his sandwich before speaking, his expression unreadable. "Is it for Carya?" he asked casually.

"Yes," Raven replied, her voice steady despite the gulp in her throat.

"Your father informed me of the plan," the gnome said nonchalantly, taking another bite of his sandwich.

"And?" Jarz chimed in eagerly.

Mug nodded, walking past them. "I have a spare one I can part ways with."

"How do you have so many?" Izarra peered over him, fascinated by all the jewels.

"I repair and sell mining equipment to the dwarves," Mug explained, finishing his sandwich and brushing off his hands. "What? You think I stand around making children's toys?"

"I'm curious to learn what's under the sheets." Jarz moved closer to the covered objects with interest.

"Me too," Raven responded. "Can we sneak a peek?"

"Absolutely not," Mug replied firmly, inspecting the diamonds. "Jarz, will this do?" Without waiting for an answer, the gnome tossed an apple-sized diamond at the swordmage.

Jarz raised it toward the light, inspecting the gem closely. "This will work."

"Thank you, Mug." Raven bent and kissed the gnome on his cheek gratefully.

"Sure," the tinkerer replied gruffly. "At least you proved I need better security."

"Tell us when we can view what you're working on," Izarra said, giving him a quick peck on the opposite cheek.

Mug blushed. "Now, you children get out of here. I have work to do, especially on a better lock."

"I'm always up for a challenge." Raven smiled mischievously as Mug huffed in response. "Do you know where my father is?"

"I last saw him headed for his work chamber at the Inn."

"Jarz—" Raven began, gesturing toward the empty space. In response, Jarz opened a subtle blue portal for her. "Let's rendezvous at sunset, Gideon's camp," she instructed, ensuring Mug couldn't overhear.

"We'll be there."

Raven entered the portal, stepping onto the familiar wooden floor of her father's work chamber. He was seated behind his desk, deeply engrossed in a tome.

"How are you feeling?" Eugor glanced up as the portal closed.

"My vision seems to be back to normal."

"Thank Blade!" Her father closed the book in front of him. "But you need to talk with your mother. She's beginning to think you're avoiding her."

"That's nonsense."

"You know how she gets," Eugor insisted gently.

"Speaking of sense. Can you talk some sense into Gideon?"

Her father chuckled softly. "He requested I do the same with you."

Raven rolled her eyes. "Where does he find the time to inform you of everything?"

"He manages." Eugor smiled. "Gideon might be right, though. I can't let you partner with the necromancer. Your mother is already distraught knowing we're related to that monster."

"Well, that monster is our only hope."

Her father stood, the chair scraping the floor. "But that's just it. I may put so much hope into saving Carya that I'm not thinking straight," he said, his voice raised. "I'm risking *you*. I couldn't handle losing a second daughter and neither could your mother."

"We won't fail," Raven reassured him confidently.

"I thought that when I allowed your sister to go to Suttiir." Eugor frowned deeply. "I don't want to make the same mistake."

"It's my choice," Raven argued, her gaze steady. "No one can talk me out of it. I need you to get Gideon to release Aushade so we can safely enter the Abyss."

A knock on the door interrupted their tense conversation. "Enter," Eugor called out, his voice strained.

Brugg entered with a canteen in hand. He wobbled to Eugor's desk and placed it down carefully, still bearing bandages on his head from the recent battle. He fixated on Raven as he approached, then without a word, he walked over and gently guided her to a nearby chair.

"I'm fine, Brugg," Raven noted, surprised by his gesture. "How are you feeling?"

"Me, good." Brugg fetched a footstool and placed it in front of her. He removed Raven's purple boot with oversized green hands and massaged her foot with surprising gentleness.

"Brugg?" Raven exclaimed, confused and amused by his unexpected attention.

Eugor's brow furrowed deeply as he approached, scrutinizing the scene from behind the orc's shoulder. "It's custom for a male orc to pamper an expecting mother," Eugor explained calmly, though his gaze remained fixed on Raven.

"Raven, mother," Brugg blurted out happily.

"Cee told you," Raven accused, realizing the bard had shared the news. The orc nodded enthusiastically. "Brugg, thank you, but maybe later," Raven said gently as the orc stood and left the room. As she slipped her boot back on, she glanced at her father, whose expression remained stoic and contemplative.

He turned away and sat at his desk, lost in thought.

"I wanted to tell you and Mother."

"But after I allowed you to enter the Abyss." His voice was heavy with disappointment, his gaze fixed on something else. "I don't know what to think right now, Nightbird. How long have you known?"

"I found out yesterday at the meeting. Along with several other people."

"Does Gideon know?" Eugor's brow furrowed as Raven shook her head. "And he's the father?" he added awkwardly, clearing his throat. "I'm sorry, Nightbird. I didn't mean it to be insulting. But the High Council has one golden rule."

"I know," Raven replied, her voice softening. "I'm not sure what they'll do."

"That rule has caused me much grief," Eugor mumbled.

"Blade?" Raven asked softly, leaning forward.

"Yes, his mother—"

"Celeste?"

"Did your mother tell—"

"No, I kind of guessed. When I arrived at the Fey Realm for the first time, she seemed extremely infatuated with you. You're all she talked about, trying to cure my eyes. 'Your father' this, 'your father' that. She must have loved you."

Eugor chuckled, and then his expression turned serious again. "Sorry, dear, but I forbid you from going to the Abyss. It's for your own good and my grandchild's."

"I'm still going!" Raven snapped defiantly, rising from her chair.

"Don't make me do it," Eugor pleaded, his voice wavering with concern as he stood to face her.

"You wouldn't dare."

"As your father and your king, I'm ordering you and the Mortal Guardians to abort the quest," Eugor stated firmly, his expression resolute.

Raven gritted her teeth, her mind racing as she fought the urge to say something she would regret. With a determined motion, she threw open a secret bookcase and stormed through the hidden tunnel into the kitchen, where she noticed someone sitting near the fireplace with her mother.

"Celeste? What are you doing here?" Raven snapped, startled to see the Fey Guardian in her home. *If not for her, Aushade would be aboard the ship, contacting the succubus.* "If Gideon—"

"She knows," Celeste said simply, glancing toward Mara, who sat unusually still.

Raven's stomach turned. Her hand twitched at her side, instinctively brushing the curve of her cloak as if shielding something invisible. "Knows what?"

"She told me the news," Mara said at last. Her voice was quiet. Toneless.

Raven's breath caught. Her eyes snapped to Celeste, who remained unreadable. The words perched like thorns on the edge of her throat. "And?"

Mara glanced at her. "You know I've lived through this once. I watched one daughter's life be taken from me. Do you really expect me to stand by while my youngest walks willingly into the inferno?"

"I'm not walking into it blindly," Raven said, fighting to stay steady. "Carya's alive—"

"We don't know that," Mara snapped, standing abruptly. "We don't know anything. You've built your hopes on fragments, on visions and dreams, and people who promise more than they can truly guarantee."

"She's my sister."

"She's my daughter," Mara shot back, voice cracking. "And so are you."

A silence fell between them. Celeste took a single step back as if the heat in the room had turned physical.

"I'm not trying to hurt you," Raven said, her voice faltering. "But I can't sit here while Carya is out there—maybe suffering, maybe calling for us."

Mara's face shifted, eyes dark with grief, fear, and something else—suspicion. "You think I haven't imagined going after her? Bargaining, fighting, clawing through whatever nightmare world she's in to bring her home? But it would've broken me."

"Mother—"

"I can't bear the thought of losing you, too."

Raven hesitated, then stepped forward and hugged her tightly. For a moment, she felt like a child again. A child with secrets pressing against her ribs. "You won't lose me," she whispered. "Not if you trust me. Not if you believe I'm ready for this."

Mara's hand lifted, brushing Raven's cheek with aching gentleness. "I believe in you, Raven. That's what terrifies me the most."

Celeste approached, her gaze flicking briefly to Raven before turning to Mara. "I gave your mother my word," she said. "I'll be by your side in the Abyss. And if it turns, even for a moment, I'll have a portal ready. I will get you out."

Mara nodded, but her shoulders stayed tight. "That helps. A little. But I hate this. I hate the idea of you in that place. There are things in the Abyss that don't just kill—they unravel."

"Carya is already in that realm," Raven said. "She's alone. She's vulnerable. Jarz has Uncle Ausharz's book, Gideon prepared us, and Celeste knows what we're walking into. We're not charging in blind—we're fighting for her."

Mara's eyes shimmered. "I would love to see Carya returned. You have no idea how much."

"Your daughter won't be alone," Celeste added. "I have faith in this group. If I didn't, I wouldn't have let this plan survive the first conversation."

"Yes, Mother," Raven said, her tone tightening like a drawstring. "Celeste always keeps her promises. She'd never betray anyone . . . not even if it meant compromising the mission."

Celeste flinched—a subtle thing, barely there. "We must be careful," she said. "The Abyss isn't just dangerous—it's deceptive. Everything there tries to twist you. Even your own heart."

Before Raven could respond, Mara rose again and pulled her into a tight, trembling embrace. "I trust you," she whispered, voice breaking. "Bring your sister home if you can. But more than that . . . bring yourself home safe. I love you."

"Love you too," Raven murmured, pressing her face against her mother's shoulder, trying to breathe through the storm in her chest.

She didn't know if her mother knew. Not for certain. But in her silence, in the way her hand lingered just a moment too long against Raven's stomach, she feared the truth had already begun to speak without her.

Mara stepped back, nodded once, and quietly exited the room. Celeste began, "I'm sorry, I—"

"There's been a change in plans." Raven turned sharply, the edges of her cloak slicing through the air like blades. "Gideon turned Aushade over to the High Council this morning. Thanks to you."

Celeste's lips parted, but no sound came. Her shoulders stiffened. "I . . . felt it was for the best."

"You specifically told me at the meeting that it was *my* decision. We need Aushade's connection to the succubus," Raven retorted. A sudden pain began to build inside her head, causing her to wince.

"Calm down," Celeste urged gently, concern etched across her face. "We don't want your vision to—"

"It doesn't matter." Raven's voice cracked as the pressure behind her eyes flared. "The mission's canceled."

Celeste's brow furrowed. "What do you mean?"

"My father knows about the pregnancy," Raven said, then louder, more brittle: "He forbade me to go. As king."

Celeste's mouth fell open. "How? I didn't—"

"Brugg," Raven answered, folding her arms and exhaling a tired sigh. "He did some kind of orcish maternity ritual right before him. Took off my boot and everything."

A long pause stretched between them. And then, the tension broke.

Raven let out a short giggle. "You should've seen my father's face."

Celeste blinked, then laughed, too, shaking her head as if to clear away the absurdity. "Of course Brugg would pick the most public way possible."

"He meant well," Raven admitted, the amusement in her voice edged with exhaustion.

Celeste nudged her gently, the mood finally easing. "Your father tries so hard to be tough on you," she said softly. "But I think he's been a father for so long, he's forgotten how to be . . . spontaneous."

Raven sighed. "Well, as soon as my mother bumps into him, she'll find out."

"Sometimes I wish I had children," Celeste mumbled softly.

Raven's expression softened. "I know about Blade."

"Oh—"

"That's why I need your help."

"To deal with the High Council," Celeste replied, understanding dawning on her face. "I might not be the best role model in that aspect. I burdened your father so I didn't have to deal with the High Council. What do you want to do?"

"Save my sister. Even if the resurrection doesn't work, I want her soul resting in the Astral Realm where it belongs."

"Eugor is a great father and always has been," Celeste pointed out gently. "He's only trying to protect you and your child."

"What about Tier?"

"I owe your father for raising Blade, so finding Carya is the priority. However, I'm hopeful that we can also find Tier. He deserves the same respect."

Raven fell silent, her gaze dropping to her belly. The weight of her decision pressed in like a storm. This wasn't just disobedience—it was exile, perhaps even death. If the king deemed her actions treasonous, there would be no leniency. And worse than banishment was the possibility that she might not return.

A sharp ache gripped her chest. She thought of the child growing inside her, small, defenseless, full of potential. What kind of mother risks everything before her child draws its first breath? But what kind of sister turns her back on family?

Raven wrapped her arms around herself, torn between fear and duty. "If something happens to me—"

"It won't," Celeste interrupted, firm and reassuring.

"But if it does, you'll look after them?"

Celeste nodded without hesitation.

Raven drew in a shaky breath. Her voice, when it came, was low but steady. "We're still going. Pray to Blade we succeed."

"I'm his mother, so I'm sure he'll bless us," Celeste replied warmly. They shared a reassuring smile. "I suggest we leave before your father alerts Gideon."

"We need a portal to the *Sea Squid* to assemble Ashley and her crew."

# CHAPTER TWENTY-NINE

# THE EDGE OF DEFIANCE

Celeste conjured a portal without hesitation, its edges flickering with cold blue light. Raven stepped through after her, boots landing on the sun-warmed deck of the *Sea Squid*. The air hit her all at once—fresh water, salt, aged wood.

Laughter drifted across the deck. Ashley, Gobs, and Ramzey were deep in a game at their makeshift table, gold coins clinking on the weathered boards. Ashley's smirk said everything—she was winning and enjoying it.

Ramzey looked up, scowling as the portal sealed behind them. "Permission granted," she muttered. No welcome, just tolerance.

Ashley casually scooped up her winnings, stacking them with theatrical flair. "Early, aren't you?" she said, not taking her eye off the table. "You missed my Dragons Versus Wizards comeback."

"No time for games," Celeste cut in, voice tight. Her wings twitched, a tell Raven didn't miss. She stood, tightening her grip on her staff. The knot in her gut hadn't loosened since they left too much at stake. That silence said enough. Gobs and Ramzey exchanged a look and disappeared belowdecks without a word.

Ashley raised a brow but didn't push. One by one, she dropped the coins into her pouch, each jingle smug. "What's the rush?"

"I'll explain later," Raven replied.

Ashley stood, stretching like she had all the time in the world. "Right, right—no fun allowed." She slung the pouch on her belt and winked. "Have you ever played? Bet you're a Dragon kind of girl." Raven didn't answer fast enough as Ashley's focus slid to Celeste. "And you . . . definitely the Wizard."

Celeste didn't blink. "I'm more the type to set the board on fire," she said, already conjuring arcane symbols in the air like she was flicking away flies.

Ashley chuckled and sauntered off, coins rattling in her pouch. "I usually do—right after I lose. But a spirit after my own heart. I like that." She left, half amused, half exasperated.

Nearby, a male elf approached Ramzey. "Saven, you're in command until my return." She sheathed her rapier and adjusted her jacket. "Watch over the *Squid*. We'll reconvene here after the mission." The elf nodded curtly and headed toward the helm.

Raven exchanged a glance with Celeste. "Portal us to Gideon's camp."

The Fey Guardian's lips twitched with amusement. "Are you certain?"

"It's the last place he would think to search."

Ashley's face turned a queasy shade of green as blue sparks crackled into being ahead of them. "A portal?" she groaned, swaying slightly as the magic twisted the air. She braced herself, clearly trying not to be sick.

Celeste stepped through, fingers carving protective sigils to shield them from unwanted magical visions. Raven followed close behind, heart already ticking faster. The portal spat them out near Gideon's old wagon, its familiar frame leaning slightly more than she remembered.

Ashley stumbled through at last and doubled over immediately. "Damn portals," she muttered, wiping her mouth with the back of her hand.

"You brave hurricanes, but this breaks you?" Ramzey leaned against a post as Ashley shot her a sideways glare. The warrior straightened, trying to recover some dignity. Ramzey gestured toward the wagon. "Gotta say, though, that's a cute wagon. It reminds me of one of my grandmothers who sold flowers out of it."

Celeste grinned. "I've always said Gideon has a touch of the old woman about him."

Raven half-listened, scanning their surroundings. The clearing was still, but the feeling that she shouldn't be there stirred. Time was short.

"When are the others arriving?" Ashley asked, trying to sound casual.

"Soon," Raven replied. "But we can't wait around doing nothing. Could you grab some firewood and start a fire? I'll check the supplies."

"I'll help you," Gobs offered, following Raven into the wagon. Inside, the air was thick with dust and disappointment. They dug through what little was left—half-empty jars, a moldy heel of bread, and what might have once been tomatoes, now liquefied beyond recognition.

Raven closed one jar, frowning. *Supplies are worse than I expected.* She picked up another jar, wrinkling her nose at the pungent odor that escaped when she cracked it open. "Ogre poop," she muttered under her breath, quickly screwing the lid back on and reaching for another.

"How are you holding up?" Gobs asked, opening a nearby drawer.

"Besides the nausea from the smell, I'm fine," Raven replied, her voice strained but steady.

"And your eyes?" Gobs pressed gently.

Raven hesitated, then exhaled. "So far they seem normal." The words settled like cool water across burning nerves. Every time she blinked without pain, every shape that held its form, was a quiet miracle. If she were still stumbling through blurred edges and shifting shadows, even these faintly lit quarters would feel like a trap. But now—now the world held steady beneath her gaze, and that steadiness felt like something she could build on.

"I'm glad *she* decided—" Gobs froze mid-sentence, mouth gaping in shock.

The jar of tomatoes slipped from Raven's hands, shattering on the floor. She turned slowly, her expression stiffening. "She?" Her voice was low, sharp with disbelief.

"I—I'm so sorry," Gobs stammered, her face crumpling. "I know it was supposed to be a surprise. It just . . . slipped out."

Raven tried to smile and keep her voice steady. "It's all right," she said as her chest tightened. She stared at the red pulp smeared across the floor. "I'm having a daughter." She stepped back, grabbing a towel off the wagon shelf as Gobs offered her a hopeful smile—but then it hit her like a crashing wave. *A daughter.*

Her knees buckled. She caught herself against the counter, breath caught in her throat. *I'm going to have a girl.*

A vision flickered—blond curls, wide purple eyes. Eyes like hers. Hair like Gideon's. But the image twisted. *What if she's like my mother? Or Carya? Graceful. Gentle. Normal.* What if she wants flowers and fairy tales?

Raven squeezed her eyes shut. Her thoughts spiraled. *I can't braid hair. I can't sew. I can barely cook without setting something on fire. Every plant I've ever owned? Dead. DEAD! How in the spell am I supposed to raise a child?*

Memories clawed up—villagers pleading with her mother for something to soothe the colic, the fever, the endless crying. Desperation. The fear. Her stomach twisted violently. She doubled over and retched into the towel.

"Raven!" Gobs was at her side in a heartbeat. "Sit down. You're pale."

She slid to the floor, her back pressed against the counter, and the towel balled in her lap. Everything felt too loud, too close. "I'm having a baby," she whispered, voice trembling. Gobs patted her back gently, trying to help, but it only made the words crash louder in her mind. "No, you don't understand." She looked up, wide-eyed, her panic raw and unguarded. "I can't even keep a plant alive."

Gobs's hands went from patting to rubbing. "Some plants are . . . delicate."

"So are babies!" Raven snapped, then winced.

"Being a mother can be terrifying," Gobs said gently. "But it's also a gift. And you don't have to do it alone."

Raven stared at her. "Promise?"

"I promise," Gobs replied softly. "I'm good with children . . . and plants."

Raven managed a thin but real laugh. "Give me a moment."

"Sure," Gobs replied as she tossed the soiled towel aside and hugged Raven. "I'll be outside if you need me."

Raven's fingers slipped into the hidden pocket of her cloak, brushing cold metal. *I miss the days when I used this pocket to store sugar cubes for Ghost.* She pulled out the phylactery.

The crystal pulsed faintly in her palm, that eerie blue shimmer like a heartbeat caught in glass. Baka's essence—contained, but never entirely still. Raven turned it over slowly, watching how the light refracted through it. It had always been a burden she carried. But now there was *her daughter.* "What does this mean for her?" she pleaded to the spirit of a copper dragon.

*What if it passes to her? What if she carries more than just my blood?* Her grip tightened, hoping to hear that low-toned laugh, that slow speech of ancient knowledge. She pictured that same gleam behind small, curious eyes. The same power . . . but no defenses. No control.

Raven stared at the phylactery, her voice barely audible. "I don't understand what I am. How can I protect her from myself? If I am part Krea, what does that make her?" She inhaled deeply, letting out a deep command, "Bakahrrato, This is Krea'tion! Answer me!" But the phylactery offered no answers—only that slow, steady glow.

*Gideon!* Her pulse quickened as the realization slammed into her like magic missiles. *Blade Naelo.* Celeste and her father had created a demigod. *Between my dragon traits and Gideon's immortality ceremony . . .* Raven tucked the phylactery away, her chest tightening with the question that hadn't been answered. *What will my daughter become?*

By the time Raven, lost in thought, stumbled toward the fire, most of the others had gathered, their attention shifting to her with quiet expectation. "Anything to eat yet?" she asked, breaking the silence and rubbing her stomach with a sigh. "I kind of lost my lunch in the wagon."

Groans answered her from around the camp.

"I lost mine first—by the portal," Ashley said, dropping onto a log with a dramatic flop. "So I'm right there with you."

Before Raven could reply, a familiar whoosh of wings caught her ear. Celeste was already in motion, her silhouette elegant against the fading sky as she unfurled her wings and untied a fishing net from the wagon.

"Hold on," the Fey Guardian said. She glided toward the lake, graceful and focused, a ribbon of purpose cutting through the evening calm.

Beside her, Gobs stepped forward, staff in hand, and began reciting a soft incantation that pulsed through the earth. "May the fish be drawn to us," she murmured.

Raven watched them work—Celeste, strong and precise, dipping the net into the water; Gobs, calm and steady, coaxing nature to provide. It was oddly soothing after the chaos in her mind.

The net emerged heavy with silver-scaled trout, flopping and shining in the twilight. Raven exhaled and returned to the wagon. Inside, she set to work. Her hands moved with practiced care—sorting herbs, gutting the fish, and prepping everything as Gideon had taught her. Familiar motions. Safe ones. But her mind refused to be still. The thought echoed again, distant and surreal, like someone else's memory she'd stumbled into. *I have a daughter.* She clung to the rhythm of her hands—herbs, fish, blade. Deliberate cuts. Clean lines. *One thing at a time.* The scent of rosemary and fresh-caught trout filled the small space. It should have been comforting.

A ripple of laughter floated in from outside, sharp against the quiet like a snapped twig. Raven paused, knife hovering over a fillet, the sound tugging her out of her thoughts.

She set the blade down and moved to the wagon door, wiping her hands on a cloth. The firelight cast a warming glow over the clearing, flickering over a table that hadn't been there.

"Go on, join your friends," Celeste said dismissing her wings. "I'll take over in the kitchen."

Raven nodded. "Thank you."

Ashley sat grinning, already amid a deal, her cards flashing between her fingers as she passed them to Ramzey and Gobs. Coins clinked as bettors placed their wagers with the solemnity of a ritual. "Room for one more if you've got the coin," she called, tapping the tabletop exaggeratedly.

Raven raised an eyebrow, glancing over Ashley's shoulder at the rustic structure. "Where did you find a table?"

Ashley pointed with a smirk. "Over in that little tree hut."

Gobs grinned. "I'm sure Avalann won't mind. We'll return it."

"The elf with short red hair, right?" Ashley asked.

"Yes," Raven confirmed, "that's Avalann."

Ashley chuckled as she shuffled the cards expertly. "I can't remember names."

"So Dragons Versus Wizards?" Raven inquired, joining them at the table.

Ashley nodded, her expression lighting up. "The card game has been a tradition in our village for years. It was created after the Dragon Wars—quite a legacy."

"It's straightforward," Gobs began, explaining the rules. "The goal is to collect all five artifacts." Ashley laid a card face down, assigning a red dragon to guard it. The druid and Ramzey groaned audibly.

"What's wrong?" Raven asked, leaning forward, excited to learn more about the game.

"She always wins with that red dragon," Ramzey sighed in resignation.

"Or maybe," Ashley teased, "I might just be bluffing."

The group continued their game as Raven noticed the sun beginning to dip below the horizon. Celeste carefully watched over the meat when suddenly, a flickering blue portal materialized near the wagon. Raven's face lit up with a smile as the rest of the guardians and Thomas emerged.

"Fantastic! Dinner's ready! I'm famished," Shorte exclaimed eagerly, making a beeline toward the spit roasting over the fire. The others exchanged tense glances.

"What's going on?" Raven stood from the table and moved toward the newcomers.

"It's your father," Avalann responded solemnly. "He confronted Shorte and me in town on our way to meet with Thomas."

"Yeah, he was on about Raven, going off about the baby and how we let you run off like that," Shorte added between bites of food.

"Baby?" Thomas choked slightly, clearly caught off guard. "What baby?"

"We told him we hadn't seen you all day and suggested you might have gone down to the pier," Avalann said, sitting next to Shorte, snatching a piece of fish from his plate.

"That's when he stormed over to our cottage, furious, demanding to know if we had any clue where you were," Jarz interjected. "We tried to cover for you, saying I'd created a portal to the windmill for you."

"What about the baby?" Thomas interjected again, still stuck on the unexpected revelation.

"He insisted the quest was off," Avalann continued, ignoring Thomas's question, her tone serious. "Is that true?"

"Only if the group chooses it to be," Celeste answered calmly, joining the circle of friends. "Raven has decided to continue the quest and rescue her sister."

Concern etched itself into Izarra's face. "But your father—"

"Is trying to protect us—I know," Raven interjected firmly. "But who will protect Carya? Besides, Gideon has returned, watching over the realm. We have a window of opportunity."

"Eugor will forgive us when we return Carya," Shorte interjected, punctuating his statement with a loud belch. "Excuse me."

"And if we fail to bring her back," Avalann added solemnly, "we'll be seen as traitors."

"No, it's on me," Raven murmured, her voice tinged with resignation. "He's not the ruler of Waterfront, Suttiir, Iron Cliff, and Thistlebane, so you all can return home safely. I'm willing to make this sacrifice for my sister."

"That's an admirable sentiment, Princess," Ramzey tossed her cards onto the table, "but our chances are slim with our Abyss connection detained by the High Council."

"We don't need that dragon fodder!" Shorte pointed at Celeste. "She's got us covered."

"I'm sorry, Master Dwarf," Celeste responded diplomatically, "but Captain Ramzey is correct. Navigating the Abyss without our connection would be perilous. We stand a better chance with the succubus guiding us."

"How do we break him out of the High Council's custody?" Jarz's brow furrowed in concern. "They'll charge him with numerous violations against the realm."

"I'll go," Raven declared firmly, her voice edged with unwavering resolve. "Breaking into places is what I do best. I'm not just an arcane assassin but a Mortal Guardian."

"No!" came the collective protest from her friends, voices overlapping in urgency.

"The baby—" Gobs started, her voice soft and worried.

"Wait, this baby. Raven, you're pregnant?" Thomas asked, visibly taken aback.

"Keep up, dragon fodder. That's old news," Shorte interjected sharply. "Should've paid attention at the meeting instead of drowning in your sorrows."

"Fine," Raven sighed, redirecting the conversation. "Who's going to sneak into the High Council?"

"We'll give it a shot," Ashley volunteered, motioning to Gobs and Ramzey.

"Sneaking into the High Council isn't like plundering shrimp boats," Jarz cautioned grimly. "You'd end up sharing a cell with Aushade."

"Ramzey might be used to that," Ashley snorted, nudging the captain.

"No one can portal into the High Council except its members and the Realm Guardians," Celeste added, her tone serious. "It has to be me. I'll do it."

"Won't they punish you?" Gobs asked.

"Only if I get caught," Celeste boasted, expanding her wings.

"They'll reverse the ritual," Jarz interjected solemnly, "and you'll lose your status as a Realm Guardian."

Raven glanced at Jarz, noting the gravity in his voice.

"Trust me, I have a plan," Celeste reassured them, her voice steady.

"What's the plan?" Izarra moved closer to her.

The Fey Guardian smiled knowingly. "Mister Fisker, I'll need you to maintain the anti-scrying spell over the camp."

"I will," Jarz said with a resolute nod.

"We shouldn't be doing this," Thomas protested, arms crossed tightly. "If Gideon finds out—"

"Ah, shut it!" Shorte interjected sharply, cutting off Thomas's complaint. "Put on your big boy breeches."

Raven smiled faintly, with worry in her eyes. "May Blade watch over you," she said, resting her hand on the Blade charm around her neck.

Celeste returned Raven's smile with a wink, then nodded resolutely, and with a swift gesture, she conjured a glistening red portal that hovered before them, leading to the heart of the High Council.

# CHAPTER THIRTY

# NEW MEMORIES

Celeste's portal glistened open inside the Great Hall at the High Council. A shiver ran down her spine as she cast a spell to open one of the gold doors, slipping inside with barely a sound. The chamber loomed dark and ominous, shadows stretching across the floor. A few light orbs hovered near the front, casting a ghostly glow over the grand room.

She tried to move softly, but her footsteps echoed in the vast space as she approached a hallway behind the head table. The five council members' chairs stood vacant, their high backs like sentinels watching over the room. Each step she took toward the passageway felt heavier, weighed down by the burden of countless histories and secrets.

At the end of the corridor, a large stone door loomed before her, inscribed with ancient Natus symbols that seemed to pulse with a faint, otherworldly light. A hum of magic in the air, a silent guardian that only relented for the Morganicule—the ritual that granted recruits immortality as Realm Guardians. Taking a deep breath, Celeste placed her hand on the cold stone. The surface was rough and rigid under her fingers, the chill seeping into her skin. She closed her eyes, feeling the magic resonate through her hand.

Or perhaps it was because she was expecting it. She leaned forward, resting her forehead against the cold, unyielding doorstone, and exhaled slowly. The chill seeped into her skin, grounding her in the present moment, even as her mind drifted back to Eugor.

His face floated into her thoughts, his expression a mix of disappointment and sadness when she told him about her decision to become the guardian of the Fey Realm. She could still see his lips pressed into a thin line, a painful plea in his sad eyes.

But then, the memory shifted. Eugor's confused expression, standing at his doorstep, staring at the wrapped infant. The lines on his face were soft as he unfolded the parchment she had left with the baby. She remembered how his features transformed, love replacing bewilderment, as he read her words.

Eugor's face was replaced by Ellie's and Joy'uss's, their gentle smiles encouraging Celeste as she gave birth to Blade in the Fey Realm. Celeste's mind raced with questions. *Did Ellie inform Elora? Was that how she earned a spot on the council?* She lowered her head, her voice barely a whisper. "It doesn't matter anymore."

"What doesn't matter?" Elora's voice pierced the silence, startling Celeste as she jerked her head up, her heart beating brisker as she met the high elf's piercing gaze. Words failed her, leaving her staring blankly at Elora as she stepped closer, her presence commanding and serene. "Let me ask you an easier question. What are you doing here?"

Celeste remained quiet, her gaze wandering over Elora's intricate wardrobe, the fine silks and embroidery reflecting her status. The Fey Guardian's mind churned, searching for a plausible response. "Any word about Tier?"

Elora sighed. "Tessk is investigating."

Celeste frowned. "How can you still trust him?"

"He's a member of the High Council—"

Celeste's laughter cut her off, bitter and unexpected. "That means nothing to me," she spat, brushing past Elora without a second glance.

"Nice chat," Elora called, her voice laced with sarcasm.

The Fey Guardian rushed through the circular chamber and down the Great Hall to the prison cells, her footsteps echoing in the corridor. She peered around the corner, her breath catching as she spotted four High Council guards stationed in front of one of the chambers. *The necromancer must be in there.*

Elora's stern face flashed in her mind as she recited, "Meta-Verto, Elora Clover," the incantation for an illusion spell. The air shimmered around her, cloaking her in the guise of Elora. With a deep breath, she stepped forward, her heart pounding. The elf guards straightened and opened the door without hesitation. *That was easy.*

Inside the chamber, two human guards stood at attention. Aushade sat on a cot, staring down at his hands, his expression blank. Celeste felt a surge of impatience. She motioned for the guards to lower the invisible barrier, her voice demanding as they hesitated, glancing at each other.

Her frustration peaked, and she cast a sleep spell with a flick of her wrist. The guards crumpled to the floor, their breathing deep and even. She twisted a wand, the barrier shimmering briefly before dissolving.

Aushade stood, staring blankly at her. "We don't have much time," she whispered, her voice low and urgent. "Let's go."

"You're not Elora," a familiar voice came from the necromancer.

"Blade," Celeste responded as *both* illusions dropped. Panic surged through her veins, and she dashed for the door. But it slammed shut with a resonant thud, and the locks clicked into place. She turned back, her heart aching as she met her son's disappointed gaze, his head shaking slowly. Desperation clawed at her as she tried to cast a portal, but the magic faded, leaving a faint shimmer.

The prison door creaked open, and Gideon stepped in first, his expression grim, followed closely by Elora. "Celeste," the Mortal Realm Guardian moaned, reaching for her arm.

Celeste yanked away, eyes blazing. "Don't touch me."

Elora sighed, her face a mask of weary resolve. "I was hoping it wouldn't be you."

"If the council did their job, the guardians wouldn't have to keep interfering," Celeste spat, her voice dripping with venom.

"You leave me no choice," Elora said softly but firmly. "I'm calling for an emergency meeting with all the guardians tonight. We'll be replacing the Fey Guardian."

Celeste's heart plummeted. "But—"

"That's three marks. After the trial, you'll be among the mortals again as one of them," Elora declared, leaving. Blade stepped out of the cell, and Gideon moved Celeste in, his grip firm as he twisted the wand to secure the barrier.

"Gideon, Raven needs you," Celeste pleaded, her voice breaking.

The Mortal Realm Guardian placed a comforting hand on Blade's shoulder, ignoring her desperation. "I'm sorry."

"She's going to the Abyss with or without our help," Celeste called out, her voice echoing in the cold, stone chamber.

Gideon paused, glancing back at her, his brow furrowed. "I'll speak with Raven after our meeting."

"By that time, she'll already be there. Remember the time difference," Celeste implored, her voice tight with fear.

"I realize that, but without you or the necromancer, she won't go. I know her," Gideon replied as he exited the room.

"Gideon!" she yelled, frustration and fear tearing at her. She turned to Blade, pleading. "You have to help your sister."

Her son gazed at her, his eyes reflecting a mix of confusion and sorrow. "When they approached me with this plan—because Gideon knew Raven would try this—I never thought it would be you."

Celeste's voice softened, pleading. "I want to help."

"For Tier?" Blade's tone was skeptical.

"Not just for him. Your father—"

"Is happy with his new family," he interrupted, with a hint of bitterness. "What are you doing, Mother?"

Celeste's heart ached at his words. She took a step closer, her eyes searching his. "Blade, I'm trying to protect all of you. This is bigger than any one of us."

Blade clenched his jaw. "You've always been about the bigger picture. But what about us? What about your *family*?"

Her shoulders sagged under the weight of his accusation. "I never meant to hurt you. I thought I was doing the right thing."

He shook his head, a deep sigh escaping his lips. "Right or wrong, it's too late now. We have to deal with the consequences."

Celeste reached out for him, her hand trembling. "Please, Blade. Help me. Help your sister. We can still make this right." She took a deep breath and stared into her son's eyes, her voice trembling with urgency. "Raven will find a way into the Abyss to save her sister. I'm the only person who can watch over her in that foul place and ensure Eugor doesn't lose another child. I love you and your father and always will. Please, help me keep Raven and the others safe."

Blade stared at her for a long moment, his expression conflicted. Finally, he twisted the wand lever, dispelling the invisible barrier.

Celeste's heart leaped as she rushed over and hugged her son tightly. "I need you to understand that I never wanted to leave you. I loved your father, but I had to move on." Tears burned her eyes as she continued, her voice breaking. "Eugor married and had two beautiful daughters, I—"

"Say no more, Mother. I understand." Blade's voice was steady as he opened the door. "Now, follow me."

A guard approached, eyebrows raised. "Sir?"

"Transferring this prisoner to cell four across from the other prisoner in cell three so we can consolidate guard shifts," Blade said, his tone authoritative.

"Aye, sir." The guard nodded, stepping aside.

Celeste followed her son across the corridor, the distant footsteps and muffled voices echoing in the hall, the cold air prickling her skin. When they reached the other cell block, Blade motioned for her to enter cell three.

As the door creaked open, Celeste glanced around, her heart pounding. The cell was small and bare, but it was a step closer to her goal. She turned to Blade, her features softening with gratitude.

"Wake up," Blade ordered sharply, his boot connecting with Aushade's cot. The necromancer stirred, casting a groggy glare at them. "On your feet."

Aushade rose slowly, stretching. "Trial time?"

Celeste, standing nearby, conjured a swirling portal of crimson light. "After you."

"I guess it beats hanging out here," Aushade muttered, stepping through the portal's shimmering threshold.

"I'll make sure the guards steer clear of this cell block," Blade remarked firmly.

"Thank you. And keep Gideon away from his camp."

"Sure."

"I'm hoping everything will be resolved by the time the trial begins, so the council won't need to hunt you down," Celeste remarked with apprehension.

"I hope so, too," Blade replied as he halted her before she could step through. "Protect Raven at all costs."

"I will," she promised solemnly.

"And save Carya, even if it means guiding her soul to the Astral Realm."

Celeste nodded, her features softening. "I love you." She enveloped her son in a heartfelt embrace, kissing his cheek.

"I love you, too," he murmured.

The wind whistled through the campsite as Celeste stepped through the swirling portal, her blond hair whipping around her face like unruly tendrils seeking freedom. Nearby, Captain Ramzey scoured through their meager supplies, searching for something warm enough to shield Aushade from the biting chill the breeze carried.

The campfire struggled against the gusts, its flames flickering wildly. Around it, the group huddled close, their faces illuminated by the dancing orange light. They plucked tender fish meat from the spit, their movements quick and precise, driven by the instinct to satisfy their hunger during the elemental turmoil.

Jarz, resolute, gathered some of the cooked food onto a sturdy plate. He approached the necromancer with measured steps, his presence contrasting with the lively bustle around the fire.

Aushade, cloaked in Ramzey's borrowed warmth, glanced up as Jarz approached, his expression unreadable yet tinged with gratitude as the sword-mage offered him the provisions.

"What took so long?" Ashley's voice cut through the crackling of the campfire, drawing everyone's attention across the makeshift circle.

"I got held up," the Fey Guardian explained tersely, her gaze flicking toward the distant horizon.

"Gideon trouble?" Shorte's voice was low, edged with concern.

The Fey Guardian nodded gravely, her expression betraying a mix of weariness and guarded resolve.

"Is he coming here?" Avalann's voice trembled slightly.

"No," Celeste interjected, her tone steady. "He's still at the High Council, preparing the necromancer's trial."

"It's a good thing she bailed you out when she did," Jarz remarked to his brother.

"Hungry?" Raven's voice broke the tension, her eyes scanning the group.

"Sure," Celeste replied with a grateful smile as Raven handed her a plate laden with fish, meat, and vegetables. "Where did you find the carrots?"

"They're magic. Gobs cast some druid spell. I didn't ask, and I don't want to know. So they may not taste the greatest."

A sudden rush of crimson light bathed the campsite as a portal flared into existence. Tension thickened the air as everyone froze, watching Aushade's armor and sword clatter through. Then, the portal vanished with a faint shimmer.

"Do I even want to ask?" Raven's voice cut through the silence.

Celeste shook her head slightly. "Best not."

"I need to find somewhere to rest and contact Courtlynn." Aushade's voice was weary, and the weight of his armor was evident as he gathered the scattered pieces.

Shorte huffed impatiently. "I can knock you out."

"Not if I beat you to it," Thomas quipped, a hint of threat in his voice.

Raven pointed toward the red and gold gypsy wagon. "You can sleep in there."

Ramzey guided Aushade toward the wagon, a silent gesture of hospitality amid the banter.

"A pirate, a demon, and a necromancer walk into a wagon—I wouldn't want to be in that triangle," Shorte quipped, earning a reproachful glance from Izarra as Jarz settled beside him.

"We have some time. Anyone want to lose more coins?" Ashley suggested, shuffling the cards.

"I want to hear another Shorte camp story," Avalann declared, propping her feet on the table and playfully blocking Ashley's attempt to deal the cards. She toyed with a fishbone toothpick, mischief curling at the corners of her grin.

"All right," Shorte began, a grin on his face. "Did you hear about the wizard and the—"

"Yes," chorused most of the gang in unison.

"I haven't," Ashley said, leaning forward with curiosity.

Izarra chuckled softly. "Basically, Shorte starts it, and Raven scares you. So I'm keeping my eyes on you, Miss Naelo."

"Raven, tell us a story about Carya," Gobs interjected suddenly.

"I don't know," Raven hesitated, scratching her head. "I'm not as good a storyteller as Shorte."

"No one is, sweetheart," Shorte belched loudly, eliciting laughter from everyone around the campfire.

A nostalgic sensation enveloped the group, a bond Celeste hadn't experienced since her days as a Realm Guardian. This makeshift family filled a void she hadn't realized existed. "Please, Raven."

"If you insist," Raven replied, her voice carrying a hint of fondness. "I remember when I was around seven, and a nightmare woke me. I was wearing my favorite purple nightgown."

"Don't you still wear it?" Shorte poked fun. "Or did Gideon burn it?"

Raven ignored the jab, continuing her story without missing a beat. "I crept down the stairs, trying not to wake Carya because I knew she would make me return to bed. I swear she slept with one eye open, always ready to catch me causing trouble."

"I think we can all understand why she would," Izarra quipped, a light-hearted smile tugging at her lips.

Raven smiled wistfully. "I don't know why I remember this so vividly, but before I ventured into the secret passage, I snagged a sugar cookie my mom had baked earlier in the day."

"Now I'm hungry again," Shorte blurted out.

"I dashed to the door leading to the hidden passage and pushed it open," Raven continued, her voice carrying the thrill of her childhood escapade. "Normally, I'd never go down there alone. I always imagined it as this long, dark, scary corridor."

"That hallway isn't that long," Jarz remarked.

"It is when you're seven," Raven protested.

"Or tipsy," Izarra said teasingly, earning a light nudge from Jarz.

"Are you two quite finished?" Raven asked with an amused raise of her brow before resuming her tale. "My father had these sconces on the wall shaped like dragon heads. The torchlight made their eyes glow eerily. I finally mustered the courage to run, but just as I did, I heard Carya yell, 'Get back to bed!' before I could take a step." She chuckled softly. "She scared the ogre poop out of me, and I dropped my precious cookie."

"Not the cookie!" Shorte exclaimed dramatically.

"I think Carya told me this story," Thomas interjected softly, a hint of nostalgia coloring his voice.

"Please continue. What happened next?" Celeste encouraged gently, sensing Raven's willingness to share more.

"Carya scolded me for getting into trouble. I don't remember exactly what she said, but I recall brushing off any dirt or dust and boldly taking a bite." Raven grinned shyly.

"You saved the cookie!" Ashley exclaimed with a grin, beating Shorte to the punchline.

"It was a good cookie," Raven admitted. "I sprinted down the hallway with Carya hot on my heels. At the end of the tunnel, a false wall created the illusion of a dead end. But if you pushed on it just right, it swung open into my father's work chamber. I remember a new tapestry hanging there, and I couldn't help but blurt out 'beauteous,' which annoyed Carya. That word stuck with me since I overheard my father tell my mother she was the most beauteous creature in Euphrasia."

Celeste caught herself mid-cough. *He used to tell me that.*

"You all right?" Shorte asked, his voice softer than usual.

"I'm fine," Celeste assured him quickly, regaining her composure. "Just the dry air from the fire."

Raven picked up the thread of her story, her voice carrying a mixture of nostalgia and perseverance. "My sister wanted us to return, but I could only think about finding my mother. We could hear voices echoing down the hallway, so I pushed open the door and slipped out before Carya could catch me."

"A rogue already in training," Celeste teased gently.

Raven shot Celeste a playful glare, sipped her drink, and continued with animated gestures. "When I finally reached the end of the hallway, a crowd suddenly screamed in unison, 'ONE!' It startled me so much, my heart nearly leaped out of my chest! I was determined to figure out what was happening, but I couldn't find anything. Everyone in front of me seemed so much taller."

"Welcome to my hell," Shorte muttered under his breath.

Raven shook her head with a chuckle. "I pushed through the crowd until I finally reached the front. My father's favorite painting was hanging on the wall—and in it, a naked dwarf with fiery red hair and a bushy beard."

"Rusty!" Izarra blurted out, her eyes widening with recognition.

"Was his butt wrinkled like Shorte's?" Avalann teased wickedly.

Shorte nearly choked on his drink. "Hey! I have a nice rump, thank you very much."

"Anyway," Raven interjected, returning the conversation to her story. "There he was, Rusty, running around the ebony tree, chased by three knights."

"I remember those guys," Izarra reminisced with a nostalgic smile. "They were surprisingly gentle when they tossed me out of the picture."

Jarz blinked, clearly intrigued by the revelation.

"I remember that night, too," Thomas chimed friskily.

Raven brushed off the interruption and continued her tale. "Carya finally caught up to me, and I couldn't help but giggle, pointing at the dwarf's arse. I had no idea how he got into the painting until my sister explained that if you touch it, it sucks you in, naked. I must've walked past that portrait a hundred times, never knowing."

"I have a confession," Celeste interjected as the group gathered around her. "Gideon and I gifted that painting to your father. Our third-year project at Waterfront was to create a magical object. Eugor didn't understand how it worked until we urged him to touch it." She blushed as she recalled the memory. "Gideon and I watched him run from those knights for a whole day before he finally gave up, and they tossed him out. After that, Euwee and I began courting."

"Euwee," Ramzey teased. "That's cute."

"Must have liked what you saw," Shorte said with a wink.

Celeste felt heat bloom across her cheeks like wildfire. She ducked her chin slightly as if that could stop the flood of warmth spreading to the tips of her ears. *Blade, help me. All the stories to resurface.* She tried to smother her smile, but the memory was too strong. She remembered that he'd looked so ridiculous charging through illusion knights in his black braies, cursing their names the whole way. But it was after—when he'd found her behind the stables, his hair stuck up in every direction, his pride bruised but his laughter genuine—that she'd first felt it. That pull. "I did," she said quietly, almost to herself. "I liked what I saw."

The fire crackled nearby, but she barely noticed. All she could think of was Eugor's goofy, lopsided, genuine smile. *Not the war-trained face he wore for others but the one he reserved for me.*

"He never told me that part of the story," Raven remarked, clearly surprised. "That explains why there are signs in five different languages that read 'do not touch,' yet people still do it anyway."

Izarra raised her hand with an embarrassing grin as Celeste beamed, glancing at her newfound friends with fondness and uncertainty. *Are we doing the right thing, heading to the Abyss?*

Raven sighed thoughtfully. "If my parents had warned me not to touch it, I probably would have done it just to see what would happen. Even if it meant everyone seeing my rear end!"

Celeste arched an eyebrow.

"I saw your arse," Thomas interjected loudly, focusing intently on his mug. "Among other things. It's a cute arse."

Raven blushed deeply as the paladin fell silent. Celeste tightened her lips behind her cup, though she felt a twist of secondhand embarrassment.

"Enough with the arse talk! Someone please take the dragon fodder's ale," Shorte declared dramatically.

Thomas stood and waved the stick he was using to cook fish. "No one is taking my ale, Mister Stone-Grin."

*He's drunker than he thinks,* Celeste noted, her gaze flicking to the uneven angle of Thomas's stick. *Or maybe he's just pretending to be. Either way, this is getting off track fast.*

"May I continue?" Raven asked, regaining control of the conversation as Thomas sat back down.

Celeste nodded slightly in encouragement. *Let her speak. I can tell she's been clinging to this story like a blade behind her back.*

"Before my sister could drag me away, a dwarf bumped into me and spilled his ale all over my gown." She glanced at Shorte, sharing a private moment. "It was Pixie."

"Ah, Pixie. May Blade watch over his soul," Shorte said somberly.

Celeste's heart pinched. She hadn't thought about Pixie in years, and the memory struck with an unexpected sting. His laughter was the way he always managed to be in the wrong place with the right kind of charm. *Especially when he ends up lost in the Fey Realm with a package because Gideon pulled a prank.*

Raven sighed. "He handed me his mug to hold and told me to take a sip if I wanted."

"Hold up!" Ashley interrupted incredulously. "He gave ale to a seven-year-old?"

"Remember, Ash," Gobs said sagely, "an elf may appear seven but be fifty-ish. Pixie didn't realize Raven was a half-elf and ages like a human."

Celeste leaned forward slightly, lips pursed. *Or maybe he realized and just didn't care. That was Pixie, too. Always trusting the world to be a little gentler than it was.*

Raven nodded in agreement. "Anyway, my curiosity got the better of me, and I was just about to take a sip when the group suddenly yelled, startling me and causing me to drop the ale. Pixie teased me about elves being unable to hold our liquor and asked how old I was. Before I could answer, my mother's voice cut through the commotion, declaring, 'She's a half-elf, only seven, and will be grounded in her personal chamber for eternity.'"

"Oh, honey! The wrath of a mom," Ashley exclaimed.

"She was furious," Raven continued, her voice tinged with amusement at the memory. "She said, 'You can explain this to your father.' The crowd parted as Gideon and my father entered."

Thomas couldn't resist. "Your future husband to the rescue, I presume." His attempt at humor fell flat, and the group fell silent, exchanging awkward glances.

"Throw this arse in the lake to sober him up," Shorte interjected loudly, attempting to break the tension.

Thomas stood abruptly, towering over Shorte with a challenging glare. "I'd like to see—"

"Enough!" Celeste's voice cut through the rising tension. Shorte and Thomas reluctantly settled down, and Celeste turned to Raven with a gentle smile. "Please, Raven, continue your story."

"My father came over and asked why I smelled of ale," Raven recounted, a nostalgic smile across her face. "So I explained the whole story to him, then pointed at the portrait and exclaimed, 'Dwarf butt.' Gideon cast a spell that pulled the dwarf out of the painting. Before my mother could drag Carya and me away, Rusty lifted his arms, revealing himself. I shouted 'BEAUTEOUS!' before my mother covered my eyes. And that's the end of that tale."

Everyone, except for Thomas, began to clap, their applause filling the air as Celeste watched Raven's face flush with embarrassment and pride. As she recounted the story, the Fey Guardian felt the deep love and connection the young half-elf had for her family.

"That was by no means a short story," Avalann remarked with a smile.

"No, it wasn't," Shorte declared with a hearty laugh.

Celeste grinned. "Raven, it was a . . . beauteous story, and we'll have your sister back again to create new memories."

"I hope so," Raven replied softly, a hint of longing in her voice, before heading off to refill her mug.

Observing the group, Celeste noted their sense of calm and camaraderie. Izarra and Jarz stole a moment at the water's edge, sharing a quick kiss. Meanwhile, Thomas, Ashley, and Gobs began setting up for a new card game, their laughter blending with the teasing banter between Shorte and Raven about dwarf butts. She took a moment to collect her thoughts, her gaze drifting toward the horizon where the evening sun painted the sky in hues of orange and pink.

Avalann's voice broke through her reverie. "Are you all right?"

"I'm fine," Celeste replied, though her tone lacked conviction. "Just thinking about our quest. I can't let them down. If Eugor—"

"You still love him," Avalann interrupted, stating the truth plainly.

Celeste sighed softly, her expression softening with a touch of sadness. "I suppose I do. Watching him raise a new family was one of the hardest things. Being immortal, with all this power, yet not having the one thing that truly makes you happy. The role of a guardian is both a blessing and a curse." She turned to Raven, who unconsciously placed a protective hand on her pregnant belly, a reminder of the vulnerabilities and responsibilities that bound them together. "But I promised to make sure all of you are safe. And that is what I intend to do."

Avalann hesitated for a moment before pressing on with her question. "What about Tier?"

Celeste pondered Avalann's question momentarily, her thoughts lingering. "He helped me through an emotional time," she finally admitted, her voice soft but resolute. "I care for him as much as my heart will allow." As she stood and stretched, her gaze drifted toward the gypsy wagon. "Has Aushade reached the succubus yet?"

Before Avalann could respond, an orange portal, indicating an unnatural source of magic, opened near the campfire, casting a flickering light across the faces of the assembled group. In an instant, Celeste unsheathed her vorpal sword, her senses on high alert as she focused on what or who might emerge from the portal.

The group gathered around, tense and ready. Thomas adjusted his grip on his makeshift weapon while Raven's hand moved instinctively to the hilt of her dagger. Shorte, ever the cautious one, positioned himself defensively, ready to react immediately. A hushed silence fell over the camp as they awaited the portal's revelation.

# CHAPTER THIRTY-ONE

# MY WORLD

Courtlynn dropped from her perch, the wind of her descent tugging at her hair. *It's time.* Her bare feet hit the obsidian floor with a soft thud, sending a ripple of excitement up her spine. She strode toward the alcove, her heart ticking faster.

Sliding into a short, black leather corset dress, a strange sense of confinement tugged at her ribs. The garment cinched tighter than expected, the cool material clinging like a second skin. On the Seventh Layer, clothing was an anomaly, a relic of forgotten modesty, an indulgence she wore like armor.

Behind her, a voice crackled with suspicion. "Someone had a nice rest," Vanessa noted, arms crossed, following Courtlynn's every move like a hawk tracking prey. "Where are you off to?"

"The Mortal Realm," Courtlynn responded, joy threading through her tone as she snapped the final clasp into place. The metallic click echoed faintly, like a closing lock. She turned, letting Vanessa see her fully.

"To visit Aushade?" Vanessa asked in disbelief. "And to battle Draklor with a handful of mortals?"

"Yes." Courtlynn stepped forward deliberately, her heels clicking with each stride, the faint heat from the basalt seeping into her soles. She placed her hands on her hips, squaring herself with Vanessa. "How do I look?"

Vanessa tilted her head, her expression unreadable. Then, a smirk broke through. "Like you're ready to stir up trouble." The smile faded as quickly as it had come. Vanessa's brow furrowed, and she stepped closer, lowering her voice. "Remember, our race only survived by surrendering the Sixth Layer to the balors without a fight."

Courtlynn flinched, her hands curled into fists, knuckles brushing the curve of her waist. "And I've been bound to Draklor ever since," she said, each word sharp with old anger. "I watched the balors conquer each layer, knowing it was wrong, but I had to obey my master."

Vanessa's gaze softened, but her voice turned flinty. "You've also helped him kill innocents."

A muscle ticked in Courtlynn's jaw. She inhaled slowly, the sulfur-scented air biting at her throat. "I know," she admitted. "But not anymore. You get numb to the carnage, but the power is intoxicating," Courtlynn admitted, with no remorse. "Whenever the balors went to war, the Demon Lords never chose Draklor to command an army. It infuriated him because he always thought he was better. I know his weakness. It's his arrogance. He believes he's invincible with his new army. However, they've only just advanced to the Second Layer and will likely remain disorganized. And now that he has his new pet, Lady Chaotica—"

"Now you just sound bitter, Lynnie."

Courtlynn's lip curled, but she caught herself before snapping back. *Lynnie.* The name grated more than it should have. She turned away from Vanessa, fingers brushing the edge of a scorched table as she walked past, her shoulders tightened. "I feel sorry for her," she said at last, her voice dipping, the edge dulled by honesty. A flicker of something warm surfaced—gratitude, reluctant and unwelcome. *After all, she stepped in and kept me from being struck again.* The memory, sudden and sharp, twisted her stomach. She pressed her palm flat against the wall, awaiting impact.

Vanessa's tone grew hushed, uncertain. "But they wouldn't dare challenge the ceredellas for the First Layer. Would they?"

Courtlynn turned back to face Vanessa, brow furrowing. A shiver ghosted down her spine at the mention of the ceredellas. Her fingers twitched at her side. "Draklor might," she said, shaking off the image of his clawed hands. "He's been working with Tessk." Her words tasted like ash.

The door creaked. Gimp shuffled in like a breeze from a broken dream— off-kilter, light on his feet but heavy in presence. Once charred stumps, his wings billowed behind him in mismatched shades of stitched velvet, silk, and old canvas. They rustled softly.

Courtlynn blinked, caught between horror and hilarity. "What happened to you?" she asked, one brow arched as she bit the inside of her cheek to stifle a laugh.

Vanessa's grin was unapologetic. "I have a friend who does this kind of stuff."

"I still can't fly," Gimp huffed, arms folding as he kicked at the floor, "but I like the colors." He paused, staring at Courtlynn's corset dress, his pout giving way to a curious tilt of his head. "Where're you going?"

Courtlynn tilted her head, a strand of hair slipping into her eyes. She flicked it back, hips shifting subtly as if to reassert control of the room. "To the Mortal Realm." She grabbed her satchel and whip.

"I want to go with you," Gimp pleaded, wrapping his arms around her leg and staring up with his big, dark eyes.

Courtlynn sighed, then smiled. "Fine. Bring your dice. Mortals enjoy games." Gimp clapped and rushed off to grab them as Vanessa shot her a concerned look. "He can guide us to Draklor," she explained as her friend nervously bit her lip. "What? I promise he won't see combat."

"Gimp ready," the imp said, returning, shaking his dice in a tall tankard.

Courtlynn closed her eyes and focused on the location of Aushade. Her body provided a natural portal, the method succubi and incubi used to travel quickly to the Mortal Realm and reach their victims—lovers. There were so many different names for their energy source. As the portal began to shimmer, Courtlynn glanced at Vanessa. "Stay safe. We'll be back soon."

Vanessa nodded. "Take care of him."

With a final deep breath, Courtlynn stepped through the portal, Gimp at her side, his tankard rattling with the promise of games. The transition was smooth, the familiar pull of the Mortal Realm's energy tingling through her senses. She was immediately met with the wide-eyed stare of the paladin she had visited the other night. His mug slipped from his hand, hitting the ground with a dull thud. The chatter around the campfire died abruptly, the sudden silence almost deafening.

"It's you," Thomas gulped, his voice cracking.

Courtlynn looked around the campfire, searching for Aushade as her nervousness spiked. The flickering flames cast eerie shadows on the unfamiliar faces that now turned toward her, their expressions ranging from shock to suspicion. Their gazes were heavy with unspoken meaning, part question, part accusation.

Gimp, sensing the tension, stayed close behind her, his tiny hands clutching her leg as he peeked out cautiously. The portal closed behind them with a soft whoosh, sealing them into this new, uncertain environment.

"Nice," one of the human females peeked over cards and snickered, breaking the silence, "she's got a whip."

Courtlynn's attention was drawn to the sound of a door opening behind her. Aushade exited the wagon with another woman, and Courtlynn's hand tightened on her whip.

"Would you care for a drink or something to eat?" the druid elf offered, but Courtlynn could only focus on the duo approaching her.

"Courtlynn," Aushade announced warmly, holding out his arms. The succubus embraced him, her eyes narrowing at the other woman eyeing her. Aushade took her face in his hands and kissed her. For one brief moment, a fire burned through her body like nothing she had ever felt with any other human or demon. She gave the brunette a snarl but then felt Gimp grab her leg, pulling her back.

"Let me introduce you." Aushade turned her around to face the campfire. "This is Courtlynn." A wave of stares and unintelligible chatter rippled through the group as Aushade turned to the brunette from the wagon. "This is Captain Ramzey Porter."

Ramzey extended her hand. "It's nice to meet you finally."

Courtlynn took the hand, her grip firm. "Likewise," she replied, though her tone was icy. She couldn't ignore how Ramzey looked at Aushade or how the others observed their interaction. Her mind raced, jealousy simmering beneath the surface. She couldn't afford distractions, not at this moment. *I need to focus on finding Draklor.* But Aushade's presence and the unexpected competition from Ramzey complicated everything.

Aushade must have sensed her loathing for this human, because he quickly moved around the campfire to finish the introductions. First was his brother. She had seen him when Aushade held him prisoner at Grey-Holg. *They look nothing alike.* He held hands with a petite blond girl. Courtlynn wasn't sure if she was a human or a naiad.

Sitting at the fire was a stern-looking red-haired elf, mistrust etched on her face. Next to her was a dwarf whose farts smelled worse than the sulfur mines of the Abyss. A human soldier and a druid sat at a small wooden table. Aushade mentioned that they worked with Ramzey. *Hearing that woman's name makes me want to scratch her eyes out.*

"Courtlynn, are you all right?" Aushade asked, snapping her back to attention.

"Sorry, just a lot to take in. Go on—"

Thomas, the paladin she had seduced to gain strength, gripped his mug so tightly it shook. *Will Aushade forgive me?*

Then, an elf—no half-elf—walked toward her with a look of pure hatred. Courtlynn knew this girl from Aushade's dreams. *She wants me dead.* Courtlynn had often seen that look on her master's face around his enemies.

Then, a guardian stepped next to Raven, holding a vorpal sword. *Celeste.* She knew all about the guardians. Tessk would tell her master what fools they were and how easily they could be controlled. That wasn't the only time she would hear that name. Nightly, when he didn't think anyone was around, Tier would whisper her name repeatedly.

"I'll recast the anti-scry to make sure it's still at full strength," Celeste said, sheathing her vorpal sword with a fluid motion. "If Gideon finds out—"

"He won't," the half-elf interjected firmly, her eyes narrowing slightly as Celeste nodded and stepped toward the wagon to cast the spell, her movements precise and controlled.

Courtlynn offered a nervous grin to the strangers staring back at her, trying to project confidence despite the turmoil within her.

The human warrior with an easygoing demeanor broke the silence. "Who's this little fella accompanying you?" she asked, curiosity brightening her voice. "I love his wings."

"This is Gimp," Courtlynn introduced, her tone softening as she glanced down at the imp clinging to her leg. "He's . . . resourceful."

Gimp peeked out from behind her, his colorful wings fluttering slightly as he shyly waved. "Hello," he said in a small voice, his eyes wide with excitement and caution.

"What are you holding there, buddy?" The dwarf's curiosity was piqued as he pointed to the tall mug in Gimp's hand.

Gimp hobbled over. He upended the cup with a flourish, letting the dice clatter onto the table. The dwarf leaned in intently, watching the dice tumble and settle. "Ignis Alea," Gimp answered, his innocent voice gaining confidence.

"It means Fire Dice," Courtlynn explained. She watched as her small friend enthusiastically explained the game's rules. The group's initial wariness seemed to melt away, replaced by curiosity and amusement. Overall, they seemed welcoming. She noticed, however, that the only person who was keeping to themselves was the paladin.

Strong fingers entwined with hers. Aushade smiled at her and then gently pulled her to the side. "Are you all right?"

"I'm fine," Courtlynn replied, still staring at the paladin. "If you'll excuse me." She made her way over and sat next to Thomas, who focused intently on the piece of trout on the end of his stick.

"I have nothing to say to you." His voice was tinged with anger.

Courtlynn's heart ached. "Thomas, please," she murmured, keeping her voice low. "I didn't come here to cause trouble. I want to help."

Thomas shot her a look, his features tightening with emotion. "Help? After everything—"

"I know," Courtlynn replied softly. "You have every reason to hate me. But I'm here now, and I'm on your side. I want to apologize for my actions that took your love away."

Thomas's face hardened. "My love, her sister"—he pointed to Raven—"his cousin, someone's daughter." The scruffy-faced man stared into the fire. "But I suppose you're here to help, so—" He pulled in his stick and offered the fish to her.

"I try not to eat," Courtlynn chuckled nervously, "but thank you."

"That's right. You seduce heartbroken men."

Courtlynn glanced around nervously to see if anyone had overheard. Aushade was staring at her intently, his expression unreadable. The others had gravitated to the table to watch the dice game. Only Raven still focused on her, her gaze cold and unyielding.

"I'm truly sorry," Courtlynn apologized, feeling the weight of their stares.

Thomas glanced away, his jaw clenched. "Sorry won't bring them back."

She wanted to explain, to somehow make him understand the complexities of her past actions, but words felt inadequate. Instead, she reached out and gently touched his arm. "I know I can't change the past, but I'm here now to make things right."

Thomas didn't pull away, but he didn't look at her either. "We'll see," he said, his voice barely audible over the crackling fire.

Raven stood, her stone-cold expression showing she didn't trust the succubus. "We should review the plan before we go."

Courtlynn nodded and retrieved the battle map from her satchel, the same one her ex-master had discarded countless times after his obsessive study sessions. Gimp grabbed his dice and put them in his tankard as she spread the map out on the table.

The group hovered around. "This is the Second Layer of the Abyss," Courtlynn began. "Before the recent battle, it was home to wasptoids and mantoids. Now Draklor and Lady Chaotica control it."

"Lady Chaotica?" Raven questioned, her voice sharp.

"Your sister," Courtlynn responded, her tone laced with regret. "He enjoys naming his pets." Raven shot her with a look of pure anger. "Because of my actions, he now has one of the largest armies in the Abyss Realm." The succubus paused, struggling to collect herself.

The feisty red-haired elf sneered, "Where was this remorse when you butchered everyone?"

Courtlynn's heart pounded in her chest. "I was under his control," her voice barely audible. "I did things I'm not proud of. But I'm here now, trying to make it right."

"Avalann—" Aushade began to defend Courtlynn, glancing at Raven, who just shrugged.

Courtlynn continued, "When your clan leaders assign you to a greater demon, you will make them proud. But I won't stand here and lie that I cared what happened to anyone in this realm. We have used this realm to feed our energy, but our nature is not to kill."

"Then why did you?" Gobs asked, her voice filled with curiosity and a hint of fear.

"For eons, my people have been controlled by the greater demons. If we disobey, we are tortured and starved to death. We have pleaded with the High Council to allow us to relocate to another realm, and they have refused, telling us we're fine where we are."

"Is it because of the whole sexual nature thing?" the warrior human blurted out, obviously trying to defuse the tension. "Because plenty of people would be into that kind of shite."

The dwarf snickered and pointed his finger at Aushade, who just shook his head as Courtlynn responded. "Yes, the High Council felt that the pleasures of the flesh are a distraction. If we were to roam freely, they feel our appetites may be insatiable."

"But you only feed on humans, right?" the half-nymph asked, leaning in with keen interest.

"Yes. Our seduction only works on humans, but succubi receive more from men. If we lay with others, like dwarves, we would not revitalize."

The dwarf grumbled, "You haven't been with the right dwarf."

"Can we get back to the plan, please?" Raven interrupted.

Courtlynn ignored the dwarf's wink and continued, "Draklor has converted thousands of souls into mindless demons by using the artifact at his command. I can try to get you in and out unseen to rescue Lady Chaotica—"

"Carya," Thomas interjected.

"Carya," the succubus corrected, her voice steady. "His army is scattered, scouting the Second Layer."

"What do you suggest?" Ramzey asked, her tone sharp.

"We need more soldiers. I can make a plea to the insectoids to help us fight—"

"Insectoids?" the dwarf huffed, disbelief etched on his face.

"Are we seriously talking about demon bugs?" the ranger elf cut in, her face twisting with disgust.

"They just lost their home after centuries of being there," Courtlynn explained, her voice steady with conviction. "Trust me, they will want revenge."

The group exchanged uneasy glances, their concern unmistakable.

Celeste stepped forward, her voice soft but edged with steel. "Would you give us a moment, please?"

Courtlynn and Gimp drifted toward the water until they were gradually swallowed by the mist curling off the lake. The group's murmurs reached her, but she let their voices blur. Her attention was pulled toward the vast, starless sky, an endless, ink-black dome pressing down from above. Only a sliver of moonlight clung to the water's surface, shimmering like a trembling secret.

The sound of the falls rose and fell in a gentle rhythm, the cascade muffling her restless thoughts. The earth had exhaled, wrapping her in something almost sacred. Her muscles eased, and the tension in her shoulders loosened.

"That's a lot of water!" Gimp exclaimed. He darted toward the shoreline, arms flailing, awe written all over his face. His feet kicked up droplets as he splashed into the shallows, giggling like a child set loose from a cage. "I like this place!"

A giggle escaped her before she could help it. "Me too." She stepped forward, slipping off her heels. The sand greeted her like an old friend—cool, damp, alive beneath her soles. It clung to her skin, grounding her in this moment that felt outside of time. Her wings flexed behind her with a low creak, stretching wide with a sigh of relief. The ache in them—ignored for too long—faded as she rolled her shoulders and inhaled the crisp night air.

Courtlynn didn't hear Aushade approach—only felt the sudden warmth of his presence beside her. Then his fingers slipped into hers. She didn't look at him immediately but stared out over the water, letting the cool spray from the lake kiss her cheeks, her hand tightening slightly around his. For now, she let herself feel it—the peace, the calm, the fragile illusion that she could still be something other than a weapon.

"They're ready for you to return," Aushade stated gently.

Courtlynn grabbed her heels and flung them into the water with a decisive toss. "They'll slow me down," she declared as Aushade smiled, a hint of admiration in his eyes, and escorted them back to the table.

"We'll split into two teams," Raven instructed, her voice firm. "Group One: Aushade, the succubus—"

"Courtlynn," Aushade blurted out, his voice carrying a note of insistence. It was a small gesture, but it made her feel more accepted, more human. She glanced at the others, noting their varied expressions—some skeptical, some supportive.

Raven paused, her gaze shifting to meet the succubus. "Courtlynn, Avalann, Jarz—"

"I want to be with Jarz," Izarra demanded, her voice firm.

"Fine, Izarra and Ramzey," Raven replied, trying to keep order.

"No," Courtlynn blurted out, her voice louder than intended. Everyone stared at her, and she thought she witnessed Ramzey give Aushade a hidden smirk. "Fine, whatever," she muttered, biting back her frustration. *Maybe I can toss her into a lava pit.*

Raven continued, "Group One will contact the insectoids. Group Two—Thomas, Ashley, Celeste, Gobs, Shorte, and I will search for Carya."

The dwarf huffed. "Oh no, the dragon fodder doesn't even have his weapon."

Thomas held up his fists, a settled look on his face. "I have two of them."

"You can't go to the Abyss with just fists," Aushade's brother advised.

Celeste carefully handed Thomas her vorpal sword, her expression serious. "Lose it, and I'll kill you myself."

Thomas swung it back and forth, a grin spreading across his face. "I've got to get one of these."

Gimp pointed to himself, looking hopeful. "Gimp?"

Raven glanced at Courtlynn for guidance. The succubus frowned, worry etched on her face. "I could take Gimp with me, but he'll be a great guide to Draklor's chamber."

"Fine, he's with us," Raven added decisively.

"Will you protect him?" Courtlynn asked anxiously. "If Draklor catches him back in the Second Layer, he'll—"

"We will," Raven answered solemnly. "I swear on my sister."

The dwarf stepped forward, putting his arm around Gimp. "I'll keep my eye on the little fellow."

A stitch of relief stung her, but Courtlynn couldn't shake the anxiety. She glanced at Aushade, who gave her a comforting nod. The group's varied emotions—determination, apprehension, and a touch of camaraderie—hung in the air as they prepared for the mission ahead.

"All right," Raven said, bringing everyone's attention back to the table. "Let's make final preparations. We leave at dawn."

As the group dispersed to gather their gear, Courtlynn took a moment to center herself. The night air was cool against her skin, the sounds of the rushing fall providing a soothing backdrop to the weight of their task. *The road ahead seems perilous, but I have renewed hope with this diverse group of allies.* She knelt in front of Gimp, who was busy admiring the sword Thomas was swinging. "Stay close to Shorte and be careful."

Gimp nodded vigorously, excitement lighting up his face with just a flicker of nervousness. "I will."

Courtlynn nodded. "I need to contact Vanessa to open the Seventh Layer portal so we can access the Second and Third Layer portals."

"I'll escort you to the wagon," Aushade offered.

Courtlynn agreed, turning to Gimp. "Behave." The imp nodded eagerly.

"Don'tcha worry." The dwarf winked.

Courtlynn rolled up the map and placed it back inside her satchel as the excited imp dumped his dice back on the table, hoping to continue the game. She laced her arm through Aushade's when he offered it. As they strode toward the wagon, her eyes were drawn again to the waterfall. "It's exquisite."

"What is?" Aushade asked, puzzled. "Oh, the waterfall."

"The Inferno-Plane consists mostly of rock, lava, and fire. We don't see a lot of water down there. I've visited this realm often but overlooked the scenery because it wasn't a priority."

"But now?"

"Everything's different when you're around," she said, a hint of sadness in her voice. "But when this is over, I'll return to my world, and you'll remain here in yours."

"We'll figure out some way for you to stay," Aushade insisted, his voice determined. "Even if I have to grovel to the Mortal Realm Guardian."

"We're not exactly on his good side."

Aushade chuckled, the sound lightening the mood. "No, we're not."

Courtlynn stopped and turned to Aushade, her expression solemn. "I want to save your cousin."

Aushade glanced at her, his expression softening. "And we will. Together."

"They won't forgive me until I do," Courtlynn said, her voice tinged with regret.

"*Us.* They won't forgive *us.* But that's not even a guarantee. We've hurt many people. I'm not sure how we can make up for that." They shared a half-grin, a fleeting moment of solidarity. "But we're in this together."

Courtlynn glanced back at the camp, her gaze landing on Ramzey. "What about the she-wolf that follows you?"

"Porter? She's just a friend who lost her grand—"

"I revitalized with Thomas," Courtlynn blurted out, unable to keep it inside any longer.

Aushade paused, his expression shifting to one of hurt and disbelief. "Wait . . . you—with him?"

She nodded, feeling guilty as she saw the pain in his eyes.

"I never laid with Ramzey. I only shared her cabin," he said, his voice filled with hurt. "I only wanted you."

"I almost perished because I couldn't find you," Courtlynn pleaded, her voice cracking. "It was only once—"

Aushade mumbled, "So the feather wasn't the only thing you gave him."

The words landed like a slap. Courtlynn's hand flew up before she could stop it—reflex, rage, heartache—*crack*. Her palm struck his scarred cheek, the sound slicing through the air like a whip. Time stalled. Her breath hitched as her hand hovered midair, trembling. The red patch spreading across his cheek . . . it was too familiar. Too *wrong*. She'd seen that same stunned stillness in her reflection once after Draklor had struck her—the raw disbelief, the moment of silence before the shame set in. Her stomach turned violently.

Courtlynn staggered back, bile and guilt rising in her throat. Without another word, she spun on her heel and fled toward the wagon, the world warping through her tear-blurred vision. Her bare feet pounded the earth, cold sand giving way to hardwood as she climbed inside and slammed the door shut behind her. Inside, it was too small. Too neat.

She collapsed onto a bench, curling into herself as sobs wracked her body. The echoes of her outburst bounced around the wagon's walls, a cruel reminder of what she'd done. Aushade's words had gutted her, but her reaction . . . *I became him. I became Draklor.*

She buried her face in her hands, tears stinging like acid. The pain of the insult paled now beside the agony of her betrayal. Of losing control. Of not knowing who she was anymore, without chains or orders.

Feeling the suffocating weight of the Mortal Realm's restrictions, Courtlynn stripped off her dress, letting the fabric pool at her feet. The cool cabin air coated her skin, a fleeting taste of freedom. She glanced out the window, her gaze falling upon Aushade moping by the campfire, his shoulders slumped in dejection. Ramzey approached him, her movements gentle and cautious. Aushade brusquely dismissed the she-wolf's attempts to comfort him. The sharp stab of jealousy mingled with her satisfaction, creating a confusing whirlwind of emotions within her.

She watched him silently, his despondent posture saying more than words could. She almost felt his misery, echoing her internal struggle. The sight of Ramzey's rejection brought a bitter smile to her lips, a reminder that she wasn't the only one wrestling with demons tonight.

Courtlynn lay on her side on the bed, maneuvering her wings to fit inside the cramped space. The recent surge of emotions left her exhausted, but somehow, it made it easier for her to rest. She couldn't shake the image of Aushade's hurt expression as she closed her eyes. The path to redemption seemed more challenging than ever, but for now, she allowed herself a moment of peace amid the chaos.

A fuzzy image of Vanessa appeared in her mind. "Open the portal," Court-lynn commanded. Her friend nodded, and as Courtlynn's meditation broke, an orange glow filled the windows of the dark wagon.

"Gather your weapons!" someone shouted outside. "Don't forget the canteens!"

Still nude, Courtlynn strutted out of the wagon, her confidence unwaver-ing. The others were preparing their weapons. The half-nymph was spinning her trident, water pulsing out of it. The dwarf banged his mace against his shield and belched. Jarz was tightening Aushade's bracers.

The party stopped and gawked at her sudden appearance, their expressions combining surprise and admiration. "Get used to it," she snapped, grabbing her satchel and whip. The cool air brushed against her bare skin, contrasting with the heat of the Inferno-Plane she was used to. She reveled in the sensation, feeling alive and powerful. Before stepping through the portal, she peered over her shoulder, her eyes meeting Aushade's. "Welcome to my world."

The orange glow of the portal bathed the scene in an eerie light, adding a sense of impending adventure. The murmurs of the group filled the air as they prepared to follow.

As Courtlynn stepped through the portal, a rush of adrenaline flooded her. *This is my domain*, a place where she had power. The familiar heat of the Inferno-Plane welcomed her, but this time, she wasn't alone. She had allies.

# CHAPTER THIRTY-TWO

# KING OF MADNESS

Eugor paced in his work chamber, glancing at the portrait on the wall and rubbing his tired eyes. Mud caked his boots after hours scouring the village paths, a testament to his fruitless search for his youngest daughter. His stomach growled as he touched it, ignoring the hunger warnings. *Raven will find me when she's ready to talk,* but the guilt of their last argument gnawed at him more than his cravings. Explaining everything to Mara made his heart pound and his brow sweat.

His wife entered, brushing off droplets of rain from her cloak. "Sorry, one of the children has fallen ill, and I—Eugor, what's wrong?"

He attempted a smile, but it felt more like a grimace. Taking Mara's hand, he noticed how cold her fingers were against his warm, calloused palm. "I need to speak with you."

"You're making me nervous."

They walked together to the window seat, the deep-red velvet plush against their weary bodies. Lightning cast eerie shadows across the room through the cathedral-style windows as Eugor squeezed Mara's hand and took a deep breath. "Raven is with child." Mara's eyes widened, her breath catching in her throat. "And all her friends know."

Mara sat frozen, her eyes squeezed shut as if warding off a sudden headache. Her fingers clutched the edge of the window seat, knuckles whitening. "What you're telling me is . . . our daughter is pregnant, and I'm the last person in Pángorbis to know."

"Well, not the last." Eugor scratched his chin, a weak smile tugging at his lips. "Gideon doesn't know either." The attempt at humor fell flat in the thickening silence.

Mara's eyes snapped open, piercing him with a look that could cut stone. "How can you jest about this?"

Eugor ran a hand through his hair, tugging at the roots in frustration. "Because I'm not sure what else to do. Part of me is delighted to be a grandpap-pap," he stumbled over the word, his voice catching. "The other part is furious that our daughter didn't trust us, and I'm bewildered at the thought of my best friend as the father of my grandchild."

Mara's lips thinned into a tight line. "Raven should have told us," she said, her tone sharp with hurt. "This changes everything. I don't care if all the Realm Guardians are there to protect her. She can't go."

He exhaled deeply, the weight of the day pressing down on him. "Our daughter said she just found out, and I believe her. But an orc ritual kind of ruined that surprise. Gideon—"

Before Eugor could finish, a knock echoed through the chamber. He glanced at Mara, a question in his eyes, before turning toward the door. "Enter."

Queen Baela Luhnar swept into the chamber, her face drawn with worry, flanked by the Greenorrs. "We're sorry to disturb you, King Naelo," Queen Baela said, her voice barely masking her urgency, "but I need to speak with you about my husband."

"No need to apologize." Eugor gestured to the chairs around his desk. "Please, have a seat."

The queen and her escorts settled into the chairs. Baela took a deep breath, her hands clasped tightly in her lap. "Since the attack here in Omlett, Edlin has become cruel and paranoid." Her voice trembled slightly. "He's shut himself into the castle and has surrounded himself with spells and objects of protection. The survivors have been forced into poverty and servitude, which goes against the wood elves' code."

"When we visited Suttiir for the funeral ritual, I thought King Luhnar seemed ill," Eugor remarked. "His pallor, how he moved—I brushed it off as exhaustion from rebuilding his kingdom."

Queen Baela's eyes darkened, and she clasped her hands tightly together. "He's become cantankerous, poisoning the city. It's as if madness has consumed him. I fled with Avalann and the others because I fear not only for my life but the lives of our people."

Mara leaned forward, her face etched with worry. "What happened between Avalann and the king?"

Arlene stepped forward, her voice filled with pride. "Our daughter freed the children and some elders," she said, her eyes shining with emotion. "It was a brave act but put her in grave danger."

Aemon huffed, his face reddening. "Only after attacking the king and becoming a traitor."

"You and I both know she had no choice," Arlene countered, her voice trembling with emotion. "She did what she thought was right."

Her husband shook his head, frustration engraved in his features. "Her temper—" A swirling red portal materialized behind him, cutting him off. The Mortal Realm Guardian stepped through, his eyes widening at the crowd.

"Brother!" Arlene exclaimed, rushing to embrace him.

"Did I miss the invitation?" Gideon teased, wrapping his arms around his younger sister.

"We're discussing Suttiir business. Nothing for a guardian to worry about," Aemon sneered, his eyes narrowing.

Gideon started, "If you need my help, I'm—"

"You've done enough," Aemon spat, his words laced with venom. "Letting your home be destroyed by demons, turning our daughter into a trait—"

"Enough!" Eugor shouted, his voice booming. The room fell into an uneasy silence, all eyes turning to him. "This is no time to bicker."

Queen Baela stepped forward, her eyes pleading. "King Naelo, I understand you have so much to deal with between your parents's deaths, Carya's loss, and the attack here. But will you try to talk sense into him?"

Eugor began, "Of course. Gideon and I—"

"King Luhnar has declared my brother an enemy now," Arlene sighed, glaring up at Gideon with weary eyes. "He feels you abandoned us."

Gideon shook his head slowly, despair flickering across his face. "I couldn't—"

"We know," Arlene said softly, her voice resigned. "Your mandate forbids you to interfere."

"Then Aemon and I will go and speak with Edlin," Eugor suggested, his voice firm. "We'll leave as soon as possible."

Mara nodded, her expression resolute. "Meanwhile, the survivors of Suttiir are welcome here. The children will move into their new home in a day. We also have temporary housing throughout the city for the elders."

"Thank you, both," Queen Baela said, her voice filled with gratitude as she exited the room. Arlene stepped forward, embracing her brother.

"We'll speak soon," Gideon promised.

Eugor watched Arlene and Aemon leave, then turned to Gideon. "Aemon's still angry about your decision to train Avalann," he stated, moving behind his desk. He noticed the way Mara sat at the window, her gaze sharp and unwavering on his best friend.

Gideon sighed, his shoulders slumping. "He never liked me, but that's not why I'm here. Do you know where Raven is?"

Mara's eyes flickered with concern. "She was home earlier, speaking with Celeste."

Gideon's expression darkened. "Celeste's been imprisoned at the High Council for treason."

"What?!" Eugor exclaimed. His face felt flushed.

Gideon nodded gravely. "She was caught trying to free the necromancer. We must call off the search for Carya. The Abyss is too dangerous right now."

The words landed hard, but Eugor felt the blow in his chest rather than on his face. As if Gideon had reached in and twisted something that hadn't fully healed. He opened his mouth to respond, but the door creaked before he could speak.

Mug bustled in, brass scale in hand, eyes gleaming with pride. "Fixed it!" he chirped, holding the scale high like a prize. His grin faltered as he caught the stillness, the unreadable expressions. "Sorry! Didn't mean to intrude."

Eugor watched the gnome—watched how the brightness dimmed in his face. Mug didn't miss much, not when it came to people.

"Don't be silly, Mug. You're always welcome, my friend," Gideon said, motioning him in.

Mug nodded and moved to the side table, the scale clinking softly as he set it down. The sound rang louder in the silence that followed.

Eugor swallowed the tightness in his throat. The moment had shifted. Not gone—but folded, hidden beneath the careful arrangement of objects and politeness. He still hadn't responded. And maybe that said enough. He took a deep breath. "Gideon, I've already called off the search. I even invoked the royal decree. Raven and the others are forbidden to enter the Abyss."

"Was that before or after I gave them a diamond?" Mug interjected with a casual tone. A hush fell over the room as everyone turned to stare at him. "What?" Mug shrugged. "They broke into the factory, searching for a decent-sized one for the resurrection."

"They broke in?" Eugor repeated, blinking once, then letting out a low whistle. His lips twitched at the corners, like he was trying not to smile. "Damn," he muttered under his breath, shaking his head. "Of course she did." *She really does take after me.*

"What are you teaching her?!" Mara's eyes widened in disbelief, "First, she breaks into Maggie's place, and now his?"

Mug waved off her concern with a casual flick of his hand. "That rogue knows her stuff. That was an advanced lock. But she's been more fearless since she learned about those dragon traits. Good thing you two kept that secret for as long as you did."

Eugor stiffened. The words landed too easily—too lightly. He didn't need to look at Mara to feel her turning toward him, the heat rising in her silence. *Careless. So damned careless.*

His eyes cut toward the gnome, sharp and warning. Not loud. Not obvious. Just a slow turn of the head, the kind that carried history behind it.

Mug didn't notice. Or didn't care.

"You two knew all this time?" Mara's voice cracked like splintered wood—tight with betrayal, brittle with disbelief.

Eugor's mouth was dry. His tongue pressed against the roof of it, heavy with what he should say—what he should have said years ago. He didn't look at her because the truth had always been heavier than the lie. He shifted uncomfortably. "When we couldn't find Ausharz's spell book, all his findings on the dragon traits were lost. It was best to wait until we knew what powers she had."

Gideon nodded, his expression serious. "Eugor and I formed a pact. We would tell her after graduating from my camp."

With a naughty grin, Mug interjected, "Then you and Raven mated, and it slipped your mind?" The three turned their heads slowly toward the gnome, their gazes murderous. Mug threw his hands up innocently. "What?"

Mara's eyes blazed as she snapped, "Why wasn't I included in this pact? I'm her *mother*!"

Eugor's voice dropped to a dangerous hiss, ignoring his wife's fury. "If they've gone against my order, Raven will—"

"They can't get into the Abyss without Celeste or Aushade. Both are locked away in the cells of the High Council," Gideon interjected, his tone calm but firm. "I'll return and get information from Celeste. I promise no harm will come to Raven or the others."

As the guardian raised his hand, a swirling red portal opened with a low hum, the air warping around it like heat over stone.

A heaviness pressed into Eugor's chest—not the kind that could be shaken off, but the type that settled in the bones. He took a step forward. *Do I tell him?* His throat tightened around the thought. The portal flickered, waiting. "Gideon!" he called, the word sharper than intended.

The guardian turned, brows lifting in quiet question.

Eugor's voice caught. His gaze shifted—almost involuntarily—to Mara. She met it, and for a moment, time thinned. Her head shook once, barely perceptible. But her eyes said more. *Not now.* He held the silence a beat longer, the unspoken words blistering on his tongue.

"Please," Mara said, her voice barely above a whisper. "Find them."

"I'll return as soon as possible," Gideon promised, stepping through the portal. The couple sighed in unison as the portal closed behind them.

"Chickened out, huh?" Mug commented, wiping down the scale with a smirk.

"You know?" they both asked in unison, their eyes widening.

"The things you hear when you're under pipes. But I'm not one to fix and tell."

Mara's voice trembled slightly. "Do you think they would disobey a direct order?"

Eugor's brow crumpled. "Raven, most likely, but Avalann and the others—"

"Will follow Raven to the Abyss and back," the gnome interrupted, his tone serious.

"Mug!" Eugor snapped. "Don't you have something else to repair or a young apprentice to feed?"

"Actually, she's been doing all the cooking," Mug replied with a shrug, heading toward the door. "But fine, I'm leaving. If you need me, you know where to find me." He nodded slightly and closed the door behind him.

The room was still, the muffled voices from the tavern below barely audible. Eugor slumped in his chair, placing his head in his hands as Mara stood beside him, her fingers gently running through his silver hair. "How much more heart-ache and loss can our family take?" he sighed.

"I have faith in Gideon," Mara whispered, her hand resting on his shoulder. "He truly loves her."

"We should've told him," Eugor murmured, regret settling in his features.

"No," Mara snapped, her eyes flashing. "Raven would never forgive us for betraying her trust. She'll tell him."

Eugor sighed, his fingers pressing into his temples. "What will happen to their child?"

Mara's expression softened slightly. "What do you mean?"

"When dragon traits and celestial traits mix?" he asked, peering at her through his fingers. "Blade, for example."

Mara thought for a moment, then grinned. "I'm not sure. Our grand-daughter will be—unique."

"Granddaughter?" Eugor replied, feeling a glimmer of hope light his heart. "Could be a boy."

"Mother's intuition," she joked, leaning in for a kiss.

Their lips had barely touched when the door flew open again, causing them both to jump. "Now what?" Eugor groaned, turning to face the intruder.

Aemon stood in the doorway, his face grim. "You need to come quickly. There's a small army marching in from the north road into Omlett. They're carrying the Suttiir banner."

Eugor cursed under his breath. *King Luhnar.* "Mara, send word to Buzz," he instructed as he followed Aemon out the door, his mind racing.

They reached the stables and quickly untethered their horses. Hooves pounded the ground as they galloped up the north road, the wind whipping past them. As they drew closer, Eugor could make out the makeshift weapons of the invading army—pitchforks and farming tools. The bannerman, the only one clad in armor, stood out among the rag-tag elves.

"Aemon, find Queen Baela," Eugor ordered, his eyes narrowing as he watched the disorganized march of the approaching group. He rode forward, raising his hand. "That's far enough," King Naelo declared, his voice carrying the distance. "State your business."

The bannerman unrolled the scroll with trembling hands and began to read, his voice shaky. "King Edlin Luhnar has declared war on the hostile city of Omlett under the charges of harboring the traitor Avalann Greenorr, kidnapping and murdering Queen Baela Luhnar, and committing treason against the rightful King of Euphrasia."

*If they attack, those poor elves will surely die.* "Zern," Eugor yelled, his voice echoing with authority. "Return home! Your king is ill. Avalann isn't a traitor. She saved the children and elders from starvation and death. Queen Baela is here of her own accord, safe from his tyranny. And everyone knows there is no one King of Euphrasia. Please set down your weapons. Stay as our guests and then return home to your families. Both of our cities have seen enough bloodshed."

Eugor's words hung in the air as Zern looked around, his eyes wide with uncertainty. The group of elves behind him shifted uneasily, their makeshift weapons wavering.

"Listen to him," one of Omlett's guards called out, stepping forward with a hand on his sword hilt. "There's no need for more fighting."

Zern swallowed hard, the scroll shaking in his grip. He glanced back at his fellow elves, who mirrored his fear and fatigue.

"Please," Eugor added, his tone softer but still firm. "Go back to your families. Let us end this conflict peacefully."

"We can't!" a young female elf cried out, her voice quivering with fear. "The king threatened our families if we didn't return your head on a pike."

"It was a halberd," another voice shouted from the crowd.

"I'm certain it was a pike," a third voice insisted.

Eugor's eyes narrowed, his rage boiling at the thought of innocent families being threatened. *This is not a professional army. They're just scared.* "Put down your weapons, and I promise I will confront Edlin now."

The rumble of Omlett's cavalry, led by Buzz's chariot, grew louder behind him, a powerful and intimidating sound. Eugor stepped forward, slowly advancing toward the small group of fighters. Zern nervously lowered the scroll, his eyes darting to Omlett's heavily armed guards flanking Eugor's sides.

"Do what he requests!" Queen Baela's voice rang out. Aemon and Arlene approached, their presence reinforcing her command.

"Take them to the Inn for food and water. Hold them in the banquet hall," King Naelo ordered Buzz. "Scrounge up some blankets from the barracks as well, Aemon. I must go to Maggie's shop and retrieve a portal scroll to Suttiir."

"That's not wise, sir." A thin elf stepped forward, handing him a scroll. "I'm supposed to give you this. It's a trap. The king placed the portal receiver in a pit of poisonous creatures."

Eugor's eyes narrowed as he scanned the scroll. "Are there any wizards among your group?"

"No, sir. He's using them to detect illusions," the elf replied, shaking his head.

Eugor exhaled sharply. "I need to ride then. Aemon, inform Mara I'll return as soon as possible."

"I'm going with you," Baela stated, her voice steady but determined. "If Edlin sees I'm safe, he may not harm you. We can talk to him together."

Eugor nodded, appreciating her bravery. He helped her onto his horse, Shadow, securing her in the saddle.

"In all my years as his queen, I have never seen him hurt or threaten his people. This must stop before more elves die."

"Agreed." He placed the portal scroll inside the pouch on his horse. *There is no time for armor, just like in my younger days.* He snapped the reins, and the horse bolted forward.

The day's journey passed in a blur, Baela keeping him company. Her presence was a comfort as they rode, exchanging stories and strategizing their approach. A piercing stab in his chest resonated as they crossed the battlefield where he'd lost his eldest daughter. The memory was sharp, the grief still raw.

As the sun dipped below the horizon, the stars began to blaze brightly, filling the ink-black sky. They dismounted from Shadow, their muscles stiff from the long ride. Torches flickered along the stone path, casting eerie shadows as the harsh darkness poisoned his homeland. "We're almost there," he said, his voice low, as they approached the guard towers.

Two human wizards, their faces stern and wands at the ready, stepped forward to block their path. "Halt!" one of the wizards commanded, his wand tip glowing faintly. "State your business."

Eugor raised his hands in a gesture of peace. "I am King Naelo, and this is Queen Baela. We've come to speak with King Edlin."

The wizards exchanged glances, their eyes narrowing as they scrutinized the newcomers. "We've been expecting you," the second wizard said, his voice tinged with suspicion. "But we need to verify your identities."

Baela stepped forward, her voice calm but authoritative. "You know who we are. Let us pass. That's an order."

The wizards hesitated, then nodded. "Very well," one said, stepping aside. "But be warned, the king is not himself."

Eugor nodded, his jaw set with steely resolve. "We understand. Lead the way."

The wizards guided them up the path, the torches flickering ominously. Eugor's heart pounded as they neared the throne room entrance.

"Step aside," Queen Baela commanded the royal guards, her voice firm and unwavering.

"I'm sorry, but no one is permitted inside," the taller guard declared, blocking her path.

Baela's eyes blazed with steely resolve. "I'm Queen Baela Luhnar, and I demand to see my husband."

The other guard moved beside them, waving a wand around their bodies. The wand emitted a soft glow, confirming their identities. "They're unaltered. King Luhnar is in the throne room," the guard said, tilting his head. "Follow me."

Eugor and Baela followed, their footsteps echoing through the softly lit halls. Firelight flickered under the door's crack. They exchanged a tense glance and took a deep breath before pushing the door open. King Luhnar sat hunched over, staring into the flames.

"Edlin!" they called out in unison, their voices filled with hope and dread. The King of Suttiir turned slowly, his face pale and worn, dark bags under his eyes that gave him a haunted appearance.

Eugor stepped forward, his voice gentle but concerned. "My friend, I've heard you're not well."

Edlin's eyes moved sluggishly to his wife, and then he pointed a trembling finger at her. "Who are you?"

The queen's voice broke with emotion. "It's me, Baela."

"My wife is dead!" Edlin snapped, his voice edged with madness. "Killed by my enemies."

The queen stepped closer, her eyes pleading. "No! *Meleth Nin*. My love, it's me."

King Luhnar turned back, his gaze locking onto Eugor with a wild intensity. He staggered forward, his steps unsteady but fueled by anger. "And you—traitor!" Edlin spat, his voice a venomous hiss. "You're in cahoots with Gideon and his guardians to take over Suttiir." He moved closer until he was inches from Eugor's face, his breath hot and sour. "You killed my queen, killed my people, and stole Celeste from me! Now you want my crown!"

*Celeste?* Eugor held his ground, his eyes unwavering as Edlin's accusations filled the room with tension. *That was close to a century ago.* Just as Edlin lunged closer, Eugor deftly sidestepped, causing the unsteady king to stagger. The guard in the corner tensed, stepping forward with a hand on his weapon.

"Halt!" Queen Baela ordered, holding up her hand to stop the guard.

"Edlin, listen to me!" Eugor's voice cut through the tension, firm and steady. "I am here to help you. Queen Baela is alive and well. Look at her!"

Baela stepped forward, her eyes filled with tears. "*Meleth Nin*, it's me. I'm right here." Edlin's eyes flickered with confusion, his rage momentarily abated by the sight of his wife. He glanced from Eugor to Baela, his expression torn between disbelief and recognition. "Edlin, please," Baela pleaded, reaching out a trembling hand. "You know me. You know I would never betray you." The king's shoulders slumped, and he took a shaky breath. Seeing the shift in Edlin's demeanor, the guard relaxed but remained vigilant.

Eugor stepped closer, his tone softening. "We are not your enemies, Edlin. We want to help you and your people. Let us do that."

King Luhnar's eyes filled with tears as he looked at his wife. "Baela—is it really you?"

"Yes, my love," Baela whispered, stepping into his arms. "It's really me."

The room fell into a heavy silence as Edlin clung to Baela, his anger melting.

"Edlin, you're not well," Eugor pleaded, his voice steady but desperate. "Let me take you to Stone-Prayer and Mara. We can help."

"You'll never take me alive!" King Edlin bellowed, his voice echoing through the chamber. He pulled out a dagger, the blade glinting menacingly in the firelight.

"Please don't do this," Eugor begged, his hands raised in a gesture of peace.

"Do you see this?" Edlin yelled, holding up the dagger. "The man you sent to assassinate me in Omlett dropped this when he was unconscious. I took it as spoils of war when Thomas was distracted."

"My friend, that wizard Astrick was working with demons," Eugor explained, his voice filled with urgency.

"Lies!" Edlin roared, his eyes wild with rage.

Queen Baela stepped between the kings, her presence a calming force. But Edlin lashed out, swinging the blade. The dagger's sharp edge ripped through her cloak, sending her stumbling backward onto the floor.

"Baela!" Eugor shouted, reaching out, but it was too late.

Edlin pounced on her, his movements frenzied and desperate. He pressed the dagger near her throat, his eyes filled with madness. "Stay back!" he snarled, his voice dangerous.

Eugor froze, his heart pounding in his chest. "Edlin, listen to me. This isn't you. Let her go."

Baela, her breath coming in quick gasps, looked up at her husband with tear-filled eyes. "*Meleth Nin*, please. Remember who you are. Remember us." The crackling of the fire rippled through the deafening silence. Edlin's grip on the dagger wavered, his expression torn.

"Baela!" Eugor shouted, lunging forward and tackling Edlin to the ground. The knife clattered to the floor, echoing sharply in the tense silence. King Naelo quickly crawled to the queen as the guard rushed to subdue Edlin. "Are you all right?" he asked, his voice laced with concern.

"I'm fine," Baela replied, sitting up slowly. Her eyes widened in horror as she screamed, "Eugor!"

King Naelo turned just in time to see Edlin wielding the guard's sword with rage and madness gleaming in his eyes. He stood cautiously, calculating every move.

Edlin stood tall, his sword glinting in the light. "You sure you want to do this without a weapon?" he taunted. With a shout, Edlin charged, his sword slicing through the air.

Eugor sidestepped, quick as a fox, as the blade whistled past him. Before Edlin could recover, Eugor lashed out with a powerful kick to Edlin's side. The impact sent the king staggering, but he quickly regained his footing, eyes blazing with resolve. He swung again, this time aiming lower.

Eugor leaped back, his movements fluid and precise, almost like a dance. Darting forward, he grabbed Edlin's wrist and twisted, loosening his grip. Eugor's knee shot up, striking Edlin in the groin and forcing him to drop the weapon. Eugor didn't relent—he spun around and aimed a roundhouse kick at Edlin's chest.

Seizing the moment, Eugor tackled Edlin to the ground. They rolled on the hard floor, a tangle of limbs and grunts. Edlin landed a solid punch to Eugor's jaw, but Eugor retaliated with an elbow to the side of Edlin's head. They grappled, each vying for the upper hand. Edlin's fingers brushed the hilt of his fallen sword, and with a desperate lunge, he grabbed it.

Eugor saw the blade flash and reacted instinctively. Twisting his body, he used his legs to trap Edlin's sword arm. With a fierce yank, he disarmed Edlin again, the sword clattering out of reach. He scrambled to his feet, breathing hard, and pulled Edlin by the collar.

Edlin swung a fist, catching Eugor on the cheek, but Eugor responded with a headbutt. Staggering, Edlin retreated a few steps, wiping blood from his lip as he searched for his sword.

Eugor, seeing the desperation in Edlin's eyes, moved in. He delivered a series of rapid punches, each finding its mark on Edlin's torso and face. Edlin blocked what he could, but the onslaught was relentless.

Summoning his last reserves of strength, Edlin lunged at Eugor, tackling him to the ground once more.

Eugor, pinned beneath him, desperately reached for a weapon. With a quick sleight of hand, he produced a hidden dagger from his boot and slashed at Edlin, forcing him to release his grip.

As the struggle intensified, Baela slid Edlin's dagger to King Naelo, who swiftly plunged it into King Luhnar's heart. To ensure he stayed down, he sliced the crazed king's throat, the blade cutting deep. A surge of twisted pleasure shot through Eugor as blood spattered across the floor in crimson arcs, mingling with the dust on the marble floor. The metallic scent filled the air, sharp and pungent.

The light in Edlin's eyes flickered, then slowly faded, leaving only a haunting emptiness behind as Baela cried out, "No!" crawling to her husband as tears streamed down her face. She cradled his head in her lap, her sobs echoing through the chamber.

Eugor dropped the blade, staring at it in disbelief before crumpling next to his fallen friend as the King of Suttiir gasped his final breath.

"What caused this madness?" Baela whispered, her voice breaking.

Eugor shook his head, his heart heavy with regret. *What have I done?* The dagger called to him with an urgency he couldn't ignore, as though his destiny hinged on responding to its beckoning.

# CHAPTER THIRTY-THREE

# NAVIGATING THE ABYSS

A searing wave of heat slammed into Raven like a hammer as she stepped through the portal, her breath catching in her throat. It wasn't just the heat of the Inferno-Plane that hit her—it was the weight of it all. Her body felt heavier than usual from the realm's brutal gravity and the small, growing life inside her. *Thirteen weeks. I should still be resting.* But here she was, leading warriors through hell. She swallowed hard, trying not to think about the risk. About the tiny heartbeat depending on her.

The air was thick and oppressive, each breath a struggle. Raven's dragon armor did its best to keep her body temperature down, but even that enchantment seemed to strain against the sheer furnace of the realm. Around her, the others staggered under the plane's gravity. Celeste, Izarra, and Gobs were already kneeling beside Ashley, who had collapsed. Gimp trembled as he reached out to the warrior with concern etched on his fragile face.

Raven wanted to help, to kneel beside Ashley and offer comfort, but as she took a step, the ground seemed to pull at her with unnatural strength. She gritted her teeth and pressed her palm to her stomach. Her reason to stay upright.

Gobs announced they needed to stay hydrated, and Raven nodded absently. She barely heard Jarz instruct Izarra to stay with her. The half-nymph nodded, a determined glint in her eye as she patted the magical ivory horn decanter hanging at her side but remained quiet.

Raven was relieved because she wasn't ready for conversation yet. Not while every instinct in her screamed to turn around and flee. But turning back wasn't an option. *Carya is out there somewhere, and I can't abandon her.*

Shorte shrugged nonchalantly, a faint smile playing on his lips. "It's not that bad," he said, his voice calm and steady. "Feels just like home when all the forges are burning." His offhand remark about the heat not being that bad grated against Raven's skin. She glanced sideways at the dwarf. Always so unbothered, so cavalier. He didn't have a life growing inside him. He didn't feel every change, every twinge, every surge of fear that something—*anything*—might go wrong.

"Forges or kitchen ovens?" Avalann teased, her voice ragged as she leaned over, hands braced on her knees, still trying to catch her breath. Shorte shot her a glare, his eyes narrowing, but his expression quickly shifted to bewilderment.

The laughter felt far away, muffled by the pounding in Raven's ears. She took another drink of water and tried to calm her fluttering heart. Everything around her was chaos. Demons, heat, memories of her father's broken tales— and inside, a baby who had no idea what world they might be born into.

Raven turned to see what had caught Shorte's attention. Before them stood groups of nude succubi and incubi, their eyes fixed on the new arrivals with unabashed curiosity. A chorus of snickers erupted from her friends, a mix of nervousness and amusement.

"I'm glad you don't have a problem with nudity," Aushade told Ramzey, a naughty glint in his eyes. The captain's cheeks flushed a deep crimson as several incubi fixed their seductive gazes on the human females, their smiles suggestive and eyes lingering.

Gimp darted forward and threw his arms around a succubus who was busy shoving the male demons away. The succubus glanced down in surprise before letting out a warm laugh, scooping him up effortlessly, and carrying him back to the group, her movements graceful.

Courtlynn moved to the newcomer and gave her a peck on the cheek. "Thank you, Nessie," she said warmly.

"So this is it?" Nessie asked, her eyes scanning the group with curiosity and appraisal. "Which one is your—" Courtlynn quickly grabbed Aushade by the arm, her friend's approving smile lighting up her face. Nessie gently lowered the imp and took Courtlynn's hand. "Be safe. All of you," she said, her voice filled with earnest concern.

"We will," Courtlynn replied, stepping back. "Now, follow me."

The group trailed behind her, their movements sluggish as they adjusted to the Inferno-Plane's environment. Raven struggled to focus on the mission, but the mesmerizing sight of the buildings and the lava river flowing alongside the town kept drawing her attention. The fiery stream glowed ominously, casting flickering shadows across the glossy rocks. She wiped beads of sweat from her forehead, thankful for the dragon armor that kept her body cooler despite the intense heat.

"No wonder everyone is nude," Avalann muttered, dabbing her face with her sleeve.

"Did you know my ancestors originated from here?" Shorte asked, breaking the tense silence.

"So dwarves are demons?" Ashley raised an eyebrow.

"Not all creatures in the Abyss are demons," Courtlynn interjected firmly.

"We were created by the god Natus to mine the Abyss, according to the legends." Shorte's voice echoed with a sense of ancient pride.

"How did the dwarves end up in the Mortal Realm?" Ramzey asked.

"Someone had to maintain the peace," Shorte responded with a solemn nod.

Raven took a slow sip of water, the cool liquid soothing her throat. "My father tried to tell us that story once, but Gideon interrupted." She secured her canteen to her belt, the memory resurfacing with a sharp twinge. "He delivered the news that the orcs attacked Fellswar—" Her voice trailed off as she noticed Jarz and Aushade exchange a tense glance.

The group approached a decorative alcove housing nine portals, each shimmering with an eerie light. Strange vines and flowers clung to the surrounding stone, their petals a vibrant burnt orange and pink, an unexpected splash of color. *There's beauty in the oddest places.* The stone structures bore chiseled markings around the arches, ancient and foreboding.

"Those are demonic symbols," Thomas pointed out, his voice tense.

"Yes, they indicate each level of the Inferno-Plane," Courtlynn replied, her tone authoritative. She flicked her whip to stop Izarra from watering the tiny flowers. "You'll drown the fire spinners."

"Delosperma have a complex root system that keeps them hydrated," Gobs added, her voice a mix of fascination and caution.

"Which portal?" Thomas asked impatiently, his eyes darting from one arch to the next.

Gimp stepped forward and pointed to the second structure from the left. "Master, here."

"Not another portal," Ashley whimpered, her voice shaking. "This is truly hell."

Gobs rummaged through her pouch and pulled out a small root. "Here, eat this," she said, handing it to Ashley.

The warrior eyed the root suspiciously. "What is it?"

"Ginger root," the druid replied with a reassuring smile. "It will help ease the nausea."

Ashley cautiously nibbled the ginger root, then took a bigger bite. "That has some kick to it. How come you're just now informing me of this?"

Gobs shrugged, a sly smile tugging at her lips. "I've tried before, but you won't eat anything from the ground until it's clean. I found some at the campsite and figured I'd bring them along."

"I could use one," Raven said, queasiness coiling low in her stomach as she placed a hand over it. *I don't think the little one is happy I'm here.* The druid quickly retrieved another ginger root and handed it to her. "Thank you." She bit into it, and the taste hit hard—sharp, earthy, and electric. The heat bloomed across her tongue like fire licking dry leaves. She reached for her canteen and took a long drink, blinking through the afterburn. "That's . . . potent," she murmured, wiping her mouth. "But it'll do."

Avalann snickered from behind, her eyes gleaming with amusement. "Can't even handle a plant."

Raven, unamused, tucked the rest of the ginger root into her satchel, fingers brushing the worn leather flap before fastening it shut. A mundane task, but her hands moved with purpose—habit was easier than thought. "Group One should head out now. Group Two will follow once Ashley feels better." Her voice didn't shake. The tension coiled beneath it like a second heartbeat, but no one needed to hear that. She scanned their faces. Some still waited on her as if she could promise safety with a sentence. She couldn't. But they needed direction, and so she gave it.

"Agreed," Jarz said, stepping forward. "Group One with me."

Aushade, Courtlynn, Ramzey, and Avalann moved to his side. They packed quickly—soldiers, every one of them.

But Raven saw the flickers behind their composed expressions. The flinches. The hesitations. They felt it, too—the thinness of this plan. The gamble. *Never split the party.* The thought haunted her. Her mind spun with calculations. Ashley's health. Avalann's tendency to hang back. Courtlynn's recent limp. Aushade's puffy eyes. *Are they truly ready for this? Am I?*

Izarra stepped in to fill canteens, the efficient rhythm of her movements grounding for a moment. Raven watched, grateful for the distraction—until Izarra turned and threw her arms around Jarz, holding him tightly. Then a kiss—brief but complete, a punctuation mark to something unsaid.

Raven turned away. Not because it embarrassed her. But because it hurt. *Gideon.* And then, she let out a breath, slow and steady, like easing weight off a wound. That kind of unapologetic love was present even in danger—a luxury she couldn't afford. Not now. She had no one to kiss goodbye. *What am I doing?* A sudden pressure hit from within her stomach. *I promised Carya. Emotions later. Strategy now. Luck is for the unprepared.*

However, there were too many moving parts and people counting on her to be solid and unshakeable. She could feel the weight of their unspoken trust bearing down on her spine like boulders—all crushing at once.

"This portal leads to the Third Layer, the new home of the insectoids," Courtlynn explained, her eyes scanning the demonic symbols around the archway.

"After you," Aushade said politely, gesturing toward the portal. Courtlynn stepped through first, her form disappearing into the shimmering light, followed closely by Avalann. Ramzey lingered for a moment, casting a concerned glance at the necromancer.

"Trust her," Aushade said before stepping through.

"May Blade guide us," Jarz intoned solemnly to the others.

"He will," Celeste responded with confidence. Izarra sighed deeply as she watched the swordmage and his brother vanish into the portal, her fingers lingering on the spot where Jarz had stood.

Raven noticed Gimp hovering near the edge of the gateway as if to follow Courtlynn, his fingers twitching at his sides. His eyes flitted from portal to portal, never settling. When Raven stepped toward him, he inched back, feet scuffing against the packed red terrain. She knelt slowly, trying to meet his gaze, but he kept his head tilted, eyes darting past her shoulder. "Gimp," she said softly, "she'll be all right."

The imp's shoulders lifted with a sharp breath. After a moment, he offered a hesitant smile—small, flickering, and gone as quickly as it came.

"Let's go already," Thomas barked impatiently. "I want to find Carya and get out of this hellhole."

Raven stood and turned to Ashley. "How do you feel?"

"I think the ginger root is helping." The warrior took another sip of water, her expression steadier than before.

Izarra raised her magical horn decanter. "Let me fill everyone's canteens."

Gimp pointed to the portal next to the one Group One had used. "Second Layer. That's where you will find my master."

"Lead the way," Raven said kindly. Shorte didn't hesitate, striding forward to follow the imp with Thomas close behind. Gobs, Izarra, and Celeste were next, their movements purposeful but wary. Raven watched as Ashley hesitated, a flicker of doubt crossing her face.

"It's just a portal, no big deal," Ashley mumbled, her voice shaky but determined.

"No big deal," Raven echoed with a reassuring smile.

"The things I do for coins," Ashley groaned, closing her eyes as she stepped through the portal. Raven followed right behind her, the familiar tingling sensation coursing through her body. This time, the group avoided portal sickness.

The Second Layer bore the scars of recent conflict: Piles of rubble littered the passages, and deep fissures marred the walls. High above them, charred spider webs clung to the ceiling. *The size of those webs—I hope I don't run into one.*

In some areas, sections of honeycombs replaced the stone walls. Curiosity got the better of Raven, and she peeped inside one as Gimp quickly grabbed her hand. "They're tombs," he explained, his voice hushed with reverence. He pointed above. "The messenger tunnels."

Izarra glanced up with unease. "Are they safe?"

"We carry important messages. We imps have one job. To deliver. We ignore everything else," Gimp explained.

"How do we get up there?" Shorte asked, glancing up at the messenger tunnels high above them.

Celeste folded her arms. "Do you want options, or should I just choose?"

"I prefer stairs," Shorte muttered, his voice tinged with reluctance.

"No stairs," Gimp responded innocently. "Mostly fly."

"You heard the imp. Fly it is," Celeste declared, her eyes twinkling. She began chanting "Tolle Fuga," her fingers moving gracefully as she touched each person on the shoulder.

A warm, tingling sensation spread from Celeste's touch, and a lightness filled Raven's body as if gravity had loosened its grip. With an exhilarating sense of weightlessness, Raven's feet lifted off the ground. The group hovered as the gravity around them seemed to lighten.

"Focus on me," Celeste called out, her voice clear and commanding. She flew past the group with effortless grace, landing smoothly at the mouth of the tunnel.

Raven fixed her eyes on the Fey Guardian, concentrating on her movements. Gimp glided beside her, his tiny wings flapping rhythmically as he tried to guide her. Raven grabbed Celeste's hand, the guardian's grip solid and reassuring as she pulled the rogue into the tunnel. Inside, her eyes widened at the sight. Thousands of imps zipped through the air at high speeds, a blur of motion above and around the tunnels. They focused on their tasks, darting back and forth with single-minded determination, paying no attention to the newcomers.

Laughter and chatter filled the air as the group ascended. Gobs floated lazily, her movements relaxed and confident as if she had done this a hundred times before. She guided Ashley by the arm, keeping the warrior steady. On the other hand, Thomas flailed comically, his arms moving in exaggerated swimming motions that had everyone giggling.

They made it safely to the edge except for Shorte, who drifted perilously close to a lava fall. The molten stream cast an ominous glow, and Raven's heart skipped a beat. Gimp swooped over just in time, grabbing the dwarf and steering him back to the safety of the tunnel.

"I thought I saw stairs," Shorte muttered, embarrassed but grateful. Gimp, now more comfortable in the air, flew around joyfully, clearly relishing the sensation of flying again.

Celeste called out, her voice cutting through the laughter, "We can continue to fly down the tunnels, or we can—"

"Walk!" the group yelled in unison, their voices echoing off the tunnel walls.

As the Fly spell wore off, Shorte quickly caught Gimp, who seemed disappointed to be grounded again. The imp sighed but then waddled off, signaling for them to follow. The group trekked down the passage, their footsteps echoing. They reached a fork in the tunnel. "Master is this way," Gimp said, his voice filled with uncertainty as he pointed to the right.

"Everyone, please drink some water," Gobs recommended, handing Ashley a full canteen.

Ashley grabbed it with a grateful smile. "If I drink any more, I'll become a fountain."

"Shorte knows that feeling," Raven jested, nudging the dwarf lightly.

Shorte huffed a twinkle in his eyes. "That was years ago. You still remember that?"

"Of course, it's cemented in my memory," Raven replied fondly. *A joke can go a long way in easing tension amid threats.*

"Oh, now you're a bard." Shorte snorted, shaking his head.

They continued down the tunnel until they reached the end. "Down there." Gimp pointed to an opening in the wall. "Master's new chamber."

Balors loomed over the worksite, their massive forms casting long, clawed shadows across the swarm of minions hauling boulders. Raven's breath caught as her eyes locked onto one—its hulking silhouette too familiar. The parchments with the fire demon images provided at Gideon's camp couldn't prepare her for their actual size. The story of a balor murdering her father couldn't prepare her for the evil aura that surrounded them. Her father's scar pressed at the edges of her mind.

Now, the stakes felt different. Higher. Raven rested a hand lightly on her belly to steady herself—or shield something not yet there. The demons below worked in frantic harmony, fire spirits tearing through the honeycomb towers with blistered hands, their touch turning ancient stone into falling ash. The towers crumbled with a scream of splintering rock, hexagonal walls collapsing into the chasm floor, already a battlefield of dust and ruin. Something was being built here. Something new. But all Raven could feel was her gut's slow churn of dread.

"Those balors are enormous," Thomas remarked, his eyes wide with awe. "They're bigger than the ogres in Fellswar."

Gimp's eyes sparkled with excitement. "Are we flying?" he asked eagerly, practically bouncing.

"No," Celeste responded firmly, "we all need to jump."

"Oh no," Thomas gulped, peering over the edge at the dizzying drop below.

"I'm with the dragon fodder on this one," Shorte agreed, crossing his arms.

"We're up pretty high," Ashley pointed out, her voice wavering slightly. Izarra and Gobs nodded in agreement, their faces pale.

Celeste's brow gathered. "I can cast a portal."

"I'll jump," Ashley yelled impulsively, stepping toward the edge. Gobs quickly grabbed her arm, pulling her back to safety.

"There's no other way we can get across without being detected," Thomas pointed out, his gaze fixed on Ashley.

"Invisibility," Shorte suggested, glancing at Celeste.

"No," Raven retorted, shaking her head. "My father taught me that balors see through invisibility."

"Did you bring your razor wire?" Shorte asked suddenly.

"Of course," the rogue answered, surprised by the random question. "Why?"

"I'm not sure." The dwarf scratched his head. "It just sorta popped into my head. Carya always complained to me that all she heard were stories about balors, razor wire, and dragon eggs."

Raven sighed heavily, her shoulders sagging. "Bedtime stories weren't my father's strong suit, that's for sure."

"Imagine the story you'll tell your child," Thomas said with a sneer, "if we survive." Ashley elbowed the scruffy-bearded paladin in the gut. "What? We're stuck in a messenger tunnel, in another realm, surrounded by balors. Maybe we should wait for Group One?"

"Scared, dragon fodder?" Shorte teased, an impish grin spreading across his face. "I thought you were a paladin. Demons should be your forte."

"Fine!" Ashley snapped, her teeth gritting in frustration. "Cast a portal."

"Are you sure?" Raven asked, concern flickering in her eyes.

The warrior huffed, her patience wearing thin. "If it will shut this fairy up."

"Don't insult the fairies," Shorte snickered, giving Thomas a teasing nudge. "He's dragon fodder."

Thomas glared, his knuckles white with tension on the pommel of the vorpal sword.

Celeste stepped back behind the tunnel wall, her eyes scanning the area cautiously. "You have to go through quickly so we're not detected," she instructed. "I'll do my best to get it as close as possible."

With a flourish of her arms, Celeste cast a blue portal, the shimmering gateway appearing before them. "Go!" she urged as everyone sprinted forward.

Raven followed close behind Shorte, her heart pulsing in her chest. They charged straight for the opening, the portal's energy crackling around them. Out of the corner of her eye, she saw Ashley stumble and hit the side of the wall, wincing in pain.

Celeste quickly reached out, guiding Ashley back toward the opening with a firm yet gentle hand. "This way!"

"Just a little disoriented, but I'm fine," Ashley whispered, her voice barely audible.

Gimp pointed ahead. "Down the hall is my master's war chamber."

Raven's fingers twitched around her staff. "How many chambers are there?" The words came out steady, but her stomach had gone tight, coiled like it was bracing for a blow. The air smelled like old blood and iron, thick enough to taste.

"Four," the imp explained. "War chamber, rest chamber, Lady Chaotica's chamber, and a large den. The den is where the army roams."

"The flox?" Celeste inquired, her tone sharp with curiosity.

"He sleeps in a cage in the war chamber," Gimp replied.

The group crept down the narrow hall, their weapons drawn and senses heightened. Raven split her staff into gleaming daggers, the familiar weight comforting in her hands. She activated True Seeing to ensure no surprises lurked in the shadows.

Celeste moved with silent grace, slipping into the war chamber first. She scanned the room, then waved for the rest of them to join her. Raven followed, her heart pounding, eyes darting around the room for any signs of danger.

The walls were veined with molten rock, lava flowing in glowing rivulets into deep crevices. Steam seeped ominously from the cracks, hissing softly and filling the air with a humid, oppressive heat. The remnants of destroyed honeycombs lay scattered across the floor, their once intricate hexagon patterns now shattered and charred.

Raven's gaze caught on the decaying body of a humanoid insect dangling from a broken tomb, its limbs twisted grotesquely. The sight made her stomach churn, but she forced herself to look away, focusing on the room's other details.

A large stone table stood in the middle of the chamber, its surface almost level with Shorte's height. The table was strewn with parchments, their edges curling from the heat. Strategic maps and hastily scribbled notes lay haphazardly across the surface. The faint scent of burning sulfur mixed with the metallic tang of blood, creating a nauseating atmosphere that clung to the back of her throat.

"These guys are massive," Thomas reiterated, his eyes wide with awe as he took in the towering forms of the balor's furniture.

"Of them all," Gimp whispered, "my master is the shortest."

"Where is Cary—Lady Chaotica's chamber?" Raven asked urgently, catching herself mid-name. Her voice softened around the revision, careful not to confuse the young imp. Gimp pointed to another tunnel, and she was moving before he finished, her pulse quickening with every step. The chamber was empty. Raven stopped cold. For a breathless moment, she stared at the disheveled silks, the untouched basin, the way the sheets were still pulled tight at the corners. No signs of struggle. No warmth left behind.

Raven prepared herself for this, but some stubborn part had expected it to be easy. A rescue. A reunion. Not . . . nothing. Her jaw tightened as the weight of disappointment settled in her chest, hot and dense like the air around her. She swallowed hard against it, forcing herself to move. "Let's check out his rest quarters," she said, her voice steadier than she felt.

She'd taken three steps before she stopped. A shape. Still. Her eyes caught the glint of metal chains sunk deep into stone, and then the figure came into full view. Her breath hitched.

The guardian was barely more than a shadow of himself. His limbs hung limp, wrists stretched high above his head, the iron cuffs biting into flesh rubbed raw. Skin-like parchment clung to the sharp bone, mottled with bruises and burns. Flies buzzed in lazy circles above his head, drawn to the open sores that peppered his arms and neck. One eye was swollen shut. The other stared ahead, glassy, not quite seeing.

The stench hit next—acrid sweat, old blood, and something sweeter, rotting. Raven gagged, hand flying to her mouth. Nausea rolled through her, thick and hot, curling under her ribs. She pressed a palm to her abdomen, grounding herself as if to shield the life inside her from the horror in front of her. Her instincts screamed to act, tear the chains from the wall, or do *something*—but she couldn't move yet. Not until her mind caught up with her senses.

"What the spell?" Raven's voice trembling. "What did they do to him?"

Celeste entered behind her. "Are you all—" The words died as she froze mid-step, her breath catching. "No, no—" Celeste's voice broke like glass. She rushed forward, sobs building in her throat as she flew up to him, wings trembling. "Tier, Tier, I'm here," she whispered, her voice raw, shaking. Her hands fumbled to find a pulse at his neck, then hovered, hesitant, over his mangled chest.

Tier stirred only slightly. His head lifted with painful slowness. One eye was swollen shut, the other was foggy and unfocused. His mouth moved, but no sound came out—only a faint rasp, like wind through broken reeds.

Four heavy chains held him, sunk deep into the stone behind and deeper still into his wrists. The skin had grown around the metal in places, fused into grotesque scabs.

Celeste hovered before him, her expression shifting, grief folding into fury. "Hold on," she said through clenched teeth. Her hands glowed, light seeping between her fingers. She aimed precisely—no hesitation—and released a blast of energy. *Crack.* The shackles exploded. Tier slumped forward. "Pluma Cadere!" Celeste shouted, her voice echoing like a prayer.

Tier's body slowed mid-fall, drifting downward like a broken marionette. Thomas rushed forward, knees nearly buckling as he reached Tier. His hands shook as he knelt to ease the Abyss Guardian to the floor. But even that small motion tore a scream from Tier's throat—raw, cracked, the sound of a soul caught in fire. Celeste dropped beside him, hands already at work, her magic pooling beneath her fingertips.

Raven flinched at the shriek. It lanced through her like a blade, scraping through old battle memories and into places she thought she'd fortified. She knelt, finally able to move. But the scent, the blood, the brutal confirmation of what had been done . . . it clung to her. *This isn't just cruelty. It's a message. A warning. A challenge.*

Celeste gathered his bloodied head into her lap. Her hands moved desperately, thumbs brushing gently across his filth-streaked cheeks.

Tier's lips parted. "Tessk," he rasped. A name dragged up from the deep, where pain hadn't yet taken root.

Celeste bent over him, her tears falling freely now. "They'll pay for this," she whispered, trembling with grief and righteous heat. "I swear it, they'll all pay."

Raven stood just behind them, her pulse pounding in her ears. She couldn't look away. Tier's body was ruined. From legs to chest, his flesh was blackened and cracked, a grotesque tapestry of fire's aftermath. Bits of charred skin curled away from raw, weeping muscle beneath. The smell—gods, the *smell*—was thick and greasy, clinging to the back of her throat like smoke in her lungs.

A memory struck her, fast and cruel, standing by the flames at Waterfront, watching Gideon carve into a roasted boar, its hide blistered and peeling. The same smell. The same texture. Her stomach turned; bile was sharp in her mouth.

And his wings. Where once they had spanned broad and powerful, only the bony framework remained, jutting from his back like the ribs of some fallen beast. The membranes had been stripped away, melted, or torn to pieces.

Raven pressed a fist to her lips, willing herself to stay upright. *This is what they do. This is the cost.* She felt the child within her shift, a flutter—life stirring beneath the weight of death.

She looked down at Tier and felt something harden deep inside. No spell—no sword—would ever balance what had been done here. But she would come close.

Gobs leaned over Tier's broken body, her usual sharpness dulled by what she saw. Her face was grim as she pulled back, shaking her head slowly, her eyes avoiding Celeste's. "The damage is too severe," she said softly. "There's nothing I can do."

Ashley gasped, hands over her mouth. "How's he still alive?"

"The Morganicule is keeping him alive," Celeste replied, voice strained as tears streamed freely down her cheeks.

"The Morg—what?" Shorte asked, stumbling over the unfamiliar term.

"It's the immortality ritual for guardians," Celeste said, barely able to get the words out. Her hands never stopped moving—tenderly brushing blood-matted hair from Tier's face as if that one small comfort might keep him tethered to life.

Raven watched, her chest tightening. She couldn't take her eyes off Celeste—not just her grief, but the fierce, aching love behind it. The way her hands shook with helplessness. The way her body bent instinctively, protectively, around Tier's ruined form.

For a moment, it wasn't Tier on the ground. It was Gideon. And she was Celeste. The thought hit hard. *Would he weep like this if I fell? Would his hands shake as he tried to hold me together? Would someone else stand by, helpless, trying to piece me back together?*

Raven pressed her palm to her stomach. Her child shifted, just a whisper of movement. This wasn't just about war or revenge. It was about what they could lose. She took a deep breath, forcing down the bitter taste of nausea that rose in her throat. "You have to get him out of here," she said, locking eyes with Celeste. "Now."

Celeste shook her head, her jaw set. "I promised you and your family I wouldn't leave your side until we found Carya."

Raven exhaled sharply. *Stubborn, loyal—just like Carya.* "Fine," she said, cutting the conversation short. There wasn't time for back-and-forth. Her mind churned, trying to sort the chaos into something actionable. "We'll check the den. Then we're done. We all leave."

"But Carya—" Thomas's voice cracked, raw with desperation.

Raven turned back toward Tier, forcing herself to *look* at him again. His chest barely moved. Celeste cradled him as if he might break further, and maybe he would. The scorched skin, the tattered wings, the way his blood darkened the stone beneath him, it was already a miracle he was breathing.

"My sister would understand," Raven said, her voice tightening around the words. *She has to.* It felt like a betrayal to say it out loud. But she couldn't justify losing more people—not now, not with Tier like this, not with a child inside her whose life could hinge on a single moment's misstep. "Maybe Group One will have better luck." She clenched her jaw and turned to Gimp. "Show us to the den."

Gimp hesitated, eyes flicking to the dark doorway behind them as if expecting his master to step through. When no shadow emerged, he nodded and shuffled ahead, quickening his pace when he felt safe.

"Shorte, Thomas—with me," Raven ordered. "The rest of you, stay here. Stay alert. Be ready to portal out on my signal."

The chasm's air grew heavier as they moved, thick with heat and the coppery stink of blood. Raven's fingers curled tighter around her weapon with each step. *Stay sharp. Focus. Time is needed, and we can buy it by finishing this quickly.*

They turned a corner, and Raven stopped cold. At the far end of the hall, a figure stood motionless. White robes, hood drawn low, staff in hand. Around them, demons wandered in twitching patterns—aimless, disjointed, like puppets whose strings had been half-cut.

Raven narrowed her eyes. Her body tensed, instincts flaring. *Something's wrong.* Something was off with the demons' stillness and unnatural sway. She raised a hand, fingers balled up into a fist directing them to halt. *We finish the mission, then we run like hell.*

The air pressed around them, heavy and stale. Raven moved first, silent as the snow, every step a deliberate promise not to make noise she couldn't take back. The white-robed figure didn't move—just stood at the end of the corridor, staff in hand, like a statue in mourning. The faint torchlight shimmered across the pale fabric of a dress.

It was cold in a way that heat couldn't touch.

"That's her," Thomas breathed. "That's her burial gown."

The words hit like a blow. Raven stopped dead, her pulse thundering in her ears. *Burial gown?* She squinted. The white robe, the trailing hem, and the delicate silver embroidery at the sleeves *were* familiar. *Carya's gown.* The one she had been laid in. The one Raven had helped fold over her sister's still hands. *No. No, no, no.* Her knees nearly buckled, but she caught herself. Her daggers hung heavy at her sides now, forgotten. Her breath caught in her throat.

*Carya?* Her name was a scream inside Raven's skull, but she didn't speak it. She stepped forward slowly, afraid to blink, fearful that if she got closer, the illusion would shatter—or worse, confirm everything. The demons around the figure twitched, some dragging claws along the walls, their eyes glassy and unfocused.

This wasn't how she had imagined finding her sister. She had braced for blood, for chains, for some prison she could lock pick—but not this. Not the stillness. Not the possibility that Carya oversaw a demon army. Raven drew a trembling breath.

"What do we do?" Shorte asked, his voice edged with panic. "Tier can't walk, and if we try to drag her away, I'm pretty sure her minions will retaliate."

"I'll deliver the message to the others!" Gimp offered eagerly, rushing off before anyone could stop him.

"Gimp—" Raven started, but he was already gone, slipping around the corner.

Shorte opened his mouth. "Maybe the others will come up with—"

"GIMP!"

The voice cracked through the chamber like a whip, deep and jagged, thick with malice. It didn't echo—it *shook*. The walls seemed to pull tighter around them, the air sharp with magic and heat. Raven's body locked up, and her breath caught halfway out of her throat.

The figure in white turned. Not all at once—just her head, as if bones had learned motion again but hadn't yet remembered grace. The hood slipped back just enough to reveal the face beneath.

Raven's heart froze. *Carya.* Not the Carya she remembered, the girl with laughter in her eyes and the blush on her cheeks. No, that Carya was gone. What stood before them was a mockery wrapped in death's elegance. Hollow eyes met Raven's across the distance, and something inside her curled.

"Carya!" Thomas's voice cracked, thick with hope and dread. He surged forward, lifting Celeste's vorpal sword, its sharp edge catching the lava glow as if it hungered for blood.

The thing in the burial gown—Lady Chaotica—tilted her head slowly, a crooked smile curving on her lips. The gesture was familiar, *almost* human, but her eyes stayed cold. Empty. No recognition. No warmth. Raven couldn't breathe. Her sister's body—that was her sister's *body.* She'd sat beside it, kissed its forehead before the burial, and whispered promises into cold ears. She had *mourned* this woman. And now, Carya stood before her with something ancient and cruel looking out through her face.

Raven's stomach shifted again, reacting to her rising panic. Her eyes began to blur into darkness, and Raven pressed a hand against her abdomen. *Not now.* Her instincts screamed—*run, fight, protect*—but her feet wouldn't move. All she could do was stare into those flat eyes.

*This is what became of her? This is what they did?* She wanted to scream. To call out her name, reach through whatever darkness held her, drag her back—but the words died in her mouth. Because part of her already knew . . . *the sister I love might not be there.*

"Help!" Gimp's voice was a raw, desperate wail that bounced off the heated stone walls, filling the chamber with his torment. "Please!" His pleas for help echoed down the hall, each cry more heart-wrenching than the last.

# CHAPTER THIRTY-FOUR

# BATTLE WITH THE BALOR

Raven exchanged a quick, determined glance with Thomas and Shorte, but her heart was already sprinting ahead. Gimp's cries clawed at her conscience, each one louder, more frantic. They had to move fast, but her feet refused to budge. Her eyes locked on Lady Chaotica—no—*Carya*.

Those eyes, once so familiar, now glinted with a glacial stillness. Was that a flicker? A tremor in her stare, a shadow of something long buried? A memory or a warning?

The amulet at Carya's throat pulsed faster, its glow deepening like a heartbeat trying to break through ice. It reminded Raven of Baka's phylactery. It had the same haunting glow.

The demons stirred, their screeches tearing through the thick, charged air, sharp and unearthly. Raven cringed, pulse hammering, and reached instinctively for her blades. But Carya raised her staff, and the creatures froze mid-charge. Not tamed—*leashed*. Held just out of reach, their black eyes burned with rage.

Thomas reached out his hand. His voice cracked—half hope, half prayer—as he called softly, "Carya, please come with us."

But Raven barely registered it. Her world had narrowed to her sister's face, pale and unreadable, and the silence stretched like a chasm between them. She swallowed hard. Her voice came out stronger than she felt. "We have to help Gimp. I made a promise." Her throat tightened, but she forced the words out. "*My sister* would help me keep that promise."

Carya didn't move. Didn't blink. Raven's chest tightened, breath catching. She tried to speak again but found only silence. The stillness was unbearable, like screaming into a void and hearing nothing back.

"Carya, uh—hello," Shorte added, voice trembling. "Shorte here—your best friend—I'm helping, too." The lich's gaze drifted to him, blank and pitiless. The amulet's glow flared again, casting eerie shadows across her face.

Raven took a half-step forward before stopping herself. *This can't be all that's left.* She wanted to scream, to shake Carya, to *make* her remember—but there was no time. And if she stayed, she knew she wouldn't leave. Her heart breaking, Raven clenched her fists and forced her voice steady. "We'll be back for you," she said, each word a blade against her throat. "I swear it." She turned before her voice could betray her.

The demons continued to snarl, their eyes following the group's every move, but they remained in place, held in check by Lady Chaotica's staff.

"We have to move," Raven whispered urgently, her eyes darting toward the hallway where Gimp's cries had come from. "Now."

The three burst into the war chamber, a vortex of chaos and heat. An eight-foot-tall balor loomed over Ashley, Izarra, and Gobs, its molten eyes blazing with hatred, wings flexing with the promise of destruction. *This must be Draklor, the one Aushade assisted and Gimp's former master.*

Celeste stood in the doorway, her hands dancing through sigils mid-air as she sustained a protection spell. Izarra's water golem surged into action, crashing into the balor with a roar of steam. The impact staggered the demon back—but only for a moment.

Across the room, Gimp was pinned beneath a snarling demon fox, its massive jaws inches from his neck.

Thomas rushed forward, vorpal blade raised. "I've got this fire demon!" he shouted. He intercepted one of its strikes with a clang of steel, taking up a defensive position.

Shorte followed close behind, slamming his mace against his shield, the sound of a battle cry. "Iron Dwarf!" he bellowed. A shimmer of iron runes coated his skin as he moved to support Thomas.

Raven raced to Celeste's side, panting. "What's the situation?"

Celeste stared at the battlefield. "We're holding him—barely. But Gimp won't last."

Raven's gaze darted across the chamber, taking in the balor's punishing blows, the golem's struggle, and Gimp's limp form. Her fingers tightened around her daggers. "I'll take the fox. You keep Tier safe."

Celeste's magic faltered for a second. "I've spent too much power shielding him. I don't know how long I can—"

"Portal him out," Raven cut in. Her voice was sharp and controlled, but underneath, she was fraying. "Just go. We'll need you focused."

Celeste hesitated, her expression flickering with doubt.

"We *need* you," Raven repeated, almost a plea.

Celeste nodded grimly, then turned to Tier. A swirl of red magic spiraled from her hands, opening a glowing portal. With another incantation, she lifted Tier's body and guided it through. And then she was gone.

Raven darted into the skirmish. Her target: the demon fox. But before she could reach it, another water golem burst apart. A blast of heat from the balor vaporized it mid-lunge. Steam billowed into the chamber, choking the air with boiling humidity.

Izarra staggered back, coughing, her hands empty. Thomas and Shorte were being driven back, their attacks deflected, their defenses cracking.

No one had a clear path to Gimp except her. Raven's eyes locked on the fox. Gimp's blood stained the stone beneath him. He was still breathing—but barely.

There was no time to think. No one else was left. No backup. No delay. Raven rushed forward from the shadows, her daggers gleaming, her heart racing.

Ashley swung her battle axes ferociously, each strike aimed at the balor. The fire demon retaliated with a pulse of searing flame, but as the smoke cleared, Ashley stood unscathed, brushing off the attack as if it were nothing. The only sign of damage was the singed mink pelt on her armor.

*Is she immune to fire?* Raven's eyes narrowed as Ashley emerged, barely charred. She had no time to process it—Gimp was still pinned, the flox's massive body coiled like a vice.

"I loved this fur!" the warrior bellowed, her voice echoing through the chamber. She charged at the balor again. "He has a fire aura," Ashley called out, her voice clear and commanding. "Don't get near him."

Shorte and Thomas, after being driven back, engaged the fox demon as it thrashed violently, its tail, a deadly whip, slicing through the air.

"Don't sever the tail!" Raven shouted, racing through the chaos. "It's too volatile!" She didn't wait to see if they heard. With a breath, she vanished— *Arcane Step.* Her body flickered, magic thrumming at her core. The battlefield blurred around her as she zeroed in on the beast's flank.

In the blink of an eye, Raven reappeared beside the flox—daggers already drawn, feet hitting the ground in a controlled slide. She crouched low, reading the creature's movement, weight, and rhythm. Then—*strike.*

Her dagger plunged into the soft tendon behind its rear paw. The flox shrieked, the sound ear-splitting. Its jaws snapped blindly in her direction, teeth missing her throat by inches.

Raven ducked under its swipe, rolled, and came up on the other side—already slashing again. Each movement, a decision. Each breath, a countdown. She wasn't just stabbing a monster—she was *dismantling* it. "Shorte, Thomas—now!"

They surged in behind her, perfectly timed. Shorte's mace cracked against the beast's ribs. Thomas drove the vorpal blade downward in a clean arc, avoiding the tail, driving the demon further off-balance.

"Keep it distracted!" Raven called, her voice strained but focused. She plunged her dagger into the flox's front paw, twisting the blade to maximize the damage.

The creature roared in agony, its attention diverted enough for Gimp to wriggle free from the flox's clutches. The imp darted away, his small form blending as Thomas stepped in front, preventing the flox from chasing.

Raven reappeared beside it, her Arcane Step dissipating as she drove her other dagger into the flox's side. The beast howled in pain, its enormous claws swatting wildly at Shorte and Thomas.

With a fierce roar, the paladin seized the moment. Thomas lunged forward, thrusting Celeste's vorpal sword through the flox's heart. The blade sank deep, its magical edge tearing through flesh and bone. The demon fox let out one last agonized shriek before collapsing.

Thomas hunched over, breathing hard, one hand braced on his knee. The adrenaline was fading fast, and Raven could see it—his shoulders sagging, the edge slipping from his stance. "It's down," he muttered, eyes locked on the fallen flox like he didn't quite believe it.

Shorte stumbled to his side, dragging his shield against the floor. His voice was thin and shaky. "Good work—"

"No." Raven didn't let herself breathe, let alone relax. Her daggers dripped with blood, hands tense at her sides as she swept the battlefield again. The air reeked of scorched fur, smoke, and something worse—the lingering sting of loss. Her gaze locked on Gimp, slumped against a shattered column, chest rising in shallow wheezes. She moved quickly. "Are you all right?" she asked, crouching beside him.

Gimp gave a shaky nod. "I . . . I think so. You saved me." His voice caught on the last word, raw with disbelief. He lifted a trembling hand and pointed. "But Master . . ."

A sudden hiss of steam exploded across the chamber as another blast of water struck the balor's flaming form. The sound tore through the room, sharp and high-pitched, like a scream swallowed by pressure. "Floxy!" The name cut through the haze—not just a cry but a warning. The balor still stood. *Still burning. Still furious.*

Raven's breath caught. *We haven't won yet.* And then she heard it—*flapping*—dozens of wings. She flinched and glanced up from a crouching position, and her stomach sank. Human-sized bats spilled from the upper tunnels like a flood of shadow and screeching teeth.

"Eyes up!" Shorte shouted. "We've got company!"

The others glanced up just as the first wave broke from the ceiling. Raven planted her feet, blades raised, blood still slick on her hands. No rest. No breath. No end in sight. This wasn't survival anymore. *This was war.*

The dire-bats swooped down with a ferocity that took her breath away as they blew past them, clawing and biting at the balor. The massive demon roared violently, swinging his fire whip wildly, the blazing weapon cracking and sending sparks flying.

Raven's eyes darted to Gobs, her face a mask of intense concentration. The druid's hands moved in intricate patterns, controlling the swarm of dire-bats with precision and skill.

The balor flailed, trying to fend off the attacks, but the dire-bats were relentless, their sheer numbers overwhelming. The air filled with screeches and roars, the chaotic symphony of battle echoing through the chamber. Draklor's attention was fractured—split between targets—and Raven knew how to exploit a crack. She slipped through the smoke and blood like a dire-snake on the hunt, daggers gleaming in her hands.

Every step was measured. Every strike, silent. One blade sliced deep into a tendon, the other aimed for a weak spot beneath the ribs—swift, precise, lethal.

Ashley moved out of the corner of her eye, her axe a blur, but the demon blinked out of reach. He reappeared behind Gobs.

Raven's breath caught. "No—"

A pulse of fire exploded. The blast sent the druid flying. Her scream cut off as flames devoured her. The dire-bats disintegrated in the explosion, their ashes swirling like black snow.

Ashley roared, charging. "You bastard!"

Raven couldn't tear her gaze from Gobs—crumpled, smoking, not moving. Not breathing.

Izarra's voice rose in a desperate chant, dousing the flames with a torrent of water. Steam hissed across the stone, but it was too late.

Raven's chest twisted. *This isn't just a fight. This is a slaughter.*

Another fire pulse detonated from Draklor's core. It flung Izarra aside like a ragdoll and knocked Ashley flat. Gobs's body skidded across the chamber floor, leaving a blackened smear in its wake.

Something cold unfurled in Raven's gut. Not fear. Helplessness.

Ashley stood again, wreathed in fire—and unmoved by it. Her grumble cut through the chaos like a war horn. The flames curled off her like water off oil.

Draklor snarled in return, tossing his flaming whip aside in disgust. Then, his hand wrapped around Tier's sword—the vorpal blade. Raven's eyes widened as firelight caught the edge, casting cruel glints across the steel as he swung straight at Ashley's head.

Raven winced, already moving, too far away to reach her in time—but the blade froze mid-air. A radiant shield shimmered into place, catching the strike with a sound like cracking stars. Shorte stood behind Ashley, arms outstretched, his magic humming around them like a living force.

"Thanks, Shorte!" Ashley gasped, stunned but alive.

Raven exhaled sharply and shakily. Relief was a luxury she couldn't afford, not when the smell of charred flesh still clung to the back of her throat. *Not while Gobs lay motionless.* Her fingers tightened around her daggers. She didn't know if they could win this. But she'd make damn sure Draklor bled.

Shorte didn't waste a moment. He charged at the fire demon with another battle cry, raising his mace. The dwarven warrior moved with surprising speed and agility, his protective shield glistening around him like a suit of glowing armor.

Draklor snarled, his eyes blazing with fury. He swung the vorpal sword toward Shorte, but the dwarf parried the blow with his shield. The clash of steel echoed, the force of the impact sending sparks flying.

Raven took advantage of the distraction, darting around to flank Draklor. She aimed for the knee joints, each strike calculated to weaken the demon further.

Thomas and Shorte continued their relentless assault from the other side, their coordinated attacks adding to the pressure on Draklor. The fire demon roared, his rage echoing through the war chamber as he struggled to fend off the combined assault.

Raven turned to Thomas, her voice cutting through the chaos. "Go check on Carya!" she yelled. Thomas nodded and sprinted toward the den.

Raven Arcane Stepped again, her form flickering as she flashed to her fallen friends. Her heart pounded as she knelt beside them, quickly assessing their condition. Izarra was still breathing, her chest rising and falling faintly, but Gobs lay unnaturally still. A cold dread gripped her heart. *Blade, no!* She barely had time to process her pain before another fire pulse struck Shorte, his iron skin glowing red-hot.

The dwarf gritted his teeth and kept fighting, but the intense heat seared off most of his beard, leaving charred stubble in its place. The acrid smell of burnt hair filled the air.

Ashley and Shorte were the only ones still in striking distance, their movements growing more desperate with each passing moment. Tears streamed down Ashley's cheeks, sizzling and evaporating in the heat. Despite the pain and exhaustion, their resolve remained unbroken.

Raven had to find a way to turn the tide. With a deep breath, she steeled herself, her grip tightening on her daggers. "Hang in there, Shorte and Ashley!" She glanced at Izarra, knowing she had to protect her friend while figuring out their next move. *I won't survive that fire pulse. May Blade welcome us all to the Astral Realm.*

Draklor's fiery aura blazed around him, and the demonic wrath in his eyes showed no sign of abating.

The blast of a horn echoed through the chamber, filling Raven with hope. *Group One must have persuaded the wasptoids to help.* Izarra moaned, her hand groping weakly for her trident. The water half-nymph slowly rose to her feet, grit etched on her face, as Ashley and Shorte distracted the frustrated balor.

Suddenly, Draklor teleported, his massive form reappearing directly before Raven and Izarra. With instinctive quickness, Izarra cast a water bubble around them. The fire pulse from Draklor hit the shield, causing it to sizzle into steam and knocking both Raven and Izarra to the ground.

Raven gritted her teeth, forcing herself to focus. She cast Darkness, shrouding the area in an impenetrable black void. But even in the pitch black, the balor charged, the vorpal sword raised high.

"I can't see!" someone yelled through the darkness. Realizing the spell was causing more harm than good, Raven quickly dropped it, the chamber flooding with light again.

As the darkness lifted, Izarra summoned another giant water golem, its liquid form surging forward to slow the fire demon. Thinking quickly, Raven touched the water elemental, her magic transforming it into a towering mud creature. The newly-formed golem roared and launched itself at the balor, its muddy fists pummeling the demon.

Raven grasped Izarra's shoulder, "Kant-Osp," casting a spell to turn her into a gas form just as Draklor swung his massive sword. The fire demon's weapon sliced through the air, wedging deep into the mud golem's side, unable to find the now-vaporous Izarra.

The balor unleashed another heatwave, the fiery blast slamming Raven against the wall. The force hit her like a sledgehammer, sending a jolt of pain through her body. She crumpled to the ground, dazed, her mind reeling from the impact. Blood trickled from her split lip, the coppery taste mingling with the smoke-filled air. Her vision blurred, shapes and colors merging into a chaotic swirl. The world spun around her, a dizzying carousel of heat and burning.

*Stay conscious*, she commanded herself, gripping the rough stone floor. The smell of burning filled her nostrils, and the crackle of flames roared in her ears. She fought against the darkness that threatened to pull her under, each breath a battle against the overwhelming heat.

As Draklor stood with a smug glaze from the strike, Raven's mind raced, calculating. The demon's ferocity made him sloppy. And for just a breath, his guard dropped.

It was the break they needed. Ashley and Shorte moved in. They flanked him like the blades of a trap snapping shut—Raven couldn't help but feel the flicker of pride amid the chaos. Ashley's face was carved in rage, axes already mid-swing. They struck true, both blades slamming into Draklor's back with enough force to send tremors through the stone beneath them.

The metal bit deep.

The balor roared, a guttural, wounded bellow that vibrated in Raven's bones. He spun, vehemence redirected, momentarily forgetting the threat at his feet.

The mud golem surged forward, answering her will. Raven could feel the link pulsing, the echo of her magic in its dense, shifting form. It moved like a wave made solid, slamming into Draklor and wrapping around him. Viscous arms clamped down with crushing weight, and steam hissed where molten fire met enchanted clay.

"Hold him," Raven breathed, her voice low, willing the creature to endure as if the golem obeyed without question, anchored by her power instead of Izarra's.

Shorte was already moving in. Raven caught the blur of his mace just before it cracked into Draklor's leg with brutal force. Another strike, then another— each one aimed to bring the monster down.

Raven slowly sat up, her head pounding like a relentless drumbeat. She wiped the blood from her mouth, her fingers trembling as she blinked, trying to focus. The sounds of battle were muffled as if underwater, her senses dulled. *Come on, get it together.* She squinted against the haze that clouded her vision. Shorte's form was a blur, standing resolute like a mountain, while Ashley danced around the balor, her axes glistening with lethal intent.

Just as Raven regained her bearings, Izarra reappeared behind the balor. With a fierce look of resolve, the half-nymph conjured a powerful water funnel. The swirling torrent of water surged forward, striking the balor with immense force. The fire demon roared in anger, his fiery aura hissing and sputtering under the onslaught of the water.

Glancing around the room, Raven's eyes fell on Gobs. Her heart skipped a beat, and she stepped closer, her breath catching in her throat. *Did she move?*

Suddenly, a snarl erupted behind her. Raven spun around, her daggers at the ready, and saw the undead flox, its eyes glowing with malevolent light. *What the spell?* Her grip tightened on her weapons. But to her surprise, the flox ignored her, leaping onto the stone table with a single bound and pouncing toward its former master. Raven's gaze shifted around the room, taking in the unsettling sight.

Nearby, wasptoid and mantoid corpses crawled from honeycomb graves, their movements jerky and unnatural. The eerie glow of necromantic energy surrounded them, casting long, grotesque shadows on the chamber walls.

A chill ran down her spine as the undead creatures slowly but surely came to life. The chamber, once filled with the heat of battle, now resonated with the unsettling presence of the risen dead. The air was thick with the smell of decay and the low, guttural sounds of reanimated beings.

Gobs's burnt corpse, now reanimated, led the charge alongside the undead wasptoids and mantoids. Their once-lifeless forms moved with a terrifying purpose, rushing toward Draklor with relentless aggression. The balor unleashed a fire pulse, the intense heat setting the undead creatures ablaze. Flames licked their bodies, but they pressed on, undeterred by the inferno.

"The tail!" Raven shouted, her voice cutting through the chaos. "It can't lose its tail!"

As the burning undead continued their assault, the balor's frustration grew. He swung the vorpal sword in wide arcs, trying to fend off the relentless attackers, but the flaming corpses clung to him, their claws and mandibles digging into his flesh.

Izarra quickly cast a water spell, dousing the flox's corpse, steam rising from the extinguished flames. Reinforcements swarmed through the front hall into the war chamber, a chaotic rush of bodies and wings. Raven's eyes widened as she noticed the wasptoids—abnormal, stripped of armor and weapons—attacking with nothing but their stingers.

The balor was outnumbered by the sheer volume of attackers overwhelming him. Even his powerful fire pulse proved useless against the ruthless undead.

Gobs's skeletal form was horrifying, layers of burnt flesh hanging off as the heat waves continued to scorch her body. Yet she pressed on, her fortitude undiminished by her ghastly appearance.

The wasptoids, their bodies ablaze, showed no signs of retreat. They swarmed the balor, their burning stingers plunging into his flesh. The chamber filled with the sickening smell of burning chitin and the crackle of flames.

A shiver ran down Raven's spine at the sight. The wasptoids' relentless assault, despite their own immolation, added a nightmarish quality to the battle. The balor, now clearly struggling, roared in anger, his fiery aura flickering as his strength waned.

Ashley's axes gleamed as she struck, aiming for the balor's weakened spots. With his Iron Skin still glowing from the heat, Shorte swung his mace with powerful, bone-crushing blows as Izarra cast another water spell, sending a torrent of water toward the burning wasptoids clinging to the balor.

"Chaotica!" Draklor screamed, his voice echoing through the chamber. "Send in my army!"

A roar from the cavern made the hair on the back of Raven's neck stand. She hurried to the tunnel entrance, her heart pulsing as she prepared to confront her sister. But nothing emerged.

Raven spotted sharp, fast, controlled movement from the corner of her eye. *Avalann.* The ranger melted into the fight with a grace Raven couldn't help but admire, her obsidian stone-tipped arrows flying one after another. Each shot struck true, burying deep into the balor's hide. The glow from her bow, a fierce orange now, blazed with demon-slaying intent.

Raven felt a flicker of hope. Fragile. But real.

Jarz and Aushade flanked the archer, calm and deadly, their faces hard with resolve. The swordmage lifted a hand, summoning a glimmering ice shield that shimmered like frost over the moonlight. It flared out just in time to absorb another blast of fire from the balor's burning frame.

Raven flinched from the heat, even across the chamber. *Good timing.*

Aushade didn't slow. He lifted his long sword, chanting low and fast. Magic wove from his fingers like threads of smoke, drifting into the skeletal forms around him. The undead army twitched, then straightened, eyes glowing, limbs steadier.

Raven witnessed the way his magic settled into them. Fireproofing their bodies. Making them last. She'd never understood the immoral practice of necromancy—too many unknowns and disturbed souls like Carya. *But right now, I don't care where the strength comes from as long as it holds.*

The undead surged forward, and Raven tensed, tracking the balor's shifting mass, watching for an opening. Then she heard the unmistakable crack of a flaming whip cutting through the air. *Courtlynn.*

Hovering above, radiant and terrifying, the succubus lashed out at the balor with surgical wrath. Each strike glowed hot, her whip igniting mid-swing, snapping against its charred flesh.

Raven felt the heat of those strikes even from below, seeing how the balor staggered under their sting. No hesitation. No fear. Courtlynn was all vengeance now.

The balor's roar echoed through the chamber, pain and rage twisted into one ragged sound. It thrashed against the growing tide of resistance, trying to fight back the net tightening around it.

Raven's breath caught. *We're turning the tide.* But she knew better than to celebrate early. That thing still had strength. Still, something bloomed in her chest for the first time. *Momentum.* And if they could keep it just a little longer, they might survive.

Her allies fought with everything they had. Every spell, every strike, a blur of steel and sorcery battering the balor from all sides, allowing Raven to move like liquid through the undead crowd, her twin daggers catching the balor as she closed in again. *Perfect cover.*

The chamber had become a maelstrom. Fire raged across the cracked stone, ice spears shattered mid-air, and spirits warped and danced under the pressure of summoned magic. The smell of scorched flesh choked the air.

Raven ducked low under a gust of flame and slid across a patch of wet stone. One of the balor's legs staggered near, thick as a tree trunk, exposed. Vulnerable. She struck.

Her first dagger sank deep behind the joint, angled upward. The demon howled. Raven pivoted smoothly, twisting the blade, then pulled free and slashed across the muscles with her second. Smoke curled where her steel kissed fire-wreathed flesh, but she didn't stop. *Strike. Move. Disappear. Repeat.*

The balor swiped wildly, missing her by inches as she darted behind a ruined column. Her chest heaved, but her hands never faltered.

A cry echoed in her mind. *Where's Ramzey?* The thought hit like a gut punch. She poked her head out, watching the battlefield through the swirl of elemental chaos. *Focus. Survive first. Find her later.*

A low voice echoed from her cloak. "Krea."

"Baka?" She pulled the phylactery out. It pulsed the blue light as usual. "Can you help?" It didn't respond. "Baka?!" She stuffed it back in the pocket of her cloak. *Krea, all traits.* Her hand patted her stomach. *We got this, kiddo. Let's end this and go home.*

Raven broke from cover, blades glinting, boots skidding on scorched stone. The battlefield fell away. There was only him now. *Draklor.*

The demon towered above her, flames coursing through the cracks in his skin like molten veins. His whip was gone. The undead minions faltered. But his eyes burned straight into hers.

Raven slowed, daggers at her sides. Her stance shifted—lower, grounded, balanced.

Not backing down. *All dragon traits.* She held his gaze.

The world hushed.

Around them, spells roared, and arrows flew, slamming into his back, but Draklor's stare didn't waver. This moment was the arena where archers stared each other down, both waiting to shoot. *A standoff.*

Then Draklor roared, and fire erupted from him, a concentrated blast, a torrent of heat and rage aimed directly at her. Screams rang out. Someone shouted her name. Too late.

The fire surged around her, a living tempest of gold and crimson, yet her skin remained untouched—no blistering, smoke-stung cough, or even a singed thread on her armor. She stood at the heart of the inferno like a monument carved from calm itself. The flames licked the air around her in furious spirals but bent away at the last moment as if repelled by an invisible force—or in awe of something greater. Her eyes reflected the blaze, not with fear, but with something ancient and knowing, like she belonged to the fire, or perhaps the fire belonged to her.

Draklor's flames sputtered out, and Raven saw it in his eyes for the first time. *Doubt.* The balor bellowed, voice booming with infernal power. "I command you, Lady Chaotica—release my army!"

Raven pressed her back to the stone column, heart pounding, as the demon's voice cracked at the edges. It wasn't confidence—it was panic masked as authority. *He's losing control. And I'm not about to give it back.* Her eyes darted toward the hall.

Thomas sprinted toward her, his face pale with fear. "They're coming," he panted, his voice tinged with urgency.

"Of course they are," Draklor sneered. "See how well you fare against them."

Carya emerged from the hall, leading a formidable demon army, poised to charge at any moment.

Shorte stopped behind them, slightly out of breath, as the lich raised her staff, halting the demons' advance at the tunnel's entrance. The air grew thick with tension, the demons snarling and growling, eager to attack but held back by an unseen force.

"Whenever she sees us, she stops the attack. Do you think she remembers?" Thomas asked, his voice tinged with a mix of hope and uncertainty. He moved slowly toward Carya, stopping halfway, his eyes locked on her.

Shorte glanced at Raven, following the paladin, his steps cautious, his grip tightening on his mace. "Maybe there's still a part of her that does."

Something pulsed—hot, insistent—against Raven's side. Her breath hitched as her fingers closed around the phylactery. Baka's. It buzzed again like a second heartbeat, thrumming through her bones. She drew it out, and the blue light *exploded*, a jagged beam shooting from the crystal, hissing through the air like a shooting star, and slamming into the undead flox.

The demon animal staggered. Its leering skull twisted toward Raven, the rotted mouth stretching wider. Then it snorted. A low, curdled sound like metal warping under pressure.

Raven froze. The flox wasn't laughing at her. It was amused with recognition. *Baka?*

The demon pet rushed Draklor, sinking its claws into the fire demon's thighs. "Flox!" It reached around—not to defend or attack—but to gnaw its tail, dragging ragged teeth through rotten sinew as if savoring something.

"No—" The word tore out of her, raw and useless. She took a staggering step forward. Her hand clenched the now-dark crystal, her pulse hammering. "Baka, don't. I need—" The knowledge she'd chased. The secrets he held. All slipping through her fingers like blood-soaked sand. The air grew heavier, stinking of sulfur and rot. The world narrowed. Her chest tightened until she couldn't breathe, not from fear but from *grief*.

"BAKA!" she screamed as the balor wailed under the undead animal's assault, but there was only the crunch of bone in the demon fox's jaw as his bushy, tail-filled smile gleamed one last time before the final yank. Her vision blurred. Her voice cracked when she realized what Baka was making the flox do. "Guardians, take cover!"

Jarz swiftly cast Wind Wall, a gleaming barrier of swirling air in front of them, as others ducked behind any large boulder they could find.

A massive explosion erupted inside the war chamber, the shockwave rattling the very foundations. Dust and smoke filled the room almost instantly, debris flying through the air. The Wind Wall strained to hold back the entire force. However, small pieces of stone and metal managed to breach the barrier.

A pebble struck Raven just below her eye, the sharp pain making her wince. *Shite that hurt!* She raised a hand to her face, feeling the sting and the warmth of a small trickle of blood. Around her, the others coughed and choked on the thick smoke, the Wind Wall struggling to keep the worst of it at bay.

Raven squinted through the haze, her vision blurred by tears and dust. The acrid smoke wrapped around them like a suffocating shroud, making every breath a struggle. She tried to clear her throat, the taste of ash and grit lingering on her tongue as she shielded her eyes, coughing as the dust choked the air. The blast had obliterated the undead wasptoids and Gobs's skeletal form, reducing them to ash. Her heart ached with the loss. *I'm so sorry, Gobs.* The sting of guilt stabbed through her.

Shattered remnants of the battle lay scattered across the chamber, the once fierce combatants now reduced to fragments. The echo of the explosion faded, leaving a heavy silence.

Jarz, breathing heavily, lowered his arm, his face grim but resolute. "It's done," he said quietly, his voice barely audible over the settling dust.

Avalann scanned the room, her bow still ready. "Is everyone all right?"

Raven wiped the grime from her face, her eyes searching for her friends. "We're here," she replied, her voice hoarse but determined. She glanced at the remnants of Gobs and the wasptoids, their sacrifice heavy on her shoulders.

"Use your circlet," Izarra managed to blurt out between coughs.

"It doesn't work that way," Raven huffed, holding her injured eye and waving the dust away from her face. They focused on where the balor had been standing. Suddenly, a heatwave blasted against the Wind Wall, shooting flames straight into the cavernous ceiling.

"Is he dead?" Jarz asked, picking up Raven's razor wire and shaking off the dust. "Balors explode when they die."

As the smoke cleared, Raven's eyes widened in horror. The other chamber entrances had collapsed. The den's opening had a small space that someone might squeeze through. "Thomas and Shorte are in that hallway," she said, pointing to the entrance.

Everyone gazed at Avalann's bow, lit up in orange.

Through a cloud of dust, the balor emerged, gripping the vorpal sword, his eyes blazing with anger and purpose.

"Jarz, maybe we should use a portal and get out of here," Izarra suggested, her voice tinged with desperation.

"We already lost Gobs," Ashley spat, her anger evident.

Raven noticed a small figure trapped under a rock. "Look, it's Gimp!" The imp appeared to have tried to escape but was now pinned and crying in pain.

Without hesitation, Courtlynn flew over to help, her wings a blur of motion. "Court!" Aushade yelled, trying to follow, but the others held him back. They watched as the succubus struggled to lift the heavy stone, her efforts frantic and urgent.

"Traitor," Draklor sneered from the smoke, his voice dripping with malice.

Raven took a deep breath, her mind racing. "Aushade, go down the hall and find Thomas and Shorte. Jarz, portal everyone out," she ordered. She cast Invisibility, her form fading from sight. "I'll distract him."

"Let me!" Ashley snapped, her eyes blazing with grit. "Think of the baby."

Raven paused, Ashley's words hanging heavy in the air. The thought of letting the warrior take her place flickered, but she quickly pushed it aside. *I have to. It's all or nothing.*

"It seems she took off already," Aushade quipped to the warrior.

*No, I'm here, arse.* Raven gritted her teeth, the frustration gnawing at her, but a deep sigh followed as she forced herself to focus. Courage settled in her bones like iron.

As the others scrambled to follow her commands, Raven slipped into the chaos, her heart pounding like a war drum. The air was thick with heat and smoke, each breath a scorching reminder of the danger they faced. She knew she had to buy them time.

Ahead, Draklor's massive form towered over the battlefield, his fiery aura casting flickering shadows that danced eerily on the shattered ground. The heat from his presence distorted the air, rippling it like a mirage. Raven's pulse quickened, but she forced herself to remain steady.

Draklor limped toward the succubus, his fiery eyes narrowing. Jarz cast a levitation spell on the rock, lifting it effortlessly, freeing Gimp. Courtlynn, acting immediately, opened an orange portal, but not before the fire demon swung his vorpal sword wildly. The blade caught her wings, slicing through them as she escaped, clutching the injured imp tightly to her chest.

Magic arrows from Avalann streaked through the air, striking Draklor's scorched hide in rapid succession. A geyser surged from Izarra's outstretched hands, crashing into the balor with thunderous force. Jarz's icy projectiles shattered on contact, steam exploding around the demon's molten frame. Ashley, immune to flame, exhaled a fiery breath that met Draklor's with equal ferocity.

Amid the barrage of attacks, Aushade dashed toward the tunnel as Raven darted through the shadows with swift movements, weaving between the debris and flames.

While the others battered him from afar, she slipped past, silently closing the distance. Where their power clashed openly with the demon's might, hers lay in timing, stealth, and a blade yet to strike. *I'm not a storm like the others. I'm the knife in the dark.*

Then, with a burst of speed, Raven moved with practiced grace, her footsteps light and noiseless over the scattered rubble. She positioned herself behind him, daggers drawn, breath steady, as Draklor, still locked onto the others, failed to notice her approach.

The fiery demon loomed, battered and bleeding, as Raven's heart pounded, but she turned the surge of adrenaline into stillness, into aim. Then, his head turned. His gaze locked onto her. He saw her.

*Balors can see through invisibility . . . but he thinks I don't know.* Raven's pulse quickened. Her grip tightened on the hilts. The comm-stone in her onyx bracelet buzzed—*Gideon. Not now.*

The balor snickered, his lips curling into a cruel smile as he pointed the vorpal sword in her direction. "You're next, little one," he sneered. "See if you can withstand my blade."

Her injured eye was swollen and blurry, throbbing with pain, but she managed to focus. Through the haze, a red portal opened in the sky behind Draklor. *Celeste?*

The portal shimmered ominously, its crimson glow casting an eerie light over the battlefield. Draklor paused and turned slightly, his grip on the vorpal sword tightening.

Raven's heart throbbed. *I have to act quickly.* "Celeste!" she called out, her voice filled with hope and desperation. The portal's appearance could be the turning point they needed, but she had to keep Draklor's attention. Just as his eyes locked onto hers, a shadowed figure emerged from the swirling vortex. Her breath caught in her throat. *It's not Celeste. It's someone else—or something else.*

# CHAPTER THIRTY-FIVE

# UNLEASH THE WAR-WIZARD

Gideon sat comfortably on his newly acquired throne, adorned with velvet cushions, deep in meditation within his private quarters at the High Council. The Mortal Realm lay in a state of tranquility. Light blue portals sporadically appeared near Waterfront, yet they were not unusual. The day's sluggish pace allowed him to devote energy to refining his vision.

Believing the flox obstructed his vision of Abyss creatures, he altered his sight to identify any anti-scry spells in the Mortal Realm. The blue image started to take on a purple hue, signaling the onset of night. *Perhaps it's time to call it a day and visit Raven.* He recalled the last encounter with his beloved at the docks, which had troubled her.

A yellow spot appeared near his campsite, cutting short his contemplation. The newly installed anti-scrying device functioned perfectly. *The flox?* Stirred from his thoughts, Gideon awoke and conjured a red portal just as a knock sounded at his door. After a moment's hesitation, he swiftly opened it. Elora stood there, her gaze drifting past him.

"Planning another escape?" she inquired, eyeing the portal.

"Realm business, but I'll probably stay there after the investigation."

"Can you brief the prisoners about what to expect at their trial?"

*Why can't she do it herself?* "If I must."

"Thank you," Elora responded. "I hope all is well in the Mortal Realm."

"It's probably nothing," Gideon lied as he went to close the door, but Elora stopped it with her hand.

"I'm truly sorry about Celeste," she said sincerely.

Gideon nodded somberly. "She made her choice." He watched as Elora walked back down the hallway before closing the door.

The Guardian of the Mortal Realm stepped through the portal to his encampment. Instantly, he sensed an intrusion. A fire still burned, chairs were scattered about, and everything suggested a hasty departure. The demon dice on the table caught his eye, and a wave of dread washed over him. "She couldn't have," he whispered. *Had Raven discovered another entrance?*

With a swift motion, he unsheathed his vorpal sword and uttered a spell, flinging the door of his wagon wide open. Inside, cabinet doors hung ajar, drawers were emptied, and spices were gone.

Gideon sheathed his sword and stepped back to the High Council through a red portal. He strode from the Great Hall to the necromancer's cell, where two guards snapped to attention upon his entry. "How did you alert the succubus?" Gideon interrogated, pacing before Aushade, who lay on the cot with his back turned. "How did you reach her?" he shouted, pounding the wall.

Silence. Gideon whirled to the adjacent cell where Celeste was positioned likewise. "Celeste, where is Raven?" he questioned the Fey Guardian, who remained motionless. "Considering the time difference, they might already be traversing the Abyss. Where are they?"

Gideon turned off the unseen barrier and approached Celeste. His hand slipped through the illusion as he reached to touch her shoulder. He glanced at the two sentinels.

"Blade?" Gideon questioned. "Why?"

Suddenly, one sentinel disappeared along with the prisoners, while the other revealed himself as the demigod of luck. "I'm sorry, Gideon."

Gideon's shoulders sagged, his voice heavy with sorrow. "How could you let your sister and mother enter that inferno?"

Elora and Tessk stepped into the cell's foyer. "What's going on?" Elora asked as they exchanged puzzled looks. "Blade, Gideon—where are the prisoners?" Her eyes darted between the cells. "Both of you, to the main chamber. Now!" Gideon and Blade trailed Elora side by side, followed by Tessk.

Elora halted and confronted them at the room's center. "Blade, I am profoundly disappointed," she said, pausing to choose her words carefully. "For centuries, I've held my tongue while you demigods act as you wish, with no sense of responsibility or consistency, unwilling to engage. It was a blessing when you showed interest in aiding the council. Unlike your peers, you were the first demigod to prioritize caring for others over yourself. I shouldn't complain, though. Despite the years' ups and downs, the council members have succeeded in maintaining peace among the realms and keeping them separate." Turning her attention from the demigod to Gideon, Elora continued, "And as for you guardians, choosing from the Mortal Realm may have been an error."

Gideon started, "But—"

"Our emotions are our weakness . . . our downfall," Elora declared as everyone stopped to consider her words. "I'm calling a mandatory meeting for all guardians. We will establish new rules immediately regarding Celeste."

As Elora mentioned the Fey Guardian's name, a red portal materialized in the main chamber. A body emerged, levitating, followed by a trembling Celeste. Gideon rushed forward to catch the body as it descended from the spell's grasp. *Tier!*

He carefully placed the Abyss Guardian's body on the head table while a tearful Celeste clutched his shoulder and stated, "I must return."

"You will not," Elora countered firmly, approaching Tier's charred remains. "You will go back to your cell. Tessk—" At the mention of the Abyss counselor's name, Tier's eyes fluttered open, and he groaned in agony. Elora commanded, "Summon the High Council guards." She then closed her eyes, chanting as Tier took one final breath before becoming still.

"What have you done?!" Celeste exclaimed.

"He remained alive solely by the power of the Morganicule. I did what was necessary," Elora declared arrogantly, "and stripped him of his immortality."

"You heartless creature," Celeste hissed, reaching for her vorpal blade.

"Have you misplaced your weapon as well?" Elora taunted. "How pitiful."

As Celeste hastily began a spell, Blade intervened, casting his own to neutralize hers. "Son, stand aside!"

Gideon laid a hand on the Fey Guardian's shoulder. "Celeste, be still."

"Tessk betrayed Tier, and *she's* the one who ended his life!"

Elora folded her arms. "Without evidence—"

"Tier confided in me!" the Fey Guardian erupted.

"All I heard was a whimper," Elora retorted coldly, "nothing but deathbed delusions."

The High Council guards shoved past Gideon and seized Celeste by the arms. "Deathbed delusions? I'll give you deathbed delusions." She struggled to break free from the guards.

Elora sighed. "Threatening a council member—"

Blade groaned with guilt. "I'm so sorry, I should have helped Tier when I first found out. I—"

"Raven's in trouble," Celeste snapped as she was dragged toward the Great Hall.

Gideon froze. Her name hit him like a stone to the chest.

"She defied our wishes," he murmured, more to himself than anyone else. His jaw tightened. "They'll make an example of her."

Celeste wrenched her arm free, her eyes blazing. "And you're going to let them?"

Gideon's gaze lifted, distant and torn but no longer uncertain. "No," the decision carving itself into his bones. "I won't."

"And she's with child!" Celeste exclaimed. "*Your* child, Gideon."

*Your child.* The world lurched sideways. Sound drained from the corridor. The guards, the footsteps, even Celeste's voice blurred into a dull hum behind the roaring in his ears.

A dozen memories flashed behind his eyes: Raven's laughter by the falls, her hand lingering in his, the quiet confession she never reasonably said aloud. *And now she's in danger.* Not just her—their unborn child, the life they had created. A deep ache settled in his chest, which turned swiftly to fire.

"No, Gideon," Elora snapped, voice sharp with command, "you mustn't—"

"Blade," Gideon shouted, unsheathing his vorpal sword, the weight of the decision and the lives hanging in the balance. The demigod lifted the Dead Magic Zone as Gideon invoked the Haste spell upon himself. He raised his gauntlet. "Noctis Avem Sermo Porta." A small red portal appeared from the gray stone. *Come on, Raven, please answer.* His heart pounded with each passing moment of silence.

Celeste wrenched free from the guards and conjured a red portal. "I can't guarantee where in the Second Layer this will take you," she said, her voice cracking with desperation.

"Gideon!" Elora protested. "You are forbidden to leave." She lifted her arm to cast a spell but failed. "Blade, what is this treason? You defy the High Council."

"You said it yourself. We demigods need to be more involved, so that's exactly what I'm doing," Blade replied, countering the councilwoman's spells. "Go save Raven and the rest."

Gideon zipped through the portal like a streak of lightning, the world blurring around him as the Haste spell surged through his veins. Time stretched, slowed—each heartbeat a thunderclap, each breath an eternity. He materialized mid-air behind a towering balor, its wings flared wide, oblivious to the danger descending upon it. The fire demon was advancing toward the back wall, blade raised, unaware of the threat.

Gideon fell fast. His grip on his vorpal sword tightened, both hands braced, muscles thrumming with magical velocity.

The guardians were clustered to his left, standing behind a shimmering barrier of Jarz's creation. But Raven—Raven was not there.

A sharp whistle sliced through the air, crisp and shrill, cutting through the chaos like shattering glass. The balor's horned head snapped upward.

"Where are you?" Gideon murmured, low and urgent, barely audible beneath the roar of fire. Around him, heat danced in warping waves, but inside, he was calm in the eye of a storm.

His knuckles whitened as he shifted his weight, every movement precise, sharpened by supernatural speed. In this bubble of accelerated time, Gideon was a force. A weapon.

The fire demon lunged. In one fluid motion, Gideon turned, blade flashing in a deadly arc. Steel met flesh. The demon's neck split open in a hiss of ash and flame, its head torn free, spinning through the air before it hit the ground with a sickening thud.

Smoke curled around Gideon as he stepped forward, boots crunching on scorched stone. He stopped near the fallen balor's smoldering form, the weight of the moment pressing down on him. "Raven!" he cried, his voice raw now, desperate, and cutting through the chaos.

Though Gideon couldn't see her, her arms encircled him, calming his fear. Hastily, he conjured a protective barrier as Draklor's colossal form crumpled to the ground. The air itself seemed to hold its breath, awaiting the inevitable cataclysm. The monstrous body convulsed violently, its leathery skin splitting with a sickening rip. A blinding light, as if of the very essence of hellfire, burst forth from the gaping wounds, illuminating the battlefield in a grotesque display of destruction.

The balor's fiery innards erupted with a deafening roar, sending torrents of molten lava and jagged shards of obsidian rock hurtling in all directions. The ground beneath it quaked and fissured, unable to withstand the sheer force of the explosion. Tendrils of dark smoke spiraled upward, twisting and writhing as they joined the hellish inferno.

Gideon activated the red gem on his gauntlet, noticing Raven's ring starting to blink as she materialized, exhaling a breath of relief. At the same time, rocks tumbled from the ceiling and walls, sealing the tunnel entrances. Across the room, Jarz lowered the protective shield around the group and activated his ring, creating a portal to the camp. The others escaped as Gideon guided Raven through her gateway.

The brisk lake air brushed against his face, starkly contrasting with the heat they had just escaped. A woman he recognized from the pirate ship emerged from a portal, clutching a guardian ring. She approached the axe-wielding warrior who shouted, "Ramzey!"

"Ash! Where's Gobs?" inquired Ramzey. The warrior let her weapons fall and wept in the pirate's embrace while the rest joined in sorrow.

"May Blade watch over her," murmured Avalann, her voice trembling. Jarz embraced Izarra tightly, tears shimmering in his eyes.

"Are you all right?" Gideon inquired, examining Raven's face. He took out his canteen and enchanted it with a spell of frost.

"Shorte, Thomas, Aushade. They're still back there," Raven stated worriedly, pressing the chilled canteen against her cheek.

"Look," Jarz exclaimed, "Shorte's portal!" The group watched with bated breath. Suddenly, Aushade materialized, cradling Carya's lifeless form.

"Carya!" Raven cried out, dashing to grasp her sister's hand.

"Take her to the wagon," commanded Gideon, as the necromancer acknowledged with a nod.

As Raven let go of her sister's hand, Shorte tumbled through the portal, landing squarely on his backside. "The dragon fodder hurled me through as soon as my Iron Skin dissipated. He still requires assistance!"

A demon burst forth from the crimson portal, nearly crushing the dwarf. With a swift motion, Gideon's vorpal sword dispatched the fiend just as another emerged.

"I'm going to seal the portal!" declared Gideon.

"Please, I beg you!" Raven cried out.

The Guardian of the Mortal Realm surveyed the weary warriors and took in a sharp breath. Wielding his blade, he impaled the infernal demon, forcing it back through the portal. The vanquished foe collapsed onto the den's floor as the gateway sealed shut after he stepped through.

With a swift flick of his wrist, Gideon unleashed Chained Lightning. The electric arc surged from his fingers, striking a beast before him. The creature convulsed, sending jagged sparks to nearly twenty others, forging a clear path. The den was teeming with hundreds of creatures charging at them. A saddled Nightmare paced in circles, seemingly unnoticed by the rest. A familiar succubus guarded Thomas, who was motionless on the ground. She brandished her fiery whip in a defensive sweep, warding off the advancing demons.

Gideon lifted another vorpal sword that lay beside Thomas. *This has to belong to Celeste.* He glanced at the succubus. "You again?" he jested. "We should stop meeting like this, or people will gossip."

"You're not my type—elf," Courtlynn retorted with a playful tone, cracking the whip at a demon. "However, I wouldn't mind your assistance in returning me and my steed to the Seventh Layer."

"With pleasure," Gideon responded, a hint of mischief tugging at his lips as he clashed the vorpal swords together. "After all"—he winked—"I'm just a male with needs." Her smile suggested that she recalled their previous encounter in Omlett.

Wielding both swords in a whirling blur of steel and light, he moved like a tempest through the ranks of snarling demons. One blade slashed in wide, graceful arcs—measured and deliberate—while the other struck with brutal precision, fast as a lightning snap. Sparks flew with each clash of steel, demonic forms collapsing in his wake.

His footwork was flawless, weight shifting effortlessly between strikes, the twin blades dancing in perfect counterpoint—offense and defense melded into one seamless motion.

Then he paused, breath steady, and lifted one blade skyward. The runes etched along its length flared brilliantly. *Time Stop.*

A power surge pulsed outward, and the blinding white light drowned the chamber. Everything fell still. A low hum resonated through the air as a shimmering barrier materialized, subtle but vast, enclosing Courtlynn and Thomas in a protective shell of suspended time. Their bodies glowed faintly within the temporal bubble, untouchable.

With his other hand, he banished the Nightmare with a gesture. The creature vanished from the battlefield in a flash of cold light, reappearing safely within the protected space beside them.

Gideon raised both arms, conjuring twin Force Walls in a sweeping V, the narrow point angled toward the oncoming swarm. He summoned a cluster of spinning blades at its tips—fast, silent, deadly.

As the bright, white light of Time Stop began to fade, he moved quickly, planting additional blades at the mouth of the tunnel, where the demons pressed forward in a frenzied tide.

With a final motion, he summoned a heavy horizontal wall above the spinning death trap, boxing the creatures in. The moment Time Stop dissolved, chaos resumed—and momentum betrayed them. The demons surged forward straight into the whirring blades. Screeches echoed as they were torn apart, their bodies shredded mid-charge. Those behind recoiled, tripping over each other in a panicked retreat.

A light tap echoed from behind. Courtlynn. She stood at the edge of the protective barrier, catching his eye. The Nightmare now stood calmly at her side.

Gideon allowed himself a brief smile, then turned back and extended a hand. A gravity well erupted near the edge of the Force Walls, dragging the nearest demons backward through the blades. More shrieks. More blood.

At the rear of the skirmish, the rest of the horde turned to flee toward the tunnel's far exit. Gideon anticipated the maneuver and raised a curved stone wall, sealing the escape by linking the ends of his V-shaped trap.

With a flick of thought, he teleported to the top of his structure and dropped into a crouch, surveying the chaos below. Demons clawed at the steep, smooth incline, their limbs sliding helplessly as they tried to scale it.

Above, winged shadows circled but kept their distance. Watching. Waiting. So was he.

Gideon surveyed his surroundings, conjuring portals linked to the Hydro-Plane of the Abyss. Torrential waves surged forth, flooding the demons at the dangerous choke point. The azure waters, stained with demon ichor, swelled against the protective barrier, soon submerging the area.

The guardian dipped his hand into the water, halting its ascent above the stone wall's crest. Sensing the ripples, he smirked as the remaining demons floundered to stay above water. Flyers descended in attempts to save some while dire-piranhas from the Hydro-Plane nibbled at the monsters' limbs during their precarious extraction.

Gideon transformed his magical projectiles into piercing missiles, launching a volley that clipped the flyers' wings, causing them to plummet into the waters teeming with dire-piranhas. The winged beasts were annihilated, leaving only a handful of demons bobbing on the surface. Concentrating, he created a portal to siphon the water and its residents back to the Hydro-Plane. Scattered puddles and the few surviving demons dotted the den's floor, drenched, weary, wounded, bewildered, and unable to move.

Gideon rose, lifted his gauntlet, and swiftly lowered his arm, collapsing the V-shaped force walls. The creatures were crushed into a pulp between the barriers as Gideon stood tall, eyes gleaming triumphantly. A balor cursed him vehemently as he soared toward the tunnel, glancing through the whirling blades.

"Lower these walls, and your end will come, mortal," the balor sneered.

Gideon lifted the vorpal swords, dismissing the spinning blades. As the balor charged, the ten-ton wall the structures had supported crashed, crushing the fire demon. "Hmm . . . I forgot about that," he sneered, standing atop the wall. He etched a message into the steel with magic: "Stay out of the Mortal Realm."

Courtlynn shook her head as the guardian removed the invisible protective cage. "And you call us demons. If I didn't know better, I'd think you were trying to impress me."

"Just having a bad day," Gideon retorted, hoisting Thomas onto the demon horse before mounting it. He extended his hand to Courtlynn to help her to her feet.

"Where are you taking me?" she inquired with suspicion. "No portal?"

"I'm taking you to Aushade," he replied. "If you stay on the Inferno-Plane, they'll hunt you down. Besides, you're injured and unable to fly."

She hesitated. "What about the—"

"Realm Guardian?" He smiled as she grasped his arm, cast a red portal to his camp, and rode the Nightmare. They materialized on the other side to an anxious audience. Gideon, sitting tall, glanced at Aushade. "Now I understand your fondness for these creatures."

The guardian assisted the succubus in dismounting as Aushade and Avalann gently lowered Thomas, carrying him to the lake.

"He just collapsed," Courtlynn reported as they stripped off his armor, and Izarra spread her blanket on the beach.

"I should have stayed," Shorte lamented. "The poor dragon fodder must be overheated." Ashley hurried over with a wet cloth to place on his forehead.

Raven exited the wagon, discarded the canteen ice pack, and sprinted toward him with open arms. Her eyes were wide with worry, and her breath came in quick, shallow gasps.

"Will he be all right?" Raven asked, throwing herself at him, her voice trembling.

"He should," Gideon responded, his tone steady and reassuring, "we just need to keep him cool and hydrated."

"We need to get Carya to the church," Raven said urgently, her hands gripping his arms tightly.

"Tell Jarz we must leave immediately." She quickly kissed his lips and strode back to the wagon, her steps sharp and confident. He watched her go, worried but pushing it aside. "Someone has to stay with Thomas."

"I can stay with him," Courtlynn offered. Her voice was calm and steady, but her eyes betrayed a flicker of worry.

"No!" Aushade interjected, brow knitting in protest. "Not alone."

"I'll stay as well," Ramzey said, stepping forward without hesitation.

Shorte mumbled, "Damn love triangles."

"Oh, honey!" Ashley blurted out, her eyes wide with amusement and exasperation.

Aushade shot them a look, then moved toward Courtlynn and Gideon as the others prepared for their departure. "How are your wings?" he asked.

Gideon's gaze drifted to the succubus. She stood frozen, frowning, her injured wings twitching with involuntary spasms. The delicate membranes were torn, with patches of holes. Once graceful, they hung unevenly at her back, useless for flight. Still, she defied herself as if daring anyone to pity her.

"They'll heal," Courtlynn responded, flexing them slightly and wincing. They watched as the necromancer walked up to the Nightmare, its fiery mane casting a warm glow on his face as he gently petted it.

"Where's Gimp?" Aushade asked, his eyes scanning the camp.

"He's safe with Vanessa," Courtlynn answered, her gaze following the necromancer's admiring look at the fiery steed. "Go for it," she added, giving Aushade a slight head gesture.

Gideon nodded. "Make it quick."

Aushade hopped on the demon horse. He guided it in circles around the camp, the wind whipping through his hair as he leaned into the ride, the horse's hooves thundering against the ground. With a determined look, he made a daring dash toward the portal, the fiery light reflecting in his eyes. He hopped off, allowing the demon horse to return to the Abyss.

Before it could slip through, Gideon dispelled the gateway, his hand steady despite the swirling energy. The fiery steed stopped and began exploring the grassy field, its curiosity evident in its careful steps. "Keep it."

Aushade's eyes widened in surprise, his mouth hanging slightly open. "Thank you, but the High Council?" he asked, his voice tinged with awe and uncertainty.

Gideon shrugged, his expression calm. "You can deal with them and the next Mortal Realm Guardian. But for now, go assist with Carya."

# CHAPTER THIRTY-SIX

# THE TOLL

Raven, the first through the portal, pushed the creaking church doors open as Aushade followed closely behind, Carya's unconscious form draped over his arms. His breath came in ragged gasps, but he pressed on, grit etched in every line of his face. Raven darted ahead, her nimble fingers quickly unlatching the final entry to the ceremonial chamber. She stole a glance over her shoulder, her eyes catching the frantic movements of Gideon, Jarz, Aushade, and Shorte as they hurried past.

Ashley moved to follow, her armor clinking softly with each step. But Raven blocked her path, gripping the door frame with white-knuckled intensity. Her eyes were hard, a muted command evident in her stern gaze.

"Oh hell no," Ashley barked, echoing through the chamber. "I lost my best friend, and I left Ramzey with a succubus to nurse-sit an unconscious paladin. I paid the toll."

Raven's arm wavered momentarily before she lowered it, allowing the warrior to push past.

"I can't," Izarra whimpered, her voice barely above a whisper. Tears welled in her eyes, her hands trembling at her sides.

Avalann stepped closer, placing a reassuring hand on Izarra's shoulder. "I'll keep her company," she said softly, a soothing balm. "And we can pray to Blade."

Raven nodded and closed the door, the sound echoing softly in the hushed chamber. Carya lay still on the stone altar, her face pale and serene. Aushade stood vigil beside her, his jaw clenched and eyes shadowed with worry. High Priest Stone-Prayer meticulously arranged the ritual items: a diamond gleamed under the flickering candlelight, and the open spell book's pages fluttered slightly in a draft.

"Should I get your father and mother?" Gideon asked, his voice a soft murmur that broke the tense silence. Raven nodded, her gaze steady but distant.

"Will you be all right?" he pressed gently. She nodded again, squeezing his hand briefly before letting go. Gideon lingered momentarily, cast a blue portal, and stepped through, vanishing from sight.

Raven took a deep breath. She moved to stand beside Ashley, who offered a comforting presence, her eyes filled with strength. "So, fire-resistant too, huh?" Raven whispered, observing Shorte as he prepared the spell book.

"When I was three, my mother caught me stomping out a fire on her favorite bear-skin rug. I didn't have a single burn."

Raven glanced at her, a flicker of apprehension crossing her face. "I'm afraid of these powers. Not just for myself, but for my baby."

Ashley placed a reassuring hand on Raven's shoulder, her touch firm. "You're not alone in this. There are more of us out there, scattered about. We need to find each other."

Shorte paced back and forth, his boots tapping against the wooden platform. "What if I mess it up?"

"I can do it," Aushade offered, stepping forward with willpower.

The dwarf pushed him aside roughly. "No, you're not. It's your fault to begin with," he snapped, anger flaring in his eyes.

"Gentlemen, please." Raven stepped between them. "This isn't the time nor the place."

"I could try," Stone-Prayer chimed in, his voice calm and steady amid the tension.

"No, I can do it," Shorte huffed, grit hardening his voice. "It has to be me." The dwarf's eyes locked onto the spell book as he began reading under his breath.

Aushade carefully removed the phylactery, and suddenly, Carya screamed, her voice piercing the air. Her hand shot out, seizing Stone-Prayer's arm. The cleric's body stiffened like a stone pillar before he collapsed, motionless. Raven and Ashley sprinted to his side, their faces etched with concern. *The lich's touch paralyzed him.*

"He'll be all right. The spell is temporary," Aushade reassured, his tone steady. "Ashley, can you take him out?"

The warrior nodded, dragging Stone-Prayer from the room, her movements swift and efficient. Meanwhile, the others struggled to hold Carya down, her body thrashing violently.

"Begin, dwarf!" Aushade shouted to Shorte, gripping Carya's head to keep her still.

"Don't you have to remove the undead curse?" Raven cried out, panic lacing her voice.

"We can't now," Jarz explained, straining to hold down Carya's thrashing legs. "It's too late to dispel it, but it shouldn't affect the ritual."

Shorte chanted from the spell book, his voice rising and falling with the ancient incantations. Aushade carefully lifted the phylactery toward the diamond, his other hand pressing firmly on the lich's head to keep it steady.

Ashley returned to Raven's side with wide eyes. Suddenly, the glass soul container shattered with a sharp crack, sending shards flying across the room. A light blue beam shot from the phylactery, reflecting off the diamond in a dazzling arc. The beam struck Carya, her body convulsing violently as if seized by an unseen force. She arched off the altar, a scream caught in her throat, before falling limp, her chest heaving as silence filled the chamber.

Everyone froze, holding their breath as they watched helplessly. Carya's appearance changed slowly; her skin smoothed and rejuvenated, while her hair turned a striking pure white.

"Oh no," Shorte muttered, his voice trembling as he continued reading from the spell book. His eyes darted to Jarz, who quickly rushed over.

"That didn't sound good," Ashley murmured, her hands tightening around the hilt of her axes as if waiting for the creature to attack. Raven bit down on her lip. Jarz's eyes flashed over the spell book's text, his face blanching.

"What?" Aushade asked, his voice edged with concern.

Raven hurried over and read the line of text Shorte pointed to. "*If a phylactery is involved, purify it,*" she read aloud, a sharp throbbing shooting through her head.

"You need to relax," Ashley instructed, "your eyes are glowing."

Raven closed her eyes, taking a deep breath to calm herself, then reopened them. "What exactly does it mean—about the purification?" Raven asked, her voice steadier.

"I can't believe I forgot about that," Jarz said, his voice heavy with regret as he lowered his head.

"What do you mean you *forgot?*" Raven asked incredulously, her eyes wide.

"Liches feed on other souls," Aushade explained, his voice heavy with concern. "It's possible another soul mixed with hers."

"How often do they feed?" Raven asked, her tone sharp. "She wasn't with him that long."

"It depends," Aushade responded.

"On?" Raven snapped, frustration boiling over.

Aushade huffed, clearly exasperated. "On what type of incantation the balor used to transfer the soul to the phylactery."

"This might not even work," Shorte mumbled, holding Carya's still hand. Her appearance seemed normal now, except for the stark white curls that mirrored her father's hair after his resurrection. But she wasn't breathing.

The door creaked open, and her parents rushed to Carya's lifeless body as others filed into the room. Her mother gently ran a hand through Carya's white curls, tears welling in her eyes. "She's beauteous," Mara whispered, her voice trembling.

"At least her body is back where it belongs," Eugor said, turning to Raven. His expression hardened. "I'm grateful your sister is back, but you're in serious trouble." Raven's heart sank, her chest tightening as Gideon put a comforting arm around her shoulders.

Suddenly, Carya's body twitched violently, arching off the altar again as she released a loud, gasping breath. Her eyes flew open, wide with shock and confusion, as her chest heaved. The room fell into a tense silence, everyone holding their breath, watching as she slowly began to breathe more steadily.

"Eugor!" Mara shouted. "She's awake!"

Everyone rushed to the table. Carya's eyes fluttered open, scanning the faces around her. Raven noticed her sister's blue eyes had turned gray, just like their father's.

"Mother?" Carya called out, her voice weak.

"I'm here, dear," Mara cried, clutching Carya's hand tightly.

"I had a terrible dream," Carya whimpered, "all those demons . . . and my body aches."

"Where does it hurt?" Shorte asked, his voice choked with emotion.

Carya's eyes darted to the dwarf. "Everywhere," she moaned, a pained expression on her face. "Father?"

"I'm here," Eugor said, moving to the other side of the altar. "Relax, take your time."

"Where am I?" Carya asked, her voice trembling.

"At the church," Raven replied, stepping closer to get a better glimpse of her sister.

"You look like ogre poop." Carya tried to laugh but winced.

"She's back." Raven giggled tearfully, relief washing over her.

Outside the church, the air was calm and still, the moment quiet between the fading echo of chimes and the murmur of distant voices.

Ashley stepped forward and placed a gentle hand on Raven's shoulder. "Congratulations," she said with a warm, tired smile. Before Raven could respond, Ashley turned to Avalann and offered back the ring, cradled carefully in her palm. "Thank you for allowing Ramzey to use this. It saved her life."

Avalann accepted it solemnly, slipping the ring back onto her finger without a word.

Raven stepped in, pulling Ashley into a tight, earnest embrace. "Thank you," she whispered, her voice thick. She pulled back just enough to meet Ashley's gaze. "And I'm truly sorry about Gobs."

Ashley blinked hard, her composure wavering. "I appreciate that," she said, her voice catching. "I'll deliver her share of coins to her family."

"She was one of ours." Raven held her friend's hands. "I'll stop by the ship in the morning—with more."

A silence settled between them, brief but complete. Then, Ashley drew a steady breath and turned toward Gideon as blue light curled around his hands. "All right, wizzy," she said, her voice more constant now. "I'm ready."

Avalann stepped forward. "I'll return with her to watch over Thomas and Courtlynn, so she and Ramzey can grieve," she said. The warrior and archer stepped through the portal, which shimmered briefly before closing.

Raven glanced back to see her sister skipping through the church door. Carya tugged at her hair and compared it to their father's silver strands. The others followed, their faces showing concern as they wandered closer.

"Thomas is injured back at Gideon's camp," Raven gently informed Carya. Her sister shrugged, still examining her hair. Silence fell over the group. "Thomas, your fiancé," Raven clarified, her voice strained.

"I heard you the first time," Carya sneered, her tone sharp. "I was asleep, not dead." Everyone exchanged worried glances.

*What's wrong with her?* An unease settled in Raven's stomach.

Eugor placed a comforting hand on his eldest daughter's shoulder. "You do understand you were dead, and they brought you back. That's why you and I have the same hair and eye color."

"Is this Trickster Day?" Carya asked, her gaze sweeping over their solemn faces. "Why does everyone look so sour?"

"Maybe we should get you home," Mara suggested gently, "so you can get more rest."

"Mother, I just woke up," Carya protested, spinning in a circle. Her legs buckled beneath her, and Aushade and Jarz rushed to help, but she pushed them away. As she struggled to stand, Gideon cast a portal to the Omlett Inn.

"I think I'll walk," Carya insisted, taking a tentative step. The guardian sighed and dispelled the portal.

"We'll escort her," Mara said, wrapping her arm around her daughter's. Eugor moved to her other side.

"Why all the fuss? I know where we live," Carya muttered, her voice tinged with irritation. "The Gypsy Corner in Omlett."

"In the Gypsy Corner?" Izarra questioned, eyeing Raven with concern.

"Close, dear," Mara responded kindly, "maybe once we get you home, it will all return." The three walked down the path, leaving the others staring silently.

Raven grabbed Gideon by the hands, her eyes wide with worry. "Something's wrong."

"Give her some time," the guardian suggested gently. "Your father took weeks to adjust, and he didn't go through what she has. He didn't get out of bed for days. For her to be up and walking already is amazing."

"She's younger than he was when it happened," Raven said, trying to see the bright side, though her voice was tinged with doubt.

"We're going to return to camp," Jarz announced, casting a blue portal. "We'll take Thomas to the Inn. Aunt Mara will care for him."

Gideon shot a stern glance at Aushade. "I'll deal with you and your demon companion later." The necromancer lowered his head in acknowledgment and followed his brother, Izarra, and Shorte through the portal. As the gateway vanished, an eerie silence settled over the churchyard.

Raven turned to Gideon, her resolve crumbling as she embraced him. Tears streamed down her face, releasing the pent-up emotions she had been holding back.

"It's going to be all right," Gideon said. "For both of you."

"You know?" she sniffled, trying to collect her scattered thoughts.

"I didn't go to the Abyss for the view," Gideon replied, his tone tinged with a hint of dark humor.

"Nor for me," Raven retorted, managing a small, weary smile through her tears.

"You and the guardians put everyone in a difficult situation. Just the act of mortals going to the Abyss could start a war among the realms. Guardians are not to interfere in quests like this. It's against the rules—you know this."

"But Celeste—"

"Celeste hoped Blade would stall long enough for you all to get there and back. It may have worked if I hadn't found out about his charade." Raven went to speak, but Gideon continued, "Celeste knew the risk of helping—Elora will take her guardianship."

Raven's guilt settled in her chest. *What have we done?*

"I didn't like the idea of you risking your life, but you're a mortal guardian and have been trained to do dangerous tasks. This is part of your chosen life—and I pray to Blade to watch over you each time." Gideon continued, his tone softening. "But I will defend our child and you from every realm till my last breath."

"You're immortal," Raven reminded him. "I don't have that luxury."

"I might not be immortal for long," Gideon replied, a note of remorse coloring his voice. "I believe the fall of the guardians is upon us."

"Is that a bad thing?" Raven asked, rubbing his cheek and gazing into his icy blue eyes.

The guardian stared nervously.

"Your hands are shaking," she noticed, gripping them with hers.

"I know you're half-human and half-elf," he said, his palms growing sweaty.

She sensed his hesitation and felt her nerves rise. "Gideon?"

"How shall I propose to you?"

Raven's jaw dropped, her heart vibrating. She frantically glanced around, searching for her friends for advice. "Human," she answered, turning back to him with a smile, her eyes filling with joyful tears.

Gideon took a deep breath and got on one knee, a mixture of iron will and anxiety on his face. "I believe this is how the human males do it."

Raven's excitement bubbled over. "They usually have rings, or so my mother says," she whispered, her voice trembling with keenness.

The guardian held out his hand, summoning an ornate silver ring with a flourish. Adorned with intricate wing engravings on either side of a brilliant amethyst stone, the gem glimmered in the candlelight. Two smaller diamonds flanked the amethyst, sparkling like stars. "Will this work?" he asked, his voice filled with hope and a touch of magic.

Raven's breath caught in her throat as she stared at the beautiful ring. "It's perfect," she whispered, tears streaming down her face.

Gideon smiled. "Raven, will you marry me?" he asked, his voice steady and filled with love.

"Yes!" Raven exclaimed, throwing her arms around him. The room lit up with joy as he slipped the ring onto her finger. She pulled back to look at it, the stones catching the light and creating a kaleidoscope of colors. "It's beauteous!" she exclaimed, kissing him. "But I want an Elven ceremony."

Gideon stood, wrapping his arms around her in a warm embrace. "I should get you home," he said softly, laying a protective hand on her stomach and inspecting her split lip and injured eye with concern. "You both need rest." He began to cast a portal, but she stopped him with a gentle touch.

"Can we walk, too?" she asked, her eyes pleading for normalcy.

"Of course," he replied as he took her hand. They exited the church together, stepping into the cool night air, the stars twinkling above them.

"What will happen now?" Raven asked wearily, her voice tinged with worry. "To you, for entering the Abyss."

Gideon sighed, his expression somber. "It's just a matter of time until the High Council summons me for a hearing. I will lose my wings, the realm vision, and immortality."

Raven's grip tightened around his hand, her heart aching at the thought. "But you did it for us," she whispered, tears welling in her eyes.

"I did," Gideon replied, his voice firm and unwavering. "And I would do it again in a heartbeat."

The night was serene as they walked, the gentle rustling of leaves and the distant chirping of crickets providing a soothing backdrop. A wintry chill wrapped around them, the cold biting at their exposed skin. Their breath formed misty clouds, the cold dirt crunching under their boots with each step. The world was hushed and serene with the distant howl of the wind weaving through the bare branches of trees. The moon cast a silvery glow on the landscape, making the slight snow sparkle like a sea of diamonds. The chill in the air was sharp but invigorating, each inhale filling their lungs with winter's pure, cold essence.

Raven snuggled closer to Gideon, his warmth a welcome refuge from the biting cold. At that moment, an overwhelming rush of emotions filled her mind. Guilt twisted her stomach. *Gobs gone. Thomas injured. And Gideon will lose his immortality.* Yet happiness bubbled within the cracks because their family would now be Gideon's priority, and then a sadness weighed on her at the thought of no longer being part of the Mortal Guardians. "What will happen to the group?" Raven asked, her voice trembling.

"Just because I'm losing my position doesn't mean there won't be threats in our realm," Gideon replied, squeezing her hand reassuringly. "Each of you can choose a new path or continue."

Raven sighed with relief, feeling the tension ease from her shoulders. "I choose you," she said, her voice filled with conviction.

He smiled warmly at her. "Of course—good choice."

They finally reached her home and stepped inside. Her father and mother sat by the fire, their faces lined with worry and exhaustion.

"How's Carya?" Gideon asked gently.

"I managed to get her to drink some herbal tea. She's asleep upstairs," Mara said, tears staining her cheeks. She turned to Raven, her expression a mix of relief and sorrow. "Raven, what you did, knowing about—"

Raven's heart sank, her breath catching in her throat. "You can say it. Baby. He knows." The disappointment etched on her parents' faces pierced her more deeply than any weapon ever could. "I'm sorry. All I could think about was freeing Carya, but we had a plan if anything went wrong."

Mara's tears flowed freely as she reached to touch Raven's cut under her eye. "We were so worried," she whispered, her voice breaking. "But you did it. You brought her back."

Eugor huffed, his face darkening. "But Nightbird, it did go wrong, or Gideon wouldn't have broken his oath by entering the Abyss. You and your friends disobeyed a royal decree, got Gobs killed, and injured Thomas, costing Gideon his prestigious profession."

This time, guilt overpowered all the other emotions in Raven's heart. *It's all my fault.*

"Eugor, it was my choice," Gideon declared, stepping forward. "When Celeste told me about the child, nothing else mattered."

Her father stared at both for a long moment, then sighed heavily, pouring another glass of mulberry wine. "Jarz used a portal to bring Thomas here."

"Shorte and Stone-Prayer are caring for him in room three at the Inn," Mara whispered, her voice barely audible. Silence fell over the room again, thick and heavy.

Raven took a deep breath. "Father—"

"Listen," Eugor cut her off, his voice firm yet gentle. "You're going to be a mother, and as a parent, you would do anything to protect your child. Even if that means laying down a royal decree." A small, understanding smile touched his lips. "You'll forgive them for their mistakes, be proud of their accomplishments, and love them until your dying breath. We rarely get a second chance, so cherish these moments, Nightbird."

Tears welled in Raven's eyes as she rushed over to him, wrapping her arms around him tightly. "I love you," she whispered.

"As for you, my friend," Eugor said, gazing at Gideon. "Back when we were young, if you had told me you were going to make me a grandpap-pap, I would have—"

"Eugor," Mara interrupted gently, placing a hand on his arm, "who else in this world would better protect our daughter and grandchild than you?"

Gideon nodded, his expression resolute. "I promise to protect them with everything I have," he said, his voice steady and full of conviction.

Eugor's stern expression softened as he looked at Gideon and Raven. "I know you will," he said quietly.

"Do you know the gender of the baby?" Mara blurted out.

Raven glanced at Gideon, a gentle smile forming on her lips. "Do you want to know?" she asked softly. He nodded, his eyes lighting up with anticipation as she turned to her parents, her smile widening. "It's a girl."

Mara beamed, tears of joy filling her eyes as she embraced her daughter tightly. She then beamed at Eugor. "See? I told you—mother's intuition."

Eugor shrugged, a twinkle returning to his eyes. "I was betting on a boy."

"We have something else to share," the guardian announced, taking Raven's hand. He held up her ring finger, displaying the new ring on it. "We're—"

"Betrothed."

The four sat around the fire, celebrating and allowing themselves to focus on the good things, burying their sorrows for the night. Laughter and warmth filled the room as they shared stories and dreams for the future.

Once her parents left to check on Thomas, Raven turned to Gideon and kissed him softly. "You'll be a terrific father."

"And you're going to be a great mother," he replied, pulling her against his chest. "Imagine what she'll become. Your beauty—"

"You're not too shabby yourself, Mister Grindal," she teased, looking deep into his eyes.

"My power."

"Hey now," Raven mused, raising an eyebrow.

"Your stubbornness," they yelled in unison, bursting into laughter.

Gideon smiled, his eyes sparkling. "And to think, you thought the rogue life was hard."

Raven's eyes widened with mock terror, but before she could answer, a soft creak broke the moment.

She turned—sharp, instinctive.

Half-shadowed in the dim stairwell, Carya crept up the steps. She moved slowly, deliberately—too deliberately. And in her hand, half-hidden by the folds of her nightgown, something glinted in the low light.

Raven's breath hitched. A quiet question spiraling in her mind.

*How long had she been there?*

# CHAPTER THIRTY-SEVEN

# REBORN

G ideon arranged the last of his gear, his movements precise and methodi-
cal as the first rays of the morning sun filtered through the canopy. The
chirping of early birds and the rustling leaves blended into a soothing
symphony. His sleepless night had driven him to clean, each task distracting
from his restless thoughts. As he tipped the washbowl, the cool water splashed
onto the ground, the droplets glistening briefly before soaking into the earth.
He paused, his gaze lifting to the roaring waterfall. Gideon took a deep breath,
the crisp, damp air filling his lungs, and for a moment, the tranquility of the
scene washed over him, easing the tension that had knotted his muscles through
the night.

Gideon absentmindedly scratched his ring finger, the silver band leaving
a faint red mark on his skin. Despite the irritation, a smile tugged at his lips.
He remembered Raven's delicate smile as he crafted the rings. Securing the
last of his belongings inside the wagon, he cast a quick, satisfied glance over
his organized campsite. He approached Avalann's table with purposeful steps,
where the demon dice lay in a messy pile. Carefully, he gathered their smooth
weight in his hands and slid them into a cloth pouch hanging from his belt.
The soft clink of the dice inside the pouch echoed the calm yet resolute rhythm
of his heartbeat.

The guardian closed his eyes, centering his mind on the task. He envisioned
his gypsy wagon, picturing every detail as he focused on teleporting it to the
horse stable in Omlett. The air around him buzzed with energy, and a deep hum
resonated through his bones as he channeled the immense magic required for
such a feat. The familiar surge of power flew through him, a tingling sensation
spreading from his core to his fingertips.

As the spell reached its crescendo, the magic pulsed and dissipated, signaling the completion of the teleportation. The guardian opened his eyes, his

breath escaping in a slow, measured sigh. Before him, the clearing near the falls lay empty, the absence of the wagon a testament to his success. He stared at the spot where it had stood, the gentle rush of the waterfall providing a stark contrast to the intense focus and effort of moments before. He felt the weight of the magic he wielded for a brief instant, a mixture of weariness and satisfaction.

"One down, one to go. I hope I have enough energy for this," Gideon muttered, rolling his shoulders to ease the tension. He tilted his head to each side, cracking his neck, then clenched his fists and stretched his fingers several times, feeling the strain of his previous teleportation. Taking a deep breath, he closed his eyes and focused once more. The air shimmered and buzzed with energy, and a dimensional door materialized before him. He pulled the cottage from the Fey Realm through it.

A wave of dizziness washed over him, and he swayed on his feet. As he steadied himself, he took in the unfamiliar sight. *It's not the same, but there's still a waterfall.* The sound of distant waves mixed with the memory of the falls in the Fey.

He reached for his gold armor lying on the ground but paused, his hand hovering over the gleaming metal. *I should get used to not wearing it.* With a resigned sigh, he turned away and stepped into his cottage. The familiar scent of aged wood and herbs greeted him. He made his way to the back of the wardrobe, pushing aside layers of armor and cloaks until his fingers brushed against the soft fabric of his old wizard robes. Pulling them out, he held the old cloth for a moment, a tangible link to his past.

Gideon slipped into a robe, the fabric familiar and comforting against his skin. The sapphire fabric that matched his boots featured wide, flowing sleeves and was adorned with the intricate embroidery of arcane symbols and mystical runes in gold thread. The robe's hem brushed the ground, its edges frayed and slightly discolored from years of dragging through various terrains.

With hands raised, he cast a blue portal, carefully placing the cottage just outside the Omlett Inn to adhere to Waterfront's rules of etiquette. Stepping through, he found himself in front of his favorite tavern, its weathered sign swaying gently in the breeze. Pausing for a moment, he soaked in the surroundings. *I'm home.* A smile spread across his face as the excitement of marrying Raven, living close to his friends, and the prospect of becoming a father flooded his mind. The thought brought a warmth that overshadowed the bittersweet reality of losing his immortality. The village was alive with the usual hustle and bustle in the morning, familiar faces passing by with nods of recognition.

Gideon took a deep breath, savoring the scent of the Suttiir River mingling with freshly baked bread from a nearby bakery. He pushed open the heavy oak door of the Inn, the wood tremendous and solid under his palm.

Gideon paused in the doorway. A lightheadedness swept over him as he adjusted to the soft, warm light inside. His eyes were drawn to the figure sitting by the fireplace, her presence almost hypnotic. She wore a short, red silk night-gown that shimmered in the firelight, casting a warm glow on her ivory skin. It took him a moment to recognize Raven's sister, her delicate hands tracing a path across the dark-skinned face of her companion.

The person beside her was the demigod of the moons, clad in gray leather armor. Gideon's breath caught as he watched her fingers glide slowly down the demigod's chest, her movements intimate and deliberate. *Allus.* The name echoed in his mind as he took in the scene. *What's he doing here?*

Allus leaned in closer, his silver eyes reflecting the dancing flames, and Gideon felt discomfort as he realized the demigod was about to kiss her. The air seemed to thicken, the warmth of the fire clashing with the sudden chill that gripped Gideon's heart. "Carya!" Gideon called out, his voice sharp with disbelief and a tinge of anger as he watched the demigod's lips brush against her neck, his hand caressing her breast over the silky fabric. Gideon's heart pounded with confusion. "What are you doing?"

Carya turned with a mischievous glint in her eyes. She bit her lip, her expression a blend of seduction and challenge. "Care to join?" she purred, her voice smooth and teasing as Allus continued massaging her nipples.

A rush of emotion—anger, jealousy, and a reluctant thrill—battled within him. Gideon stepped forward, then stopped, his fists clenching at his sides.

Her companion smiled and then casually grabbed a drink, leaning back nonchalantly. The moon-elf greeted Gideon by waving his mug and splashing its contents all over the floor. "Hello? Giddy? Hello?"

Gideon shook his head, trying to escape the daze that clouded his mind. The two figures straightened, their eyes fixed on him with curious intensity. He returned their gaze sternly, feeling the weight of the situation pressing on him. *Was that all in my head?*

Carya sauntered over, her movements smooth and confident. "Hey there, handsome. Got something on your mind?" she asked, her fingers lightly tug-ging at his wizard robe. He stared into her gray eyes, searching for a hint of Raven's sister. "Where's the gold armor?" she continued, her voice a mix of teasing and genuine curiosity.

Out of the corner of his eye, Gideon saw Allus vanish into thin air, leaving behind a faint shimmer where he had been. The sudden disappearance sent a chill down his spine. "What's going on here, Carya?" he demanded, his voice steady but laced with concern. "This isn't like you."

She tilted her head, a wicked smile dancing on her lips. "People change, Giddy. Maybe you should, too."

"Thomas is right down the hall, with demon poison coursing through his veins," Gideon stated, his voice heavy with sorrow. "He risked his life, like many others, to bring you back."

Carya shrugged, a dismissive gesture that felt like a punch to Gideon's gut. "I know," she said, her tone casual. "My parents explained everything to me last night on our walk home."

"And?" Gideon pressed, his eyes darting to the empty seat where Allus had been moments before.

"And what?" Carya glanced back at him, a smile playing on her lips.

"You were just—"

"Talking," she interrupted, her voice dripping with innocence. "We were talking. Were you jealous, Giddy? What's going on in that head of yours?" she teased, her eyes gleaming with a knowing look.

"What were you talking about?"

"The Shadow Realm. Oh, did you know moon-elves live there?"

"Yes," Gideon replied, his mind still reeling from the earlier encounter. His thoughts scattered, unable to focus.

"All these years, and I had no clue. So it makes me wonder, what else is out there?" Carya mused, her tone light and curious.

"There are rules for the realms that we must abide by," Gideon said, struggling to regain his composure. His emotions were a tangled web of frustration and protectiveness. The flickering firelight painted shifting patterns on the walls, heightening his sense of unease.

Carya's smile faded slightly, and she stepped closer, her demeanor softening. "Gideon, I'm grateful for what Thomas and the others did. Truly. But I must find my own path to understand my place in all of this. It's just when I want something, I get it," Carya said, her voice sultry and confident.

Suddenly, Gideon felt an unexpected pressure against his groin, catching him off guard. A wave of instant arousal surged through him. *Both her hands are on my robe. How is this happening?* The invisible pressure grew more insistent, massaging him with increasing intensity. "Carya," Gideon pleaded, his voice strained with shock and desire. He quickly gathered his focus and cast Dispel Magic, feeling the spell's energy flow through him as he aimed to dismiss her Mage Hand spell. The sensation abruptly stopped, leaving him breathless and flushed. He glanced at Carya, who smirked, clearly unfazed. Gideon realized with a jolt how much he had depended on his gold armor to deflect and dampen magic. Without it, he was vulnerable in ways he had almost forgotten. The memory of its protective weight felt like a distant dream. "Carya, this isn't right," he said, trying to regain control over his racing heart.

Carya gripped his robe tighter, pulling him closer. "Did you enjoy that?" she whispered, her breath warm against his ear.

Gideon stepped away, his movements deliberate as he removed her hands from him. He shook his head, trying to clear the lingering fog of arousal and confusion.

"You're no fun," she said, crossing her arms with a pout. "I see why you're with my sister. You may appear young, but you and my father may as well build matching rockers, sit on the porch, and have an interesting conversation about the weather."

"Carya," Gideon pleaded, "what's wrong?"

Her eyes flickered with mixed emotions—anger, frustration, and something he couldn't quite identify. "What's wrong?" she echoed, her tone mocking. "What's wrong is that everyone expects me to be the same." Her expression softened momentarily, a flicker of something unreadable passing through her eyes. "I just wanted to remind you that I'm not the little girl you remember. I have power, too, Gideon. Don't forget that. So nothing's *wrong*," Carya snapped, sitting on the table before him and pulling him closer with her legs. "I've seen death, and unlike my father, I won't settle down in a tavern and hide. It feels like I was reborn, and I want to explore the realms." She wrapped her legs tighter around him, her hands sliding to his waist, gripping firmly. A mix of alarm and desire overwhelmed his senses. "Do you know the difference between a demigod and a guardian?" she asked, her eyes locking onto his with a fierce intensity.

"Demigods are naturally immortal," Gideon replied, trying to maintain his composure.

"Wrong! There's no difference. It's just a title. Because right now, you're a demigod."

"Carya? What? No. That's not how it works."

"Allus is no different from you. You're both immortal."

"For now, but the High Council can remove it. I've seen it done."

"Anyone's immortality can be taken away if someone has the right tools."

Gideon's heart skipped a beat. "What? How do you know this?"

"A girl has secrets, and I can keep secrets," she said seductively, her hands exploring his body with deliberate slowness. She reached into the cloth pouch at his side and pulled out the demon dice. "What's this?" she asked, her voice dripping with curiosity.

"They're not mine," Gideon choked, his voice barely above a whisper.

"You naughty elf," Carya murmured, getting on her knees on the table, her eyes gleaming with a dangerous glint. "I knew deep down you had a dark side." She pulled him closer, their faces inches apart, her finger tracing the outline of his lips. "We could play," she purred, her words dripping with seductive promise. "Remove an article of clothing for every fire symbol we roll." He shook his head, trying to resist the intoxicating pull of her presence. She leaned in closer, her lips brushing against his ear. "And I'm only wearing this," she murmured, lowering the strap of her nightgown over her right shoulder. The silk slipped down, revealing the smooth curve of her skin.

A robust and overwhelming urge to touch her flashed through Gideon's mind, his self-control wavering. The firelight cast a warm glow on her exposed shoulder, highlighting the delicate lines of her collarbone. He swallowed hard, the temptation almost too much to bear. "Carya, please," he managed to say, his voice strained. "This isn't right."

Her eyes sparkled with mischief as she pressed closer, her breath hot against his skin. "Why not? Afraid to lose control, Giddy?"

*How is she doing this?* Gideon fought off the trance, shaking his head to clear his thoughts. "Carya, you're not yourself."

"Then who am I? Do you want me to be Raven? I can do that, too," she mocked, her voice dripping with sarcasm as she placed the dice down and tied her white hair into a ponytail. "Oh, Gideon, boo-hoo, no one understands me. Can we go to my room so you can teach me magic tricks?"

Gideon fought the powerful urge coursing through him. "That's enough," he said, his voice trembling but resolute.

Carya hopped down from the table, her gaze piercing as she stared into his eyes. "But Giddy, I can perform things without magic. We could create a godly child. Even more powerful than your daughter."

Her words struck him like a blow, and for a moment, he was speechless, the air between them thick with tension. He took a deep breath, his heart pounding, and forced himself to remain calm. "Carya, you don't understand what you're saying."

"Oh, I understand perfectly. You're afraid. Afraid of what we could be together. Afraid of our power."

"*Ah-hem*! What's going on?" Raven demanded, stepping into the room with a bag slung over her shoulder. Her sudden presence snapped Gideon out of the daze, and he quickly backed away from Carya, who laughed and undid her ponytail, letting her hair cascade down.

"I'm just playing," Carya teased, shaking the dice and handing them to Raven. "I never realized how powerful he is. It's no wonder you gave yourself to him," she snickered, then growled seductively.

Raven blushed deeply, her cheeks flushing with both embarrassment and anger. "Stop it."

Carya's playful demeanor shifted to one of sternness. "But you should have waited until marriage. I'll forgive you. You're my sister, and he's a god." She reached for the coin pouch in Raven's hand. "What's in there?"

"Payment for the help of bringing you back," Raven replied, her grip tightening on the pouch.

"I didn't realize I was worth that much."

Raven's eyes softened, and she stepped closer to her sister. "Gobs paid the ultimate price, and there isn't any amount of coin to compensate for that."

Carya's expression faltered, a flicker of genuine emotion crossing her face. "Gobs . . . she's gone?" her voice breaking with sorrow.

"She gave her life to save you. We all did what we could, but . . . she didn't make it."

"I'm sorry." Carya frowned, but the sadness quickly switched to a chipper tone. "Well, all right then. I'll meet you for lunch."

Cee moved behind the bar with a basket from the pantry. "Carya, I'm looking forward to your breakfast arrangements again."

"Get your *own* damn breakfast," Carya called out, her voice cutting through the room like a knife as Cee's gleeful face fell, replaced by a gleam of embarrassment. "I have things to do." She turned on her heel and walked down the hall toward their father's work chamber.

"What about Thomas?" Raven shouted, her voice echoing in the corridor.

"I'm sure Mother is doing a superb job with Mister Goody Two-Boots," Carya responded, her tone dripping with sarcasm.

"You mean Two-Shoes?" Raven mumbled, struggling to hold back her temper. "He traveled through hell for you! We all did."

Carya ignored her sister, then turned back and called out to Gideon. "My offer still stands. You know where to find me." She blew him a kiss before slamming their father's door shut.

Raven's eyes narrowed as she glared at him. "What offer?"

Gideon shook his head, a troubled expression on his face. "There's something wrong with her."

"Can you help?" Raven asked, her voice laced with desperation. "A spell or something?"

"Resurrections are rare," the guardian stated, his voice thoughtful. "It's possible something changed her."

Raven frowned, her worry deepening the lines on her face. "Why is she acting like this? She's excited about our baby and engagement one moment, then scolds us the next. I don't understand."

Gideon sighed, placing a comforting hand on her shoulder. "It's not uncommon for those brought back from the brink to be different. Sometimes, they're not entirely themselves. It could be a lingering effect of the resurrection spell or the trauma of returning from death. It hasn't even been a full day since her return," Gideon pointed out, his voice calm but firm. "We need to give her more time."

"Have you—" Raven began to ask, her eyes drifting to his robe.

"Not yet," he answered, understanding her unfinished question. "Time moves slower at the High Council, so I have some to spare."

"Are you nervous?" Raven asked, handing him back his dice.

"Not really," Gideon said, quickly tying up the cloth pouch. "I view it as a new chapter in life. As someone said, 'reborn.'"

They walked down the hallway to Thomas's room, their footsteps echoing softly on the wooden floor. Inside, Thomas lay asleep, his face pale and glistening with sweat. Mara was by his side, rinsing out another wet towel with meticulous care.

"How is he?" Raven asked, her voice filled with concern.

"Still has a fever," Mara replied, glancing up with tired eyes. "The demon poison is still spreading slowly."

"Has Carya stopped by yet?" Gideon asked, his brow creasing.

"Not yet," Mara replied.

"Poor Thomas," Raven said sadly, her gaze resting on his unconscious form. "I'm not sure how he'll handle Carya if she doesn't feel the same way about him anymore."

"Let's stop the poison first and deal with that later," Mara recommended, her voice gentle but firm. "Love has a way of healing everything."

Gideon grabbed Raven's hand and kissed it tenderly. "Speaking of love, are the necromancer and the succubus comfy at the windmill?"

"I hope so," Raven replied, a hint of worry in her eyes. "It's the only place I could think of where people won't bother them. But they can't hide there forever."

Mara sighed sadly, her eyes reflecting the weight of her words. "Forgiving Aushade and that . . . demon . . . for what they have done will take time. But your father and I are trying out of love and respect for Ausharz. That's why we agreed to banishment and not execution."

"I'm giving them my cottage," Gideon said.

"They can't stay in the Fey Realm," Raven countered.

"It's outside the Inn now, but I'll move it to my camp along with our unicorn rescues, Aerica and Trotter," Gideon explained. "It would be interesting to watch a succubus and a necromancer care for unicorns and a Nightmare. Let's hope the new guardian will be more lenient than the last one." They shared a laugh, the tension easing slightly. "But I should return to the High Council and face their wrath."

Raven kissed him softly. "I need to get the payment to the *Sea Squid* and return the diamond to Mug." Gideon held her hand as she escorted him outside, the cool breeze brushing against their faces.

"Will you still love me"—Gideon hesitated, the words caught in his throat as Raven gave him a dumbfounded look—"when I'm sitting on the porch talking to your father about the weather?"

"Of course," Raven responded, her eyes softening. "What kind of question is that?"

"Things are changing—"

"Of course they are—we're becoming parents—but it doesn't mean we stop living." She tugged on his robes, a twinkle in her eye. "We may need to work on your wardrobe, though. I think these went out of style about seventy-five years ago."

Gideon chuckled, feeling the warmth of her love. "Noted." He pulled her into a tight embrace, their laughter mingling with the rustling leaves around them.

Raven's face tightened. "I'm sorry—I'm the reason you're losing your guardianship."

Gideon tilted her chin with a gentle finger until her purple eyes met his. "Honestly, there's some sadness. But then I think of our new life with the little one," he said, pulling her close. "We'll just have to find a way to have different adventures."

"I'm sure my parents will watch *our* daughter if we need to escape."

"A daughter," he repeated, his voice filled with wonder.

Raven hugged him tightly. "Now go tell those High Council dung beetles you don't need them."

"Portal?" he asked, raising an eyebrow.

"I'll walk. I need the exercise." She gave him another quick kiss. "I'll be here when you return."

Gideon cast a blue portal to his camp and retrieved his gold armor. He donned the familiar weight, feeling a sense of resolve as he summoned his white wings and sheathed his polished blade. *Do I keep Celeste's vorpal sword?* He cast a spell to spawn it inside his wagon back at Omlett. *They think she lost it in the Abyss.*

The guardian cast a red portal to the High Council. He entered the Great Hall, where the gold doors stood imposingly closed. Inside, the air was thick with tension. Celeste was bound between two guards, wearing a white tunic and breeches similar to what he'd worn in the holding cell. Gideon stopped beside her in front of the guard.

"Because of you," Celeste sneered at him, breaking the silence.

"Celeste—"

She smiled. "They changed how the privy works."

Gideon shook his head and laughed. "It was an honor serving with you."

"All good things must come to an end," she boasted.

The other two guardians stood together, whispering among themselves. Meliae, a wood nymph and the Astral Realm Guardian, wore a thistle branch headpiece that adorned her short brunette hair. Krut, the half-orc and the Shadow Realm Guardian, looked rugged with his black cropped hair and beard as if he had awoken from a long meditation session. Both were clad in their gold armor and white wings, their expressions dark as they shot murderous looks at the two elves, seemingly blaming them for this disciplinary meeting.

"They'll thank us later," Celeste mused, a hint of defiance in her voice. "At least you don't need security."

"I might be joining you," Gideon teased, his tone light but with an undercurrent of uncertainty. "You never know."

The gold doors slowly opened with a creak. "This will probably be the last time we go through them." Celeste sighed as the guards pushed her forward.

Elora stood in the middle of the head table as all four guardians assembled in the center, awaiting their fate. The doors closed behind them with a finality that echoed in the vast hall. The head councilwoman smacked her gavel on the table, the sound sharp and decisive. "The votes," Elora called to her fellow council members. A water elemental from the Water-Plane had replaced Tessk in the Abyss chair. Gideon's mind raced with questions. *Did they finally realize he betrayed them? Or did he flee back to the Abyss?*

"Let us begin," Elora stated, her voice carrying the weight of authority. The water elemental raised its paddle, the watery form shifting as it did so. The motion felt agonizingly slow and deliberate. Finally, it settled on red. Gideon's stomach churned.

Ozul's red eyes beamed as he held up the same. Elora followed suit, her scowl deepening. *It's already a three-to-none vote.* Gideon's heart sank.

The atmosphere in the hall was thick with tension. Meliae's and Krut's eyes bored into him, their wordless accusations blatant. He glanced at Celeste, who stood tall despite her bindings, her eyes locked on the council with a mixture of defiance and resignation.

"Elora, this isn't right," Gideon began, his voice steady but urgent. "We've always served the realms faithfully. Can't you see there's more at play here?"

Elora's gaze softened for a moment, but the sternness quickly returned. "Gideon, your loyalty is commendable, but actions have consequences. The council must uphold the laws that govern us all."

Gideon's heart pounded as he awaited the final votes. Their fates hung in the balance, determined by the very people they had served alongside. The tension in the room was almost unbearable as the last council member, Ellie, raised her paddle. She hesitated, her gaze lingering on Gideon and Celeste before slowly lifting the red paddle.

"Four to none," Elora announced, her voice echoing through the hall. "Gideon and Celeste, you are hereby stripped of your titles and banished from the Guardian Council."

The words hit Gideon like a physical blow. He glanced at Celeste, who met him with a determined look. Gideon locked eyes with another new arrival, Henry Owens. The elderly wizard's presence only heightened the tension, and Gideon knew that if Blade had been replaced, the verdict would be severe. Henry's expression was inscrutable as he slowly held up the red paddle. The chamber fell into an expectant silence as everyone waited to hear the results.

Elora cleared her throat, her voice cutting through the quiet. "The vote is unanimous. The council hereby declares the abolishment of the Realm Guardians."

A murmur of shock and disbelief rippled through the room. A cold dread settled in Gideon's stomach as one of the High Council guards stepped forward, his expression stoic and adamant. The guard moved to collect their vorpal swords, the symbols of their authority and power.

Gideon reluctantly unsheathed his polished blade, the weight of it familiar yet now tinged with the bitter taste of loss. He handed it over sorrowfully. Beside him, the other guardians did the same. Meliae whimpered, Krut huffed, and Celeste sighed. *My protection of the Mortal Realm has officially come to an end.*

Meliae was instantly lifted into the air as her wings and armor disappeared, replaced by a cinnamon-colored tunic and breeches. Krut followed, his gold armor and white wings vanishing, leaving him in his familiar black cloth garb.

Gideon closed his eyes, bracing for his turn. It wasn't the first time he had experienced this, but it felt different now—more final. His feet lifted from the ground, and he held out his arms to welcome the procedure. The ritual removed his armor piece by piece, and as the last of the golden plates dissolved, he was gently lowered to the floor. Celeste floated upward last, her prisoner attire stark against the grand hall's backdrop, before returning to the ground.

He didn't feel any different physically, but mentally, there was a sense of freedom. Once a comforting burden, the weight of his duty had been lifted. He opened his eyes and saw Meliae and Krut, both appearing as disoriented as he felt.

"This is a new era," Elora declared, echoing through the hall. "The members on the High Council bench will now oversee each realm. Change is coming, and we remind you that our law is final. Disobey and spend the rest of your lives locked in cells. We wish you the best."

*After serving as a guardian for almost two centuries, all I received was a "We wish you the best." Raven was right.*

Gideon watched portals open for Meliae and Krut, and the council members began to exit, their expressions neutral and unreadable. Henry Owens and Elora lingered, staring intently at the remaining guardians. Gideon met Owens's gaze, trying to decipher the emotion behind the old wizard's eyes. *Is it pity? Curiosity? Regret?*

Owens finally spoke, his voice low but carrying a weight of sincerity. "Gideon, Celeste, the council's decisions are not always just, but they are the law. Remember that not all battles are fought with swords and spells. Sometimes, perseverance and wisdom can lead to greater victories. Mister Grindal, you are dismissed."

"What about Celeste?" Gideon called out, desperation edging his voice.

"She's returning to her cell immediately," Elora ordered, her voice cold and unyielding. "Guards."

"No, no," Celeste cried out as one of the guards grabbed her roughly. "Gideon!"

Gideon instinctively cast a spell to stop the guards, but it fizzled before it could take effect. He turned to see Henry Owens, his hand raised, eyes stern, countering the spell. Before Gideon could react, another guard shoved him through the portal.

He stumbled out in front of the Omlett Inn, the night air cool against his skin. He looked around, disoriented, the reality of his situation sinking in. The Inn's warm lights glowed softly, starkly contrasting the turmoil inside him.

"No!" he shouted, trying to cast a portal to return to the High Council. The spell sparked and died, his connection to the council's magic severed.

Gideon hastily returned to his wagon next to the stables. The cold winter air filled his lungs as he took a deep breath, trying to steady his racing thoughts. The frost-covered ground crunched under his boots as he approached the wagon, his sanctuary amid the chaos.

He opened the door and stepped inside, the warmth and familiarity of his space offering a small measure of comfort. He undressed quickly, the fatigue of the day's events weighing heavily on him. Climbing under the sheets, he allowed himself a moment of stillness, the first in what felt like an eternity.

*This will be the second time I can sleep without visions of the realm in almost a century.* A bittersweet realization. Gideon's mind, however, was far from quiet. Concerns for Celeste gnawed at him, mingling with the uncertainty of the past few days. He could still hear her cries and see the desperation in her eyes as the guards dragged her away.

Gideon closed his eyes, willing himself to find some semblance of peace. The weight of his guardianship had been lifted, but the burdens of his heart remained. He thought of Raven, her unwavering support, as a beacon of hope in the darkness.

His mind drifted to their plans, the journey to the Enchanted Forest, and the uncertain path ahead. They would need allies, strength, and courage. But they had each other, a foundation he could build upon.

A gentle hand brushed his bare skin. Gideon glanced up and saw purple eyes staring down at him. "Raven," he whispered, sitting up as she stood at the edge of the bed. "It's done. I'm no longer a guardian."

She smiled, a warm, reassuring expression, and began to remove her purple gown. A rush of emotions—relief, longing, and love—as he pulled her slender body over him, kissing her passionately. "I'm aging again, so let's use our time and count the stars," he murmured against her lips as Raven nodded. He embraced her again, his hands gliding across her cold skin as he pressed his lips to her neck. Her hair swept against him. The usual scent of lavender was missing.

Gideon reached up and gently removed the tie, holding her hair back. The soft black strands fell free, cascading over her bare chest. He paused, his fingers threading through the unfamiliar texture, his mind racing.

Gideon gently laid her on the bed, positioning himself between her legs. The warmth of her breath on his neck sent goosebumps across his skin, intensifying their connection. As they moved together, their bodies rhythmically entwined, her skin glistened with a sheen of sweat, catching the dim moonlight of the room.

With a swift motion, she rolled him over, pinning him to the bed. Gideon closed his eyes, surrendering to the sensation of her hands exploring his chest. A sharp sting broke his reverie. "Hey!" he exclaimed, feeling her nails scratch his side.

She smiled, a wicked glint in her eyes, and kissed him again, silencing his protest as their bodies merged. For a moment, the world outside ceased to exist. The intensity of their passion drowned out all other thoughts.

Gideon's senses were overwhelmed by the feel of her skin against his, the taste of her lips, the sound of their breaths mingling. Yet, a small part of his mind remained alert, wary of his earlier unease.

As the climax of their lovemaking approached, Gideon opened his eyes, catching a fleeting glimpse of something in her gaze that sent a jolt of uneasiness through him. As they finally rested, their bodies still intertwined, he whispered, "I never want this to end."

Raven's smile widened, a hint of satisfaction in her eyes. "Neither do I, Gideon. Neither do I."

Breathing hard and exhausted, Gideon guided Raven into his arms. *She seems different tonight*, a nervous feeling tugging at the back of his mind. She reached over and touched his silver ring. "It's not as glamorous as yours," he said, "but I thought having one, too, would be nice." He pulled her hand closer, his eyes narrowing as he realized she wasn't wearing her ring.

She yanked her hand away, quickly standing. Slipping on one of Gideon's old wizard robes, she kissed him and headed for the door.

"Where are you going?" Gideon asked, rising to his feet, concern tightening his voice. "You're not staying?"

She paused in the doorway, her back to him. Her shoulders lifted slightly—like a breath caught halfway. When she turned, her eyes weren't wet, but they shone with something brittle, like glass under strain. "Thomas passed." The words landed flat, hollow. Her voice wavered on the last syllable, like it might shatter if she spoke again.

Gideon's breath caught. He stepped forward instinctively, his expression darkening with shock. "Raven . . . I'm sorry." He searched her face, trying to read the space between her stillness and her silence. "Do you want to talk about it?"

She grinned with a strange, almost detached smile and kissed him. Without another word, she exited, leaving Gideon leaning against the wall, a deep frown creasing his brow. *That was strange*, his mind racing. *Something isn't right.* The way she moved, the way she spoke—it all felt off. He replayed the events in his mind, searching for clues. The missing ring, the unfamiliar scent, her cryptic behavior. *That wasn't Raven.*

Cyndi's voice called out from the stable, startling him. "Carya! Your sister is searching for you."

Without thinking, he dashed out the door into the cold, completely nude, as the bard eyed him awkwardly. "Which way did Raven go?" he asked frantically.

"Raven?" Cee questioned, raising an eyebrow. "She's in the tavern having some late-night tea. Carya just skipped by on her way to the Inn."

His heart raced. "What was Carya wearing?"

Cyndi blushed, glancing away. "More than you!" The bard shook her head. "And I thought Brugg lost his mind."

A sharp pain shot through Gideon's head, causing him to lose his balance. His vision blurred, then cleared again.

"Gideon! Are you all right?" She wrapped him with her long fur coat.

"Where's Raven?" Gideon asked, disoriented. "Having tea?"

"In bed, most likely," Cyndi replied, concern in her voice. "You might want to get dressed."

"Carya?" Gideon mumbled, trying to piece together his thoughts. "Was she wearing my robe?"

"No, but I think you need to lay off the ale there, pal," Cee suggested, shaking her head. "Why would Raven's sister be wearing your . . . oh. Nobody but us and the horses. Are you sure you're all right? I can summon a cleric."

"I don't know," Gideon mumbled, stumbling back to his wagon. "She's in my head again."

"I'll pick up my coat later today," the bard called out as he slammed the door behind him. He heard her faint voice through the walls. "Try not to spill ale on it!"

Gideon collapsed onto the bed, his mind racing. Trying to make sense of what had happened, questions swirling. The effort to untangle memories and visions caused a throbbing headache. He needed rest to clear his head, but as Gideon lay there, wrapped in the fur coat, unease gnawed relentlessly. He couldn't shake the feeling that something was terribly wrong. *Was it really Carya, or was it someone—or something—else entirely? Was it even real?*

# CHAPTER THIRTY-EIGHT

# THE MORNING OF
# THE MOURNING

Raven lay still in her bed, her eyes tracing the soft rise and fall of Carya's breath across the room. The morning sun trickled through the curtains, painting her sister's serene face with a golden light. Almost a week had passed since Carya's sudden return, yet the disbelief lingered like a ghost in Raven's mind. She couldn't reconcile the joy of reunion with the disquiet that had settled in her chest. Carya's eyes would dart around the room, her fingers tapping incessantly on any surface, constantly circling back to questions about Gideon and Blade. Once full of shared secrets and laughter, her voice now brimmed with an unsettling urgency whenever the demigods were mentioned.

Raven took a deep breath, trying to shake off the unease, and slipped out of bed. She gathered her bathing bucket, careful not to disturb the fragile peace, and tiptoed from the room, the floorboards whispering under her careful steps. They'd spent the last couple of nights mourning the loss of Thomas. The demon poison had taken its course, leaving confusion and heartache in its wake. Her mother was relentless, insisting that something else was to blame, even pointing the finger at Aushade's new partner, Courtlynn, her voice sharp with accusation, until her father's calm reasoning finally subdued her.

*It feels like an eternity since I saw anyone.* Raven's friends were in seclusion, nursing their wounds and spirits after the fierce battle. With the orphanage now complete, it was a hive of activity, with Jarz and Izarra busying themselves, guiding the children to their new home. Even Shorte found a way to help, tirelessly preparing oatcakes and stew, the comforting aroma wafting through the air, a small beacon of normalcy amid the chaos.

Avalann cherished the fleeting moments with her parents before they departed for Suttiir. The warmth of their laughter and the comfort of their familiar voices filled her with a bittersweet nostalgia. Queen Baela sent an urgent message, requesting the Greenorrs' expertise in bolstering security, and duty called them away.

Ramzey's ship swayed gently with the current at Fischer's Docks. Raven visited the anchored vessel, the breeze ruffling her hair and the calls of seagulls echoing in the background. The deck was eerily quiet, lacking its usual bustle, and her heart sank a little as she realized they weren't on board.

*I hope to see my friends tonight.* Her father was hosting an honor tribute for Gobs and Thomas, and the air buzzed with excitement and solemnity. Her familiar, Shorty, flew through the streets, extending the invitations, determined to ensure everyone knew of the gathering.

The sounds of rehearsals drifted from the courtyard where the Cee Sharps were fine-tuning their performance. Cyndi's voice rang out clear and strong, blending seamlessly with the melodies of her band members, their music adding an upbeat note to the otherwise somber day.

Even Gideon, still grappling with losing his guardianship, found solace in activity. He moved through their new home purposefully, arranging furniture and manually painting the walls, trying to focus on the future. His hands were steady, but his eyes betrayed a flicker of sadness whenever they caught a familiar glimpse of the past.

Raven hurried back from the bathing hole, the cool morning air prickling her damp skin. Her heart sank when she saw Carya's empty bed, the covers neatly pulled back, and she shook off the uneasy feeling. She moved to her wardrobe, her fingers brushing over the familiar fabrics as she selected a waist-length, lace-up, purple eyelet tunic that perfectly matched her boots. The rich, deep color contrasted beautifully with the black onyx set in her circlet and the sleek black breeches that hugged her legs.

Dressed and ready, Raven gathered her hair with deliberate care, the motion as familiar and grounding as the rhythm of her own breath. Her fingers moved with practiced precision, sweeping back the long strands and smoothing them down, each motion a quiet act of control. This was her ritual—one last moment of calm before the storm. She tilted her head slightly, ensuring every strand was in place, then wrapped the tie around the bundle with a few firm twists. Her lock pick clip slipped into the base of the ponytail, secured and invisible but always close—her small insurance against the unpredictable. The high tail swayed lightly as she moved, its shine catching the light, a signal to anyone watching: She was focused, steady, and ready.

Raven took a deep breath, feeling anticipation about the day ahead. Hurrying down the steps, the old wood creaked beneath her feet. Rounding the corner, she collided with Brugg, his broad frame nearly sending her sprawling. "I'm taking care of some errands before the ceremony tonight," she said, adjusting her tunic.

"Be good," the orc replied with a broken-toothed smile, his gruff voice softened by the warmth in his eyes. Raven couldn't help but smile back, appreciating his rough kindness.

As Raven stepped outside, the early morning sun glowed over the town. The streets were bustling with activity: vendors setting up their stalls, children darting between them, their laughter ringing. She inhaled deeply, the scent of fresh bread and blooming flowers mingling in the breeze.

She made her way along the dirt roads as her mind buzzed with a mental checklist of tasks, but she couldn't shake the lingering unease about Carya's absence. The overcast sky left a gray pall over the town, signaling impending rain. Raven welcomed the warm breeze across her face, carrying the scent of wet earth and blooming wildflowers. She stopped by the stable and checked on Ghost.

"Hey, girl," Raven murmured, ruffling the unicorn's silken mane. Ghost's soft, steady breaths and the familiar, comforting scent of hay filled the air. "Looks like we're both going to be mothers. If only you could talk." Ghost neighed softly, her large eyes reflecting affection.

Raven reached for the grooming brush, but as she turned, she froze. Carya was walking down the path, wearing a short red nightgown that clung to her figure, the neckline plunging to reveal more cleavage than any of her previous outfits. The sight was jarring and out of character, making Raven's heart race. Her sister clutched a bucket, her steps purposeful as she headed toward their secret spot.

*I need to find out what's going on with her.* Urgency tightened her chest as Carya disappeared down the path, the red of her gown a beacon against the muted landscape.

Raven quickened her pace to catch up with her sister. "May I keep you company?"

"Sure," Carya replied, her tone light. "Just going to freshen up for the party."

"I don't think it's a party," the rogue blurted out, her brow furrowing. "What about the tub?"

"Nah," her sister responded. "It's not roomy enough for two people."

"Why would—" Raven began, but her words trailed off as she noticed someone waving from the waterhole. She squinted, trying to make out the figure of a shirtless male elf floating about. "Saven?" Raven questioned, her voice edged with surprise.

"He's a great wizard," Carya said nonchalantly, slipping out of her gown and stepping into the water as the elf's eyes followed her every move.

"I know," Raven replied, kneeling by the water's edge and shaking her head in disbelief. "Saven, please excuse us."

The wizard's expression fell, disappointment etched on his face as Carya signaled with a nod for him to leave. Raven turned her head, catching a glimpse of the elf's bare backside as he reluctantly climbed out of the water. He muttered a curse under his breath, hastily dressed, and summoned a shimmering blue portal.

"He's not built like Gideon, is he?" Carya said with a wink, mischief dancing in her eyes.

*How does she know?* Raven wondered, her mind racing.

"Still cute, though," her sister continued blushingly.

"Carya, you have to stop," Raven pleaded, her voice trembling with urgency.

"What's wrong, sis?" Carya asked, her tone dripping with sarcasm. "You've always nagged me for using the tub. Raven Naelo, the carefree one, with no worries and no rules. Now you want to talk to me like Mother would because I've chosen to flesh-dip with a person I just met. Didn't you do that with Thomas? Trying to steal him from me?"

A deafening silence fell between the sisters, Carya's accusation hanging heavily in the air. Raven's heart pounded in her chest, the sting of her sister's words hitting her like a physical blow.

"Make up your mind, little sister. Should I go back to being boring or be bold like you? You can't have both."

With a mental punch to the stomach, Raven's breath caught in her throat. *Is she right?* Doubt gnawed at her, the guilt of past actions surfacing.

Carya huffed, crossing her arms defensively. "What more do you want from me? I sat and cried with you, mourning Thomas. I boarded the *Sea Squid*, a pristine ship, I must say, to thank Ashley and the captain for Messybeans's sacrifice. Which, by the way, is how I met Saven."

"It's Gooeybeans," Raven grumbled, her voice barely above a whisper.

"I didn't request that you and your misfit band of heroes come to rescue me."

"But Carya—"

"The loss of Mess—Gobs—and Thomas is on you, and you're using me as a scapegoat. I can feel your guilt and don't even have to try."

Raven bit her lip, trying to hold back the flood of emotions.

"If you truly want to honor them, accept me for who I have become. Let me live my life."

"Fine," Raven snapped, the words tumbling out before she could stop them. "I'll let you live your life, but if you touch Gideon again, I'll put you right back in the Abyss myself." *Did I just say that?*

Carya's eyes widened before a slow smile spread across her face. "There's my sister!"

Raven straightened, her posture rigid. "The ceremony starts at dusk. Don't be late."

"Yes, *Mother*," her sister teased, diving under the water, her laughter bubbling up to the surface.

Raven turned away, her anger simmering. *Did my sister intentionally make me feel this way?* She shook her head, trying to clear her thoughts, as she took a shortcut through the brush to the banquet hall.

The hall was a hive of activity, with her father and Gideon making the final arrangements. Eugor wore his royal robe, resplendent in red with gold trim, his stature commanding as he directed the preparations.

With his blond hair tied back neatly, Gideon wore a long-sleeved, white cotton eyelet tunic and dark blue breeches. The frantic shopping trip with Izarra the day before, selecting the outfit to replace Gideon's worn wizard robes, rushed back.

"The Cee Sharps will set up over there, but I think everything else is ready," Eugor said proudly, scanning the hall. "I have the medals for Miss Nell and Captain Smyth in my chamber."

Gideon nodded, his expression serious. "It was nice of William to travel from Brindell to accept Thomas's medal on behalf of the Paladin Guild."

"He should be here by sunset," Eugor replied, adjusting the collar of his robe. "He refused a portal." The atmosphere in the hall was a mix of solemnity and anticipation, the weight of the upcoming ceremony heavy on everyone's shoulders.

"Raven and I will deliver Aushade's medal once Jarz and Izarra arrive," Gideon added, glancing at her. She tried to smile but her anger with Carya lingered. She nodded at Gideon, appreciating his calm presence.

Eugor huffed, his face reddening with frustration. "It took every ounce of goodness in my body to make him one."

Raven grabbed her father's hand, her eyes earnest. "It's the right thing to do. He helped bring Carya home."

"He was the cause of all this," Eugor retorted, pulling his hand away. "I wouldn't reward a pyromancer if they set the Omlett Inn on fire and then decided to help me extinguish it after half of it was torched."

"I have to agree with your father on this one," Gideon interjected, his tone grave. "He's lucky we banished him to my cottage at the camp."

Raven's anger flared. "Well, if the orcs slaughtered my family when I was only a child and my only companions were hatred and the undead, I probably would have gone mad and done the same thing. I would want to see the world burn."

Gideon and Eugor stared at her, their faces a mix of shock and concern. The intensity of her outburst hung in the air.

Irritation followed Raven as she stormed away, her footsteps echoing through the hallway as the bustle of the banquet hall faded behind her, replaced by the rhythmic pounding of her pulse in her ears. She needed to clear her mind and escape the suffocating weight.

Rushing past the bar area, she pushed the front doors open and stormed down the stone steps of the Omlett Inn, each footfall echoing with a hard thud that reverberated through the hushed surroundings. Her breaths came out in short, angry bursts, and she flung herself down onto the stoop without pausing. The cold, rough surface of the stone bit into her legs through the fabric of her pants, but she didn't care.

She glared across the landscape below, her jaw set and eyes blazing, the tension in her body evident in the rigid line of her shoulders and the tight grip of her knees against the step beneath her. Raindrops began to fall. The cool droplets mingled with the warmth of her tears, the rhythmic patter on the ground matching the tumult in her heart. She lowered her head between her knees, seeking solace in the brief solitude.

The sound of approaching footsteps pulled her from her thoughts. Izarra and Jarz arrived, their sea-blue attire standing out against the dreary backdrop. Izarra's floor-length dress sparkled in the fading daylight, casting tiny reflections around them. Jarz's tunic was finely embroidered with intricate patterns of golden stitching.

"You all right?" Izarra asked, stopping beside her, concern etched in her eyes. "Carya?"

"This one is on me," Raven replied, her voice heavy with guilt. "I had a vision that everything would be normal once my sister was back."

"I'm sorry," Jarz said, his tone sincere. "I still think it's because we didn't purify the phylactery."

Raven began, "Is there—"

The swordmage shook his head, his expression grim. "This is uncharted territory."

"What about Courtlynn? Would she know?" Izarra asked, a glimmer of hope in her voice.

"I'm not sure," Jarz pondered, rubbing his chin thoughtfully. "It's possible she knows what Draklor did."

Gideon joined them at the steps, his presence bringing a comforting solidity. He handed Raven Aushade's medal, the cool metal pressing into her palm. "I apologize, and you're right. None of us can understand what the poor guy went through."

Raven hugged him tightly, her earlier anger melting like snow under the sun. She held him for a moment longer, savoring the warmth and reassurance of his embrace. "Let's give my cousin a chance," she said softly, pulling away and meeting his eyes with a newfound resolve.

As they stepped back, the group shared a brief moment of lightness. Gideon and Jarz, ever the competitive pair, attempted to cast a portal simultaneously. Their synchronized efforts caused the air to shimmer and flicker humorously, like ripples on a pond disturbed by sprightly fish. Laughter bubbled up, breaking the tension that had settled over them like a heavy fog.

A smile tugged at Gideon's lips as he glanced at Jarz. His eyes twinkled with amusement. "Please do," he said, his voice carrying a note of encouragement.

The swordmage, grinning widely, finally stabilized the spell. With a flourish, Jarz launched a portal to Gideon's camp. The swirling vortex cast a soft, otherworldly light over their faces, illuminating their features in shades of blue.

Raven took a deep breath, stepping toward the portal. The future was uncertain, but surrounded by her friends and buoyed by their support, a renewed sense of purpose washed over her.

As they stepped out, they saw Gimp splashing around at the lake's edge, his joyful laughter mingling with the sound of water. The two unicorns, Aerica and Trotter, lay peacefully in their stable, their sides rising and falling gently. Across the lake, the Nightmare steed, Blaze, roamed the tall grassy field, his fiery mane flickering like distant flames.

Aushade stood by the fire pit, the savory scent of roasting meat wafting through the air. Courtlynn waved from a nearby table, a joyful expression on her face. The succubus had multiple mugs lined up in front of her. After tasting one, she cringed, her wings fluttering in displeasure.

The necromancer hugged his younger brother tightly, a rare smile softening his usually stern features. He kissed Izarra's cheek and shook Gideon's hand firmly. When his eyes met Raven's, she leaned in, feeling the warmth of his brief kiss on her cheek.

"I can't thank you enough, Gideon," Aushade said, his voice earnest. "I know we don't deserve this kindness, but we'll do what we can to make amends for what we've done."

Gideon began with humility, "It's no castle—"

"It's perfect." Aushade hesitated, then, with a curious tilt, said, "We did want to ask, what's with the bedchamber's invisible ceiling?"

"It's for counting stars," Gideon explained, a hint of a smile on his lips. Raven blushed, the thought of such a romantic touch stirring her emotions.

The succubus joined the group, lazily wrapping her arms around Aushade, trying not to spill her drink. Her presence was as striking as ever, and her eyes glinted with mischief.

"Any luck with eating and drinking mortal food?" Raven asked, raising an eyebrow.

Courtlynn crinkled her nose playfully. "Still an acquired taste." She lifted the mug and took a tentative sip. She winced, her wings giving a slight flutter. "But I'm getting there. I seem to enjoy the meat, but all the drinks are sweet. I'm currently limited to water, but it has no taste," Courtlynn said, a hint of frustration in her voice.

"Try demon whiskey," Jarz suggested, then an awkward expression crossed his face as he wondered if it was inappropriate. "We could bring you a bottle next time."

"A demon trying demon whiskey," Courtlynn snickered, her eyes twinkling with amusement. "I guess it's worth a shot."

"I see your wings are healing nicely," Izarra remarked, her gaze softening as she looked at Courtlynn.

"We've been counting stars," Aushade winked, a flirtatious glint in his eye. "I'm glad it's a big Astral Realm."

Courtlynn smacked his arm, her wings fluttering slightly. "It's how I heal."

Gideon shook his head, his eyes flashing with mock exasperation. "I keep informing Raven I pulled a muscle, and all I get is an ice bath." Raven shot him a death stare, but a smile tugged at the corners of her mouth.

As if sensing the need to save Gideon, Aushade asked, "Did you two find a place yet?"

"We did," Raven replied excitedly. "We built a family cottage on the river's east shore, across from the Omlett Inn."

"Enough room for three, I bet," Aushade mused, then nudged his brother with a knowing look. "What about you?"

"The Fey builders constructed a house right next to the orphanage," Jarz stated proudly.

"It's not by water, but we plan on creating a pond with some fountains," Izarra added.

"Sounds . . . lovely," Courtlynn managed to say, searching for the right word.

"Enough room for three?" Aushade teased again, making Izarra blush and hide her face in Jarz's shoulder.

"Yes, there's room for her mother," Jarz snickered, his eyes gleaming with trouble. The group burst into laughter as the half-nymph elbowed him lovingly.

Gimp ran over, his clawed toes kicking up dust when he approached the group; Aushade picked him up and swung him in a joyful arc.

"I wish we could have given this to you at the ceremony tonight," Raven said, her voice softening as she handed the medal to the young imp. "It's actually for all three of you. We couldn't—Carya—"

Aushade shifted Gimp in his arms and grabbed Raven's hand with his free one, his grip firm and reassuring. "You're welcome, cousin. It's the least we could do. Any information on the new Mortal Realm Guardian?"

"It's going to be Elora," Gideon answered, his tone serious. "It's probably only a matter of time before she finds Courtlynn and Gimp."

"Enjoy your time here," Jarz insisted, his voice filled with earnestness. "But if we have to keep hiding you, we will."

"We appreciate that," Courtlynn replied, her eyes softening with gratitude.

"We should return," Raven suggested, glancing at the darkening sky. Jarz nodded and cast a portal, the shimmering blue vortex opening before them.

"Oh," Gideon said, suddenly remembering. He removed a cloth pouch from his belt and handed it to Gimp. "I believe this belongs to you."

The young imp's eyes lit up with excitement as he handed the medal to Aushade, then eagerly reached into the pouch, pulling out his beloved dice. Gimp's face broke into a wide grin, his earlier shyness replaced by pure joy.

"I want to play again!" Gimp shouted excitedly, his eyes sparkling with enthusiasm. Aushade lowered him to the ground, and he dashed to the table where Courtlynn was already settling in, her laughter trailing behind them.

"Izarra and I will return later tonight," Jarz reminded his brother, his tone turning sincere before stepping through the portal. "We need to discuss Carya's situation."

Aushade nodded as Jarz and the others entered the portal, the sparkling light enveloping them. Moments later, they found themselves in front of the Omlett Inn.

As the portal closed behind them, the familiar scent of rain-kissed earth greeted Raven once more. The Omlett Inn stood tranquil in the dusk, its lights warm and inviting against the evening gloom. Yet, inside her, a different storm had begun to settle.

Raven paused at the threshold. The laughter from earlier still echoed faintly in her chest, but the weight of her sister's words—and her own—pressed heavier.

She let out a slow breath and looked toward the distant horizon, where night had begun to swallow the last of the light. Carya still shimmered like a memory too bright and wild to hold somewhere out there. Raven didn't know who her sister was anymore but knew she'd fight for her. She'd fight *with* her if she had to. And if Carya truly walked a dangerous line, Raven would be the one to draw it.

But not tonight.

Tonight, they would pay their respects to the fallen. They would carry their names forward, not as shadows that dragged them down, but as torches they held high.

Raven glanced at Gideon beside her. He wasn't looking at the horizon—he was watching her. She could see the questions in his eyes, the concern, the steady patience. She didn't flinch from it for the first time in what felt like forever. "I'm ready," she said, her voice steady.

As they walked together up the steps of the Inn, Raven paused again at the door, her hand resting on the handle. Her reflection in the glass caught her eye—tired, yes, but unbroken. Changed, but not lost.

Gideon opened the other door for her, his voice gentle. "Are you all right?"

"Let me live my life," Raven murmured, echoing Carya's words from earlier, not as a question but as a decision.

"All right," Gideon said, the weight in his voice matching the one in her heart.

Raven wasn't sure if her sister's words meant *stepping aside* or *moving on*. But this much, she knew. *I'm ready.* "Maybe it's time I start living mine." Her hand drifted instinctively to her stomach. Then, reaching out, she laced her fingers with his. "We're ready."

# CHAPTER THIRTY-NINE

# HONOR THE FALLEN

Raven gripped Gideon's arm tightly, grateful that he allowed Aushade to hide at the camp. *Maybe Aushade can redeem himself.*

Izarra grasped Jarz's hand and swung it excitedly, giggling. Jarz paused and glanced back, his excitement giving way to a serious expression. "Gideon, I wanted to talk to you about my father's spell book," he uttered, his voice filled with resolve and apprehension. "I will destroy it once we figure out what's wrong with Carya."

Gideon raised an eyebrow. "Destroy it? That's a significant decision. Are you sure?"

Jarz's jaw tightened, and a steely glint shone in his eyes. "Yes. The power in that book—it's too dangerous. It's caused enough suffering already."

"It's your choice, but it's a powerful book handed down through generations of Fiskers. You may want to ask your Aunt Mara if she wishes to keep it," Gideon responded. Jarz nodded, absorbing the advice. "And speaking of powerful objects, we must find someplace safe for the Artifact of the Stolen Souls."

Raven's fingers absently traced the intricate design of the necklace, feeling the weight of responsibility it carried as she wrapped her hand around the pendant, still holding the illusion of the sword charm. "You will not touch my ASS," she replied, the mischievous glint in her eyes revealing her enjoyment of the pun. Then, more seriously, she added, "Blade said—"

"I know what he said, but with the current situation in the Abyss, I think it would be safer locked away with the demigods." Gideon noticed her unease and softened his stance. "I understand your attachment to it. But sometimes, the best way to protect something precious is to keep it where others can't reach."

Raven sighed, nodding slowly. "You're right. We'll ask Blade."

The evening air chilled, and the stars began to poke through the darkening sky. A loud grunt from the stables made Raven turn to see Brugg carrying large bags toward Gideon's wagon, his muscles straining under the weight.

Confusion knitted her brows as Carya tossed her belongings inside with hurried motions. *What the spell?* "Gideon, why is—"

"I told her she could have it after we found a new place," Gideon said defensively.

"Don't you think maybe you should have consulted me before making that decision?" Raven's voice was tight with frustration.

"It's not yours," Gideon replied, his jaw set stubbornly.

Raven's eyes widened in shock as Jarz and Izarra groaned behind them. "But we could've given it to our daughter." Her voice softened as she thought of their future child.

Gideon attempted a fake smile. "Carya will be tired of it before our daughter arrives. She can't move it as easily as I can." Suddenly, orange sparks whipped wildly around the wagon as it began to disappear. Raven tilted her head, waiting for Gideon's explanation, her patience wearing thin. He shook his head in disbelief. "She must have found my spell book."

"Why was your—"

"I'm not perfect," Gideon replied defeatedly. He wrapped his arm around Raven. "Still want me?"

"Carya shouldn't be able to do that," Jarz stated as he processed the situation. "Did you see the orange sparks?"

"Yes," Gideon replied, his brow furrowed. The wizard and swordmage turned to each other, realization dawning simultaneously.

"Gypsies?" they asked in unison.

Gideon gasped. "Or a succubus. That would explain . . ."

"Explain what?" Raven demanded, her eyes narrowing suspiciously.

Gideon lowered his head with frustration in his eyes. "She's been visiting me in my dreams."

"She *what?*" Raven asked rhetorically, her voice rising, pulling from his arm.

"She—"

"I heard you!" Raven's tone was sharp, her anger barely contained. "When did you plan on telling me?"

"Nothing happened between us," Gideon explained, his voice earnest. "She pesters me about the demigods and the High Council."

"Is this the first time?" Raven's heart pounded.

"No. The first night was when I returned from the High Council. She entered my head as you. And we—It wasn't real—I don't think."

"What?" Raven turned away from Gideon, her hands clenched into fists. "I'm going to kill her."

Izarra grabbed Jarz's arm, her expression concerned. "Jarz, they need our help at the banquet hall." The two slowly walked away, giving the couple some privacy.

Gideon wrapped his arms around Raven, his touch gentle yet firm. "It was just a dream," he promised.

*I hope so, for his sake.* Raven took a deep breath, willing herself to calm down. Her pulse gradually slowed. "Promise me, you'll tell me everything from now on."

Gideon nodded, his eyes locking onto hers. "I promise."

The wagon reappeared in its original spot with a faint shimmer, and Carya opened the door, stepping out with a graceful flourish. When she noticed them, she waved at the pair, wearing her new dress from Omlett OutFitters.

The lacey, black bell sleeves fluttered as she spun around, showcasing her outfit. The dress, made of luxurious satin, hugged her figure perfectly, accentuating every curve. The leather corset, laced tightly with delicate ribbons, accentuated her waist and added a touch of sophistication to the ensemble. The short skirt flared slightly, allowing a playful peek of her thigh-high boots gleaming with polished leather.

Why are you making Brugg work?" Raven snapped, her eyes narrowing with anger. "You know he's injured!"

"Whatcha think, Gideon?" Carya asked, completely ignoring her sister. She twirled again. "Mother mentioned black attire is appropriate for the ceremony." Raven held her tongue, her fists clenching at her sides as she seethed internally. "Not sure why. It's so depressing and not very flattering."

Gideon shifted uncomfortably, glancing between the sisters. "It's . . . It's stunning, Carya."

Raven's jaw tightened, her teeth grinding together. She took a deep breath, trying to calm the emotions swirling inside her. "Carya, you can't just ignore Brugg's condition. He needs rest."

Carya finally glanced at Raven, her expression dismissive. "He's a big fella. He can handle a few bags."

"Wow," a husky voice shot from behind them. The three turned to see the new arrivals.

"Shorte?" Carya asked, her eyes lighting up with recognition. "Is that you?" Avalann stuck out her arms for a hug, but Carya brushed past her, focusing on Shorte and rubbing his bare face. "I knew there was a handsome face under all that hair."

"I had no choice. The fire bastard burnt it off." Shorte puffed out his chest, his voice tinged with pride and a hint of irritation. "It wasn't an easy battle."

He relaxed and eyed her appreciatively. "But your beauty surpasses any water nymph."

"You're too kind." A delicate pink colored Carya's cheeks.

Then he whispered, "Don't tell Izarra I said that."

"I'm sorry about Thomas," Avalann said solemnly, her eyes reflecting the sadness of the loss. Shorte took Carya's hand to comfort her, his rough fingers gently squeezing hers.

"You mean dragon fodder," Carya teased, nudging the dwarf.

"Carya!" Raven snapped.

"That's inappropriate," Avalann added, crossing her arms over her chest.

Carya snickered. "Place another moral compass chair by my sister." She squeezed the dwarf's hand flirtatiously. "I don't have anyone to accompany me. Will you?"

Shorte seemed baffled but managed to nod.

"Be careful," Raven warned the dwarf, her voice laced with concern.

"Nothing to be scared of," Carya retorted, her eyes glinting mischievously. "I don't bite—ask Gideon." She winked.

Raven clenched her hand into a fist, her nails digging into her palm. Avalann, sensing a fight, quickly grabbed the rogue's purple tunic, gently restraining her.

They watched as Carya pulled Shorte toward the banquet hall, her laughter echoing in the evening air.

"Where's Miley?" Gideon asked, trying to shift the focus.

"She escorted my parents home," Avalann responded.

"Will you be returning as well?" Raven questioned, her eyes still fixed on Carya.

"Eventually. But I'm going with Shorte to visit Iron Cliff. I heard one of his brothers needs bow lessons," the elf jested, a twinkle of amusement in her eyes. "Then I'll return to Suttiir."

At that moment, Carya let out a loud, raucous cackle.

"I'm thinking succubus," Gideon murmured as they walked toward the hall.

Avalann gasped, "Carya?"

Gideon continued, his voice low. "I think a succubus soul was mixed with hers in the phylactery. But it's odd. She's affecting males of all races, not just humans."

Raven moaned, rubbing her temples. "And we must learn to live with that?"

"I have to do more research," Gideon replied as the three entered the hall, the warm glow of torches casting long shadows. "But I don't think I'll be welcomed back to Waterfront anytime soon."

Cyndi's band struck up a lively tune, the music filling the banquet hall with a vibrant energy. Raven scanned the room. She spotted Ashley, Ramzey, and Saven deep in conversation with Carya and Shorte, their faces illuminated by the soft glow of the chandeliers.

The hall was bustling with activity. The smell of roasted meat and freshly baked bread mingled with fragrant flowers adorning the tables. The clinking of glasses and murmured conversations created a symphony of social engagement. Gnome caterers bustled, setting up the last food on the long, decorated tables.

Raven's gaze drifted toward the front of the room, where Izarra and Jarz sat, their heads close together in a hushed discussion as High Priest Stone-Prayer moved gracefully around the room with his imposing yet gentle presence, greeting guests with a firm handshake and a warm smile. His deep voice carried over the clatter, a reassuring presence amid the lively conversation.

Mug and Eugor stood near the open doors that led to the stables, their conversation animated yet respectful. The evening breeze drifted in, carrying the scent of hay and the soft sounds of the horses shifting in their stalls.

Prominently displayed at the front of the room were beautifully detailed sketches of Gobs and Thomas. Ramzey had drawn them, capturing their likenesses with a kind of quiet devotion that only grief could teach. Every stroke of charcoal seemed to know them.

Raven approached the sketches slowly. Her eyes locked first on Gobs's grin—the caring one she wore when she talked about her daughter. Then Thomas, his gaze steady, shoulders squared, drawn in the way he used to stand when he thought no one was watching. The way he looked at her when they first met at Miss Crinkly's bakery. *Spellbinding. He said my eyes were spellbinding.*

Her chest tightened. The ache was sharp and sudden. *Gone, but returning to the Astral Realm.* She reached out, fingertips hovering just above the parchment, a breath caught in her throat. For a moment, she wanted to press her hand to the page—to remind herself they'd been real. That this wasn't some Fey dream conjured by sorrow.

But she pulled back. She wouldn't smudge them. Wouldn't risk disrupting the careful reverence of the lines Ramzey had drawn. They deserved to remain untouched.

The gnome caterers finished their preparations, stepping back to admire their handiwork. Platters of food glistened under the warm light, inviting guests to partake in the feast as her father swiftly moved to the front of the room, his presence commanding attention. "Everyone, please take a seat," Eugor announced, his voice resonating through the hall. Cee brought the music to a graceful halt, and a hush fell over the guests as they found their seats.

Mara entered, her white and gold robes flowing elegantly around her. She moved serenely, escorting a newcomer who drew curious glances from the assembled guests.

"I hope I'm not late," said a handsome, dark-skinned male wearing paladin armor that gleamed under the hall's chandeliers. The intricate designs on the armor resembled those Thomas had worn when he first arrived in Omlett, stirring a wave of nostalgia among those who recognized it.

"Please take a seat, Captain." Eugor smiled warmly. "I'm glad you could make it."

William nodded appreciatively and moved toward the front. Carya quickly stood, leaving Shorte for the front row and patting an empty chair beside her. "Here, Captain," she said with a charming smile. As Captain Smyth sat beside Carya, the energy in the room shifted slightly. He carried an air of confidence, and his presence seemed to command respect effortlessly.

"Welcome, Captain," Carya said softly, her eyes twinkling with admiration.

Raven overheard Ashley tell Ramzey, "Here we go again." Avalann, seated next to the warrior, stifled a laugh. Raven's eyes flicked back to Shorte, who sat alone, his face reflecting disappointment and a touch of hurt as he watched Carya leave him for the new arrival. Raven caught his eye and gave him a slight, reassuring nod.

"Let's begin," Eugor stated, his voice steady and commanding. However, the door opened once more, drawing everyone's attention. Celeste entered. Her gown, crafted from luxurious satin, clung to her curves like liquid gold, accentuating her every movement. Intricate beadwork adorned the bodice, catching the light and casting a delicate sparkle. The off-the-shoulder neckline framed her collarbones and shoulders with a sophisticated allure, while the fitted waist flared into a flowing skirt that swirled around her with every step. Tiny, hand-sewn sequins were scattered across the fabric, creating a mesmerizing effect as they glittered in the flickering light.

Blade followed, wearing formal Elvish attire in pale green, highlighting his regal bearing. The tunic, woven from fine silken fabric, clung to his muscular form with tailored precision. Embroidered vines and leaves, crafted with silver thread, traced intricate patterns along the hem and cuffs, evoking the natural elegance of his homeland. A high collar framed his chiseled jawline, while the fitted trousers tucked neatly into knee-high, supple leather boots. A finely crafted belt cinched his waist, adorned with a silver buckle shaped like an ancient Elvish rune. They sat behind Raven, leaving an empty chair directly behind Gideon.

As they exchanged polite smiles with those around them, a moon-elf clad in a silver robe hurried to the empty seat behind Gideon. "Giddy," the stranger teased, patting Gideon on the shoulder.

Gideon's expression shifted to one of annoyance. "Allus," he responded in a low voice, "what are you doing here?"

"I'm going to be around a lot more," the moon demigod teased, a wicked gleam flashed in his eyes.

Eugor, undeterred by the interruptions, cleared his throat and raised his voice slightly. "As I was saying, let's begin." The room fell into a respectful silence, the air thick with anticipation.

Raven's ears perked up as she overheard Allus whispering to Celeste and Blade. "Giddy and Carya were—" He leaned in closer, his voice dropping to a conspiratorial murmur. Raven strained to catch his words, but they became garbled, lost in the room's ambient noise. She shot a frustrated glance at the trio, her curiosity piqued. As she tried to refocus on her father's speech, a wave of anxiety rippled through her. *What had Allus been about to reveal?* Her mind raced with possibilities, each more unsettling than the last.

Eugor's voice cut through her thoughts, bringing her attention back to the front. He spoke with a solemn grace, his words a heartfelt tribute to Gobs and Thomas. Raven tried to concentrate, but the nagging sense of something unspoken hung heavily in the air.

"Miss Nell, please accept this medal on behalf of my family for the bravery of Gooeybeans," Eugor announced, his voice filled with emotion.

Everyone clapped as Cee signaled the band to play a soft, respectful tune. Ashley approached the podium with a composed grace. Her armor creaked as the fresh leather broke in. She accepted the award with a solemn nod, then raised the medal high, blowing a kiss toward the Astral Realm. The crowd responded with heartfelt applause, honoring the fallen hero.

Raven's gaze wandered through the room, eventually landing on Carya. Her sister's usually confident demeanor seemed to falter, her eyes darting nervously. *Is she upset?* Then she saw the source of Carya's unease: Captain Smyth deliberately ignored her. His posture was rigid, his eyes fixed ahead, refusing to acknowledge Carya's attempts to catch his attention. *He's the one guy in Euphrasia who seems immune to her advances.* A mix of curiosity and admiration stirred within her. *I wonder what his secret is.*

As the band continued to play, Raven's mind buzzed with questions. She observed Captain Smyth closely, trying to discern what set him apart. His dark eyes were focused, a hint of resolve in their depths. Unlike others who were drawn in by Carya's charms, he remained steadfast and unmoved. Carya's expression shifted from distress to frustration, her lips pressing into a thin line. She glanced around, perhaps seeking another target for her attention, but her eyes drifted back to the captain.

"Next, we want to show our appreciation to Sir Thomas Wellington. Not only was he an honorable paladin, but he was also part of our family. Please, Captain Smyth, accept this award on our family's behalf," Eugor announced, his voice filled with deep, heartfelt reverence.

The room fell silent as Captain Smyth approached the podium, the medal gleaming. "I would be honored to say something briefly," he said, his voice steady and resonant. Eugor stepped off to the side, and the music came to a gentle halt, the room now enveloped in a respectful silence.

Captain Smyth took a deep breath, scanning the room, reflecting the solemnity of the moment. "Sir Thomas Wellington was more than just a paladin. He was a beacon of hope and a paragon of virtue. His bravery and unwavering commitment to justice inspired us all."

A lump formed in Raven's throat as she listened. The captain's words echoed in her heart, each a poignant reminder of Thomas's legacy.

"He faced every challenge with courage and integrity," Smyth continued, his voice filled with emotion. "And in his final act, he gave everything to protect those he loved and the principles he held dear. We stand here today to mourn his loss and celebrate the extraordinary life he led and his impact on all of us."

A tear slipped down Raven's cheek, and she quickly brushed it away, not wanting to lose her composure.

"Thomas was a noble paladin and part of the guild family. He wrote to me whenever he could. His first message was how much he loved the town of Omlett and the diversity of its citizens. He also spoke about how much he admired the half-elf princess with purple eyes and truly loved her sister, his angel, Carya." Raven glanced at her sister, who watched Captain Smyth intently as he continued. "He shared with me his adventures, like riding an orc's shoulders as he hung decorations. I was away on a mission when one of his messages arrived," Smyth continued, his voice steady. "It was an invitation to Omlett's twenty-fifth-anniversary celebration, which I could not attend. However, his final message reached me just as I returned. It was an invitation to a wedding, which unfortunately never happened."

A hush fell over the room, the weight of lost possibilities hanging in the air. Smyth's eyes glistened briefly before he composed himself. "If Brindell had known about the evil attacks, I swear on our king we would have fought by your side," Smyth declared, his voice filled with conviction. "Thomas loved this city, and because of this, we'll be allies forever. Thank you."

The guests clapped as he sat back down. Raven turned her gaze back to Carya, who sat still, her usual vivacity replaced by a contemplative stillness. *Did it finally hit her?*

As the applause died down, the band began to play a soft, soothing melody, filling the hall with gentle notes. Eugor returned to the podium, his expression somber yet resolute. "Thank you, Captain Smyth, for those touching words. Let us carry Thomas's memory with us as we move forward, united in our shared purpose. Without Gooeybeans's and Thomas's sacrifices, our eldest daughter would not be with us today. Mara and I will never be able to repay them, her shipmates, or Gideon's Guardians for their heroism. Their acts of bravery will never be forgotten. I truly wish I could return everyone who perished," Eugor stated, trying to hide his emotions. "Please enjoy the refreshments and celebrate the lives of these amazing heroes."

As the room buzzed with muted conversations and the gentle clinking of glasses, Raven finally had a chance to hug the warrior and pirate, feeling the warmth and sorrow in their embrace. "I'll always remember Gobs," she said, her voice thick with emotion.

"She admired you," Ashley replied, her eyes glistening. "Gobs said she had a magical connection with you and me. Maybe it was because of our traits."

Raven smiled through her tears. "I decided my daughter's middle name will be Gobs."

"Aww, Baby Gobs," Ashley snickered, a bittersweet smile spreading across her face. "She would love it."

"Will you be staying a while longer?" Raven asked, her tone hopeful.

The warrior shook her head, her expression resolute. "We're sailing to Mizzendale. We have leads on two more Gooners—or Draakgoons."

"I prefer Draakgoons," Raven said with a smile, appreciating the levity.

"We sail first thing in the morning," Ramzey stated, her voice firm.

A mixture of admiration and gloom washed over Raven. "Be safe, both of you. And thank you for everything."

Ashley squeezed her hand. "You, too, Raven. We'll be back with more stories."

The three friends shared a moment of silence, their heartache and fortitude forging a deeper bond between them. The soft notes of the band's music drifted through the hall, adding a gentle backdrop to their farewell.

Ashley pulled a small, ornate box from her pouch and handed Raven three dragon cards, each adorned with intricate red, green, and black illustrations.

"Three down, four to go," she said reassuringly. "Take care of Baby Gobs, and let us worry about Cadence and the dragons for now. I promise to keep you informed if we find anything."

Raven nodded as she took the cards before embracing Ashley and Ramzey tightly.

"Don't lose my cards!" Ashley called out with a playful wink. "I'll be back for them soon."

Raven watched them leave, pride and worry swelling in her chest. As the door closed behind them, her eyes scanned the crowd in search of Gideon, the soft murmur of conversations and the clinking of glasses creating a gentle hum.

Raven spotted Carya sitting alone and staring blankly at the wall in the front row. Her heart ached at the sight of her sister's isolation. She crept through the room, weaving between clusters of guests. Reaching Carya, Raven hesitated momentarily, unsure how to break through her sister's trance. She gently placed a hand on her sister's shoulder.

Carya blinked and turned to look at Raven, her eyes glassy and distant. "Thomas loved me," she replied, her voice shaking, holding back tears.

"We've been trying to tell you that since you returned," Raven said gently, her voice filled with empathy.

"I killed him," she whimpered, her voice breaking.

"He chose to save you," Raven stated firmly, hoping to reassure her.

"You don't understand, I—" Carya began, but her words dissolved into sobs as she flung her arms around her younger sister. Raven held her tightly, raw suffering echoing in her sister's embrace. As Carya's tears flowed, the rain outside tapped insistently on the ceiling.

Carya pulled away, staring into the distance as if in a trance. Raven, dumbfounded, watched her sister's gaze drift around the room. Suddenly, a smile broke through Carya's tears, and she grabbed Raven's hands. "Come on," she urged, her voice tinged with a surprising excitement.

"Carya—" Raven started, but her sister was already skipping toward Cee's band, urging them to their feet. With infectious enthusiasm, Carya guided them outside under the stable as the rain poured in earnest.

The guests watched in amazement as Carya pulled Celeste into the rain, dancing with wild abandon. Laughter and joy rippled through the crowd. Allus quickly jolted out and joined the two ladies in the shower, his movements adding to the spontaneous celebration.

Standing under the awning, Gideon's arms wrapped around Raven, his warmth a comforting contrast to the cool rain. She leaned into him.

"Congratulations on your engagement," Blade announced as he approached. His eyes were fixed on Raven's hand, where the ring gleamed softly.

"Thank you," Raven replied, her voice filled with sincerity. "We hope you'll attend the wedding."

"I wouldn't miss it," Blade responded with a smile.

"Elora may have something to say about that," Gideon pointed out, his tone cautious. "When did she release Celeste?"

Blade beamed wickedly, and a sly sparkle lit his eyes. "Elora Clover is *tied* up at the moment. She won't be searching for my mother or anyone. I've also handled your Waterfront problem because Taiker Gavan went into hiding. Henry Owens is the new headmaster."

"How?" Gideon asked, incredulous. "He has a seat at the High Council now."

"Luck," Blade winked, his grin widening. "I guess he will be a busy man. But I would stay clear of the island until things settle down."

"If Gavan is on the run, will he come after me?" Raven held up the Artifact of Stolen Souls, its blood-red surface reflecting the flickering light from the torches. "What should we do with this?"

"The safest place is *still* with you," Blade responded confidently.

Gideon fidgeted. "But the Abyss—"

"It's not your concern anymore," Blade interrupted, his tone firm. "Trust me, having two of the Forbidden Realm Artifacts with Gideon's Guardians is only the beginning."

"Forbidden?" Raven asked. The word echoed in her mind, laden with untold secrets.

"Wait!" Gideon cried out, a note of desperation in his voice. "What's happening with the forbidden artifacts?"

"Blade," a soft voice spoke behind him, drawing his attention.

"Avalann? My dear, how you have grown," the demigod admired, his demeanor shifting to genuine affection. "Care to dance?" The elf-archer nodded, her eyes bright with excitement and nostalgia. She took Blade's arm gracefully as he paused, turning back with a cryptic smile. "That's a story for another time, my friend. Enjoy the evening." Blade escorted Avalann into the rain, their laughter blending with the sound of the falling droplets.

"What the spell is he talking about?" Raven asked, her brow furrowing in confusion.

"I'm not sure," Gideon responded, shaking his head. "I don't trust it when demigods talk about the forbidden artifacts. They were separated for a reason."

As Blade and Avalann moved to the dance floor, the significance of the Artifact of Stolen Souls in Raven's hand loomed more in the wake of Blade's revelation.

Carya grabbed Shorte, dragging him into the rain with a teasing grin. Celeste followed suit, pulling Eugor into the downpour. The spontaneous dance turned the night into a celebration of life, a defiant joy amid the sorrow.

Mara stood at the edge of the doorway, her expression mixed with amusement and concern. "Don't stay out in the rain too long," her mother urged, her voice carrying over the sound of the rain. "We don't want you getting ill." Despite her words, Mara couldn't resist the pull of the moment and rushed into the pouring rain straight into Eugor's arms. Seeing her parents embracing in the rain made Raven smile.

Izarra nudged Jarz, pushing him out to join the others. They swayed slowly in each other's arms, their movements gentle and synchronized, a stark contrast to the energetic dancing of the others.

Raven and Gideon stood under the awning, watching the scene unfold. The dancers' laughter and joy were infectious. But a blend of sadness and happiness tugged at Raven's heart. She wrapped her arms around Gideon's waist, leaning back into his embrace. "How do you feel about the name Carzarra Gobs Naelo?" she asked, a hint of respect in her voice.

Gideon nibbled gently on her neck, sending a pleasant shiver down her spine. "Grindal?" he murmured against her skin.

Raven snickered, shaking her head. "We'll discuss it later."

As they swayed to the music, the paladin captain stepped out of the Inn, the rain immediately pelting his armor. "This will be a wet trip back," he commented, his tone good-natured despite the weather.

"Would you like a portal, sir?" Gideon offered, his voice carrying over the rain.

"No, thank you," the captain replied, a determined glint in his eyes. "That's the easy way."

"You're more than welcome to stay at the Inn," Raven offered, her voice filled with genuine warmth.

"That's very kind, Princess Naelo, but I have a long diplomatic journey to Iron Cliff," he said, bowing slightly.

"Thank you for allowing us to keep Grail," Gideon added, extending his hand in gratitude.

Captain Smyth shook Gideon's hand. "A warhorse for a war-wizard."

"Thomas would be pleased that his steed is being cared for by his friends," Raven added, her smile sincere. "Especially since it is the father of Ghost's fetus."

Captain Smyth's eyes softened, a hint of a smile touching his lips. "I'm glad to hear it. Thomas had a deep bond with Grail, and knowing he's in good hands brings me comfort."

Raven nodded, a swell of emotion building at the mention of Thomas. "Have a safe journey, Captain."

"Oh, and if I were you, I would keep my eyes on that one," Captain Smyth said, pointing to Carya, who was soaked and dancing happily. "Thomas used to write about how pure her aura was. I don't know if his death changed it or the resurrection. It's not red, but it's damn close."

Raven gripped Gideon's arms tighter, fingers digging in without realizing. Her heart hammered against her ribs like it was trying to warn her before her mind caught up. She saw William dash toward the stable in a blur—too fast, too sudden. "What does that mean?" she yelled, her voice sharp with fear, already knowing she wouldn't like the answer.

Captain Smyth paused, rain slicking his gray uniform to his frame, droplets streaking across the brim of his hat. His face had gone stiff, searching—no, *bracing*—for the right words.

Then thunder cracked, as if the world itself were being split open. The band went silent. The last note hung and died. Around Raven, the courtyard stilled—too quiet, too still.

"It means she's evil, my dear. *Evil,*" Captain Smyth shouted, and without the music, his voice rang out like a bell in an empty cathedral.

Carya stood motionless, her back to the crowd, white hair plastered to her spine like a warning banner. Her clothes clung to her soaked frame, rain cascading down her shoulders in steady sheets. The storm lashed at everything around her—but she didn't flinch. The moment stretched—warped—until she slowly turned, as if summoned by the weight of all those stares.

Lightning flashed. Carya's face lit for one heartbeat. Eyes like polished steel. A sneer curling her lips.

"What the spell?" The chill that ran down Raven's spine wasn't from the rain or wind but from something that shattered deep within.

*What have I done?*

# CHAPTER FORTY

## SIX-SIDED REALM ROLE

Blade Naelo, the demigod of luck, adjusted his black padded armor, the soft leather creaking as he settled into his chair at the head of the table. The main chamber of the High Council, recently redesigned by Blade and his fellow demigods, now featured a grand central area tailored for the six rulers. Above them, a chandelier made from rare pink diamonds cast a soft, rosy glow, its facets scattering light like the twinkling of stars.

Blade stood, the scrape of his chair against the floor slicing through the air, bringing the room into an immediate and respectful silence. "Reports." His voice was firm and authoritative, the word hanging like an unspoken command.

He glanced to his right at Solas, a female demon with skin the color of freshly spilled blood and long black hair cascading over her shoulders. The demigod of energy, draped in a burnt orange robe that seemed to crackle with an unseen power, met his gaze with a nod.

"The Astral Realm is in order," Solas announced. Her voice was like a low hum of electricity, steady and charged. The words resonated with an underlying power, a testament to her domain.

Blade winked at his beloved, Fharla, a fiery red-haired fey elf whose presence seemed to soften the rigid atmosphere of the chamber. The demigoddess of love, passion, and fertility, Fharla, was adorned in a light blue robe that flowed like water, its delicate fabric shimmering as if woven with threads of moonlight.

"Everything is in order in the Fey Realm," she beamed, her voice a melodic lilt that infused the room with warmth. Her smile was radiant, a burst of sunshine that chased away any lingering shadows.

Blade's smirk widened into a genuine grin, a rare and treasured sight. The way Fharla spoke, with such joy and assurance, brought a sense of peace to his heart. Her eyes, sparkling like emeralds, met his, and the weight of his responsibilities felt lighter for a moment.

He turned to Nerull, a female human, Natus's daughter, clad in a robe adorned with intricate patterns resembling nature's cycles, flowing gracefully as she moved. The fabric shimmered with subtle hints of green, gold, auburn, and white, reflecting the ever-shifting balance of life. Her hair was a cascade of earthy reds and browns that seemed to mirror the changing leaves of autumn. The demigoddess of the seasons huffed, her expression one of exasperation. "The Shadow Realm is, well, the Shadow Realm."

Blade's brows furrowed slightly. "What's wrong?" he asked, his tone a blend of curiosity and concern.

"It's so dark and gloomy," Nerull replied, her voice hinting at frustration. "Why can't Allus and I switch? He's a moon-elf. It's his home realm." Blade considered her words, glancing over at Allus, who sat a few seats away.

With his silvery hair and ethereal presence, the moon-elf glanced up with a slight smile. "Gloomy to you, maybe. We appreciate the darkness as much as the Fey appreciate the light. I would rather be home gazing at the full moon and stars in Lunathil than deal with this crazy mess in the Mortal Realm," Allus stated, his voice carrying the chill of a moonlit night.

"How so?" Blade asked.

"The dwellers there don't follow the rules. There are artifacts and creatures from different realms. Plus, the anomaly, your sister—"

"Carya," Blade interrupted, giving Allus a stern look to tread lightly on this subject, "what about her?"

Allus sighed, his expression turning serious. "I had a fascinating conversation with her until Giddy interrupted, acting all strange," he sneered, his disdain evident. "He stared at me as if he caught us doing something inappropriate."

"Were you?" Blade questioned, his tone sharp.

Allus huffed. "No. We were discussing the moon-elves, demigods, and the High Council."

Blade considered the request for a moment, then nodded. "Very well, the two of you may switch," he conceded, glancing at Nerull, who appeared relieved. "It makes sense."

"Speaking of the Mortal Realm, I need the unicorns to return to the Fey," Fharla interjected, her voice softening the tension in the room.

"Please don't touch Raven's unicorns," Blade pleaded, his expression almost comically serious.

Fharla rolled her eyes, her patience clearly wearing thin. "I'm only here to help you clean up this mess the others made. I do have better things to do."

"I know," Blade replied, "but the unicorns have lost their magic, so there's no harm in allowing them to stay." She nodded in agreement. "Weejas?" Blade turned his attention to a dwarf, the demigod of inventions.

Weejas's sturdy frame was adorned with intricate tattoos of gears and cogs, each glowing faintly with a celestial light. His fierce red beard, braided with mithril and copper wire strands, reached his broad chest. A pair of goggles with lenses of polished sapphire rested perpetually on his forehead, ready to be pulled down over his piercing emerald eyes. "The Abyss is insane, but I'm learning," Weejas jested. "I haven't been down there for eons."

"I'm glad you're adjusting." Blade beamed. "But I need another favor."

"Certainly," the dwarf replied, leaning forward with interest.

"Work with Nerull and introduce the Mortal Realm to our new calendar concept. Our names will represent one day of the week, reminding them who's in charge."

Weejas stroked his beard thoughtfully. "I can calculate the day length and the seasons. It'll work. It'll line up with the 360-day system they use now."

"That's just pure luck," Allus laughed, his silver eyes gleaming with amusement.

"You know it," Blade simpered. "It's time for our reign of the realms to begin." The group began to shout in agreement, their voices rising in excitement. Blade raised his hand, commanding silence. "But there is one final piece of business. I wish to allow my family to visit here in the Astral Realm." A murmur of surprise filled the room, eyes widening in disbelief. "I *understand*"—he raised his voice to quell the rising objections—"that this is sacred ground, but I wish for us to become more involved with the beings of the realms."

"I think it's a lovely idea," Fharla responded, her voice like a soothing balm to the tension. "Especially a wedding!"

"Of course you do," mumbled Solas, her expression skeptical. "Our father built the High Council for higher beings. It's not meant for mortals to roam."

"This is where Weejas comes in," Blade replied.

"How can I help?" Weejas asked, curiosity piqued.

"I would like a magical atrium built on the castle turret facing Cenergy," Blade responded thoughtfully.

"Are you insane? The mortals will certainly go blind," Solas protested, her voice rising alarmingly.

"Weejas can place a tint on the dome, shielding them from the harsh light," Blade countered, his tone firm yet reassuring.

Weejas nodded slowly, considering the request. "I can design a special glass that adjusts to the light levels, ensuring their safety."

Blade smiled, grateful for the dwarf's ingenuity. "Thank you, Weejas. This will be a step toward bridging our worlds."

The council murmured among themselves, the initial shock gradually giving way to contemplation. Blade glanced around the room, seeing concern and hope reflected in their eyes.

"If your family is allowed, does that mean all of ours are?" Allus asked, his tone measured and thoughtful.

"Yes, as I stated," Blade replied. "We need to be more involved with all realms."

The council members murmured among themselves, discussing the implications and possibilities of this new decree. Blade watched, sensing a mixture of excitement and apprehension in the air.

Nerull finally spoke, her voice carrying the weight of consensus. "We agree."

"Wonderful," Blade said, a smile touching his lips. "Then, if nothing else, you're all dismissed."

The demigods rose from their seats, the room buzzing with renewed energy and purpose. Blade remained seated, watching as his fellow rulers exchanged ideas and plans, their previous concerns giving way to a sense of unity and collaboration.

Fharla lingered beside him, her hand resting lightly on his shoulder. "You did well, Blade," she whispered, her eyes filled with pride and affection.

The couple held hands as they exited the High Council's main chamber and entered the ritual chamber, encased with a clear magical dome. The dome allowed the ethereal beauty of the Astral Realm to be seen in all its glory—swirling nebulae of vibrant colors, distant stars twinkling like diamonds, and the soft glow of astral light bathing everything in a serene luminescence.

Fharla moved to the far side of the chamber, her light blue robe flowing behind her like a gentle river. She stared into the Astral Realm, her thoughts lost in the infinite expanse. Blade watched her momentarily, appreciating her inner strength and the calm she brought to his often-tumultuous life.

He then turned and approached the central fountain, its crystalline waters sparkling in the light of the dome. Sitting at the fountain's edge, he dipped his hands into the water, feeling its cool, soothing touch. The liquid shimmered with a life of its own, its surface reflecting the cosmos above. As he ran his hands through, he mumbled, "The Celestial Water of Life," the words a reverent whisper.

"What, dear?" Fharla asked, her eyes filled with curiosity.

"It's nice knowing the Artifact of Stolen Souls is with my sister. The Dagger of Chaos is in Suttiir, and the Spell Book of the Wysards is with a wizard named Jarz. The Fey Chalice is locked up at Waterfront. That's all five Forbidden Artifacts discovered in the Mortal Realm." Blade's voice was steady, but there was an undercurrent of anxiety.

"Why didn't you confiscate them?" Fharla's brow furrowed with worry.

"The dagger drove the King of Suttiir mad. When he sent a message to Waterfront that he wanted to hire ten covens to protect him, I had to investigate." Blade's hands moved through the Celestial Water, creating ripples that mirrored his troubled thoughts. "I feel terrible that my father had to end the king's life. The blade's powers amplify the person's current emotions. The king must have been overwhelmed with fear between the attack on his life and the desecration of his city." He paused, hoping the blade would not harm the Queen of Suttiir before he was ready to remove it from there. "I must ensure I'm well-prepared to handle all of the artifacts when the time is right."

Fharla wrapped her arms around him, lowering her chin to his shoulder. "Sounds like we need some luck."

Blade chuckled softly, then spun around, pulling her into his lap. He kissed her deeply, their connection momentarily dissolving their worries.

As they broke the kiss, she laid her head on his shoulder. "How did you learn about the artifacts anyway? Only my family knew. As far as demigods go, you're considered young."

"It began with my father's beheading," Blade explained, his voice tinged with sorrow. "I wanted to know what item could be worth my father's life. Over the years, I traced the artifacts to the headmaster at Waterfront. He has ancient texts from the Realm Wars. He wants to capture the dragons for their magic and destroy the Gooners, the dragon protectors, and now the legendary Draakgoons."

"Is that why you confronted the headmaster?" Fharla asked, piecing together the fragments of his story. "So he ran?"

"Yes, my love," Blade replied, his voice firm. "My sister, Raven, is a Gooner. He just picked on the wrong family." He guided her off his lap and kissed her again, a kiss filled with love and reassurance.

She glared at him with concern. "Just be careful. My father destroyed my sister, the demigod of dragons, for plotting something he didn't like."

"I heard that Elora and the new council betrayed Draconia to Natus. That's why I replaced her on the High Council."

"Draconia wanted to return the dragons to the Fey Realm, so she would betray my father's orders. He warned that if anyone else tried to help the dragons, he would destroy all the demigods."

"When I was first assigned to the Astral Realm, Guardian Meliae pointed out Draconia's soul orbiting Cenergy. God's and Goddess's souls do not return to the soul pool. So, when it disappeared, I knew Draconia would end up in the physical world again."

"And most likely to save her dragons. We're allowed to protect them, but Natus's orders are that they must remain in the Mortal Realm." Fharla looked troubled. "Why don't you take your sister to Draakland?"

"Because Raven must learn from the past and embrace her heritage. She won't be any help if she doesn't believe in what she's doing."

"But the moon-elf Cadence?" Fharla began. "She's growing weaker every passing year."

"I've already done my part—left the marks at Waterfront, replaced Headmaster Taiker." His voice echoed with finality as his image wavered, distorting like heat rising off the stone. "Now, I must tend to the institution." The illusion melted away in the fountain's reflection, revealing not the dark, sharp figure of Blade, but a frail, elderly man with hollow eyes and parchment skin. "After all," he murmured, staring at the old man's reflection, "I'm in charge now."

Fharla stepped forward, smoothing the collar of his robe. "This Henry Owens disguise does you no justice," she teased, brushing her lips across his withered cheek. "Go get 'em, Headmaster."

Blade—Henry—didn't smile. His expression hardened. "If Draconia returns . . ." His voice softened, heavy with dread. "Then I must prepare the Mortal Realm for Draconia's wrath. For war."

Koport

Northern
Euphrasia

Plattnims

Mizzendale

Sonny-Mikula
Village

Eastern
Euphrasia

hrasia

Sand Storm

Port Easter

Seastral
Haven

n Euphrasia

rey Tunn

Ir Island

Euphrasia

# ABOUT THE AUTHORS

**Rachel Ann Fischer** is an author from Harrisburg, PA. After serving time in the Army, she attended technical school for Auto-Cad and Interior Design. Her creativity began at an early age when she discovered the world of fantasy role-playing games. This sparked Rachel's imagination and passion for creat-

ing worlds and characters. She wrote two play scripts that were produced by a local drama department. The process made her fall in love with writing dialogue and gave her the confidence to write this novel. The story is based on a role-playing campaign that began many years ago in her cousin Kevin's kitchen.

**AnnMarie Knorr-Fischer** is an author from Harrisburg, PA. Her love of the arts began at a very young age. The first memories of writing that she can recall date back to elementary school, where she wrote short poems and stories. Ann's love for the written word progressed over the years as she wrote for school literary publications and completed a full-length movie script in her senior year in college. Working with Rachel, she directed and produced two plays. Currently, she works as an entertainment consultant in Hershey, PA.

R.A.Fischer Authors

www.rafischerauthors.com

www.ingramcontent.com/pod-product-compliance
Lightning Source LLC
Chambersburg PA
CBHW020253030726
47499CB00001B/189